PRAISE FOR
THE SPECIMEN

"Propulsive and lush, Fixsen weaves an exquisitely Gothic tale that explores the power of a mother's love to transcend all things, even the grave. From the first to the very last page, this novel kept me riveted, needing to know that Isobel would prevail against all odds. Fans of Hester Fox and Paulette Kennedy will adore this one."

—Jess Armstrong, *USA Today* bestselling author of *The Curse of Penryth Hall*

"*The Specimen* is a fantastic read! Tense, gripping, and full of fabulous characters you grow to love or hate! I devoured it in two sittings."

—Gareth Brown, bestselling author of *The Book of Doors*

"*The Specimen* is a dark delight! Jaima Fixsen has crafted a dynamic cast of characters with real heart and set them against a riveting backdrop of science, witchcraft, and scandal. I couldn't put this book down!"

—Emily Ruth Verona, author of *Midnight on Beacon Street*

"*The Specimen* unfolds a haunting tale of secrets, sacrifice, and obsession. This is a brilliant story that delves into the darkest corners of the human soul, where the quest for knowledge collides with the primal instinct to protect what matters most."

—Kim Taylor Blakemore, author of *After Alice Fell* and *The Companion*

"*The Specimen* offers a fascinating glimpse into the shadowy world of nineteenth-century medicine, full of historical detail. A vivid and atmospheric read!"

—Ritu Mukerji, author of
Murder by Degrees

"Part Gothic horror, part detective tale, Fixsen's smart narrative peels back the surface of respectable doctors seeking knowledge from anatomical studies to reveal an underbelly of theft, murder, and questionable medical collections, sending the reader along the path of the woman at its center, Isobel Tait, who's determined to reveal the truth and seek vengeance, both for herself and for the innocent victims... A compelling gem of a novel!"

—Amiee Gibbs, author of
The Carnivale of Curiosities

"Fixsen's ghost story is the most haunting of all: a tale of the real-life evil that shapes our world and the heroines who dare name these men monsters. With a meticulous hand, Fixsen conjures Edinburgh and its history of music, immigration, murder, ghosts, and above all, love."

—J. R. Dawson, author of
The First Bright Thing

THE
SPECIMEN

JAIMA FIXSEN

Poisoned Pen
PRESS

Originally published as *Traité des Poisons Tirés des Règnes Minéral, Végétal
et Animal ou Toxicologie Générale* © Matthieu Joseph Bonaventure Orfila,
1814. Translated and abridged from French by Joseph G. Nancrede.

The characters and events portrayed in this book are fictitious or are used
fictitiously. Apart from well-known historical figures, any similarity to real
persons, living or dead, is purely coincidental and not intended by the author.

All biblical verses are used as reflected in the King James Version
(KJV) of the Christian Bible unless otherwise noted.

Published by Poisoned Pen Press, an imprint of Sourcebooks
P.O. Box 4410, Naperville, Illinois 60567-4410
(630) 961-3900
sourcebooks.com

Cataloging-in-Publication Data is on file with the Library of Congress.

Printed and bound in the United States of America.
VP 10 9 8 7 6 5 4 3 2 1

To Ashley, for getting me away from my desk,
and Sarah, for keeping me at it.

To Edward and Isla and Jeff,
who journeyed to Scotland with me.

And to Kanapawamakan,
who founded a family.

...written not with ink, but with the Spirit of the living...not in tables of stone, but in fleshy tables of the heart.

2 Corinthians 3:3 KJV

PROLOGUE

I believe in ghosts. Restless, deceived, disappointed: they talk to me as I dust the shelves and darn the socks, as I push my way to market in the crowded street. There must be dozens altogether—some I only feel because they are too sullen to speak.

Even though I am, I do not feel alone. In the quiet of my room, one ghost—my ghost—curls up beside me, cold breath shifting my hair and smoothing my cheek.

Never alone.

{ 1 }

My son, Thomas, snuggled deeper into my side, and I looped an arm around him, glad to be watching the water wash down the windowpanes, after another day of him too listless, too flushed, and too lightheaded. "Aren't you hungry?"

I'd brought up a cup of sweet tea with toast soldiers and a dollop of raspberry jam, but he'd stopped eating after a few bites.

Thomas shook his head. "You eat it."

"I'm not hungry." I smiled as I said it, but in truth, it was the stone's weight of worry sitting in my middle that kept me from eating.

"Let's share." The glint in his eye made me laugh in spite of myself. He was a crafty one, my Thomas, well aware that his story wouldn't come until his supper plate was empty.

"Fine, then. You first." Two could play at that game.

He nibbled the jam off a toast soldier, then offered the bare end to me. "Your turn."

"You ate all the jam," I said reproachfully, so he swiped it through the sticky puddle on his plate and thrust it at me again.

I snapped the bit of bread from his fingers like a puppy, knowing it would make him laugh, and he did, his cheeks getting even pinker, his breath fast. "Your turn," I told him.

I moved the toast at the last minute, dabbing a bit of jam on the corner of his mouth.

"Mam!"

"Not on your sleeve, Tommy."

He huffed, but minded me anyway, stretching out his tongue to clean up the mess. But he got his own back with the next bite, leaving me with jam on the end of my nose.

"Uggh. You know my tongue can't reach that far." I tried anyway, setting him off in a fit of giggles that quickly turned to breathless wheezing. He curled forward, struggling to draw in more air while I reached for a camphor-scented handkerchief and rubbed circles on his back. He was frightened enough; I couldn't let him see how these gasping spells terrified me.

"Let's have a quiet game, mmm?" I suggested, when his breathing slowed and his color faded.

"A story," he said, nodding.

"Not a scary one." Ghosts, witches, ogres, girls who cut off their toes to outsmart cunning goblins, knights with treachery-strained hearthrugs—these were always the stories Thomas preferred, but I was too old now to believe in the inevitably triumphant endings.

"I want the one about the blood that speaks," he said.

I got up to open the window, hiding my grimace. My mother had told that one, and to this day I recalled her exact inflections. The tale was eerie and sad, not one I wished to think on today.

The window sash stuck, only giving way when I gave an extra push and a grunt. Outside, the rain had slowed to a drizzle, glittering against a purple dusk that blew gently into the room, soft and cool against my cheeks.

"There." I turned around, dusting my hands. "The fresh air will do you good." I climbed back into the bed and settled him into the crook of my arm, watching the breeze stir the lace curtains.

"My story?" Thomas prompted.

"I told that one yesterday," I reminded him.

"Tell it again," he begged, his cheeks so flushed, his eyes so big and shadowed it was impossible to deny him.

"All right, then." I pulled him a little closer. "When Thomas left home to see the world—"

"He was the bravest boy in Scotland, wasn't he?"

"He certainly was. And when—"

"Mam—" His hand closed urgently on my arm.

"What's wrong?" Even as I spoke, something black moved at the corner of my eye, streaking across the room and flapping with impotent rage against the wall. It veered back, right toward us.

"Bat!" I gasped, yanking the covers over my son and curling around him as the shadow passed overhead in a buffeting squall. "Stay down."

I'd once helped a trapped bird back outside after it'd come down the chimney, and in spite of the goose bumps climbing my arms, this couldn't be that different. Except the frantic wheeling of these black stretched-skin wings was sinister, not sad. I could have borne a peck from a bird; I quaked at the thought of a bat's bite. Finches slept at night, but a bat, sailing about in the dark, silent and sharp-toothed, must be a monster. His fluttering at the ceiling seemed to stop my heart.

"Don't move, Thomas," I said, reaching for the shawl on the nearby chair. "I'll get it out."

I flapped the fabric, trying to drive it away from Thomas, toward the open window, but the animal wheeled away, batting against the ceiling, then the opposite wall. "Out!" I hollered, flapping again, and the bat careened into the mantelpiece, knocking a flower-filled vase to the floor, shattering the pale blue porcelain and strewing stalks of lily of the valley across the hearthrug.

The bat dove and I pitched to the floor, terrified it would tangle in my hair.

"Mam!" Thomas called, frightened—I must have let out a scream.

"It's all right," I promised. "Just stay there."

Lips pressed together, I pushed onto my feet and sidled behind the panicked animal. Once I caught it in the folds of my shawl, I could toss it outside and never wear the thing again. Poised on my toes, I waited. It veered close, and I sprang, but before I could gather up the cloth with the bat inside, it fought free in an explosion of beating wings, darting around the room.

"No—"

Too late. It crashed into the wall above the mantelpiece, and knocked off my only remaining ornament, a brass hourglass sized to fit easily into my hand, a gift from my father after Thomas's birth, when I began teaching piano lessons to keep and feed us. Time slowed as the glass turned end over end in the air. I lunged for it, hand outstretched, but I never got within a yard of it. Flying past my fingers, it smashed into the floor, pelting me with shards of glass and a spray of white sand.

For a moment, I stared at the broken remains. Then I wiped my forehead, and realized my hand was oozing blood. "Damn beast."

I chased the thing around like a madwoman, thumping and cursing, until the landlady and Mr. Mitchell, one of the downstairs tenants, helped me corner it.

"There," Mr. Mitchell said, hurling it outside. It fell, righted itself halfway down to the street, then flapped away into the shadows. I yanked the window shut.

"What a demon!" Mrs. McPherson said, surveying my wrecked room. "You all right, Thomas?"

His eyes were twice their usual size, but he nodded.

"And you, Isobel?"

I took my eyes away from the broken bits littering my hearth and swallowed. "I'm fine." The brass fittings were intact, but there was no way the hourglass could be repaired, and even if I bought myself another, it wouldn't be the same. "I'll sweep this up."

"What about your hand?" Mr. Mitchell asked.

I glanced at it, but the cut was small. It had stopped bleeding. "It's fine," I said, and fetched the broom. Mrs. McPherson helped, muttering prayers under her breath.

"'Twas just an animal, Mrs. Mac. Probably as frightened as we were," Mitchell said, then gave me an apologetic smile. "Though I'm right sorry about your things, Mrs. Tait."

I nodded in response. Now that the creature was gone, it was easier to be sensible. Few things are as dull and deadening as a dustpan. With the help of my neighbor and landlady, soon the room was just as it was, save for my empty mantelpiece. They left, and Thomas, tenacious as ever, reminded me I owed him a story.

"I don't know if I can." My heart wasn't racing anymore, and I felt drained, hollow as an empty cask.

"Were you very frightened?" Thomas asked.

I nodded automatically. "Those wings—" I stopped, noting the frown on his face. "I thought it would eat you," I finished with a laugh, tickling his ribs. "Silly of me. Horrid beast, but far too small to eat a fellow like you. You did well to stay hidden. We might have tripped over you, and just think what a tangle that would be." Skirts flying everywhere, Mrs. McPherson beneath her gentleman tenant, and a crazed bat wheeling above. I shook my head.

"I'm sorry about your things," Thomas said.

"No use crying over them." I produced a smile and wiggled into the bed beside him. "Let's have your story. No more interruptions." I tucked the blankets extra close and cleared my throat.

"When Thomas left home to see the world, his mama had nothing to give him, for they were poor. So she took her kerchief and pricked her finger, putting a drop of blood in each of the four corners. 'Magic—'"

"To protect you," Thomas put in. He knew this tale well.

"Aye," I said, brushing his soft skin. "'Ever and always, no matter where you will go, my blood will sing to you and save you from harm. Always keep it with you,' she said. And he promised he would. So she tied a knot in each of the four corners, blessed him and kissed him, and sent him on his way."

"Does he meet a giant this time, Mam?"

I shook my head. "Not this time, love. Because down the road, he came to a farm with a thatched roof and a stable full of horses, all with golden manes." No more monsters for me tonight. We'd take this story a different way.

I told him a long and lovely adventure, until my voice cracked, and Thomas told me to drink a cup of tea. His eyes were heavy, his breath slow and even, like waves on the shore of a calm sea. "Let's finish tomorrow," he said.

"Mr. Craig?"

The surgeon straightened away from my boy, still limp and list-less in his wee bed. Except for the bright flags of color high on his cheeks, Thomas was as white as his shift.

Mr. Craig gave Thomas his usual smile and patted his head fondly. "Good job, little man. I had a good listen."

Without turning to me, he packed away his wooden stethoscope. Mr. Craig was a fine surgeon, well versed in the new methods championed by lecturers at Edinburgh University. I'd always been used to doctors pressing their ears right to my chest, but Mr. Craig said the quality of sound through a stethoscope was better.

"His lungs sound fine," Mr. Craig said, when he finally faced me at the door of the room, far enough from Thomas's hearing.

While that was some relief, I'd learned enough to wait for more. "And his heart?"

"Still struggling. The murmur"—it was too friendly a word for what Mr. Craig had described to me, but I was no surgeon—"is still there, plain to the ear."

He'd taught me hear it myself, leaning over my formerly brawny boy, though the sound was not easy to distinguish between the allegro counterpoint of his pulse. Barely audible, the shushing was ominous as the whispering petticoats of my onetime schoolmistress. Her professed sensibility had never once tempered her excellent hearing, her rigid bearing, or her preference for applying the cane. Papa hadn't left me as a boarder there long, but three months in the young ladies' academy had been enough. Beneath the sleeves of my dress and my lightly freckled skin, I had lumps on the bones of both forearms. Mr. Craig, who'd tended to me then, had feared the bones were broken.

Even my worst memories were preferable to considering the state of Thomas's heart, but I made myself focus. "You said it might heal."

Mr. Craig nodded. "I hope it does. His heart was fine before the scarlet fever."

Thomas had survived the fever, but he'd failed to regain his strength. Even now, a year afterward, his breath left him every time he climbed the stairs. He never ran anymore.

"Rest, good food...they will help." Mr. Craig's kind smile and his sorrowful eyes told me the rest.

Thomas was a green leaf that had withered, still clinging to the tree, but liable to be carried off by the next strong wind. Not, I admit, an unexpected diagnosis. I'd seen the short lives of invalids, even the most cosseted ones, but hadn't wanted to believe this would be Thomas's fate. I'd never seen a bigger, fatter baby than he, or one with a livelier laugh. Even now, every so often he'd flash a roguish smile, silently telling me this was all in fun, that he'd tricked me into thinking him ill, that all this was just pretending.

I wanted to climb into bed beside him and inhale his soft blond hair.

"He's a fine lad, with a fine mother," Mr. Craig said, buckling his bag.

I swallowed. "Thank you, Mr. Craig. I'll be by to teach the girls their lessons tomorrow as usual."

"No need, Miss Isobel." He still addressed me as if I were a girl, but I liked that. "Take the day. You can make up the missed lesson in a week or two."

He was a kind man, who still insisted on paying for his daughters' piano lessons, though he treated Thomas without charge.

"I will keep on with the chest liniment," I said. Thomas complained that the camphor scent of his greasy ointment stung his eyes, but it did aid his breathing, temporarily.

"Yes, at least once a day," Mr. Craig agreed, but not with any conviction.

Miss Minnie Low finished the last bars of Beethoven's moonlight sonata and sighed—more noticeably, but no less deeply than I did. Maintaining composure throughout our one-hour lesson took more effort than I knew I had. Today, even breathing hurt.

Minnie shifted closer, so our sides abutted on the piano bench. "Mrs. Tait, what if they make me play?" Her eyes brimmed with mute misery. Though she tried mightily, even the most beautiful melodies emerged loud and inflexibly from her dainty white hands, and in a month, she was visiting her fashionable cousins in Harrogate. Both her parents had high expectations of the visit, but no matter how patiently I taught her or how sternly the dancing master drilled her, poor Minnie couldn't keep time with a beat.

"I'll make such a fool of myself."

In spite of the weight on my own heart, I felt a twinge for the suffering in hers. Laying a hand on her shoulder, I bent close so the shepherdesses on Mrs. Low's toile wallpaper couldn't overhear. "Play the Radetsky march if you have to." The thumping cadence was easiest for Minnie to follow, and the piece was short. As for the dancing—"Early on in the visit, I suggest you sprain an ankle."

Minnie's brow cleared. "Thank you, Mrs. Tait."

I returned her smile, ignoring a kick from my conscience. Minnie was a good girl, not the type to conceive a deception unprompted. "My pleasure. Good luck."

I gathered my gloves, hat, and reticule, and went to pay my respects to Mrs. Low before going out.

She was writing letters in the morning room, as usual. In spite of her hopes for her daughter, she was realist enough to retreat to this room at the back of the house during our weekly lesson. With my hands clasped in front of me, I waited for Mrs. Low to set aside her pen.

"Mrs. Tait."

"Good afternoon, Mrs. Low. Miss Minnie is finished for the day." With Minnie off to Harrogate at the end of the week, I needed to collect payment for the last month's worth of lessons. Mrs. Low wasn't interested in piano lessons for her younger sons.

"We'll miss you," Mrs. Low said. "And of course, if Minnie comes back, we'll resume her lessons."

I nodded, perfectly understanding the hope that Minnie would instead be moving on to a life and a home of her own. All the genteel mothers for whom I worked wanted the very same thing.

"You've worked hard with her," Mrs. Low said.

"She's a diligent student." Minnie lacked aptitude, but I liked her.

Mrs. Low had a stack of coins ready on her desk, but she took an extra one from the box in the drawer and began pushing the little stack of comfort and security toward me. Before I could thank her, she paused with her hand over the money and tilted her head at me. "How is your son?"

Always over the past year I had smiled and said he was recovering. Today the coming loss was too great. My smile broke. Mrs. Low, a mother with her own losses contained in some quiet, hidden-away cupboard, immediately understood. As the corners of her eyes fell, the dammed-up tears in mine began to leak.

"My dear Isobel," she said, and stretched out her hands.

By the time I was drying my nose with her handkerchief and halfway through a cup of tea, Mrs. Low had paced a half mile between her writing desk and the door.

"But he survived the fever. Surely something can be done." There was music in her walk, in her clipped syllables, in the swish of her skirts.

Lulled by it, I shook my head. "Mr. Craig says—"

"Yes, Mr. Craig." Mrs. Low waved her hand dismissively. "An excellent surgeon, but have you—" She hesitated. "Have you called in anyone else? A doctor?"

"Dr. Munro saw him while the fever was at its worst." But I couldn't afford him again.

"That old slow top. You need an expert opinion," Mrs. Low said. "And you shall have it."

Before I could protest, she was kneeling in front of me, holding my hands. "Let me, Isobel. My sister-in-law consulted Dr. Burnett last year and said his services are excellent. If there is any way to help Thomas—well, you simply must."

"You know I can't repay you."

"You ought to know I wouldn't ask." Her grip tightened on my hands. "Think of it as a favor to your father. He and my husband were such good friends." She dabbed at my cheeks with the handkerchief. "My dear, you cannot bear this all on your own."

I nodded, overcome. Mrs. Low had hired me as Minnie's teacher years ago, certainly as a favor to my father. But he had died two years before; this boon was for Thomas and me. "I—"

"Don't speak," Mrs. Low said. "I will arrange it before Minnie and I leave. If anything needs to be done, Mr. Low will attend to it."

I gulped. "What is the name of the doctor again?" I knew little of the physicians currently making a name for our city, besides that they had done so. Two of my students had fathers working at Edinburgh University.

"I've heard him lecture. Dr. Conall Burnett. Wonderful man. A genius. They say there are few like him."

Later I learned that was true. Too late for me, though.

{ 2 }

The door to the consulting room opened, revealing a lean man with weathered cheeks and a pair of side whiskers much redder than his sandy blond hair. He smiled. "You must be Mrs. Tait."

I nodded, used to the lie after this many years. "Thank you for seeing us, Dr. Burnett."

"Think nothing of it, my dear. I'm happy to help any friend of Caroline Low's."

I passed by him through the door, hand in hand with Thomas, blinded briefly by the spring sunshine pouring through the long windows—a marked contrast from the dimly lit corridor.

"Morning, Isobel." The unexpected greeting caught me like a surreptitious tap on the shoulder. I turned away from the light and discovered a friend occupying one of the chairs, his warm smile dispelling my unease.

"Mr. Craig! How good to see you."

"Dr. Burnett was kind enough to invite me," Mr. Craig explained.

"I'm very happy to hear firsthand his management of your son's case." Dr. Burnett shut the door. I glanced between the two of them, not sure where to go, until Dr. Burnett rescued me. "If

Thomas will be good enough to lie on the sofa, you can take the nearest chair."

My eyes had adjusted now. I crossed a softly fading carpet to the red patterned sofa, taking in the array of tools neatly arranged on the dusty walnut desk. And behind it, shelves full of books and—

I stopped, a shiver passing over me.

"Don't mind my specimens," Dr. Burnett said.

I pulled my eyes away from the wired bird skeleton poised on the second-highest shelf—an evil-looking thing with hollow eyes, knife-like beak, and widespread bone wings ready to swoop and pounce.

Mother Mary, there was more. A rank of jars occupied the shelf below, all filled with murky liquid and—I gulped, trying not to stare. One held an unidentifiable gray cauliflower-esque lump, but I recognized the kidney right next to it. This one bore a blossom-like growth on one side. "What are they?" I asked, a little breathless.

"Nothing to alarm you. Just part of my collection. There's more in my drawing room. Essential to my teaching work, but I'm sorry if you find them alarming. Most people are eager to take a look."

Mr. Craig chuckled. "They pay for the privilege, if you can believe it, Isobel. Not just students and medical men, but quite ordinary folk."

I tore my eyes away from a pale floating hand with the third and fourth fingers joined together. It was, I supposed, not that different from paying to look at the freaks at the fair, but I'd always disliked the ugliness of selling tickets and staring.

"Just pretend there's nothing there," Dr. Burnett suggested.

I closed my eyes and took the last three steps to the sofa. Thomas, always shy among strangers, didn't protest when I let go of his hand and motioned him to sit down. He lay back promptly, familiar enough with medical men to know what to expect.

"What a well-behaved boy." Dr. Burnett smiled down at him. "I'm glad to see you are so good to your mother."

"He's an excellent chap," Mr. Craig said, with a quick smile at me. He knew how I felt about homilies. Why so many strangers took it upon themselves to instruct every child they came across, I'd never understand, but luckily, Thomas never seemed to mind. I was the one who bristled like a cat at well-meant advice. But then, we received more than most, since I was a "widow."

"Mr. Craig has kindly acquainted me with Thomas's history," Dr. Burnett went on.

"Dr. Burnett is wonderful with the stethoscope," Mr. Craig said. "He can tell, just from the sound, precisely where the trouble is."

"And why does that help?" I asked. It wasn't as if Thomas was a clock they could open and fix.

"Some murmurs heal on their own," Dr. Burnett explained, "so identifying the variety informs the prognosis."

I smiled, like women do when they are pretending to understand something. Dr. Burnett didn't need to know I was better read than my circumstances warranted.

And the kind of murmurs arising from fevers? What's their prognosis? I wanted to ask, but couldn't, not with Thomas beside me. He was quick-witted too.

Dr. Burnett worked like a born showman, selecting his instruments and shooting his cuffs, bending, listening, his face creasing, clearing, turning pensive. He straightened and offered the stethoscope to Mr. Craig. "You hear it, Stephen? The opening snap?"

Mr. Craig bent, but after a minute he shook his head. "I fear my hearing's not as good as yours."

"It's in the mitral valve—chronic, not acute, probably stenosis. Wait, let me show you."

Striding to the bookshelf, he retrieved a heavy volume and laid it open on the couch, flipping through vivid color plates until he found the one he wanted. I peered down at the drawing of a heart, purple with vessels of blue and crimson, sliced open to reveal its inner chambers. The parts were lettered, and the sides of the page lined with columns of incomprehensible names.

I'd ask Mr. Craig to explain to me later, I decided, but then Dr. Burnett resorted to a language I knew. Perhaps the one I knew best. He tapped a short, syncopated beat on the nearby table. "One *two,* one *two,* one *two*—is what we expect, but Thomas here is going at more of a gallop—da-di-*la,* da-di-*la.* Try again," Burnett urged, offering the stethoscope with an eager grin.

"May I?" I asked.

"Y—you would like to try?"

It was an unusual request, especially from a woman, but Burnett's surprise indicated he'd quite forgotten me. I didn't blame him—if anything, I liked him better for it, knowing myself how it was, caught up in one's passion. If his intense focus hadn't betrayed his, the gruesome collection certainly did. Thomas needed a doctor who made medicine his whole life, not only our gentle, generous Mr. Craig.

"I'm considered to have quite a good ear," I explained, and stretched out a hand for the stethoscope, smiling apologetically.

"Mrs. Tait teaches pianoforte. She's very accomplished," Mr. Craig put in.

Burnett hesitated and glanced at my son. "You do not mind, Thomas?"

Why Thomas should mind me more than him, a stranger, I couldn't think, but I reminded myself that genius is often tactless. My father had always thought so, and he'd counted enough geniuses among his acquaintance to know.

Thomas gave a small shake of his head and allowed Burnett to reposition him and place the wooden tube. "Lean in, Mrs. Tait. I'll hold it for you."

"Thank you, doctor."

I closed my eyes and trained my ear, letting go of everything else around me, filling myself with the irregular trot of my son's heart: almost the cadence of a Vivaldi concerto, the pastoral dance of spring, or the rustic dance of summer, much quicker than the slow tread that sometimes sounded in my ears when I lay awake and overtired.

Be strong, little heart, I silently ordered, and straightened, leaving Thomas with a passing caress. "I hear it." Yes, his heart was bruised, but surely if we took good care...

I retreated to my chair while they consulted, smiling at Thomas to remind him to be patient. Finally, Dr. Burnett turned to me.

"Come into the garden, Mrs. Tait. We can talk there."

A tight heaviness warned of the alchemical transformation beginning in my own chest, and I followed him out, my face stiff.

"I'm afraid your son's case is very grave." His tone was measured and rational, and he had his feet braced slightly apart, as if anticipating from me a faint or an emotional storm. All I did was nod dumbly. Foolish to hope, but how does one go on not hoping? I stared at a profusion of roses climbing the garden wall, unable to watch his face.

"I cannot cure or even treat his condition. It is incredibly rare. Most patients with this defect die within three years."

I took a breath. We had time still. Years, even, but every day would be the best. Stories every bedtime. Naps together in the bed beneath the window before I taught my lessons. I would tell him the truth, and we would fill each day with as much joy as we could cram into it.

Burnett was talking about tonics, how he could prescribe nothing to better Mr. Craig's current prescription, but that rest and a judicious amount of gentle activity was advisable. I scarcely heard, but then he offered me his handkerchief.

"I'm so sorry, Mrs. Tait."

I scrubbed at my cheeks. "I'm all right. Thomas and I will be all right."

"Perhaps it will be better if I write my advice in a letter. You'll give me your address?"

I recited the direction gratefully while tidying my face. "Thank you. I'll take him home now, Dr. Burnett."

Thomas set aside his spoon. "We have custard every day now."

I patted his hand. "Well, you know why. I promised you enough for a lifetime." Eggs and cream were good for him.

It hadn't, after all, been so very hard to tell him. Thomas, wise thing that he was, had known for some time. Now each day was special, a quiet celebration. I was more wounded than he was by the fact he'd never grow up. Buoyed by his robust child's confidence, he seldom seemed afraid, telling me he was going ahead, that heaven was a fine place to wait for me.

"But will you still have custard without me?" he asked. "You mustn't be reckless with money."

He was good at throwing my words—old words—back at me, and his sidelong look meant he was truly concerned.

"Thomas," I said. "It's my job to do the worrying. I'll always have custard, and I'll always remember you eating all my raisins."

He scooped up another spoonful, his dimple winking at me from his right cheek. "Enough for a lifetime, you said."

Soon enough, our bowls were empty. I set them aside for the landlady and peered out the window. The sky, a muddle of grays—warm, cold, light, and dark—favored the warmer tones just now. "Shall we have a walk?"

"I'll get my kite," he said.

He carried the sturdy assemblage of sticks, glue, and brown paper in one hand while I carried him down the three flights of stairs on my back. He was light enough that it wasn't hard, though I always had to pause at the landings on the way up. If I let him climb on his own, he lost his breath so quickly. Out in the street, instead of running ahead, as he had formerly, he trotted at my side, our hands clasped together, the tail of the kite writing cursive loops in the air behind us.

"'Tis a fine day for flying," he told me.

"Aye."

The sun pierced the clouds, lightening the gray and smoke-stained stone walls lining the street and reflecting off the window-panes so brightly I had to avert my eyes. The wind was brisk, the air smelled clean, the cobbles were freshly washed by the morning's rain. Pitched roofs, dotted with tiny dormers, blinked down at us like so many just-awoken eyes.

The buildings here were older, plain, a little higgledy-piggledy: a patched roof here, a rickety set of wooden stairs there, clinging desperately to the shabby house on the end of the row, when most of the other buildings had sufficient manners to hide their staircases indoors.

Tatty laundry hung from every railing, and one of the residents was playing a poorly tuned fiddle.

Jarring notes aside, the tune was a jaunty, pleasant one, and Thomas and I matched our steps to the fiddler's tempo. It wasn't very poor here, not like the steep and filthy closes beyond the university, higher up the hill, where buildings pressed so tight you could spread your arms and touch the walls on either side of the street. But it wasn't rich here, either. This was the home of shopkeepers, tradesmen, tutors, students, spinster gentlewomen, stretching meager livings. People with enough, but not plenty, like Thomas and me.

My son smiled, eager to reach the end of the road and the green meadow beyond. With tree-lined paths and wide stretches of grass, the place was popular for walking and for games like golf. Plenty of folk were enjoying both here today. Leaving the path, Thomas and I found a place away from most others and clear of the trees. I tossed the kite up, and the wind caught it and carried it away.

"Look at it go!" Thomas said, laughing as the spool of string spun in his hands. The kite soared above the steep slate rooftops edging the field and the church spires beyond, kicking and spinning. I tugged my shawl closer and craned my head up, watching it shrink in the sky.

The wind eased, and Thomas reeled it in, tightening the slack in the string until another gust bore it upward. My cares lifted, too, and I drank in the sight of Thomas playing, eyes bright, patches of scarlet high on his cheeks. When it was my turn, I sat down on the grass, holding the string, making a pillow for him on my lap, so we could stare up into the sky.

We followed the kite's swaying dance, until a chance movement caught my eye, drawing it to the nearest path—and I flinched. Embarrassment burned my cheeks; I turned my face away and regretted it at once. I knew better. The unfortunate man on the path didn't deserve this.

I dared a glance back. He'd stopped a dozen yards from us,

pausing to light his pipe, intent on shielding his flickering match. Maybe he hadn't noticed my start. In any case, he must be used to people taking fright and looking hastily away because he looked like no human I'd ever seen, his features melted away, falling down his neck like so much melted wax. Without brows or lashes, his eyes were dark blots in a pale void, his mouth stretched out of shape by the taut scars that marred him. My heart clenched; he must have been burned terribly.

I looked down at Thomas, still focused on the kite. "If I buy more string, will you make us another? Then we could each fly one."

He settled deeper into my lap, his hand slipping into my free one. "It's good to share."

He tired so fast. I brushed the hair off his forehead and looked at the kite, letting the wind cool the burn in my eyes. When I glanced sideways, the man was still lingering, but upon catching my eye, he began shuffling away.

I shifted on the grass. It was a public path. Just because he looked different—I frowned at my lap and told myself that it wasn't his appearance. I'd be perturbed by anyone loitering this close without a reason. But he'd gone. I could put him from my mind.

"Mam, you keep jostling."

"Sorry, love. My foot's tingling."

Thomas sat up.

"I have to teach the Duncan girls soon," I said, reminding myself as much as him. "Mrs. McPherson said she'd sit with you till I come home."

Thomas made a face. Our landlady, though kind enough to watch him, never diverted her attention too far from her knitting. "It's not the Duncans' day."

"I know. But Marjory had a cold on Monday." All three sisters studied the piano, so when I could reschedule them, I did. "I'll give you your story before I go."

He huffed, only partly appeased. "I hope they practiced."

I bit my lip, hearing my grumbles thrown back at me. "It doesn't matter so much if they do or don't," I admitted. "They pay."

I pinched his ear, now cold at the edges. "Home again? It's chilly." His hands had burrowed into his pockets without me noticing. Next time I'd keep better watch, so he wouldn't get cold. "A cup of tea for you now, then a nap and—"

I broke off as Thomas turned and froze, locking eyes with the melted man. He'd come back. Perhaps he'd intended only to walk to the end of the row, then reverse his direction, but his presence again was unsettling.

"Come along." I jumped to my feet and took Thomas firmly by the hand. As we hurried away, I ducked my head and murmured, "I know, love, but we mustn't stare."

"But he stared at me," Thomas said indignantly. "When I caught him at it, he didn't even look away."

"Then we should be sorry for him," I said. "He must not be right in the head."

Thomas glanced back and stuck out his tongue. I quickened my steps, but quickly regretted it when Thomas began puffing at my side.

"Do you want to sit?" There was a low wall ahead, wet and green with moss.

Thomas shook his head.

"I'll carry you, then," I said, unaccountably relieved not to be detained, yet half-ashamed of myself for it. The man wasn't to blame for his deformity. People were cruel, and wearing a face like that...

I shook my head, settled Thomas firmly on my back, and set off up the hill. Back in our rooms, I brewed tea for us both and filled a hot-water bottle for Thomas, ignoring the prickling at the back of my neck. As he sipped tea and warmed his toes, I set out the evening's candles—one for Mrs. McPherson to knit by, and another for Thomas—and happened to glance into the street.

The ruined face wasn't visible, but I started at the shape of the shoulders hidden behind a loose brown jacket. Then I snorted. Brown jacket? The city was full of them, and every butcher and builder and canal worker—and many other men besides—had wide shoulders. This wasn't the same man. I was simply unnerved by my earlier encounters with that face.

I didn't own the road. If a man wanted to lean against a lamppost and talk with a fellow in a finer coat and hat, I couldn't stop him, even if he did have a frightening face.

And this one couldn't have. The idea was absurd. I narrowed my eyes anyway, straining for a better look.

"Don't forget my story," Thomas piped up. "You promised."

"So I did." I consulted the watch I kept in my pocket, now that my hourglass was broken. It had been Father's. Only half an hour until the Duncans' lessons. Closing the curtains would have to suffice.

I squeezed into the chair beside Thomas, our bodies conforming to each other's as comfortably as cats

"Back, far back when the world was young—" I paused, waiting for Thomas to prompt me.

"Let's have a monster story," Thomas said.

I shook my head, sharply enough to make Thomas's brow crease with a question. "Not when I'm about to leave you with Mrs. McPherson," I said quickly, forcing brightness into my voice. "You'll let your imagination run away with you, and then you'll be too afraid to sleep."

"I will not," Thomas asserted, disgusted I'd even imagine such a thing.

"Better safe than sorry," I said, drawing a quick finger down the length of his nose. "No monsters today, but don't fret. I'll give you a good yarn."

"All right, then." He subsided, resting his cheek on my arm.

"A boy built a kite, you know, big as a cow, big as the kirkyard gate. And on a windy Wednesday, he went to the meadows, his pockets full of apples and the kite string tied round his waist—"

"Red apples?"

"Of course they were. Red and round as his cheeks." I grinned and pinched his softly.

Soon, I set out for the Duncans' with my father's old walking stick tucked under my arm, a precaution I sometimes carried when I wasn't sanguine about everyone I might meet on my way. Foolish, especially when most days a firm step and sharp sense of purpose were more than sufficient protection. As I locked the door behind me, I glanced over my shoulder. The place by the lamppost was empty.

Of course it was. *You're being ridiculous*, I told myself. But my eyes darted to the place automatically when I came and went the next day and the day after that.

The sky was thick and mizzling as I hastened home the following Thursday after another afternoon of lessons. Henrietta Maitland and Barbara and Marion Innes were sound musicians, competently executing their Beethoven and Mozart to their parents' satisfaction. Emilia Hunter had a lovely touch but never practiced, so her fingers had stumbled repeatedly over her studies and scales. But she had no mother, and her indulgent papa didn't mind. She was a tall girl who liked her books, with a sharp sense of humor, and though at this rate she would never make a musician, I liked her best of the bunch.

Balancing my umbrella in one hand and clutching my leather portfolio of sheet music in the other, I leaped from the curb over a fast-growing puddle and scurried across the street, stepping aside for a trio of university students. Their conversation, punctuated by urgent hand gestures, was so intense they'd have barreled right though me if I hadn't dodged. The shortest, spotting my maneuvers belatedly, flashed me a look of apology and touched the brim of his hat.

I returned a frown and lowered my umbrella like a shield against the next gust of wind. My cloak needed a good drying in front of the fire. Beyond the university's stately halls and domed edifices, I passed bookshops and instrument makers, many with reputations as celebrated as the professors and surgeons and scientists they supplied. Ornamental stonework abounded, embellishing doors and windows, cornices and downspouts, but it all looked gloomy under today's downpour.

At last I reached my front step. Shaking the rain from my umbrella, I stepped inside, surprised by the unlocked front door. "Thomas?" I called, my voice ringing in the silent house.

Perhaps he'd fallen asleep.

I let myself into our rooms, where Mrs. McPherson was sleeping by the fire. The other chair, a wooden rocker, was empty.

It shouldn't be. I'd left Thomas tired, after a long indoor game of hide-and-seek, anticipating that he'd rest quietly in the older woman's company.

"Mrs. Mac?"

This wasn't the first time she'd dozed off. The years were beginning to tell on her face, matching the bright silver filigree spreading through her dark hair. I nudged her shoulder, and her head drooped.

"Thomas?" I called again.

No response, and Mrs. Mac didn't even start. I knelt, giving her a rough shake. She jerked and mumbled sleepily.

"Izzie? Sorry, I—"

"Where's Thomas?"

She blinked heavy eyes but couldn't seem to focus. I darted into the bedroom. The bed was empty, the covers smooth and untroubled. My heart, already thumping noisily, sped to a canter.

"He must be with Miss Clark," I said aloud. The middle-aged spinster who lived across the hall, a teacher in a nearby academy, always made him welcome, offering biscuits, books, and snowflakes of cut paper. With Mrs. Mac asleep, he could have grown restless and wandered beyond our door.

I rapped on Miss Clark's with unaccustomed sharpness. "I've come for Thomas," I said breathlessly.

"He's not here," she said, surprise lengthening her face. "I've not seen him since the day before yesterday. Is something wrong?" She caught my hands, and I realized they were shaking.

"I can't find him. He wouldn't have gone outside," I said, forestalling her question. The only place he'd venture without me was here. Or Mrs. McPherson's kitchen.

"He'll be downstairs, then," Miss Clark said, relaxing into a smile. "I'll help you search."

She talked soothingly as we made our way to the tiled room in the basement. Mrs. McPherson's day girl was sleeping in her chair, next to the bowl of abandoned potatoes she had been scrubbing for our supper.

Her too? I scowled, banishing wispy half-formed thoughts of affronted fairies stealing children or cursing them and putting whole castles to sleep.

"Wake up, Gracie!"

She jolted awake, unlike Mrs. Mac.

"Have you seen my Thomas?" I asked, desperation deep in my voice.

"Naw." She scratched a cheek, marred with bright red spots that might have caused another girl despair, but placid Gracie didn't let these or anything else concern her. "Why? He missing?"

I recoiled from the word, despite her flat tone. "Did you hear the door?" I demanded. "It was unlocked." I always locked it.

"I never went out," Miss Clark put in.

Gracie tipped her head. "Might have heard it, but I never mind it. There's always plenty of coming and going."

Mrs. McPherson had two more lodgers, not enough, in my mind, for Gracie's claims. Miss Clark spoke before I could. "We need you to help us look."

"Thomas! Come out. This isn't funny!" I called.

We searched the larder, the cellar, the kitchen cupboard, an enormous basket of laundry, and behind a sack of carrots too small to conceal a cat. No sign of him.

Mrs. McPherson met us on our way back up the stairs. "I'm so sorry, Izzie. I must be unwell. I wasn't even tired when you left, and now I feel like I've been trampled. I'm sure he's only playing. He wasn't belowstairs?"

I pursed my lips, swallowing the bile-tinged words crowding my throat.

"My rooms, then." Mrs. McPherson turned around, retracing her route upstairs. "We'll find him soon enough."

Her words ran like a litany in my head. *He's only playing,* I told myself, but I knew my son. He'd never done anything like this before. I rushed through Mrs. McPherson's rooms, tore open the cupboards and dove under the bed, then did the same in mine. Thomas wasn't behind the curtains or curled up behind a door. He wasn't in Miss Clark's rooms or Mr. Mitchell's on the other floor. By now, everyone in the house was searching.

"We have to look outside," I said finally, arms heavy.

Miss Clark caught me by the shoulders and forced me into a chair. "Miss Simpson's already gone next door and Mr. Mitchell's looking down the street."

My chin shook. And my hands, still empty. If not for my nerves, tight as the spring of a rat trap, my very bones would be jostling apart. I gulped, afraid of the tears behind my hot eyelids, the first sob that would tear me wide open.

"Why did you fall asleep?" I wailed, turning on Mrs. Mac. "Thomas wouldn't have—"

"I know. He's a good boy. And too tired, most days, to venture far." She blinked and swallowed. "Isobel, I—" The lines in her face lengthened, etching deeper. "I don't know. It doesn't make sense. And Gracie—" She shook her head. "We'll find Thomas. Ten to one, he's someplace we haven't thought to look."

"He wouldn't leave," I insisted. "And he wouldn't hide from me."

Mrs. McPherson licked her lips. "If he was asleep, like I was..."

"What?" I demanded.

She swallowed, speaking as if uncertain. "I doze sometimes. You know that. But I'm a light sleeper. You were all calling and banging about for a good while before I even stirred. Thomas and I shared a pot of tea. And I poured a cup for Gracie before I carried it up."

I fixed my gaze on the table, on the two cups, one empty, one half-full. Beside them stood a little blue-glazed, two-handled earthenware mug. Only dregs remained in the pot. I sniffed them, then passed the pot to Mrs. Mac.

"Smells different," I said.

She inhaled. "I can't tell," she said helplessly, and passed it to Miss Clark.

"It is a little unusual," she said. "Did it taste—"

"Where did you get it?" I demanded.

"Bought it this morning," she said. "A man came early, a cripple, with things to sell. I thought I should help him."

Inexplicable fear shot through me, like lightning, all the way to the tips of my fingers. "What did he look like?"

Mrs. McPherson licked her lips, hesitating.

I choked. I had no words. I couldn't even breathe.

"What's wrong, Izzie?"

I gripped my knees. Told myself that the air couldn't be solidifying around me. It was air. Meant to flow in and out of my lungs. "The man," I croaked. "The cripple. Was it his face?"

"He had a scarf," Mrs. McPherson said. "So I couldn't see all of him, but I understood why he didn't want—well, he must have been burned, you see. I felt so badly for him."

My lungs folded, sticking on themselves like wet paper. "I've seen him," I rasped. "Loitering in the park last week. He followed us home."

"That doesn't make any sense," Miss Clark said.

"We need the police," I told her.

I clutched my cooling cup of tea and stared at the window, at my ghastly reflection, thrown back by the dark. Thomas would never have stayed away, not at this hour.

"Anyone else, Mrs. Tait?" Across from me, the detective narrowed his eyes, like he'd asked this more than once.

I glanced at the tight lines of scratchy handwriting in his notebook and shook my head.

"There's the bookseller's down Guthrie Street," Mrs. McPherson put in desperately. "They know Thomas. He might have walked there."

More scratching from the detective's pencil. "It's important," he said. "Anyone we can ask who might have seen him. Any outing you might have planned but forgotten—"

"I haven't forgotten," I said wearily. "Thomas is an invalid. I told you before. He doesn't go anywhere without me."

"If he was vexed at being left alone—"

"Mrs. McPherson was with him," I repeated. "I never leave Thomas alone."

"Naturally, naturally," he said, waving his pencil soothingly.

"And something was put in their tea," I said. "I told you about the man selling—"

"The burned fellow, aye."

I flinched at his offhand tone, as casually delivered as the caning at school that had left bumps on my arms. "You have to find him," I snapped. "I told you. On Saturday that man followed me and Thomas home from the park—"

"I've six officers looking, plus the local watch. Plenty of your neighbors searching as well. We'll find your boy."

But the world was wide, and Thomas only seven, facts this man certainly understood. Yet somehow, even when I explained... I set my cup down with a clang and made to rise from my chair, but the man stopped me, trapping me with a sandbag hand plopped onto my knee. "Mrs. Tait, I need you here. Is there anyone else Thomas knows or might have gone to?"

I fought not to writhe within my chair, but I'd spent time with the others, dashing up and down the streets, to no avail. "Thomas isn't like that. He doesn't run off."

The detective nodded. "But if he did, who might—"

"I've told you everyone! Besides Mrs. McPherson and me—"

Still blocking me, he turned his face away. "Mrs. M., you wouldn't be able to bring us a fresh cup of tea? This one can scarcely be warm by now."

My guts twisted, as they did with each reminder of the hours slipping past, minute by minute. Thomas might be miles away by now. It was still raining. He'd barely touched his supper. Where was he? I couldn't stop thinking but didn't dare guess. Every terrible thing I'd ever read or overheard kept slicing apart my control.

A sob punched through my aching ribs, sore from spells of weeping.

The detective passed me a handkerchief and glanced over his shoulder at the door by which Mrs. McPherson had left. "Your land-lady," he said, voice low. "Does she like a tipple?"

I straightened, glaring until he moved a few inches back. "Mrs. McPherson is a teetotaler," I spat. "She doesn't allow spirits in the house."

"Of course, of course," he said, with an infuriating lack of conviction, jotting another line in his book.

"Your notes aren't going to find Thomas," I said. "Why can't you—"

"Ah. There you are." The man in front of me looked over my shoulder and sighed in relief. I turned around. Another dark-coated officer stood in the doorway, one hand resting on the frame.

"This is the mother?"

A muscle between my shoulder twitched. *Your boy. The son. The mother.* We had names. These convenient categories were too much like the harrowing alternatives that ought to be impossible, but which I was forced to consider. *The victim. The body.*

The man in front of me nodded, the one with sandbag hands, and the new arrival stepped into the room. In appearance, he was as unlike the first as could be: tanned instead of freckled, and dark of hair and eye compared to the other's familiar ginger and hazel coloring. His shoulders were stiff, and his mouth bracketed with lines, like it was used to holding back words.

"This is my colleague, Mr. Adam Kerr," the first one said. "He's circulated your boy's description."

"It'll be in every station house within the hour," Kerr promised. "We're putting every man on the search. Have faith, Mrs. Tait."

I swallowed. I wanted to, but—

He took Sandbag Hands's abandoned chair, and brought it next to mine, settling into the worn upholstery and depositing a leather case on the table, next to a splash of tea from my neglected cup.

"This fellow you say sold the unusual tea to your landlady. What was he like?"

"Terribly scarred. Burned, I imagine. His eyes—"

"Give me a moment, if you please." He reached into the case resting on the table and drew out paper and charcoals. With a few quick strokes, he'd drawn the outline of a head. "How's the shape?"

"Longer," I said, and bit my lip. "But I saw him days ago, and Mrs. McPherson—"

"I'll speak to her afterward," he said. "For now, it's best to keep your recollections separate. And two drawings—it will make it easier for us to find him."

"And easier to see if I'm telling the truth." I wasn't an imbecile, and wanted him and his friend to know it.

Kerr smiled again, conceding the point. "His ears?"

"Crumpled," I said. "Like this." I traced a finger over the paper. His charcoal quickly followed, pulling features from the void of empty paper.

"His face looked stretched. The bottom lip turned down." I demonstrated. "And large pouches underneath the eyes."

The other detective, restless on his feet, peered down at the drawing. "Face like that, he won't be hard to find. Howling ugly, he is." He stuffed his hands in his pockets.

I kept my attention on the paper. Kerr's hand moved quickly. He had no wedding ring, not like the other detective, and most of the constables. "No, he didn't have any eyebrows," I corrected.

Kerr frowned and rubbed the eyebrow off his sketch.

The other detective, increasingly restless, bounced on his heels. "I'll see about that tea," he told me. Then, to Kerr, "Have to nip home for a moment. The wife's expecting me, but I'll be right back. You won't miss me."

I opened my mouth to argue, but he was already gone, treading heavily down the stairs.

"My son's been taken," I said, to no one in particular, since I didn't exactly expect sympathy from Adam Kerr, who'd said nothing about his colleague's desertion. "He can send his wife a message."

Kerr shook his head. "I don't give Hugh orders."

"Why not? Doesn't he like you?" I snapped. I didn't like either of them, that was certain.

"He likes me well enough." His head bent over the paper, giving me a view of nothing but his carefully cut dark hair.

"Then it must be me he doesn't care for."

Kerr didn't contradict me. I reached for my abandoned teacup and gulped the cold brew until it was empty.

"The mouth is like this?" he asked.

I nodded. Then, unable to help myself, "Why can't you—"

"Your boy hasn't been missing long," he interrupted. "That's a point in our favor."

"Thomas didn't wander away on his own," I insisted. "Someone took him."

Kerr finished darkening the shadow below the monster man's bottom lip before studying me across his portrait.

"Abductions happen, Mrs. Tait. But they are rare. That's why Detective Fraser and I must keep open minds. It isn't a matter of either of us liking or disliking you."

Frustration swelled in my chest, pressing against my ribs and tightly closed throat. "It matters if you don't believe me. It matters to Thomas."

"Our men are looking," he said. "A clear drawing will help."

Perhaps it would, but how many more minutes had passed? Unwilling to cry or scream (I'd done plenty of that already), I pushed up and marched to the window, resting my pounding forehead against the cool glass.

{ 3 }

At noon the next day, there was still no sign of him. Sapped by
the long night's waiting, by hours of walking and searching in
mist and rain, I couldn't remain in the house. Detectives Kerr and
Fraser had left, but Miss Simpson and Mrs. McPherson wouldn't
leave me—a monumental kindness, but their continual reassurances
were becoming unbearable.

Miss Simpson didn't think going out was wise, not in my current
state. Neither did Mrs. McPherson. "The police are searching," she
said pleadingly. "We can't do any better than them."

I nodded, because it seemed churlish to disagree. "I know. But
I can't be inside."

"Very well. But don't be long." She patted my hand, tied my
bonnet for me, and hastened me out the door.

The street—wet, gray, forlorn—was unchanged from an hour
ago, when we'd returned again empty-handed, damp, and shivering. I'd been up and down it numberless times, begged for news of
Thomas from everyone I met, knocked at every door.

But there was more that could be done. Not just by the police,
so I buttoned the collar of my cloak, pulling it close, and turned
north toward New Town. Used to walking up and down hills, my

gasping breath wasn't from the steep streets. Alone, I let despair take me, because I couldn't beside the women who were trying so valiantly to help.

Sobbing as I walked, I ignored the parade of shocked, pitying, and embarrassed looks, coursing along the Royal Mile. Thomas and I used to walk here, up the wide street from the old tollbooth. We'd point out steeples and peer in shop windows all through Lawnmarket to Castle Hill, until we stood below the great fortress presiding over the city. Thomas liked seeing the garrison patrolling the walls and hearing the gunfire, giving the time to the ships in Leith Harbor far below. Since his fever, I'd never let him try the climb. He wouldn't have had strength for it and—

I stuffed down my emotions again, wresting back a facade of control. I would need it.

Imagining my fingers marching through scales—C major, C minor, then D—I slowed and lengthened my breaths. The Stevensons lived on Moray Place, a sweeping circle of houses in a comfortably assured part of town, surrounding a private garden. I'd sworn never to visit the house, though I passed it several times a week, walking from one student's home to the next, averting my eyes and refusing to glance into the windows.

The steps were swept, the knocker polished, the window shades drawn, as if the house was ignoring me in turn. Stubbornly, I rang the bell and gave my card to the butler, face up, though there was nothing to stop him from turning it over and reading the penciled message on the reverse.

Help please. Thomas is missing.

"I'm here to see Mr. Stevenson."

Tearstained and exhausted, with muddled hair and splashed skirts, I wasn't his usual sort of visitor.

The butler shut the door—no surprise, since my appearance certainly didn't merit waiting in the parlor. I paced the front step, reminding myself of the reasons John Stevenson would never agree to see me.

"Mrs. Tait?"

I turned and saw the butler beckoning me inside. "This way."

John was in his study. The gray at his temples surprised me, but nothing else had changed. Still clean-shaven, still with the same style of knot in his cravat, and surrounded by books. An inkstand with bronze elephants sat precisely on his leather-topped desk. The bust of his father, John Stevenson Senior, watched from the table beside the window.

John Stevenson—the younger one—looked handsome as ever.

"Mrs. Tait."

Hands at my sides, it was impossible to stretch my fingers inside my gloves without him noticing. Everything I wore felt far too tight.

"Mr. Stevenson. Thank you for seeing me."

"I haven't much time." He glanced up briefly from his letter, his hand not slowing.

"I understand." I watched as he dropped a stop at the end of his sentence and pushed the paper away. "I know I'm not supposed to come here, but Thomas—" I stopped, swaying on my feet, and John forgot his papers, coming around the desk and leading me to a nearby chair.

"Isobel." His voice dropped from the polite, indifferent tone to a gentle whisper, the one that had played prelude to our poorly composed duet.

"Why don't you tell me what's wrong?"

Tears came, a smattering and then a flood of them, with a storm of incoherent words. When the deluge stopped, I was holding his hand, sipping his whisky.

"And they can find no sign of the boy?"

"Thomas," I corrected. "No. They've found nothing."

He got up and walked to the window, adjusted the curtains, thought better of it, then put them back. "I wanted you to leave him with me," he said.

"Please don't," I said, tight with pain. "I know. And I've thought it often enough since yesterday." It didn't matter now that I was Thomas's mother, that I loved him more. I'd fought to keep him for myself, away from John. This was my fault, and no one else's.

John, perhaps swayed by my tears, didn't add anything more. "I'll speak to the police," he said quietly. "Our families knew each other. It would be natural for me to help."

I kept my chin down, my hands clasped around the whisky glass. His last words weren't spoken for me, but I needed him to believe them.

"I hoped—perhaps you could offer a reward. Because of the old friendship between our families. As you said, it wouldn't be a very singular thing to do."

He hesitated, knowing as well as I did that there still might be talk.

"Please, John," I whispered. "I don't know what to do."

"Aye, of course. What are the names of the detectives?"

"Adam Kerr. The senior officer is a Mr. Hugh Fraser."

"And you're certain Thomas wouldn't have run off on his own? It's the kind of thing a headstrong child might do."

"Thomas isn't headstrong. And"—I swallowed—"he's sickly. Has been for over a year. Since catching scarlet fever."

He frowned. "You didn't tell me."

I set down the glass and focused on the row of miniatures displayed on his desk: his wife, Helen, and two daughters. They'd be five and six now, but I hadn't heard any noises signifying they might be in the house. Both girls were too young to take music lessons, not that I'd ever agree to teach them. And John would never ask. "That was our agreement. We said—"

"I know. But you ought to tell me that sort of thing, Isobel." He sighed and shook his head. He poured himself another dose of whisky and downed it with a grimace. "Well, you came now. I care about him. And you. I'll see what I can do. I just hope it's not too late."

I took that as a dismissal. Pressing my lips together, I reached for my cloak.

High above, a wind from the sea teased apart tangles of cloud. Down on the ground, it drove people indoors and buffeted me along the streets. The sky brightened, and my heart sped. Surely they'd found him by now. Something had happened; I couldn't think what, but there would be a rational explanation. I hurried up muddy steps along a narrow close, leading me to the Mile again, the high spine of Edinburgh's aged back. Pushing past carts and stalls, I walked eastward along the Mile, then hastened into another narrow passageway, Borthwick's Close, to conduct me downhill and home.

Thomas might very well be found by now. Mrs. Mac would cry and hold him and put him to bed in my absence, but the thought of me not being there... I darted past an old woman, steadying myself on the wall to keep my footing on the steep, slippery cobbles.

Not much farther. I rounded the last corner and raced up the steps, through the front door, my heart pounding.

But the house was quiet, save for Gracie singing off-key in the kitchen. I swayed into the wall, letting my forehead press against the faded floral paper. I squeezed my eyelids together until sparks danced in the heavy dark.

For a long, long time, I hid there. Then, like a bent old woman compressed by the weight of a lifetime, I forced myself up the stairs. I rapped on Mrs. McPherson's parlor.

"I'm home." Then, before she could try to comfort me, I escaped to my empty rooms.

{ 4 }

The offices for the detectives of the Edinburgh Police were sparse, utilitarian, and dirtier than I'd imagined. But this wasn't my first visit, not even my fifteenth, so I was used to the old gray fingerprints on the whitewashed walls. The few windows in the building looked onto the mercat cross and the even dirtier square, but this side of the building, rubbing shoulders with St. Giles, didn't seem to have windows at all. Not that Mr. Kerr appeared to mind.

He greeted me patiently and offered me a chair. "How do you do, Mrs. Tait?"

"How do you think I'm doing?"

He had the grace to look ashamed. "We know this must be impossibly hard for you."

It was. And I wasn't in the mood for platitudes. "You don't know. You don't have children." I'd gathered this fact sometime in the last month, but not much else about him.

"Aye, I do not."

Under other circumstances, his tone might have made me pause, but I refused to be distracted. I spread my hands on the desk. John had offered a generous reward and spurred the police on multiple occasions. Detective Hugh Fraser, who led the investigation, had promised the might and energy of every man at his disposal, but twenty-three days had passed, and Thomas wasn't found.

Twenty-three days. I moved through each one like a broken clock, springs popping, gears grinding, parts of me falling off as time marched me around and around.

"As you know, numerous sightings continue to be reported since Mr. Stevenson offered his reward," Kerr said. "We've been presented with more than a dozen children, but three were girls, and none of the others were Thomas. We wished to spare you the distress of—"

"And the burned man? Have you found him?" My description, despite his doubts, had proved an uncanny match to Mrs. McPherson's.

"We tentatively identified him as Eoin Brennan."

"Yes. You told me."

"I spoke to his former landlord. Brennan paid his shot the morning after your son vanished. He was talking about going back to Ireland."

"And someone will look there?"

"We're making inquiries."

"Are you?" I challenged. "I came yesterday, and Mr. Fraser wouldn't see me."

I was still angry about it.

A line appeared between Kerr's brows. "Yesterday? I'm sure you're mistaken. If Hugh happened to be busy, he would have asked you to wait." His forehead smoothed. "I know—"

"You don't." My voice was tight with emotion. Embarrassingly so. I couldn't keep coming here and crying. Pressing my hands against my skirts, I forced an even tone. "Mr. Fraser told me to come another day. That's why I'm here again."

"Mrs. Tait—" Kerr looked pained.

I leaned forward. "This is a job for you. Thomas is my life."

He sighed. "I wish I had better news," he began, throwing me the same threadbare phrase. I wasn't having it.

I slapped my hands on the table. "I can't give up. I can't stop looking, and I can't let you stop either. Please, Mr. Kerr." Twenty-three days, and each one harder than the last.

He reached across the desk, one hand landing on mine. I glanced down, and saw I was wearing two different-colored gloves. "Your buttons are wrong too," he said quietly.

My eyes, dry and hot with anger a second ago, started leaking.

"You're unraveling," he said. "And no wonder. But are you eating? Sleeping?"

I swiped at my eyes with the back of my wrist. "How can I?"

"You must," he said gently, and my helplessness coalesced like quicksilver into impossible frustration. Too many would-be friends—Mrs. Low, Mrs. Clark, John's wife, Helen—had said the same to me. And more.

Even if they find him, how much longer—
You'd have lost him soon, anyway.

But I wanted these twenty-three days. I wanted the next week and the next year. I wanted my son back.

Kerr wasn't finished. "Falling to pieces won't help us find him," he said. "I'm sorry if Fraser was short with you, but the thing is—"

"Yes?" I snapped.

"We've seen a few similar cases, Fraser and I." Kerr sighed, and shifted his eyes to a space above my head. Reluctantly, he continued. "They are always hard, and yours is—well, these cases aren't always hard in the way you think. You'd give your eyes to have Thomas back, but not all parents would." He paused. "Often, you see, we end up investigating the family."

My breath rushed from me like I'd been punched. Fumbling for composure, for words to describe the impossible suggestion taking shape in my mind, I whispered, "You think I—" My voice broke. "You think I did this?"

"It would surprise me very much if you were responsible," Kerr said, his voice so low, I realized he didn't want his colleagues overhearing. They'd all decided I was guilty, and even if Kerr didn't agree, he didn't have the authority to press his opinion. "But I'm afraid Mr. Fraser is quite cynical."

"You're cleverer than he is," I mumbled, wanting to plead, but doubting it would matter. It was true, though. Kerr was better spoken than his colleague. He looked slightly older, and he'd clearly studied things Fraser hadn't, like drawing. "You know I'd never—"

"Hugh's been longer with the police than me," Kerr said quietly. "We regularly see things that make it easy to lose faith in humanity, even people we might be inclined to trust."

The smart of his accusation wasn't as strong as the fear freezing my heart. It chugged sluggishly, loudly, as cold spread from my chest to the tips of my fingers. "What kind of things?" What did he think had become of Thomas?

Kerr looked at me, and I almost flinched at the calm resignation in his dark eyes. "Mrs. Tait, please. I really can't say."

I wasn't sure if silence was really kindness, but I could tell he thought it was. On the floor below us, a woman started screaming, hurling curses at someone—probably a police officer. It was a fitting accompaniment, but I wasn't concerned with the fracas downstairs.

"My apologies," Kerr said. "We get all kinds brought in by the watch. Most remain here until they are sober."

"Did you investigate me?" I asked.

Kerr dipped his chin.

"But *you* don't think it was me."

"No." He wove his fingers together and stared at the papers neatly arranged across his desk. "You are everything you claim to be," he said, smiling thinly. "Almost. Can I help you home, Mrs. Tait?"

If I'd wondered, the slight emphasis on the surname and the *Mrs.* told me what he'd found. I fought down a blush, and waited to rise from my chair until he belatedly offered his arm.

"I'm glad *you* don't think I would hurt him," I muttered.

He didn't speak until we were well away from the station, in a street crowded with booksellers and student lodgings. "You need to be kind to yourself," he said. "It's not necessary to come to the station so often. I'll find you as soon as there's more to know."

"If," I corrected dully.

He patted my arm but didn't contradict me.

"Naturally, we'll keep Mr. Stevenson apprised as well," he said. "Your work is to press on, and to keep body and soul together."

Except I hadn't done that for Thomas. If he was still alive, the sand in his glass was quickly running out.

"It's hard to want to," I admitted. If I didn't go to the police station every day, what else could make me wash and dress and leave my rooms?

"Try," Kerr said firmly. "You really must."

Detective Adam Kerr was relieved, the following day, not to face another conference with Mrs. Tait. He didn't see her the next day, or the day after that. As the supply of spurious informants dwindled, their stories grew more far-fetched—snatched by Roma, stolen by

Irish witches—forcing Adam to examine the ideas Fraser and the superintendent were accepting as truth.

It was easy to blame Mrs. Tait or fasten fraying threads of suspicion on to her. Adam couldn't fault them for it. The Edinburgh Police came across too many infanticide investigations, too many wives and elderly fathers who fell down the stairs to accept at face value anyone's protestations of grief. The suspicion that Mrs. Tait had invented her late husband didn't help her credibility, particularly with Superintendent Maxwell, a strict Presbyterian.

Unlike him, Adam understood the expediency of camouflaging uncomfortable secrets. If it were possible to conceal his history, he would, but there were too many hints in his bronze skin and strong-featured face. His Scots name and accent couldn't cover those, and even if most of the constables never said anything to him, he knew they thought he was different. They joked with Fraser, but not with him. They drank with Fraser at the nearby pub, and while Adam occasionally trailed along, it was more comfortable to stay behind, do his work and accustom himself to being alone.

There were worse things than being perceived as different, though. It took very little to elicit judgment or persecution, so it had been shrewd, and probably necessary, for Mrs. Tait to hide some things about herself, if what he suspected was true. Unfortunately for her, the convenient story about a young soldier husband, now deceased, was a little too plausible. It wasn't helping her now and made her an untrustworthy witness—but in the absence of any proof against her, the Edinburgh Police would let things lie. Thomas's disappearance was unusual, but within the city's narrow wynds and dark closes, people vanished all the time.

"No more leads for us to follow anyway," was how Fraser put it.

Adam disagreed. There was one. He wasn't hopeful about it, but he owed it to Thomas Tait to try.

As he shrugged into his overcoat, Fraser looked up from his desk. "Off already? You have dinner with the stepmother tonight?"

In spite of his young wife, Fraser had a persistent weakness for faces like Emily's. According to him, she was wasted as a widow, and the least Adam could do was invite Fraser along to her family suppers, the ones Adam usually worked late to avoid.

"There's a call I have to make," Adam said.

Fraser raised his eyebrows expectantly, but Adam refused to be more forthcoming, clapping his hat on his head and hurrying from the office. "I'll see you tomorrow morning."

Fraser would try to dissuade him if he knew, arguing that they didn't need enemies, especially in the prosecutor's office. Besides, John Stevenson received his updates on Thomas's case at the police station, presenting himself punctually every morning, frowning over their lack of progress and offering to increase the reward. Given his likely connection to Thomas and Isobel, it was reasonable of him to receive updates at the police station, not his house. No point flaunting the boy in his wife's face.

But Adam wasn't interested in being reasonable and keeping life comfortable for Mr. John Stevenson, so he walked to New Town, and rapped impatiently at his front door.

"Detective Adam Kerr, for Mr. Stevenson," he said crisply, holding out his card.

In this neighborhood, Adam was used to being refused or admitted with startling alacrity—so neighbors wouldn't see. The Stevenson's butler swept him inside so quickly, Adam felt like he'd been dropped into the hall by the wind gusting down the street.

"Mr. Stevenson will see you in his study," the man said.

Not the parlor, where the ladies of the house sat, their murmurs simmering behind the paneled door. The study was at the end of the hall, after the last dark-toned oil painting.

"Detective Kerr to see you, sir," the servant announced, then faded away like a line written in disappearing ink.

Adam stepped inside. The room was overwarm, especially after his walk in the evening chill. The bookshelves seemed to lean in, as if they meant to close around him.

"Kerr! I didn't expect you today," John Stevenson said, setting aside a book and rising from his chair. "I planned to call at the station tomorrow as usual." He pushed his lips into a smile. "But if there's any news..."

"Nothing credible, I'm afraid," Adam said, dismissing the man's optimism with a recital of sound fact. "Though I questioned another twenty-two claimants this week." And stomped, again, on the failing hopes of a breaking mother.

Stevenson grimaced. "Nothing at all?"

Adam shook his head.

"I haven't wanted to bring this up, but you know it's been weeks—"

"Twenty-five days," Adam supplied.

"Do you think there's any hope?"

Adam hesitated a half second, partly to quell his reaction to the difference between Stevenson's tentative question and Isobel Tait's desperate ones, and partly because he hated his answer.

"Not if I'm being honest," Adam admitted.

Stevenson deflated, sinking back into his chair. "I suppose I've known for a while. And"—he swallowed—"my involvement in the case is difficult for my family."

Adam regarded him stonily. *I'll bet it is.*

"For their sakes—" Stevenson gave up, then tried again. "For their sakes, I have to distance myself from the inquiry. I—I'm no longer able to offer a reward for finding him." He licked his lips once, then a second time.

"I trust you've informed Mrs. Tait?" Adam asked.

Stevenson shook his head. "It seems cruel to tell her. And if, as you say, there's little chance he'll be found, I don't see the need of mentioning the matter."

Frigging rabbit. Adam pressed his lips into a smile, speaking the insult with his eyes.

At this stage, a lack of a reward probably didn't matter. Alive or dead, whoever had taken the boy wasn't giving him up. But if Stevenson was connected to Thomas the way everyone in the station thought he was, Adam expected better from him.

"Some of the officers think Mrs. Tait is responsible. Not through neglect. On purpose," Adam said.

Stevenson's chin jerked up. "That's ridiculous. Isobel would never harm her child."

"It's not the theory I prefer," Adam admitted, inspecting his fingers coolly. "But if my colleagues can conclude young Thomas was too much trouble for a struggling mother, he could be a danger or a liability to others. His father, for instance."

Silence, as Stevenson touched his cravat.

"We've gone nowhere with this case," Adam went on. "So I want to know your exact connection to Thomas Tait. If he or his mother are any threat to you."

"I told you, I—"

Adam lifted a hand, forestalling another threadbare explanation. "Your exact connection, Mr. Stevenson."

"You have a wild imagination, detective." The prosecutor's tone was frosty. "If your idea wasn't so ludicrous, I might be insulted."

"You are quite welcome to be," Adam returned. "I'm not interested in feelings—yours or anyone else's. I'm looking for Thomas. He was born in Bo'ness in 1819, to Isobel Tait and her deceased husband, Hamish, according to the local church register. No record of their marriage, though. She moved there four months earlier, with her father. Before that, I learned she lived in Lomond, where he was employed by your grandfather, Mr. Alexander Anstruther.

"The servants there report that you and your elder brother visited frequently in those years. But the interesting thing is that when Thomas went missing, Isobel didn't ask your grandfather for help, though you also describe him as a friend to her late father. She didn't write to his wife, Lady Margaret, or your brother either. She came to you."

"Of course she did. I live in Edinburgh."

Adam waited. It hadn't been hard to piece this together. The story was common enough, though Fraser and Superintendent Maxwell were willing to accept Stevenson's version and find proof of innocence in his offered reward.

Adam's life would be simpler if he did too.

"Mr. Stevenson?" he prompted.

The man didn't shout or swear. He sighed, motioning tiredly to the other armchair. "Have a seat, Kerr."

A glowing coal shifted in the grate. Neither one of them turned to look.

"Will you have a drink?"

"No, thank you."

Stevenson kept his next sigh in, though Adam saw it pass over him like the shadow of a cloud. When he spoke, his voice was resigned.

"You know I golf every fortnight with your superintendent."

Adam nodded. "Only since joining the prosecutor's office." Before that, Stevenson had spent his time with other barristers from the Faculty of Advocates, notable men skilled at defending criminal cases. The recent split between them and Stevenson was rumored to spring from the others' hoarding of high-profile work. John Stevenson was ambitious.

"You and Superintendent Maxwell are fairly new friends," Adam said.

Stevenson's eyebrows rose an inch. "That's true, Kerr. So why are you here, and why is Maxwell your superintendent instead of the other way round?"

"Mr. Maxwell is possessed of a little more tact," Adam said. He'd never have been promoted to detective without the influence of his late father. He was good at his job, so he'd probably keep it in spite of needling Stevenson today, but now that his father was dead, Adam knew his dubious parentage would keep him from ever rising further.

He wouldn't have liked Maxwell's job, anyway.

Stevenson laughed roughly and poured another amber splash into the glass at his elbow. "Sure I can't persuade you?"

Adam shook his head.

"I understand the challenges of your work better than you think," Stevenson said. "Law enforcement depends far too much on paid informants. When you can't pay anyone to come forward with the truth—" He shrugged. "I suppose I appreciate your effort. You're correct. Thomas is my son, and though I have never known him, I very much wish him found.

"It's true my grandfather was a patron of her father's. James Hay was a remarkable musician. So is Isobel, though of course it's impossible for her to make as good a living at it."

If he felt any guilt for her circumstances, Adam saw no sign of it. "Your daughter is three months younger than Thomas. That can't have been convenient for you."

"It certainly wasn't. At the time, I couldn't afford notoriety." He paused, perhaps waiting for Adam to offer reassurances, but none came.

"I planned to take the boy," he continued. "Raise him as my ward, pretend he was the orphaned son of a friend. But Isobel refused." Stevenson's hand tightened briefly on his glass.

"And you were persuadable?"

"She threatened me," Stevenson said. "So you aren't entirely wrong. She and Thomas were a danger to me—then. My wife and I were engaged to be married—the arrangement was between our families, had dragged on for years, and it would have harmed my career if the marriage were called off.

"Isobel was quite practical about it, and reasonable in her demands. I gave her a sum of money and she promised discretion. She confided in her father and he took her to Bo'ness, with the understanding that Thomas was hers. I allowed it, because that was our bargain, until this May, when he disappeared.

"So you see, detective, if she meant to threaten me with Thomas, she went about it all wrong. My wife and I married, just as planned. You must have gathered, from my public involvement in Thomas's case, that my wife has some inkling of what happened. My marriage and my career are well established now, and though she is uncomfortable with the speculation my involvement has caused, I have nothing to gain by hurting Isobel or Thomas."

"And you never tried to take him back?"

Stevenson glowered. "You may not think it, Kerr, but I am a man of my word. I might have hoped, when Thomas was old enough for school..."

He broke off, and Adam saw real pain in him, contorting his face for brief heartbeats before smoothed ruthlessly away. "She didn't even tell me he was dying," Stevenson muttered. "That's what I'll never forgive."

Another coal fell, its brilliant glow dying in just a few seconds on the stone hearth.

"Are you satisfied, detective?"

No. He was farther than ever from finding who'd abducted Thomas Tait.

"I believe you, Mr. Stevenson," Adam said. "I'll leave you to your work."

Stevenson nodded, his gaze fixed on the little pile of crumbling ash. "I suppose I won't stop in at the station tomorrow. Not much point."

"I'm afraid not, sir." Adam buttoned up his coat collar and let himself out of the house.

{ 5 }

The desperate will believe anything they can hang a hope on. I pray. I even have my palm read and look for answers in the lay of the cards. It is all as useless as anything else, but I can't stop trying.

Weeks and seasons pass, my thoughts stained with the troubling connection between bodies and souls. Mine are, regrettably, tethered together. I cannot believe the same for Thomas, yet I've felt nothing. No sundering between earth and heaven, no whispers or premonitions, no leave-taking from the spirit that should have been so closely tied to me. I've been watching and listening for signs; I can't have missed him.

I don't know what I've done wrong.

{ 6 }

Wednesdays I taught piano in the mornings, followed by tea with Miss Clark. The Bethune School for Young Ladies didn't teach lessons in mathematics on Wednesdays, so every week she sat me down in her parlor, our knees almost touching between her two green brocade chairs.

They were massive things, with curving arms and backs on legs of dark walnut, brought from the house she grew up in. Miss Clark hadn't married and she didn't get on with her sister-in-law, so she and the chairs had come to Edinburgh to Mrs. McPherson's rented rooms.

In the twelve and a half months since Thomas's disappearance, Miss Clark's benevolence had ripened like a sharp cheese. I smelled it before I saw her. No matter how cheerily I spoke or how falsely I smiled, I didn't fool her. I certainly didn't fool myself, and the futility of it only proved how badly I was failing, grappling my shattered life with numb hands and trying to mash it into a recognizable shape.

I drank tea with her every Wednesday, and tried to pretend the spaces where my mind seeped between one minute and the next didn't hurt.

"Will you pass the scissors?"

My voice emerged, smooth and ordinary. Usually we passed the time with embroidery, an amusement that, according to Miss Clark, never failed to soothe the mind. The elegant crane-shaped scissors were cold in my hand, and the snick of the blades severing my orange silk strands pinched at my ears. I tied a knot and located my next stitch. As the needle pushed through the cloth, it made a soft puff, like a dying gasp.

Miss Clark knotted her thread and held out her work. "What do you think?"

She'd stitched her initial—M, for *Margaret*—into the corner of a pristine white handkerchief with crimson thread, and added a tiny brown bird perched on the last curling flourish.

"Pretty," I admitted, but the answer sounded in my ears like someone else's.

"And what have you got?"

I held out my half-finished embroidery, unsure if the spray of brilliant blossoms I was working in the corner of a pillowcase would ever be finished. It was almost unchanged since last week.

"Beautiful. And you're working only from your imagination?" Miss Clark asked. "I'm not one of those who can work without a plan."

I hummed a noncommittal response.

"How are your pupils?" she asked.

"Progressing, when they practice," I said—my usual reply.

"Mine are exactly the same." She smiled and threaded her needle with a skein of bright gold. "You know, I never hear you play these days."

I played often enough for my students, teaching them not to trip in their scales, but I hardly touched the case piano standing on slim folding legs in my sitting room anymore. My father had bought it for me when I was sixteen, when he first went to Lomond, with Mr. Anstruther's healthy annual stipend filling his pockets. An expensive gift, he was worried about my healing arms, and grateful to have a place where he could bring me, away from Edinburgh and my awful school. So he'd excused the purchase, saying every musician needs her own instrument.

I stabbed my needle through the heavy linen with unnecessary force. "Just as well. It must be horribly out of tune."

"Perhaps next Wednesday we can walk instead of sew. If the day is fine," Miss Clark said, changing tacks.

She'd suggested the same last week, but that plan to rehabilitate me had been thwarted by today's wet and windy skies, so here we were, sipping oolong and ruining our eyes with close work.

The truth was, I'd prefer walking through the wet, because on sunny days, I risked spotting children with kites. If next Wednesday was fine, I'd invent some letters to write. That meant copying out verses to nonexistent correspondents, but if I spent the afternoon alone, claiming to write letters and producing none, Miss Clark would notice. So would Mrs. McPherson.

On every side, I was hemmed in by well-meaning women united in quiet conspiracy. It kept me moving through the days, but I knew, for them, that wasn't enough. For me, it was often more than I could manage.

"There's a music concert tomorrow evening," Miss Clark said.

I hummed and made another stitch.

"I'm attending with my friends. The other ladies in the literary circle. I've already invited Mrs. McPherson. We both thought you might like to come."

I shook my head.

Miss Clark set down her embroidery. "You're allowed to forget for a while, Izzie. You used to love music. Come hear some Mozart. It'll do you good."

If I said no often enough, would she and Mrs. McPherson give up? But maybe I shouldn't let myself float away.

"Please, Izzie," said Miss Clark. "I worry."

Friday evening, I sat through Mozart's *Requiem*, my hands in tight fists.

When the concert finished, one of the ladies, with a sharp nose and an artistically arranged bonnet, proposed another outing the following week. The ladies mooted possibilities—I smiled and paid no heed—and I found myself at a lecture a week later. The week after that, I was arm in arm with Miss Clark when she followed the other women around the corner onto Newington Place.

I missed a step as my heart lurched to a halt. "Here?"

The ladies in front of us turned around.

"Didn't I say? Dr. Burnett's collection is at his house—so much better than the sorry-looking specimens on display at the university." Mrs. Muir, a published botanist and close friend of Miss Clark, smiled archly. "Here, we won't be disappointed."

I balked, then realized none of these women knew I'd visited Dr. Burnett with Thomas. It hadn't been that long before he'd disappeared and ever since then, consciously or not, I'd avoided this place. Burnett was the one, after all, who told me unequivocally that I would lose him—just not how, and how soon.

No wonder I'd stayed away.

"Is something wrong?" Miss Clark asked. She was adept at reading my face.

I looked down and smoothed my gloves. "Don't laugh, but I

must be mistaken. I thought we were attending another musical concert this evening."

Mrs. Muir chuckled. "That's next week. You needn't come, you know. Skeletons are quite different than Beethoven, even if you are expecting them."

"I can walk home with you, if you'd rather not go," Miss Clark offered.

But I could tell she looked forward to this, and the tickets had already been paid for. I couldn't avoid the places Thomas and I had been—or custard or kite-flying children—forever. I lived in the same rooms, after all. Burnett's house couldn't be any worse. I'd been sad there, yes, but still ignorant of the worse things to come.

"I do want to see the curiosities," I lied. "But you can understand why I was caught off guard, loving the sonatas like I do. A silly mistake." I closed the distance between Mrs. Muir and me, and smiled at the handful of impeccably attired women who'd joined tonight's expedition and had paused their animated chattering to stare at me.

"You won't regret it," Mrs. Muir promised me. "His specimens are incredible." Since the acquisition of a platypus, Dr. Burnett's collection was all the rage, featuring in newspapers and sitting room conversations everywhere. Most of my piano students had already been.

We advanced down the street, and Miss Clark beamed at me for my effort, as if I were a child who'd presented a sheet of correct sums. She leaned her head to mine, murmuring confidingly, "You're doing so well."

I couldn't agree, though I was doing at least. I couldn't seem to do anything else.

"That must be the one," Mrs. Muir said, squinting at the print on her ticket. "These houses look exactly the same."

They did appear interchangeable, a solid rank of gray stone, three floors of identical windows girded by a palisade of wrought iron. Another party, a mixture of ladies and gentlemen, was already waiting outside the front door.

I wondered what Dr. Burnett's neighbors thought of him housing his collection here.

"I hope it won't be crowded," Mrs. Campbell said. She was a widow, who lived with her only son.

"Only ten at a time are admitted," Mrs. Muir explained. "And we will have an hour to view the collection."

I held back a sigh.

"They say his specimens are even better than Dr. Hunter's in London," Mrs. Muir went on. "I saw his collection two years ago, but if not for the zebra, I don't think—"

I rubbed at a spot on my glove, and wondered how long it would take for Miss Clark, Mrs. Muir, and the others to satisfy their curiosity. I'd taught six lessons today; perhaps the noise of so many abused pianofortes was starting to tell. I could hardly expect to move through this evening in my usual automatic fashion. Already, I was remembering the warm softness of Thomas's hand in mine as we waited outside the consulting room, and bending to listen at his chest. My hands felt sticky inside my gloves.

As the nearby church bells struck the hour, the door opened, emitting Dr. Burnett's latest batch of curious guests. They were talking energetically, dispersing in threes and fours. Most were male, in their twenties—probably medical students.

An unfamiliar man, whose mostly smooth cheeks still carried two or three youthful spots, introduced himself as Dr. Burnett's assistant and conducted us inside the house. I was relieved not to see the doctor, and that the assistant ushered us into a room at the front of the house, well away from the consulting room. Even so, as I stepped into the drawing room, my heart began to pound.

The ceilings were high, an array of lamps banishing the shadows. On the tables, in jars and in cabinets, the specimens waited to shock and amaze. Beside me, Miss Clark drew a hushed breath; eyes widened; one of the gentlemen muttered under his breath.

At first, I saw nothing. Mist curled from the edges of my vision, clouding my eyes—no doubt the work of my nerveless lungs. With an effort, I set them moving again, taking slow, painful breaths until the room steadied. Others were moving about, examining the curiosities on display, studying the neatly lettered placards or listening to the assistant describe the peculiarities of three massive whale vertebrae displayed in the center of the room.

I moved away from the group, to a wide glass bowl set in one corner. It was exactly the kind of vessel a child might use to keep a frog or a fish, except it was fitted with a lid. Inside, what appeared to be a balloon of dried parchment was displayed for all of Edinburgh to see.

"This is a particularly unusual item." One of the other guests, a university student by the look of him, moved alongside me.

I smiled noncommittally and returned my attention to the specimen, to no avail. The student adjusted his spectacles and kept on speaking, explaining how remarkable this urinary bladder was, dried and varnished, from a sixty-three-year-old teacher who'd lived in Leith.

"Oh?" was all I could think to say.

"You see the pouch protruding on the left?"

It was impossible to miss, the size of my fist. "Is that normal?" I asked.

"Not at all, madam. We call that a diverticulum. It can cause great difficulty and discomfort when passing urine."

"Not at all diverting, then," another man put in.

A woman tittered.

"And on your left, on the top shelf in this case, you can see a thigh bone from a retired soldier. I saw him in hospital, you know. Mr. Grant suffered a gunshot wound and—"

"Surely a bullet didn't do that," the man said, gesturing at the frond-like growth reaching out from halfway down the bone's length.

"No, you're quite right." This from the lanky assistant, coming over to reclaim the attention of the little crowd. "The bone was cracked but healed. It was over the course of the next twenty years that this tumor grew. It would have been exquisitely painful. To my knowledge, no doctor has ever collected a larger specimen."

"It's called a traumatic osteoma," the student added.

I followed them around the room, distracted and mildly amused by their duel of facts and Latin. As the student informed a pale-faced Miss Clark about some pickled infant's lungs showing signs of tuberculosis, the assistant loudly instructed others on a forearm disfigured by something he called keloid scarring, which lay like a slug on the skin, red and raised and bulbous.

"And in the cupboard over there is an excellently dissected male urethra, but any interested viewers will need to open the doors," he added. "Dr. Burnett uses it primarily for instruction of his pupils, and wouldn't want to discomfort any lady visitors."

Mrs. Muir immediately darted to the cabinet. The man at her elbow, initially just as curious, turned away from the specimen jar, slightly green.

Beside me, Miss Clark shifted from foot to foot.

"Go ahead and look," I whispered to her. "I won't tell."

She made a display of grimacing. "No. I couldn't."

We moved to the next case and stopped still.

"Mercy," Miss Clark said.

There was no name, age, or place written on the card for this skeleton, but it was plainly a child's, not more than three or four years of age. Unlike the wired, white bones we'd already passed, this body still had the muscles attached. There were vessels remaining, too, I noted queasily, dried like the muscles and artificially colored red. There was a foot something like this across the room, bare bones surrounded with a branching network of circulatory vessels. The medical student had explained the technique, saying doctors injected the arteries with wax, before dissolving the tissues away with acid.

The bones and bladder hadn't seemed so awful, but the sight of an entire child, dried and displayed—

I swallowed and turned away.

"How is this possible?" Miss Clark gasped.

The assistant, mistaking her horror for amazement, hastened forward.

"Yes, this one is particularly impressive. It was prepared by Dr. Barclay, who began this collection and bequeathed it to Dr. Burnett. Back then, Dr. Burnett was the junior partner," he explained. "Dr. Burnett had a reputation for skill even then, but he was not nearly so famous as he is now.

"We call this a natural skeleton, because it's still joined by the normal tissues."

I stepped away, nerves recoiling, unable to accept that there was anything natural about a dead child on display.

"Are you unwell?" Miss Clark called after me.

"Fine," I retorted. I edged away, out of the path of the assistant and Miss Clark. Mrs. Muir had finally abandoned her inspection of the display of male genitalia. A pulsing headache was coalescing behind my eyes, but it wasn't strong enough, yet, to push me into asking to leave. The whole point of this excursion was to prove I could appear normal, with interest in the world about me instead of my own grief.

I steered my feet to a benign-looking shelf of specimens floating in jars, and stared at the distorted image of my face in the glass.

La-da. La-da.

I blinked, trying to dispel the beat in my temples, then realized it didn't originate there. I glanced around, but no one else seemed to hear, even as it grew clear and louder.

Da-di-*la*. Da-di-*la*.

Maybe I wasn't hearing so much as feeling these reverberations. They seemed to come from all around me: down from the ceiling, up through the floor. The hairs on my arms prickled as I closed my eyes and drew a breath, willing away a twist of light that danced, just for an instant, at the corner of my eye.

The beat grew louder, and when I opened my eyes, I found the troublesome light flashing in time with it. The room, though spacious, was overwarm, and though my mouth was dry, my stomach was far too unsettled for me to want a drink.

I rested a loose hand on the lowest shelf, and pretended interest in the handwritten cards.

Foetal spine

Caecum with interssusception

Whatever that meant.

Da-di-*la*. I rubbed surreptitiously at my right temple. Of the two, it felt the worst, and if Mrs. Muir ambushed me with her smelling salts, I feared I'd start retching.

Juvenile heart with mitral valve scarring.

Da-di-*la*. My heart stilled as I forced myself to reread the carefully inked words.

Juvenile...mitral valve...

Behind the card was a crimson and purple heart, floating in a jar and neatly sliced open to display its crumpled white tissues, as delicate and fragile as the wings of a newly hatched moth.

My breath sped to the rapid tempo of an angry concerto as the heartbeat grew louder and louder. Ears about to burst, I reached out another steadying hand as the room dissolved into a whirlpool of dark and glistening pinpricks.

"Madam? Madam!"

I cried out, flinching from the hand on my arm. My eyes cleared and I found myself panting, crumpled in a heap on the floor.

"The heart, the heart," I sobbed, pushing away a camphor-scented handkerchief. "Whose child?"

"What is she talking about?" the student asked.

"Let me up!" I demanded, but my legs might as well have been stalks of grass.

"Hush, Isobel," Miss Clark urged desperately. "You aren't yourself. You've had some fit or spell."

"A faint, probably," the assistant put in. "It happens to some ladies when they visit, I'm afraid."

I braced myself and surged away from Miss Clark's arms, flinging one of my own accusingly at the jar on the shelf. "Whose heart is it?"

The assistant blinked. "It could be decades old, madam. I'm not familiar enough with the collection—"

"You said the osteoma was from a Mr. Grant," I countered.

Miss Clark murmured something in his ear. At once he stiffened, becoming coldly solicitous. "I'm afraid you are simply overwrought, madam. The exhibits can be alarming, and..."

"I want an answer," I demanded. "Is this heart Thomas's?"

"You aren't thinking, Isobel," Miss Clark said pleadingly. "Take a moment to clear your head."

I slowed my breath, so this room of staring people would see past the well-stoked furnace inside me. They needed to understand and hear.

"My son had a mitral heart defect. He was stolen from my home a year ago." My voice shook, and someone thrust the camphor-soaked handkerchief at me again. I pushed the hand away. "How long has this heart been on this shelf?"

Miss Clark gasped. A slow wave of whispers heaved across the room, sloshing off the walls.

I stared at the assistant, my heart drumming.

"Just what are you implying?" he challenged.

"Isobel!" Miss Clark tugged my arm. "Let's just go home."

I licked my lips, refusing to look at her. "I want to know when that heart came here."

Silence, but for the strange tangling of beats inside my head—my fevered pulse, and the limping cadence of Thomas's.

"If you insist on it, I'm certain that can be arranged," he said. "Dr. Burnett and his anatomy school are both above reproach, with nothing to hide. Your name, madam?"

"Tait," I told him. "And as I said, my son was Thomas. Dr. Burnett may still have his name in his patient records."

More whispering, which the assistant pretended not to hear.

"You will hear from the doctor shortly, I'm sure," he said.

He offered his hand. I stared at it, then wheeled around and stalked out, the percussive snaps of my heels jarring against the other beat filling my ears.

Da-di-*la*, Da-di-*la*.

{ 7 }

D r. Conall Burnett set down his glass. Down the length of the table, behind an array of candles and half-filled wineglasses, the doctors and surgeons of the Aesculapian Club listened intently. "My examination of the specimen was most informative. If you should care to visit my collection and see for yourselves..."

Only in the last year or so, Conall had taken up fishing. Tonight's endeavor felt much the same—flickering lures in front of wary minds and cold eyes. It had worked, though. The eyes around the table were admiring and appreciative now. Dr. Andrew Duncan, the eighty-three-year-old founder of the society, was about to cede his place.

Conall wanted it.

There were plenty—too many—anatomists in the Edinburgh medical clan, and the Aesculapians admitted only eleven. No one had been invited since the death of Dr. Angus Moncrieff had created a vacancy four years before. It might be years until the next one.

This invitation to speak at their regular dinner was, in fact, an audition. Conall had considered his topic carefully. These weren't men he could impress with a seamless flow of Latin or his ency-clopedic knowledge of human anatomy. Nor could he, at this point in his career, hope to compete with his former mentor's brilliant deductions in comparative anatomy. Dr. Hamilton, on his left, was unassailable in midwifery; Dr. Kellie, two places down, could rest comfortably on the fame of his doctrine on intracranial pressure and pathology.

Edinburgh abounded with clever and talented men who'd never be invited to one of these select suppers in the exquisite rooms of the George Hotel. This was Conall's first—of many, if he had anything to do with it.

"I'll take you up on that offer, Burnett." Dr. George Ballingall, a leading professor of military surgery, said. "I always think there is nothing like tactile learning."

Conall smiled. "For you, sir, I will take it out of the glass."

Kellie chortled. "That'd be something—if only to see George's reverent face when you put it in his hands."

"I have a great interest in diseases of the heart," Ballingall returned equably.

"An excellent presentation, Burnett," Dr. Duncan said, from the other end of the table. Nestled against the plum upholstery of his chair, his face was too shadowed to reveal his expression. "You've given us much to think about."

Hopefully, it had been enough. As the conversation localized to smaller groups and scattered topics, Conall smiled and sipped his port, exchanging pleasantries with the men at his elbows. Three different fowls had been served, along with mutton and venison. Conall had never seen such an array of dishes or so many gilt-edged plates, and though he might have dined at the George Hotel at his own expense at any time these past ten years, he'd chosen not to, waiting for this.

When his glass emptied, he gathered his notes and made his excuses; although he'd like to linger, he wanted to give them time to consider his membership now, while the glow of good food, excellent wine, and his meticulously crafted presentation was strongest. Other doctors might have theories about heart murmurs—so far as Conall knew, he was the only one with an actual example to back up his suppositions.

Even if Ballingall was the only one to view it, once he saw the rest of Conall's collection, others would follow, as would his admittance to the club. Other men in Edinburgh might approximate his knowledge and skill, but he was on his way to building an incomparable museum. The club wouldn't be able to resist.

At the door, Conall took one last look at the gathering: Professor Chistison's high forehead shining in the candlelight, Kellie slouched in his seat and chewing ruminatively on his pipe. "Good night, gentlemen. Let's speak again soon."

When he returned home, Ferguson, his assistant, was waiting for him.

"Your evening went well?"

"Quite." But Ferguson's must not have, else why was he here? The last group of visitors would have finished by nine. Conall scanned the shelves and cases. Everything seemed in order. "Another fainting spell?" he guessed.

Ferguson nodded.

It wasn't unusual. Even among his students, there was always at least one who fainted during their first dissection. It would be unreasonable to expect more fortitude from the general public, though they were simply looking, not wielding a scalpel. The sense of danger only added to the museum's popularity, and Conall intended to capitalize on it.

"This episode was complicated by an unlucky coincidence," Ferguson said.

Conall frowned, and Ferguson's cheeks reddened as he hastened to explain.

"She came with a ladies' literary circle. This caught her attention, and she swooned." Ferguson waved at the beautifully preserved juvenile heart, displayed prominently on the center shelf. "She had a son with the same condition. He went missing some time ago and was never found. She demanded to know whose heart this was and when you obtained it. She was quite insistent. Unbalanced, almost."

Conall composed his face. "Understandable, I suppose, given her terrible circumstance. I'm too old now to be surprised by any coincidence. When you've practiced as long as I have, the most unlikely things—"

"Exactly," Ferguson said, nodding.

"Unfortunately, that kind of claim can be very damaging," Conall went on. "It must be set right immediately. You have her name? I must write her, I suppose."

"I said you would contact her. She said"—Ferguson swallowed—"that you would have her direction already. Her son was a patient."

Conall waited until Ferguson met his eyes. "Not surprising, given my area of specialty," he said gently.

"No, so I said."

"I hope you took her direction anyway. It would be very tedious to try and unearth her name from my files—if I even could. You know how many there are."

"It's written here. Her friend provided it. I thought it expedient to encourage them both to leave without delay. Such an uncomfortable scene—"

"Quite right," Conall said. "Thank you, Ferguson. I trust all that brouhaha didn't disturb my mother?"

Ferguson smiled. "You know better, sir. She doesn't miss a trick. She came downstairs, but by then Mrs. Tait was gone. I reassured her, and took her back to her sitting room."

"I'll make sure to speak to her. Thank you, Ferguson."

"It's nothing, sir."

After Ferguson left, Conall walked around the drawing room, inspecting his shelves. An outstanding collection, yet a light layer of dust coated the shelves, and there were fingerprints visible on one of the glass cases.

Something must be done.

{ 8 }

The following afternoon, I received a letter by messenger. Mrs. McPherson brought it up, informing me in hushed tones of the method of delivery.

I cleared my throat. "Will they wait for a reply?"

She shook her head. "The boy's gone. I didn't think to suggest—"

"It's no matter," I said quickly, not wanting to betray that I was needled by her treating this missive like a royal summons. She was my friend, not Dr. Burnett's.

And not responsible for your moods, either, I reminded myself.

"I'll be in the kitchen, if you want company later," she promised as she withdrew, wearing the sympathetic smile I knew far too well.

Alone at my window, I stared at the street, then at the heavy paper, clasped with a blot of black wax. There was no beat in my head today, and Miss Clark, though nothing but kind, had clearly been mortified by my outburst. What's more, she'd mentioned the episode to Mrs. McPherson; the extra concern today, bringing up this letter, proved it.

They probably think you're demented.

My own fault. Desperate for answers, I'd secretly turned to palm readings, and lobbing my questions at a deck of tarot cards.

I'd bought them last month and kept them hidden at the back of a drawer because if Miss Clark saw them, she'd scold me for being irrational.

My episode at Burnett's was just additional proof. In spite of the strength of that pulse, I'd heard nothing unusual since leaving his house. And why would I? There was nothing to hear. Miss Clark was right—the sights had simply been too upsetting for me.

"You shouldn't expect to be unchanged," she'd murmured last night, putting a cup of tea into my unsteady hand. "We all understand." But they didn't. And here was my letter.

I couldn't explain what had happened. I'd never felt anything like it before. I didn't faint and my imagination was rusty, now that I no longer needed to invent bedtime tales. Speculation of any kind was torment. I only had one question—what had become of my son?

According to the detectives, it was better not to know the answer.

My cheeks heated. I shouldn't have gone out, broken as I was, liable to embarrass myself. I should have heeded my misgivings outside the house, made my excuses, and walked away, someplace where I could be alone, safe from memory echoes that my tired, grieving mind must have magnified into feverish illusions.

I stared at the square of paper, half wishing to hide it away. I didn't want to read it and hear Burnett's voice in my head, placating me like a hysterical patient. Those sounds had been real to me at the time. But there was no point pretending or hiding from the truth. I tugged the letter open.

Mrs. Tait,

While I respect your tragic loss, I'm wounded by your suggestion that a heart in my collection may have come from

your son, Thomas. The items on display are an important
catalog of medical knowledge and a tool for advancing the
health and well-being of humanity, and I resent your claim
that any of my specimens have been obtained by unwholesome
means. I have consulted my records, and the heart in question
was a gift from a colleague in London, the date of acquisition
17 September 1823, long before your son's regrettable
disappearance.

Though a loss such as yours must cause considerable
strain on the nervous system, your unfortunate spell, with
a public audience, will cause considerable trouble and
tarnish my name. I have written a letter to the editor of the
Caledonian Mercury, so that the citizens of Edinburgh
can be acquainted with the facts. I expect it will be
published this week.

I remain your humble servant,
Conall Burnett

Setting the sheet aside, I leaned back in my chair and gazed out the window.

Not so placating.

In fact, his tone felt angry, but if he intended me to smart from his stinging reply, he'd erred. I was numb to minor slights, insensible to paper cuts because I was walking on crippled limbs. Didn't mean I didn't see them, though.

It puzzled me that he wasn't kinder.

I put on my bonnet and set out for a walk, skirting the Meadows and trekking downhill to Holyrood and, rising above it, the rough mound of Arthur's Seat. It sat on the east, opposite the queenly

Castle Hill, with the city spreading out on the ridge between them like a vast banqueting table.

I took the shortest way up, toiling along a narrow cleft between a bare crag and a steep precipice dotted with bracken, my cheeks hot with shame, goaded by the accusations in Burnett's letter.

Strain on the nervous system.

Unfortunate spell.

I wasn't used to this climb, so I stopped only a third of the way up, gasping and clammy with perspiration. It took only seconds for the wind to pierce my cloak and freeze my damp skin.

I'd made a fool of myself in front of a crowd, and I couldn't even comfort myself with the knowledge that judgment would soften with pity.

Pity was no comfort to me.

I had to turn back. I'd never make it to the peak on this rabbit track. As I picked my way down the steep hill, bracing myself against boulders and clutching at roots, a thought came to me.

If Burnett had come by the heart in 1823, why, when I visited him with Thomas, had he explained Thomas's condition with a picture?

I weighed the question, and sifted it, peered at it from different angles all the way home.

"Well done, Charlotte. I can tell you've been practicing." My current pupil's confidence was improving. I was beginning to hear a story moving beneath the notes. "In a year, you'll be transporting listeners to a whole other country."

She ducked her head modestly, as well-bred girls were taught to do, and thanked me.

I set the study aside and gave her another, constructed around variations of familiar scales. She bobbed her head twice, silently setting her tempo, then unleashed her fingers. They scampered over the keys, rising and falling like the surrounding hills. I walked them every day now, pursued by wild thoughts I couldn't speak aloud, chastened by Burnett's letter and his crisp rebuke in Edinburgh's largest newspaper. Only yesterday, the *Mercury* had printed another letter, this one from the university's chair of military medicine, decrying the calumny heaped upon his profession by foolish laypeople—namely me.

He hadn't identified me, not like Burnett, but anyone could tell that I was who he meant, since his letter followed so hard on the first complaint.

Reacting without thinking at Burnett's house, I'd inadvertently prodded a bear—or several, and they wouldn't be appeased until they'd devoured me in public.

Charlotte stumbled on a fiendishly difficult arpeggio, and I recalled myself, pointing at the music score so she wouldn't, in her flustered state, forget the repeat. By the time she launched the last triumphant chord, she was flushed, but smiling.

"Well done! That's a tricky one, but you carry it off beautifully," I said, and she reddened even more.

"Pay particular attention here," I said, penciling a star over bar forty-two. "And keep on with your scales."

As I buttoned my cloak, a mousy-haired maidservant appeared in the doorway.

"Mrs. Findlay wants to speak with you."

I gave my pupil a parting smile and followed the maid to her mother's sitting room. Mrs. Findlay was known as a bit of an invalid, fond of tinctures and traveling to take the latest cures. Today she was clothed in a muslin wrapper, anxiously picking at the ruffle adorning one sleeve.

"This is all so unfortunate, Mrs. Tait. Charlotte is terribly fond of you."

"I'm fond of her," I said. "What is the trouble?"

She glanced at the tray beside her on the divan and the folded newspaper.

My smile hardened. I remembered, belatedly, that her much older husband was also a retired physician. Was he going to take a bite out of me too?

"My husband insists. It's all been very trying for me. He told me we must have a new teacher for Charlotte. That he has no interest in employing hysterical women."

"I'm sorry to hear that," I said evenly, without flinching. "Charlotte is progressing very well."

I'd lost two pupils already, so this was unwelcome news. If this kept up, I wouldn't be earning enough to cover my room and board. "Perhaps I could speak to your husband." I'd seen Dr. Findlay once or twice in passing. He might be mollified by an apology.

"Oh, no, that wouldn't do at all." Mrs. Findlay shook her head, setting her tremulous ruffles quivering. "I couldn't upset him. Not when he's so clearly spoken his mind."

I dipped my head, recognizing it was useless persuading her. "Well, I must thank you for the opportunity to work with your daughter. Charlotte is a wonderful student."

She tugged at the ruffles again. "Your wages will be waiting in the hall."

I left her with a nod, and collected my money—flimsy paper, today—on the way out.

Conall adjusted the flame of the lamp and held out a brass and mahogany-handled magnifier to George Ballingall.

"I can't tell you how much I've looked forward to this," Ballingall said.

Conall smiled. No need to reply. He understood. In fact, there was almost as much pleasure watching his colleague examining the scarred valve of the heart as there was studying it himself.

"Hard to believe such a small thing can be so deadly," Ballingall murmured, fingering the delicate tissues. "The damage is hard to see. Easier to feel."

"I was quite astonished myself," Conall said. "Though I'd read a French report of a posthumous dissection and examined some excellent drawings." Hearing murmurs through a stethoscope was tantalizing, but seeing proof and holding it in his hands...

"It's a miraculous organ, when you think about it—all hearts, not just this one," Ballingall said, still busy with the glass. "Whether the mind is awake or asleep, it pumps tirelessly, automatically, adjusting to changing demand without any application of will. The lungs, automatic much of the time, can still be mastered by the mind. But the heart—" Ballingall straightened. "It's almost an independent creature, living inside us."

"An interesting theory," Conall said. "But I am, alas, no poet."

"Neither of us can make that claim." Ballingall snorted. "And we aren't philosophers, either, though I admit the heart engages an astonishing collection of minds. The cleric, the artist, the sentimentalist."

"Again, you overestimate me," Conall said. "My mind is the pragmatic sort."

"The best, in my view," Ballingall said. "We are two of a kind, Burnett." He set down the magnifying glass, and stepped back, allowing Conall to collect the heart and slide it gently into the jar. Nose and eyes stinging, he carefully replenished the spirits, then replaced the rubber stopper. Wiping the jar with the linen towel he had laid across the table, he restored it to the shelf.

Ballingall was on the other side of the room now, admiring the natural skeleton of a three-year-old child that Conall had inherited from his mentor, John Barclay. Barclay had been a member of the Aesculapian Club. No invitation had arrived for Conall, but he hadn't given up yet.

"I saw your letter in the *Mercury*," he said. "Your support is most heartening."

"Was that on purpose?" Ballingall said, turning around with a smile, and Conall realized, belatedly, the pun.

"Not intentional," he said with a laugh. "Though I'm sure you understand the matter has weighed heavily on my mind."

Ballingall nodded. "Public sentiment is so volatile. They don't understand the importance of our work. Don't worry. We're behind you."

"That's a relief." He'd worried not just about that woman's claim but the timing, with his admittance to the club in question. No one would want him if he was under a cloud. They wouldn't want to be tainted by association, but with Ballingall and—if he was lucky—others in the club on his side, the matter would quickly disappear. The success of the university and the reputation of the medical fraternity were bound together too closely to allow an insider to be pilloried by all and sundry.

Was he one of them now? He couldn't be crude and ask, but the signs were encouraging.

"I'm so glad you've seen the specimen," Conall said instead. "It's really too marvelous to keep to myself. Thank you for coming."

"Not at all," Ballingall said. "Truly, the pleasure is mine." With uplifted eyebrows, he motioned at the varnished bladder. "However did you come by this one? I want to wince just looking at it."

Smiling, Conall launched into the story. He'd dusted this room himself yesterday, in preparation for Ballingall's visit, before he saw the man's supporting letter in the paper. He'd been tempted to invite him to dine, but his household simply wasn't fit for that kind of event. His mother wouldn't admit it, but the housekeeping was getting too much for her to manage, and though she had tried, neither of them was brought up to the station Conall felt himself stepping into.

He'd have to make changes, he decided, leading Ballingall around the room. It was time.

{ 9 }

Notoriety had served a purpose when Thomas went missing. More people knowing bettered the chance of finding him. But as I tallied the week's expenses in a cheap cardboard-covered ledger with a worn-down pen, I knew exactly how much Burnett was hurting me, and the cost wasn't merely financial. I didn't care for his portrait of me, a pitiful survivor, half-mad with grief.

...while I have every sympathy for Mrs. Tait's loss, her hysterical claims are an assault to my reputation...

I'd read his letter to the newspaper only twice, but I couldn't forget his words. Hysterical was, I supposed, one way of calling it. There was too much strangeness about my episode in Burnett's house. Unfortunately, Burnett's assertions about how he'd acquired the heart were rational and perfectly believable.

But hysterical or not, I'd heard that pulse, and I was reasonably sure if Dr. Burnett had owned the heart a year ago, he wasn't the type to show me pictures. He was a showman, and I'd grown up with one of those. Burnett handled his stethoscope just the same way that my father had lifted onto his toes, trilling the high notes on his violin.

The more I thought, the more I seemed to understand Burnett, and the less there was to like. Of course, a man needn't be likable to be an honest one.

But I wanted to be sure. I could hardly think of anything else, and that was no way to convince anyone, myself included, that I was still rational.

Three days later, I presented myself at the station house, only yards away from the site of the Old Tollbooth, where generations of Edinburgh watchmen and gaolbirds had worked, suffered, and slept. Although that eyesore had been demolished ten years before to make way for the new building and the city's modern police, I never could pass the place without remembering the way I'd shrunk within myself, walking this way as a child. Nor could I forget coming here to watch a hanging, when I was ten years old and clasping the hands of two older girls from the house next door. Though I tried to join in with them and the screaming, jeering crowd, frenzied by the spectacle of death performed on the Tollhouse roof, I'd returned home, sick and sore.

Papa hadn't allowed me to play with those girls again. Death isn't entertainment, he told me.

Old memories.

I stepped through the leaning shadow of the building across the way and latched my gaze on to the new station house. Things were different now. This building didn't house prisoners. Now they served their time in the new gaol on Calton Hill, with only a small cell here for temporary storage of rascals and drunks.

Sidestepping a burly watchman setting out on his rounds, I slipped through the door, where I was immediately confronted by a hard-faced constable with crossed arms. I didn't recognize him. A year ago, I knew most of the faces.

"May I help you?" he asked.

"I need to speak with Detective Sergeant Kerr."

Something shifted in his expression, but I couldn't tell what it meant.

"He's out," the man said, not bothering to glance at the logbook. "So's Fraser. You'll have to settle for—"

"I'll wait," I said. I couldn't explain myself to him.

"We haven't any comfortable chairs."

"I don't need one," I said.

He looked skeptical, but I took a seat on the nearest bench, knitting my hands together, testing an array of scripted words.

Constables came and went, along with a child caught picking pockets, a woman with swaying limbs and incoherent speech, and a handful of sharp-faced folk who came and went so surreptitiously I assumed they must be informers. Perhaps that was what the desk sergeant took me for, though my dress and speech didn't fit with that assumption—and if there was another reason for my sort to dress and speak this way besides setting ourselves apart, I hadn't found it. Clean cuffs and careful vowels proclaimed that though I wasn't well off, I wasn't indigent, and the words I chose should indicate I was far from unlettered. I'd learned early how to assert my claims. I suppose most people did.

I bounced my heels to bring the feeling back into my numb legs and shifted in my seat to push away the tiredness in my back. I'd hoped, wrongly, that Kerr would return quickly, but each bell tolling from St. Giles came with a chiding glance from the desk sergeant— *See? I told you*, his eyes seemed to say.

When Kerr finally arrived, carrying a half-eaten pie, I jumped to my feet, wincing as pins and needles filled my feet and my carefully composed words deserted me.

"Mrs. Tait. How do you do?"

"I need to speak with you," I said, trying not to sound flustered.

"So I gathered."

"She's been here all afternoon," the desk sergeant put in.

Kerr looked from me to the sergeant and back again, taking in the bustling room, the other petitioners waiting on the bench, and took another, bigger bite of his handheld meal.

"Would you like to join me in my office?" he suggested.

It was unseemly to be here, since I was a woman with properly enunciated vowels and immaculate cuffs. It was unseemly to pester law officers, to closet myself with Kerr, alone. But I nodded, and followed him up the stairs, my feet steadier now, to a door on the left side of the hall.

"Didn't you and Fraser work across the hall before?" I asked, balking at the threshold. Hard enough to say what I wanted to Kerr. I'd never manage in front of both of them, and had no hope of persuading Fraser anyway.

"Advancement is a wonderful thing, Mrs. Tait. Hugh's been promoted. Our superintendent deems him worthy of a larger window." If there was rancor between them, I couldn't find it. But then, Kerr had always been well collected.

His window was small and topped with a dingy blind, but as this room held only a single desk, it was possible to walk around all the furniture without having to turn sideways.

"This wouldn't by chance be about that heart?"

Of course he read the papers. My mouth fell and I breathed a curse, not as silently as I intended. Kerr's eyebrows swept up.

"Sit down, Mrs. Tait," he said. "Make yourself comfortable."

I couldn't tell him about the phantom heartbeats. What was I going to say?

"Mitral valve defects are relatively rare," I began.

Kerr blinked at me.

"That was the affliction Dr. Burnett diagnosed in my son," I explained. "He could hear the injury through his stethoscope. When he made the diagnosis, he didn't show me the specimen, which he claims to have had then in his possession. He showed me an illustration from one of his books."

Kerr studied me. "And?"

"I'm not hysterical," I asserted, hoping this was true. "But I am a mother, and that inclines me to be suspicious. The heart is from a child. The condition is rare. It's too much of a coincidence."

His forehead creased.

"Dr. Burnett claims he received the heart years ago from another doctor. I can't verify his claims, but you—" I faltered, marshaling my flagging courage. "Wouldn't it be possible for you to check?"

Kerr's fingers drummed on the cover of his notebook. "I'm a law officer," he said. "I can't harass the man because you have a hunch. You've stirred up a hornet's nest, and these doctors are touchy."

"All it would take," I argued, "is for you to find out the name of the doctor who gave him the heart and confirm with him it's true." Even as I said it, I spotted the flaw. Kerr hadn't said Dr. Burnett was touchy. *These doctors*, he'd said.

Other doctors had sprung to Burnett's defense immediately, writing letters and telling their wives to dismiss me from their employ. It would be so much simpler, and such a small thing, for one to lie for him.

Kerr's resigned expression said not just that he knew this, but that he'd read something of my thoughts. His eyes creased, burdened with pity.

"I wish I could help you," he said quietly. "I know it's a distressing subject, but I'm sure you're mistaken. You saw that specimen and realized it was afflicted in the same way as Thomas's. It must have been overwhelming, especially when you've been through so much. No wonder you fainted."

My eyes burned and my back stiffened.

"You don't have to believe this heart is your son's," he said. "It could be anyone's. These things come to doctors, you know, in the usual way."

I fought down a sputter, countering evenly, "And what is the usual way?"

Kerr spread his hands on the desk and stared at his notebook, answering reluctantly. "Besides Dr. Munro at the university and Dr. Burnett, there are two other anatomy schools in Edinburgh. We don't execute nearly enough criminals to supply all of them. People die for numerous reasons, and those bodies find their way to lecture theatres and study halls. It's a shadowy trade, but not, as the law stands, illegal. Your son was sickly. Even if what you think is correct, we have no idea how the owner of that heart died." His hands flattened on the wood surface briefly. "I'm afraid that, as a detective, I can only concern myself with actual crimes."

"Kidnapping is a crime," I shot back.

"Aye, and I regret that we couldn't find your son, but you know that we tried."

This, I couldn't argue with. I knew, from my repeated visits, from hearing from the constables, how long they'd worked. They'd interviewed scores of men and women in the city, and hired agents in Ireland to search for the burned man. They'd followed every hint and listened to every reported lead, but been unable to find him, and though I insisted a man with such singular looks couldn't have vanished without help, no one had admitted to it, at least not to the police. No one had informed on any hypothetical allies either.

Fraser, in my earshot, had said there was probably nothing in it—there were cripples enough, and no good evidence to tie this particular one to anything.

The police had tried, but some had tried harder than others.

"Here." Kerr reached into his coat and thrust his handkerchief at me. I hadn't realized I needed one, and jabbed angrily at my welling eyes.

"After last Thursday's paper," Kerr began, "I would be very cautious about approaching Dr. Burnett. You can't risk a defamation suit, and neither can I, even if my superiors would permit it."

I hid for a moment, dabbing my face with his lemon-scented linen, wishing I hadn't come. As Kerr had reminded me so succinctly, he was a law officer. If called on, he would testify that I'd sought him out and made accusations—if Burnett thought to ask.

Kerr wasn't my friend. Lately, I didn't seem to have any of those. Even Miss Clark and Mrs. McPherson wouldn't believe me.

I expelled a shaking breath and pressed my lips together. I'd have to be cautious in what I did next, like Kerr said, even though the wild ideas springing up in my head weren't at all what he'd meant. Swallowing, I made a show of stowing away my emotions, rubbing my cheeks, and smoothing down some loose strands of hair.

"I understand, Mr. Kerr. I overreacted. It's—it's all very difficult."

"Of course," he said quietly. "You know if there was anything I could do—"

But there wasn't, and I must never again mistake him for a friend.

He consulted his watch. "The hour's growing late. You'll allow me to escort you home?"

I nodded.

"You're still at the same address?"

I nodded again, almost hearing his unspoken thought: *Same house, so she's been paying her rent at least.*

He was putting a mark on my ledger, a credit on the "not a madwoman, not yet," side. Clearly, I'd amassed some debits on the other.

I tugged down the veil on my bonnet before walking through the station. On the walk home, Kerr chatted determinedly about ordinary things, and once we arrived, he took the opportunity to give his regards to Mrs. McPherson.

He was checking up on me.

I should never have gone.

The fewer people I shared my suspicions with, the better, because tomorrow I intended to visit the specimen collection again.

I presented myself at Burnett's house during evening viewing hours in a borrowed pair of high-heeled shoes, a bright blue pelisse I'd purchased from the secondhand stalls, with a close-woven veil hanging from the brim of my hat.

Interest in his collection had increased since my first visit and the subsequent outcry. Today there were well over a dozen ticket holders waiting. I joined the line, trusting my veil would discourage any attempts at conversation. I'd drunk a pot of tea and eaten an oatcake with butter before coming. I'd even taken an hour's nap. My head felt fine, and I'd seen the collection already, so there wouldn't be anything to alarm me. Today, I'd be able to stare and shudder as dispassionately as everyone else, hopefully extinguishing the embers of my "unreasonable suspicion."

I shifted from one foot to the other, easing my growing discomfort from the impractical high heels, and watched a brown bird dart from the wrought-iron fence to a nearby windowsill. Someone must have scattered it with crumbs, for he pecked and hopped, chirping belligerently when another winged, brown-waistcoated fellow swooped by.

Twice, select guests were whisked ahead of the waiting crowd through the doors, but the scattered grumbling this caused wasn't overly resentful. A person arriving in a coach-and-four always took precedence over those who walked on their own feet.

The door opened, and I caught a partial glimpse of the man conducting tours today. My shoulders tightened. The same assistant was here tonight, the man who'd caught me in my faint.

But I was two inches taller today, and my face was obscured. I tapped a toe in time with the whistling of the man behind me.

"How much longer, d'ye think?" he asked his friend.

The other man shrugged.

The front door opened, and the next batch shuffled in.

"One more," a voice called from inside.

I hurried up the steps and found myself face-to-face with Burnett, who was holding open the door.

"Welcome. Thank you for coming," he said, smiling to allay my sudden start.

I nodded and stepped to the side of the hall. Ignoring my paralyzed lungs, I discreetly tucked the veil closer to my chin, striving to show a calm I didn't feel. Burnett and his assistant were both present today, but they didn't seem suspicious of me, the jumpy, veiled woman at the back, and went on thanking the guests.

"I'm delighted to personally conduct you through my collection of curiosities tonight," Burnett was saying, "and perhaps acquaint you with some recent medical discoveries. We are truly on the threshold of a great age and faced with a great work. Promoting the health of mankind is the aim of every doctor and surgeon, as well as my life's calling."

His words landed amid scattered applause, and I joined reflexively, still stiff with surprise.

"My patients and students claim most of my time, but it is a particular pleasure to introduce visitors to my work." He swept us with a beneficent smile, and I held my breath until his eyes passed. "This way."

I surrendered my shilling to the assistant in exchange for a white card with Burnett's name printed on it and the date written in blue ink. Then I followed the group to the salon. Pretending interest in Burnett's grandiloquent patter, I gave attention to each and every specimen so I could linger when the time came without arousing suspicion. Latin words and case histories slipped past me in a meaningless blur. All I registered was the pull I felt to the other side of the room, and the shelf with the mysterious heart. But when we reached the place, the only item on display was a wax cast of a bronchial tree, an item Burnett passed with a brief description, before urging us to regard his gigantic whale bones—tonight, he'd set out some of the human variety nearby for comparison. I scanned the shelf again and the cupboards we'd not approached, but the heart was gone.

My own raced erratically, my brow beading with sweat, just as the assistant's attention landed on me. "Madam? Forgive me, but do we know each other?"

I shook my head. "No, I'm afraid not," I said in as repressive a tone as I could manage.

"And you came alone?"

I turned my face away. "I've been off leading strings for many years, sir."

"You are not too warm?" His eyes lingered on my veil. I lowered my voice.

"The temperature is very comfortable, but I'm afraid the wait was rather long. I wonder if you could direct me to the necessary."

He nodded deferentially. "Of course, madam. You'll find everything you require at the end of the hall."

Five quick strides carried me out of the room.

Alone in the hall, I turned toward the front door. There was no point in staying. I'd been foolish to come, risking discovery and endangering my reputation even further. Anxious to escape, I missed the thudding—it was muddled with the beat of my sharp heels on the tiled floor. But as I neared the door, it swelled louder, *da-di-la*, overpowering my footsteps, my rapid pulse, the muffled conversation penetrating into the hall.

I stopped. The syncopated thudding didn't. Alarmed now, I glanced about, left, right, and behind me. Still alone, but I couldn't count on this for long.

I turned around, paced back in front of the drawing room door, but the sound faded the nearer I came. Breath left me in a rush. I'd imagined it.

Another about-face, but I'd only taken a single step when I heard the pulse again. Frightened, I walked faster, but I couldn't outpace the sound, growing with every stride until, by a door on my right, it throbbed in a deafening drumbeat.

Here, I thought. Hesitating only a moment, I shrugged aside the idea that this was impossible. The pulse was too loud to ignore, filling my ears, reverberating across my skin. I turned the handle.

The room was dark. The door clicked shut menacingly behind

me. With trembling hands, I reached into my reticule for a match. Striking a light, I held it high, surveying the curtain-shrouded room. There, on the mantelpiece, was the thing I sought, a weird lump of flesh that seemed suspended in midair.

Da-di-la.

In my mind, words sprang into being, matching the heart's faltering cadence. I could almost hear Thomas whispering, *Mam, I'm here.*

Heat singed my fingers. I yelped and dropped the match, plunging myself into dark. I stamped frantically, but the light must have gone out before touching the carpet.

Something creaked, and I started like a deer, ears pricking. I couldn't be found here.

Dashing out to the hall, my heart stopped when I spied an elderly woman clutching the banister, halfway down the stairs.

"That room isn't open to visitors," she said accusingly.

"I was only looking for the necessary," I blurted, but before she could speak, I rushed out the front door.

Mam, I'm here. Da-di-la.

The sound faded as I fled, deadened by the snap of my heels on the pavement, accompanying my own drumbeat message.

Thomas. My Thomas. I'll come back.

{ 10 }

Adam brushed crumbs of pastry from his fingers and drained the last swallow of ale from his glass. The crowd in the pub was lively, singing along with a girl both clear voiced and comely. The warm room felt like a reprieve after tonight's dinner—though his stepmother and half brothers shared the blood ties and legal bonds to make them family, they didn't feel like one, at least to him.

"It can't be easy, since your father died," Hugh Fraser said through a mouthful of fish pie. Adam had already finished his, chewing like the movement would churn out a headful of hurt and exasperation. Dismissing his earlier resolve, Adam signed for the barmaid to refill his glass.

"It wasn't easy before," he mumbled. "We're like a puzzle with half the pieces missing." Maybe the trouble was that he came from a different box.

"So you left dinner early and came back to work." Fraser shook his head. "You need a hobby."

Fraser was married, with a young daughter, but took every chance he could to fish, golf, and while away his time at the pub. He claimed it was necessary for his equilibrium, working with the police.

Adam shook his head. "Was my own fault tonight. Too much on my mind." Thomas Tait, mostly, and his mother's incredible claims. They weighed on him like wet clothes, dank and chilling, because no matter what he'd told her, Burnett's story rested atop one great, uncomfortable coincidence.

He thought about telling Fraser, then decided against it. Fraser would only scoff, like he had when Adam had tried to explain his irrational distrust of a particular witness, years before. Something about the woman had set him on edge, reminding him of what his grandmother had said when a party of traders stopped at their settlement, a tiny outpost, weeks away from anywhere on white men's maps.

"Don't let them in," she told the others. "They smell wrong."

He'd been only five then, but he remembered her warning, and that no one heeded it, because a week later, the traders returned—and his time, not with friendly smiles and news from Montreal.

Fraser called Adam "bloodhound" for an entire month after confiding that story, even though the witness soon proved herself a liar.

This wouldn't be any different, and Adam couldn't afford to alienate his friend. But the coincidence of Burnett owning that heart...it didn't smell right either.

Fraser took another bite, chewing ruminatively. "Superintendent says he's nearly talked the Commission into hiring another two detectives. Not sure if that will make things better for you or not. Sometimes I think you don't want a life outside of work."

Adam rolled his eyes, and Fraser shrugged and turned his attention to finishing his meal. "I'll go back with you to the station," he said, as they buttoned up to face the evening's rain.

"Go home," Adam said. "We don't both need to be there." Fraser didn't need to hide away in a pile of constables' notes and informer's reports. "Your family is waiting."

"Wee Sarah won't be asleep yet." Fraser grinned. "She'll be keening for at least another hour, so I best not go home quite yet."

It was a weak excuse, one Adam knew better than to take at face value. Fraser was offering company, something Adam refused far too often.

"All right, then. Let's go." Fraser would certainly blame Adam when his wife complained about the long hours, but that was only fair, considering.

Leaving the pub's warm fire and amber-filled glasses, he followed Fraser into the rain, trudging uphill from Canongate to the station, ready for the usual allotment of drunkards, brawlers, and thieves.

And there seemed to be plenty waiting when they stepped inside, but there was also a young girl with untidy brown plaits and an angry mouth, standing with folded arms in front of the desk sergeant.

"Detectives." The man's ruddy face creased in a smile of relief, and he practically leaped from behind the desk, herding the child to him and Fraser. "The constables will have spoken to you about Miss Burt."

It took a moment to register the name. Nan Burt was a young girl who, four days ago, reported a missing mother. Four constables had been detailed with the search. Adam had listened to their reports and questioned the woman's employer himself.

He knew, from the notes, that Nan was ten. He'd expected her to be thin cheeked and sickly, like so many neglected children in the nearby wynds. Instead, she was tall for her age and well fed, wearing a stout pair of shoes. The distress of the past week was writ plain

across her face, but not deeply enough yet to dislodge the stubborn-
ness in her forehead. She was here for answers.

"Hugh—" Adam turned around, but Fraser wasn't there.

"Have to nip into my office," he called from the stairs. "Reports
for Maxwell."

The desk sergeant nodded sympathetically, but Adam pressed
his lips together, annoyed with the excuse. Nothing urgent had
existed in Fraser's office an hour ago. There was seldom good news
in this type of case, and unfortunately, they didn't have any for
Nan. Hugh was simply choosing to leave Adam to deal with the
child alone.

Coward.

Well, friendship only stretched so far. As his heart and lungs
transmuted into lead, Adam motioned the girl to a quiet corner,
away from the erratic recitations of a woman too full of whisky to
speak any sense, but not full enough to sleep off the drunkenness.

"We're still looking," Adam told the child, pitching his voice for
her ears alone. "But we haven't found her yet." The only promising
suggestion was a story of a man, going west to Glasgow to work in
his brother's printshop. Apparently he'd expressed interest in the
girl's mother, and it wasn't uncommon, at the start of a new relationship, for a parent to walk away, leaving children behind. Adam had
instructed the constables to notify the parish, but—

"Who is looking after you, Nan?" he demanded.

"I'm staying with my auntie on Chapel Street," she said, the
shields behind her eyes closing in tight, holding him off.

There was no auntie, not on Chapel Street or any other. Adam
was familiar enough with the case to know. He softened his voice.
Lord knows, he wasn't angry with the girl.

"You've been sleeping rough." It was plain from her wet cloak, sodden skirts, the thick band of dirt on her hems, and though she'd done well with the braids, they didn't quite hide the tangles in her hair. Adam sighed. If she was savvy enough to lie to him, she'd be wary of coming into his office, and he knew better than to disturb those instincts. "Wait here, Nan. I'll only be a moment."

As he left, he locked eyes with the desk sergeant. "Don't let her leave."

Up in his desk, he had a blue woolen scarf, thick and wide enough to serve as a shawl. There were also, tucked in a tin at the back of the drawer, a few ginger biscuits.

Pocketing three, he returned down the stairs, passing Hugh, who was on his way out with some folders tucked under his arm. "Taking these with me," he said. "Decided I best not keep my two Sarahs waiting."

Adam nodded absently, trying to peer ahead, around the body of the desk sergeant.

Nan was still here. Adam kept in a sigh of relief.

"Biscuit?" he offered.

The child took all three. With her mother gone, it wouldn't have taken long for the landlord to kick her out. Perhaps, if he questioned the sergeants, he'd discover why she was here, alone, instead of someplace safer, and why she was magicking away his biscuits like they'd never been, instead of eating the two meals a day she'd receive from the parish.

"I can't let you back out there alone," he told her.

She took a moment, arranging the scarf around her shoulders, before consenting to look at him. When she did, her lower lip wobbled.

"Mam wouldn't leave me," she insisted.

Adam nodded, hating himself and his work and the many

failures—big and small—that left him doing this. "But you must keep safe until we find her. You have to let me take you to the orphan's home."

If he'd said it before bringing food and the scarf, he was certain she'd have run. He'd prepared for that, choosing to stand between her and the door. As it was, she slumped a little, drawing the thick wool closer.

"Keep it," Adam told her. "Will you go, if I take you there? We can ride in a cab. It will be easier for her to find you there. And I'll visit to tell you about our search. You'll be just fine, Nan."

Seconds slipped by, each one shifting the girl's life another point on the compass. Adam prayed she wouldn't cry. He did his best, but tonight he didn't feel competent for tears.

"All right." She swallowed.

After she'd vanished behind the door of the orphan's home, stoic to the end, he wished she had cried. Or that he'd at least given room for it, if she needed. Better for her, though, this way.

He rode home alone in the dark.

{ *11* }

A nd you still haven't heard?"
   Conall smiled at his mother with more assurance than he felt. "The club waited six months after Moncrieff died before filling his place, so making a decision may take a while. I'm not concerned."

But he was, because although he could quite fairly claim to be Edinburgh's most popular teacher of anatomy, there were always other considerations. The sort that always tripped him up. Birth shouldn't count, not with the Aesculapians, who claimed to choose members for their knowledge and skill, but whatever anyone said, connections mattered. The old hierarchies still helped their own and shut out others.

"I'm easily the most compelling candidate," Conall repeated, for both of them.

"*I* know that," his mother said. "And if *they're* too fool to know it, you're better off without them."

He returned a mechanical smile, because he'd learned the hard way that belligerence over the slights he'd suffered didn't help. He didn't want to fight them. He wanted to *be* them, and he nearly was, now. After joining the Aesculapian Club, it would be ludicrous to keep him out of the university.

"What time do you want your dinner?" his mother asked, handing him his hat from the rack in the hall.

"Don't worry about me. I'll be working late." This was his usual day for deliveries, and if he wanted tomorrow's exhibit ready on time—

"You'll eat something, though?"

"I'll send Jones out." He put on the hat, inspecting its angle in the hall mirror. No, too waggish. People wouldn't take him seriously. He tilted the brim to a more conservative position.

"Make certain those young men are helping as they ought. They're lucky to be working for you," his mother said as she passed him his umbrella.

She angled her face, drawing herself up an inch, and Conall bent to brush his lips across her cheek. The skin felt dry, and bore so many fine wrinkles it looked like crepe. For a long time, he'd ignored the proliferation of gray in her hair, the gradual clouding of her irises, but Mother was old now. He smiled to hide the pang of knowing that someday—maybe soon—he'd lose her.

"When these fellows accept you, you'll let me know?" she asked.

Conall nodded. "I'll send word immediately. Have a good day, Mother. I'll see you tomorrow."

Outside, he surveyed the translucent porcelain sky with satisfaction. The air was cool—good dissecting weather. Alighting from the front steps, he turned right, walking along the row of houses, his bag swinging at his side. It wasn't far to Surgeon's Square, just a left at the end of his street, then a half mile uphill. But the slope here was gentle, unlike other parts of the city. A quarter hour's walk, at most.

Perhaps he should go home for dinner and see his mother. He might even have good news.

But the food from the pub would be better, and his mother

wouldn't expect him to stop working early. His success mattered to her, and she'd always felt his injuries like her own. She cared about his admission to the Aesculapian Society as much as he did.

Once he got it, that was another thing he'd have over Munro, who, in spite of his position and family legacy, had never been invited to join.

Conall grunted, drawing a glance from a boy dodging past him on the pavement. It probably had been a trifle bold, applying as a lecturer at the university so soon after leaving medical training with the army, but the fact was, he'd done more surgeries there than some doctors did in their entire careers, and had ample bodies available for his own private study. Those were the years he'd acquired his first specimens: bladder stones, a hand he'd dissected and dried, a fractured and healed elbow joint. Modest pieces, but all displaying his talent. He'd brought them to his interview, where Alexander Munro, the third of his name to occupy the chair of anatomy, had sniffed and sent him packing.

"Adequate work, I'm sure. But this institution has a reputation. A history."

Conall didn't.

Scowling at the blameless passersby, Conall stepped from the pavement onto the street, landing his left foot in a puddle.

"Shite." With his anxieties over the club admission, this misstep seemed symbolic of his struggle. Mother would roll her eyes and take this as an omen.

"Shite," Conall said again.

He had no patience for portents and superstition, but these shoes were new, and now he had filth all over his beautiful brown leather. Whipping out a handkerchief, he bent to wipe it clean, then reconsidered. He wasn't the type of man who shined his own shoes, not anymore. He'd ask the porter to do it for him, once he arrived at the anatomy school bearing his name.

He was nearly there, and the damage would be averted in a manner much more fitting.

Conall's wasn't the only private anatomy school on Surgeon's Square, but it was the busiest and the largest, if one counted the number of courses offered and enrollment, which Conall certainly did. It was no small satisfaction to him that a good portion of his students were disgruntled and frustrated pupils of Dr. Munro.

"Morning, Sam." Conall greeted the porter, and waved at the slime adorning his left foot. "Hoping you can help me with my shoes this morning."

"Of course, Dr. Burnett."

Sam didn't think anything of the request, hustling out of the cloakroom, rag in hand. Why hadn't Conall asked him to do this before? It was so easy.

When his shoes were once again sporting a pristine shine, Conall surrendered his coat and umbrella. "Has the delivery arrived?"

"Not yet, doctor. Last time I went round, Mr. Jones was still waiting. Mr. Ferguson isn't here yet, but I believe he's running this evening's tutorial?"

Conall nodded. He was no longer able to conduct all the smaller sessions, so he'd recently taken to assigning some to his two assistants, who worked from his detailed notes. It allowed him to increase enrollment, but it also increased his need for specimens.

"A letter's come for you," Sam said. "From a Dr. Kellie?"

Conall's breath stopped. "Give it here."

He took the missive with shaking hands, cracked the seal, and spread it open, skimming over the salutation, the polite nothings that filled half the page.

...am pleased to invite you to fill Dr. Duncan's place in our society. It's true that there are few who can, but after much discussion, we agree that you are up to the challenge.

He fumbled the letter closed, struggling to fit it into his pocket, his heart pounding fit to burst.

"Is everything all right, doctor?"

I've done it, he thought. *I've done it.*

"Doctor?" Sam put a hand on his shoulder.

"I'm quite all right," Conall said, shrugging the porter off, and collecting himself with a deep breath. "I've just been invited to the Aesculapian Club."

Sam nodded, blinking owlishly, pretending to understand. "Congratulations, sir."

"Thank you, but I'd best get to work." He straightened his sleeves, and plucked the letter from his pocket, smoothing it between his fingers. He'd crumpled it without realizing, but it could be fixed if he pressed it between the pages of a heavier book. "Perhaps you'll be good enough to show this to my mother. She'll be pleased for me."

Walking past the lecture theatre, through the laboratory, into the yard behind, Conall found his other assistant, Jones, arguing with his supplier outside the icehouse.

"She's worth more," the deliveryman argued. "This one's young. Not fat. Possibly pregnant."

Conall's eyebrows rose. "How did she die?"

The deliveryman, a thick-fingered Irishman named Will, turned and immediately swept off his cap. "Good morning, doctor. Sir."

"May I take a look?" Without waiting for an answer, Conall leaned over the open trunk. The body inside was wrapped in a muddy shroud but smelled fresh enough.

"This one drowned. Two days ago," said a sturdy-looking girl standing to Will's side.

"Dug her out of Canongate Kirkyard last night," Will put in. "Wanted to bring her to you in timely fashion."

Conall fought down a grimace at Will's words. He had a habit of trying to talk better than he was, but nothing could counter his work-roughened hands and Irish accent. Still, this was good news. A fresh body, and a possibly pregnant one was a lucky find, and a valuable one.

"You're certain of the pregnancy?" Conall asked.

"Why else would the little fool drown herself?" Will answered with a shrug.

Conall exchanged glances with Jones, who looked skeptical, then hooked his thumbs into his waistcoat pockets. "So you're not certain."

"No, but—"

"I do pay more for the pregnant ones. But only confirmed cases, I'm afraid. This one"—he peered into the box again, trying to size up the folded form—"it's hard to tell, and even if she were, it's doubtful we'll see anything useful this early." Lies, but Will wouldn't know that.

Jones nodded, taking his cue. "We'll give you the usual ten pounds."

Before Will could protest, Conall added placatingly, "How about eleven, since you brought her in such good condition?"

"I'm afraid not."

Surprised, Conall turned to the girl, who'd folded her arms.

"She's worth fourteen. If you won't pay it, I'll take her across the square."

Frowning, Conall returned his attention to the deliveryman. He didn't know her, and didn't like her forcing a way into his business negotiations. "Will, we have a long-standing arrangement. You and your family have supplied me for a long time. I pay good prices. More than fair."

Will shifted his weight, and glanced at the girl, who looked unimpressed.

Who was she?

"Prices go up, Dr. Burnett. Will told your man so last time, but he didn't seem to understand."

Quite a bold piece, this one. Again, Jones knew what to do, having tended to the disagreeable aspects of Conall's business for some time.

"I'd think it over before trying to take advantage of the doctor." Deliberately, Jones matched her stance, folding his arms, and dropping his eyes to the neck of her gown, where a white muslin frill framed a pretty expanse of pink flesh. "Dr. Burnett trades with Will. He doesn't know you."

Will coughed. "Er—Mr. Jones? Sarah's right. Costs more to do business these days. There's watchmen by the graves. Have to pay them off. You can't have this one for less than—"

"You can have twelve," Conall said. "If you're bribing the watchmen with more than that, it's your foolishness, not mine." Ignoring the girl, he smiled at Will. "I value your work. You and your cousin have always brought me the very best."

He reached into his pocket for a roll of notes and began counting them out for Will, but the man stepped back, waiting for a nod from the girl before signaling with his eyes for Conall to hand her the money.

"So who are you?" Jones asked, also noticing this exchange.

"Friend of Will's," she said sweetly. Her voice was Irish tinged too.

"How good a friend?" Jones shifted his weight onto one hip. "Care to make any more?"

Her eyes narrowed into slits, and she pushed past Jones, upsetting his balance, and thrust an open palm at Conall. "If you could hurry, please. I have other business today, doctor."

Conall might have slowed, but the notes were already counted. He handed them over, and she tucked the notes inside her gown, holding Jones's eyes, as if daring him to let his gaze wander. Then she stalked from the yard, calling over her shoulder. "Will, you can come for your share tomorrow." The back gate clanged shut behind her.

"Mr. Jones, sir." Will's voice was soft, unusually hesitant.

"What?" Jones sounded annoyed, and he was scowling at the gate.

"I always think it's best to know a thing or two about a lass's family before"—he coughed—"offering friendship. There might be a husband or father or brothers who take offense."

Jones grunted and motioned impatiently at the box. "Help me carry this inside."

Obedient, Will picked up the far side of the box, but he wasn't done talking. "Sa—she—" He grunted, as the two of them lifted the heavy load off the ground. "That woman, you know, doesn't need any help. She dunna like you, she'll gut you herself."

Jones snorted, and Conall returned the roll of notes to his pocket and took out his watch. "Kind advice. Thank you, Will, but I'm afraid Jones and I must get to work."

But his smile had vanished by the time he entered the icehouse. If the next corpse was this expensive, he'd have to raise his prices too.

Students queued to enroll in his courses and now he was a member of the Aesculapian Club. He intended to dazzle them all.

{ *12* }

I lay awake all night, not knowing what to do, only that I had to do something. It was possible that Thomas had died and his heart had been taken, but I suspected worse—Thomas was taken because of his heart.

Either way, I wouldn't leave it on display in Dr. Burnett's collection.

I was sharp with my students the next morning, and when Miss Andrews couldn't find her way through a difficult passage, I said it was a reflection of her practice. I didn't attempt to demonstrate the fingering myself—crippled by impotent fury, my hands were in no state to contest Mozart. After finishing my lessons, I walked to Surgeon's Square and stared at the unfeeling facade of the halls. Burnett's anatomy school was immediately beside the university's and almost as large, with arches and pillars that would have dwarfed his comfortable, unpretentious home on Newington Place, had the buildings been placed side by side.

As it was, the sight of these academies, shoulder to shoulder, dissuaded me from any lingering hope of finding help here. I'd gain nothing approaching one of his colleagues with my claims. In the entire city, I was probably the only one who perceived anything sinister. If Burnett and the doctors used as many corpses as Detective Kerr claimed, what chance was there that anyone would remember the body of a small blond boy, over a year ago? Even if they did, there was no chance anyone connected with this medical fraternity would tell me about it.

I stepped aside to the edge of the square, away from the procession of students arriving in greater and greater numbers as the hour drew to a close. Each man presented a card at the door before being allowed inside.

I couldn't get into Burnett's school. Try as I might, I couldn't even see a way to draw a passing student into conversation. What would a lone woman want from one of them anyway? If I was a man with a bit of money, I could join the ranks of students, but as a woman, even one with more money than I'd ever have at my disposal, that goal was impossible. Slouching away, I realized I wouldn't even be allowed to buy one of Burnett's books on my own.

If there were answers here, I wouldn't find them.

The way from the square to Newington Place was straight and quick. Having a house close by was, no doubt, a convenience for the famous medical man.

Feet flagging, worn by the futility of my task, I leaned against the railing separating Burnett's house from his neighbors. Out here, I heard nothing but the noise of the street, though I listened for long minutes, waiting for that low drumming, wishing there was some way I could beg Thomas's forgiveness. I'd failed him, first by insisting on keeping him, when he might have been fostered quietly in the country, then sent to a boys' school by his father.

If I hadn't insisted he needed a mother's care, he might never have contracted scarlet fever, which always spread so quickly in cities like Edinburgh. If I hadn't kept him living with me, he wouldn't have been taken. He'd have a degree of privilege, belonging to a guardian who mattered. And he'd have had a whole and healthy heart.

I'd loved him too much to give him up, so I'd lost him. Even if his heart was here, he wasn't, and he wouldn't know if I told him I was sorry.

The edges of the buildings blurred, and I swiped roughly at my eyes. As I cleared away the tears, my gaze landed on something white, visible in the corner of the window next to Dr. Burnett's front door—a small placard propped against the glass with a message in large black letters.

A message for me. It read: *Housekeeper needed imdtly. Experienced applicants pls inquire.*

I didn't pause or question if I could do it. This was the way to reclaim my son's heart, and perhaps uncover the murky history of his disappearance.

Before, when I'd come here, I heard Thomas, but now the voice surfacing from my memories was older, richer, and achingly familiar.

My father had always been an optimist. When I'd confessed my pregnancy and my decision to keep and raise my child, he'd taken it in stride. I heard him again, his voice soft and steady.

Where there's a will, there's a way, Isobel. Let's put our heads together and see what we can do.

There was, unfortunately, so little time.

Immediately on returning home, I penned a letter. Then I read it through, tore it to bits, and drafted another.

I needed a name, references, a history, an entirely new appearance, a plausible way of disappearing from my real life into another.

I paced and plotted and thought. Perhaps, if there'd been more time, I'd see the folly of considering this, but I was certain it was the best chance that would ever come my way. *It would be folly not to try.*

By the following dawn, I had a lengthy shopping list, two letters to dispatch in the morning post, and a plan.

Shopping first.

Impossible to obtain what I needed without selling as well as buying. I brought a basket with me of things I owned that would fetch the best price. Books, sheet music, the violin I could play, though never so well as my father. He said it was a man's instrument, and I'd taken immediately to the pianoforte, providing me with an acceptable pastime and a potential career. He'd only taught me violin so I could partner with him in duets on the rare occasions we had alone.

I emptied my basket, then called at my bank.

"You wish to withdraw everything, madam?" The clerk at the wicket looked surprised.

"I'm moving to the country," I explained.

It took an hour, though they knew I was a widow, so there was no one to appeal to besides me. A gentleman in a brown coat tried anyway, explaining that I wasn't being sensible. I quite agreed with him, but didn't admit it. Behaving sensibly wasn't my concern.

"I'm quite decided," I told him. "Edinburgh is too full of painful memories."

At last I left with a roll of pound notes—my little legacy from Papa, the scant savings eked from eight frugal years, the last of the money remaining from John, paid secretly for Thomas's maintenance. The folded bills went immediately down my bodice. I was too poor to trust such a sum to my purse.

I left the Royal Exchange for the Canongate and bought myself neat brown gowns cut large and a collection of close-fitting caps, all from shops and stalls I'd never visited before. At a shabby pawnbroker's, I traded my make-believe wedding band for a pair of spectacles with plain glass instead of corrective lenses, and bought a bottle of brown hair dye with money from my father's violin.

Then I purchased a traveling case and a pot of brown paint and a supply of beeswax candles. I took everything home and carried it up to my room, where I dyed my hair, and began experimenting with beeswax padding on the insides of my cheeks, drawing myself darker, more angular eyebrows. I folded a shawl and pinned it around my middle, thickening my waist before donning one of the brown gowns.

Saturday morning, after making sure Mrs. McPherson was out and I could escape the house unseen, I marched back to Newington Place, wearing my new persona.

"Yes?"

I must have prayed with sufficient fervor, guessed correctly, or acted while the stars aligned, because Burnett answered the door himself.

"Dr. Burnett?" I inquired, as if I didn't know.

"I'm afraid this isn't my time for patient consultations," he said, assessing and dismissing me with a glance.

"I'm not a patient," I said quickly. "I wrote you yesterday. My name is Ross. Janet Ross. You're looking for a housekeeper."

His frown cleared at once. "Ah. Yes, I saw your letter. I'm afraid I haven't had time to respond—"

My pulse faltered. "Has the position been filled?"

"Not yet." His lips compressed in what might pass as a smile as his eyes brushed over me in a quick, dismissive sweep. "I'm still looking for someone with the right qualifications. I have quite particular requirements."

I stared back, waiting for recognition to spark in his eyes and silently reminding myself of each alteration I'd made to my appearance. "What exactly do you need, doctor?" My tone was clipped, confident, as if I'd never had a panicked thought in my life. If a story is simple and said with conviction, folk tend to believe it, like when I began telling the world I was a widow.

Burnett relented with a quick glance at the hall clock, likely judging that I wouldn't take much of his time. The door swung wide, and the moment I stepped across the threshold, that pulse thrummed across my skin.

Da-di-lah.

"This way." Instead of guiding me to the study, where I'd last seen Thomas's heart, he brought me into the drawing room.

Quiet, love, I begged silently. *I need to think.*

The beat in my ears subsided, but I had no time to consider how or why. Burnett was looking back at me from the middle of his blue and gold carpet, freezing me midstride. I ran my tongue over the layer of beeswax lodged inside my cheek and told myself he'd have thrown me out already if he recognized me.

"Well?" he demanded. "If you're going to faint or have the vapors, better get it over with."

I exhaled and took a long, leisurely look about me, pretending to take it in for the first time while slowly arching my brows. "Hmm. Sorry to disappoint."

Burnett's rough bark of laughter made me jump, sending a tide of blood into my cheeks. "Don't be angry. I didn't mean to startle you. I'm just delighted by your sangfroid. I've brought a dozen applicants to this room, and not one of them was willing to stay, let alone clean the place."

I stepped to the nearest shelf and ran a finger along it, noting the dust collected on the tip of my glove. "I can see it requires some care."

"Just so," Burnett grunted. "My assistants don't like being tasked with it, and it's not something I can trust to a kitchen girl. People pay to see my collection, and the specimens are immensely valuable, not only as curiosities but as tools for study, so I am particular about how this space is maintained."

"Yes." I rubbed my fingers together to dispel the lingering dust.

He flushed. "Finding reliable help is a challenge. You, however—"

I interrupted him. "I have not, in fact, worked as a housekeeper before."

His face fell.

"But I was upstairs maid at a large establishment in Lomond, for Mr. Alexander Anstruther, and his wife, Lady Margaret."

Burnett's eyebrows lifted at the mention of these notable gentry, known for their wealth and their patronage of the arts. I thrust a folded paper at him.

"Here is my reference, from Mr. Sibbald, her ladyship's butler."

Yesterday I'd posted, among other things, a finely wrought construction of omissions and truths for Walter Sibbald, the kindly butler who'd taught me the cleaning of clocks. I was thirteen at the time, and my father and I were living within the big house's shadow, in the Anstruthers' lodge. I spent my days following him about, and "helping" the Anstruthers' housekeeper, a kindly woman, who liked my piano-playing and quiet ways.

Papa was composing music and performing at the Anstruthers' many parties. Sometimes they asked me to perform, too, and I'd always enjoyed the attention, until I turned nineteen, and caught John's.

My lips thinned at the thought. His attention hadn't lasted.

So I'd left Lomond, but yesterday, I'd written Mr. Sibbald, saying I needed a change after losing Thomas, asking him to give me a suitable reference, and to support my appropriation of the name Janet Ross. I thought it likely he'd agree to it out of compassion, but I couldn't be sure—a worry to keep for another day. Mr. Sibbald's qualms of conscience wouldn't matter if I didn't convince Burnett today, and his pleased surprise in me was fading, quickly replaced by wary skepticism.

"You are younger than I expected," Burnett said.

"But energetic," I said firmly. "And capable of managing a home without staff." I looked around, as if calculating his annual income from the size of the house and his furnishings.

"My mother manages the servants," he informed me. "Until recently, she also acted as housekeeper. She prefers it, but the work is beginning to be too much for her. You would have all the usual duties," he warned. "And I should like, occasionally, to entertain."

"Naturally," I replied. He might not care for my almost scornful tone, but I could tell without it, he'd belittle me.

"You're sure you can care for the collection?" he demanded. "It's one thing to stand here with me, but this room must be cleaned thoroughly and regularly by you alone. You don't object?"

I smiled thinly. "These things don't terrify me." The imaginings that haunted me were much worse. If not for the chance of recovering the heart, I wouldn't be here.

Still, I pretended to consider. "It's not what I'm used to," I began. "But naturally you wish these"—I faltered—"specimens to be treated with care. I can do that, sir. In fact, I was charged with cleaning Mr. Anstruther's collection of snuffboxes."

Untrue, but I had, on occasion, helped Mr. Sibbald. He'd let me handle them, telling me the history of each, considering it a high treat.

"You're a sensible young woman," Burnett said, nodding approvingly. "I'm glad to see that. But why did you leave the Anstruthers?"

I shifted my feet. "They have an excellent housekeeper, sir, and she's only forty-three. If I stayed, it would be another twenty years before I could even think of being housekeeper. And, forgive me, doctor, but I did want to see something of the world, and it seems like there's more opportunity in a place like Edinburgh." I surveyed the shelves again, then added, "I understand, doctor, why you must be careful. Other women might let their imaginations run away with them and hurry through this room, neglecting it. You can trust me not to. I would treat this place as if it was filled with fine art."

"You are right on point, Miss Ross. That is exactly what these are." The skin on my arms prickled at Burnett's widening smile. He was expansive now, his earlier reticence gone. "You are very confident, for such a young woman."

I was good at smothering emotions; hopefully I appeared nonplussed. "I'm very competent, so that shouldn't surprise you."

He laughed again, studying me sideways and stroking his chin. "Well, much as I'd like to take your word for it, I will need to confer with Mr. Sibbald."

"Please do," I said, exuding counterfeit courage impossible to actually feel. I was gambling on Mr. Sibbald's sympathies. He knew what had happened to Thomas and would believe me when I said I needed a change. But I didn't know if his morals were sufficiently flexible to lie for me to Dr. Conall Burnett. Though kind, he was also scrupulously honest.

All in, it was quelling, counting up everything I was hoping for.

"Your relative youth," Burnett mused. "I suppose that is not always a disadvantage. Would you like to hear my terms? If you are willing, I can offer you a two-week trial. If your work and your reference is satisfactory…"

My heart leaped and I fought down a shiver of alarm. No balking now. I'd be careful, guarding my identity and my secrets. I wouldn't need to be here long, just enough to take the heart.

"I'd be extremely happy with that, Dr. Burnett."

{ *13* }

That night, wearing my usual face and a cap over my dark brown hair, I told Mrs. McPherson and Miss Clark that I was moving away. Monday morning, I moved to Newington Place to begin keeping house for the doctor.

This time, an elderly woman greeted me. She had hunched shoulders, cloudy eyes, and a pinched face.

"Miss Ross. I'd have preferred a widow."

She was alone and didn't offer anyone to help me with my case. But I'd lugged it all the way from Drummond Street, so another twenty yards or so to the basement didn't matter. "Will you show me where to put my things?" I asked.

She grunted and conducted me downstairs to an unswept room with dirty windows and an unmade bed.

"I've had no one but a charwoman in the last few months," she said.

Not frequently, apparently. "It will take time to put things right," I said.

"That's what you're here for, isn't it?"

I nodded, ignoring the bite in her voice. "Why don't you show me around the house? Once I know where I am, I'll need an hour to tidy up this room and unpack my things. Then I can make a list of what needs setting in order." I could tell, from my first look at her face, that if I knuckled under, I'd never be able to stand straight here again.

She muttered something under her breath in Gaelic.

My fingers prickled, so I rubbed my hands together to take away the numbness—must be from carrying my box. I should have hired a porter.

"You can unpack now," she said, and instead of turning away, she shuffled over to the chair, smoothing her skirts over her knees and weaving her mauve-tinged fingers together.

"You have nothing else to attend to?" I asked.

"Not at present." These words carried less of a lilt, enunciated aggressively, as her eyes swept languidly over me and the room. "I'm more interested in seeing what my new housekeeper is made of."

Huh.

I tugged off my gloves and bent over my box, unpicking the knots of cord and reassessing. When Dr. Burnett mentioned his mother, I'd imagined an elderly lady, frail and a little snappish, not one radiating dislike and suspicion. I was concealing plenty of both myself, so dealing with her should have been challenging enough without her staring at me, forming battle plans for a war I couldn't afford. I had enough foes already.

Today, against her, I needed to win.

Humming softly, I rearranged my features into a tranquil mask, as smooth-cheeked and imperturbable as a pastoral-styled portrait. I pushed apart the dusty curtains, hung up my cloak, then returned to my box, where I reached past my hairbrush and extracted a set of crisply folded sheets.

"We have—" Mrs. Burnett began.

"Yes, but for now I'll use my own linen," I told her, and proceeded to strip the bed and inspect the mattress. It was lumpier than the one I'd had at Mrs. Mac's.

"Where can I find the broom?"

She shifted in her chair. "The charwoman brings—"

"Don't worry. I'll find it." It was easy to flit from the room and close the door behind me before Mrs. Burnett's stiff joints released her from the chair. Alone, I hurried through the neglected kitchen into an even grubbier scullery. The usual supplies—pail, rags, broom, and mop—were strewn about the floor. I collected the broom and dustpan, then inspected the pantry, cellar, and laundry. Another room, wedged alongside mine, would house the cook, though I could see no sign of one. The kitchen, dim and dusty, had only a half-eaten loaf on the table and a pot of something warming on the stove.

"Found it," I said, breezing back into my little room.

No mutters from her now, as I swept and scoured the corners. No smiles or conversation, either, but I took my time, ridding the place of dust and prying open the window to freshen the musty air.

If Mrs. Burnett resented watching me and spoiling her afternoon, she was too stubborn to retreat. When she said that hot water and vinegar was best for cleaning windows, I nodded at her suggestion, but when she kept on pronouncing advice, I agreed with some and told her other times that the Anstruther's housekeeper had instructed me differently. When her lips twitched in irritation, I blinked blandly and turned my attention to my work, humming another line of song.

I'd made no music of my own accord this past year, but it was possible to pretend contentment as Janet Ross, even with Mrs. Burnett's scrutiny. She didn't know about my son.

I tucked sachets of herbs into the drawers along with my shifts, stockings, and caps, and aired out my gowns.

"Lavender?" Mrs. Burnett asked.

"No, this is a recipe of my mother's," I said. She held out a hand, so I passed her one of the bundles.

"Rose petals and chamomile," I said, but she only sniffed it scornfully and passed it back.

When my sheets were stretched tight across the mattress and creased at the corners, with Mrs. Burnett's worn counterpane on top and my own blue and green wool blanket folded at the foot of the bed, I dusted my hands against each other and took a moment to stretch my shoulders.

"I think things are in good enough order here," I said.

Mrs. Burnett nodded sourly. "Much improved."

"Where is the cook?" I asked.

"I turned her off," Mrs. Burnett said. "She wasn't satisfactory."

If she meant me to be cowed or impressed, my reply must have been disappointing. "What a pity. But at least you have a Rumford fireplace. It won't be hard to engage another."

She must have been ordering food from a nearby cookshop—I couldn't believe she'd managed everything on her own.

"My son generally takes his meals away from home," she explained.

Maybe so, but I gathered he wanted the choice of dining here and inviting his colleagues. If Mrs. Burnett had already dismissed one cook, it shouldn't be hard to persuade him to allow me to hire another, and if I had the choosing, it shouldn't be hard to recruit an ally. With two of us, it would be simpler to keep his mother in check.

"Will you show me the place?"

She grunted an affirmative, and stumped for the stairs, never slowing her pace, though one leg clearly pained her.

Back in the hall, she detached a ring of keys from her waist. "My son's collection is in here. He said he already explained his requirements for this room to you."

I nodded, trying to peer past her into the dim space, but she closed the door and locked it again. "It must be cleaned every Tuesday and Thursday, before the next lot of visitors."

I swallowed my disappointment. There'd be plenty of time to plan just how I'd take the heart while I was cleaning.

"And his consulting office?" I asked, hopefully.

"Just here." She motioned across the hall to the room where I'd seen Thomas's heart, when I'd returned here, veiled, on my second visit. My heart sank as she searched through her key ring and fitted a small brass one into the lock.

"You'll have to ask my son when he wants this room cleaned. Except for when he's seeing patients, he wants it kept private."

I wanted to believe the locked door wasn't a response to my earlier intrusion, but couldn't allow myself to be that great a fool. Burnett, and perhaps his mother as well, were on guard.

She fingered the key for a moment. "I'm not the one to give instructions here. You'd best speak to my son about it." With a quick nod, she returned the keys to the clip at her waist, leaving me no choice but to follow her upstairs to the other rooms.

Burnett's personal quarters were precise, in better order than the basement floor of the house, though his cupboards revealed a distressing accumulation of laundry. Besides a cook, this house needed a girl to tackle that. A single charwoman, even if she came daily, couldn't keep up with everything.

"And that must be your room," I said, pointing to the door at the other end of the upstairs hall.

Mrs. Burnett's pause told me how little she wanted me there, but—"Your son made it clear that he only wants you to be happy and comfortable," I said.

A grunt, as she marched away with stiff shoulders. I followed, lifting my chin. I didn't like her either.

Her room was an awkward space with new furnishings in need of a good polish, costly drapery, and no personal touches whatsoever: not a single book, picture, or letter. If not for the clumsily made bed and the basket of mending by the fireside chair, I wouldn't have thought anyone lived here.

"Will you want—"

"You can leave me now," she snapped.

I closed the door softly behind me and hurried away. Any ordinary house could be comfortable after a good cleaning and the hiring of a competent cook. I doubted that cure would take effect here. Mrs. Burnett was a puzzling, frustrating woman, who resented my presence in her house.

But I didn't plan to stay long, just enough to arrange for Thomas's remains and me to disappear.

Dr. Burnett didn't return home until late, long after his mother consumed the simple meal of bread and cheese I'd prepared for her and retired to bed. I was nodding with fatigue myself, filling the time by washing the crockery, because some of the shelved plates bore crumbs and grease smears.

When I heard his key scratch in the front door lock, I closed my eyes to gather myself, then dried my hands and hurried upstairs.

"Doctor?"

He started when he saw me but recovered quickly. "Miss Ross. I didn't expect to find you awake."

I pushed a falling strand of hair off my face. "Plenty to do. And I wanted a chance to speak to you. I know you are busy, but I'll require the keys and your account book." Hiring other servants, ordering foodstuffs and other household supplies were all responsibilities of the housekeeper. "I can't really begin work properly without them." And if I had to negotiate everything with Mrs. Burnett—

"My mother will—"

"I'm afraid she has not." I'd rehearsed this conversation all through the evening hours, so it wasn't hard to infuse my voice with practiced warmth. "I'm sure this isn't easy for her, ceding duties she has worked so hard to fill, but she'll accustom herself. Soon, she won't be able to remember how she ever managed without me."

"I very much hope so," he said. "I should have thought. It will be much easier for you to have those things from me."

"Yes, I thought so too," I said.

He rubbed at his neck. "I'll—"

"If you can leave them for me before you set out tomorrow morning, that will be fine," I said. "I left the household inventory—as much as I could do today, at any rate—on your dressing table. I'd have put it in your study, but the room is locked."

He flushed. "Merely a precaution against wandering visitors. I've no reason to keep you out."

"Not if you want the room dusted," I agreed, ignoring the hairs rising on my arms.

"The room with my collection is also locked, except on Tuesday and Thursday evenings, when the visitors come."

"Yes, Mrs. Burnett told me."

"And I see patients on Monday, Wednesday, and Friday mornings. Did my mother tell you...?"

I shook my head, and he sighed.

"Be patient with her, Miss Ross. She'll warm to you in time."

I replied with a smile and no words.

"I'll make sure you have everything you need first thing tomorrow," he promised.

"Thank you, doctor." I would have the keys. Just now, I was too tired to fight for anything more.

Burnett turned away and climbed the stairs. When I heard his door close, I went back to my room. My eyes were dry and burning with fatigue, and my hands, still shriveled from washing the china, were cold and damp with sweat.

Not once in the long day, in the hours I'd prowled around the house, writing down contents of the unlocked rooms, had I sensed anything that might have been Thomas. But I had keys now. I'd find him again tomorrow.

Next morning, I tended to the fires and carried up hot water, promising myself I'd hire a girl to take over these duties as quickly as possible. Mrs. Burnett, who must have done some of this herself, responded to me with majestic sulks. If a small boy hadn't arrived with a pot of broth and fresh bread—"from the Old Bell Inn, Mrs. Burnett's usual order"—there'd have been no breakfast for anyone.

I brewed tea, dished out the broth, cut bread, spread it with butter, and set everything out in the small parlor. Dr. Burnett came down first and presented me with the household ledger, money, and a set of keys, then departed for the anatomy school.

Mrs. Burnett chose that moment to ring—God knows where she'd found a bell—and I found myself trooping up and down stairs, bringing up breakfast and taking out the chamber pots. With my nose turned away and my lips mashed together, I lugged Burnett's shit to the cesspit behind the house.

Not for long, I told myself. Soon, I'd find the heart, and maybe something about how it had come here, though that thought made me feel faint, even more than the cesspit's smell.

I rinsed the chamber pots and washed and dried my hands, though this did little to settle my roiling stomach. Finally taking advantage of my first moment without the chiming of that blasted bell, I hurried to the consulting office. Though I'd sensed nothing unusual in my time here, surely once I passed through the door, I'd sense Thomas again.

The key was in my hand before I reached the hall. It slid easily into the lock. I was in the room before I could count to three, parting the curtains and filling the space with light. Drawing a deep breath, I turned to the mantelpiece.

The jar was gone.

Impossible. Burnett wouldn't have given it up—he'd fought hard to protect it. But he might have hidden it somewhere.

I darted to the bookshelf, scattering a dozen volumes to the floor, but the shelves were too shallow to conceal an object so large. The desk drawers were locked, and didn't yield to any of my keys, so I rummaged through Burnett's black leather bag and looked behind the curtains.

Thomas's heart was gone.

I sank into the chair at the desk and buried my face in my hands, squeezing my lungs into submission and stifling every sound.

The bells of the nearest kirk sounded the half hour. Mrs. Burnett rang, but I didn't budge from the chair. She rang a second and a third time, rattling the thing so vehemently it should have flown right off the handle.

I thought about walking out the front door, but the heart was somewhere. I wanted it, even if I had to work and wait. So I rose, reshelved the books, and hurried upstairs.

"Coming, ma'am."

She must have heard me, but the bell jangled again.

{ 14 }

Conall plucked at a bit of fascia, drawing it away from the nerves plunging into the pectoralis major muscle with his forceps, detaching the clingy tissue with a touch of his scalpel and flicking it into the bin with the other scraps.

"Today we're blessed with an individual of admirable musculature," he said, gesturing with the point of his blade at the subject's chest. "So look well and take good notes. A surgeon's work isn't as easy on fleshier subjects."

Flourishing the easy command of Latin and attention to detail for which he was famed, Conall guided his students from pectorals major to minor, explaining the motion and attachments of each, as well as their protective functions to the structures beneath.

"Next week, when we have a female subject again, you'll see how the muscle aligns with the mammaries, as well as the glandular structure of that organ..." It took little effort to carry on, for Conall knew his subject well, but his mind traveled to the previous year, when he'd been lucky enough to obtain the body of a lactating woman in time for the course. His students had been captivated throughout the dissection—and it had been a novel experience for him as well.

He had a body ready for next week, waiting in a barrel of spirits in the storehouse behind his school. She was a relatively young subject, though not in good health. According to the description from Will, this one had probably died of tuberculosis—and that would be a valuable experience for his students, if his tentative diagnosis turned out to be true. Conall had similar specimens in his collection, but students always appreciated the chance to observe pathologies in situ.

"Are there any questions?" Conall stepped back and surveyed the group filling the room. Burns, a student who usually made a point of demonstrating his attentiveness in front of the others with at least one inquiry, had already filled his quota today. His last question, on the innervation of the muscles, was so misguided it had been answered by a classmate at Burns's elbow, which seemed to have silenced him for the day.

"Come take a look, then. Mr. Ferguson?"

Yielding his place to his assistant, Conall stepped away from the table and carefully wiped his hands. His fifty students would be occupied for some time. Trusting them to Ferguson's care, Conall stepped outside the theatre and crossed the hall to his laboratory, poured out a measure of whisky, and drained his glass. Lecturing through most of the afternoon was impossible without regularly wetting his throat.

Pausing to examine his record book—yes, his stores were adequate until the end of the month—he returned to the lecture theatre in time to field a question about the branches supplying the radial nerve. By the end of the session, forty-five minutes later, he was sore in the shoulders and ready to take the weight off his feet.

While Ferguson and Jones wrapped the body in wet linen and carried it back to the icehouse, Conall tidied his forceps, probes, and scalpels, inspecting the blades for nicks and polishing the mono-grammed ivory handles. It was a beautiful set, purchased on credit when he was finishing his apprenticeship and headed for the army. Though he and his mother had lived on broth and porridge for months afterward, he didn't regret the purchase. These tools were a pledge to himself; he was meant for better things.

Ferguson returned just as he placed the last blade within the velvet-lined box.

"I believe I'm on for tours this evening, doctor."

"Yes, I forgot you traded with Jones last week."

"I'll see you at six," Ferguson said, setting aside his leather apron and donning a finely woven wool coat. Unlike Jones, Ferguson came from money.

"Why don't you come by now?" Conall suggested. "Dine with me. I'd enjoy the company—unless you have other plans," he finished hastily.

Ferguson's mouth twitched in a tentative smile. "I've no plans. That would be—I'm very happy to join you, sir."

Conall hadn't issued invitations to his assistants before. Oh, they visited his home often enough in the course of their work, and there was nothing to be ashamed of in his address. But he never admitted them beyond the salon with his specimens or, occasionally, his consulting room.

The rest of the house hadn't really been fit for company before now. And he couldn't invite anyone over to share the scones and stews his mother usually had sent over from the Old Bell Inn.

Such lamentable housekeeping wasn't really his mother's fault. She was of simple stock, uncomfortable around and distrustful of servants. Nor did she understand the nuances of polite behavior. Though she prided herself on keeping things trim and neat, over the past year, the rheumatism in her knees had worsened, making it impossible for her to keep pace with even the most spartan arrangements. She wasn't pleased having Miss Ross in the house, but at least she couldn't find any fault with Miss Ross's work. In only a fortnight, the house was just as he'd dreamed it could be.

"Come along, then," Conall said, beckoning casually. "I can't promise anything elaborate, but you'll be well fed."

Even the exterior of his home looked different, thanks to Miss Ross. The steps were newly whitewashed and the door knocker shone. Though his mother considered Miss Ross's liberal use of candles almost criminally extravagant, the light from the ground floor windows was welcoming, a pleasant sight at the close of the day. Inside, the scents of beeswax and lavender greeted him, followed, a second later, by Miss Ross herself.

"Good evening, doctor."

Midway through a perfectly proper and dry exchange with her, Conall realized Ferguson was frowning.

"What time shall I tell Cook to serve dinner?" Miss Ross asked.

"Right away, please."

"Of course, doctor."

Ferguson's eyes followed her departure, a crease between his brows. Conall couldn't think what she'd done to offend him. He'd witnessed similar exchanges between many of his colleagues and their servants. There was no point, yet, in the stiff formality of butlers and footman. That was beyond his current means, and therefore pretentious.

"She's very efficient," Conall said, briefly. Then, to change the subject—"Join me for a drink?"

Miss Ross had taken it upon herself to display his liquor in an array of costly decanters, instead of tucking it away in the original bottles, as he had always done. What's more, any glass he used disappeared almost the moment he quit the room, and there were always clean glasses sheltering beside the decanters on the matching crystal tray. Suppressing a smile, Conall poured out two whiskies and offered one to his assistant.

But Ferguson, who liked a dram as much as anyone, merely swirled his glass.

Conall lit a spill and brought it to the pile of wood shavings in the middle of the neatly stacked coal waiting in the fireplace. "Something troubling you?"

"It's nothing." Ferguson took a quick sip, then changed his mind. "Actually, it's your housekeeper. She looked familiar. Caught me staring. I hope I didn't embarrass her."

Conall straightened his cuffs. "She's quite a modest woman, you know. A stare would have disconcerted her."

"It was stupid of me. Just my imagination. I didn't even get a good look at her, what with the spectacles and cap."

"Understandable. I've had the same thing happen," Conall said, smoothing away the awkwardness. Ferguson's invitation was an experiment, one he wanted to succeed. "Just last week I thought I saw one of the doctors who trained me walking to church. And he's been dead for years." He sighed and settled into a chair.

"John Barclay?"

Conall nodded.

"I hear such good things of him. You must miss him," Ferguson said.

Conall nodded. "It was so unexpected. He died well before his time."

Ensconced in the warm, bright room, it was easy to move on to anecdotes of his famous mentor. Ferguson was an eager listener.

"Of course you know that Munro was chair at the university then, too," Burnett finished, shaking his head at the injustice of it.

"Which one? Tertius?"

Conall nodded, annoyed at the question. He wasn't that old. Munro's father, known as Munro Secundus, because he had also succeeded an Alexander Munro as chair, had died more than ten years before.

"Yes, Tertius is dreadful, not at all like his father or grandfather—or so I'm told," Ferguson said quickly. "Jones told me after two years' classes with Tertius, he still hadn't touched a cadaver. And everyone knows he reuses his grandfather's notes." He shrugged. "In one way, I suppose the genius of Primus and Secundus are still with us."

Conall snorted. "A perfect example of the failings of a hereditary system. Science must be a meritocracy or what good is it?"

Ferguson nodded. He was a younger son. Ambitious, too.

They finished their drinks, then ambled into the dining room, where Miss Ross had laid the table and set out an assortment of his new cook's dishes: game pie, cucumber salad, and thinly shaved ham. The slight tension gathering around Conall's heart eased. For somewhat of a potluck meal, this fare was excellent.

By the time Ferguson reached dessert (a truly outstanding trifle), his tongue and manner had loosened considerably. Conall congratulated himself. Miss Ross was just who he'd needed. There was nothing to worry about. He could take those next steps, make invitations, and work his way into the circles where he belonged.

"I'm so glad you joined me tonight," he said aloud to Ferguson. "You must dine here more often."

{ 15 }

Half an hour after the last of Dr. Burnett's paying visitors quit the house, the redheaded assistant finally left. I watched him from an upstairs window, trying to work some order into my thoughts.

In all my speculation, in all my half-baked plans, I hadn't considered this particular danger. Of course, I hadn't planned on staying this long, and Burnett's assistant, the man who'd conducted me and Miss Clark's literary circle around the collection, had seen my face much more recently than Burnett. It was sheer luck he hadn't come by until now.

I'd heard my name through the keyhole of the consulting room door, as well as him saying I reminded him of someone.

Drawing the curtain closed, I rubbed the knot in the back of my neck. I still hadn't found Thomas's heart, and feared Burnett might have removed it to his anatomy school on Surgeon's Square.

And Ferguson would be back; if he placed me in his memory, it might be better to abandon my endeavor now. It was too late to alter my appearance, even if I could dream up a way to augment the changes I'd made already. And though I intended to avoid him, that wouldn't be possible, with Burnett set on playing host and Ferguson's assistant duties.

But giving up now meant giving up for good. I couldn't quit without thinking this through and weighing the decision carefully. Tonight, I was too tired to consider which nightdress was warmest, let alone anything else.

I pushed the silver spectacles up onto my forehead and palmed my eyes, wishing for familiar voices, faces, and friendly company. I missed Miss Clark, and her insistence on tea with me every Wednesday, but I'd cut myself loose, and the best company I had was waiting downstairs, thinking my name was Janet Ross.

Still, I'd rather be there, in the kitchen, than here, alone with my worries and tangling thoughts.

Burnett was closeted in his consulting office; the dining room was cleared and the candles within long since extinguished; Mrs. Burnett hadn't stirred from her room since her last demand for fresh candles. I'd retreat to the kitchen, where Mrs. Williams, the newly installed cook, would be sitting with a cup of tea, a slice of cake, and her feet propped on the fender. Maggie, the girl who helped Mrs. Williams and me with the rough work, would be knitting on the bench nearby. Their easy chatter would tease away the anxieties of the evening.

I resettled the spectacles on the bridge of my nose and made my way through the tilting shadows painting the stairs.

Just as I'd pictured, Mrs. Williams was talking and gesturing with her teacup, toasting her stockinged feet. Maggie was nodding along, too tired to say much. Even after the day's scrubbing, scouring, and dozens of trips up and downstairs, her hands were busy, knitting a half-finished gray stocking without conscious thought.

What surprised me was the presence of an unwelcome

third—Mrs. Burnett sitting in the chair I usually occupied, a matching gray stocking materializing row by row on her aproned lap.

I stopped on the threshold. "Good evening, ma'am. I didn't expect—"

"Miss Ross." She looked older than ever in the firelight, her features deepened by dark shadows. Her formal nod told me I ought to turn tail and run, that I was the interloper here. But I was on friendly enough terms with Maggie and Cook.

"Is anything amiss, Mrs. Burnett? You could have rung for me."

Cook sniffed. "Why shouldn't the mistress join us? Day's work is done, and it's cozier here away from the visitors and the gentlemen."

I forced a smile. "No reason at all. It's very kind, ma'am, to give us the pleasure of your company." I glanced at her cup and offered to refill it before pouring my own tea. Then I sat down next to Maggie on the bench, recalculating—and drank without thinking, burning my tongue.

"Careful, it's hot," Mrs. Burnett warned, with a catlike gleam in her eye.

"Help yourself to a slice of cake, Miss Ross," Cook said, motioning to the plate.

I shook my head, appetite gone.

"Shall I fetch your sewing?" Maggie offered.

"Not tonight. I'll—I think I'll read a book. I have *Ivanhoe*, if you care to hear it?"

"Cook's in the middle of a story," Maggie said, and I noticed, belatedly, the wideness in her eyes. I'd interrupted them. Mrs. Burnett had fought and failed to stop me from taking control of household affairs. Confident that I had her son's approval, I hadn't thought to look for a counteroffensive here.

"Won't you go on?" Maggie begged.

I cradled the cup in my hands and leaned back against the wall. This wasn't at all the respite I'd hoped for, but Cook was a fine storyteller. And I was tired enough I might just fall asleep where I sat, completely forgetting Mrs. Burnett for now. I closed my eyes and let Cook's warm brogue fill my ears.

"The evil-looking glass was shattered into splinters, ground down to dust, the frame broken beyond repair. But 'thon Bo'ness witches vowed to take their revenge. Calling on the devil, they raised a great wind..."

Beside me, Maggie shivered. "Can they do that, Mrs. Williams?"

"There's tell of evil winds, girl, in the Bible," Mrs. Burnett put in, knobby fingers knitting, never slowing. "The book of Job—'Terrors are turned upon me: they pursue my soul as the wind: and my welfare passeth away as a cloud.'"

The fire snapped, and Maggie and I jumped, then laughed guiltily together.

"And so it was with the people of Monadhliath," Cook said, widening her eyes dramatically. "For the wind carried the bits of glass, and pierced the heart and eyes of every last one of them. Wounded so, they fell under a curse, for they could see no goodness or brightness, and their hearts turned hard and cold. Their faces became sharp, their words cutting, and there wasn't a bit of kindness to be found."

Close by the fire, pressed in by the dark, I could almost feel the sting of glass fragments blowing into my face. And the indifferent faces, the unpitying hearts...I didn't have to imagine those. I'd seen plenty: John, the impatient police constables, Detective Adam Kerr. The medical fraternity and their satellites, including former employers of mine like Mrs. Findlay.

No one had helped me, not in any way that mattered. I let out a breath and smoothed my skirts. Without realizing, I'd crumpled the cloth into my fist.

"Only one soul was spared," Mrs. Williams went on. "She was a young maid, the chief witch's daughter. Thin as a rail, with a mop of ink-black hair, she was forced to slave for her wicked mother, with nary a kind word or a crust thrown her way. Only reason the girl didn't starve was the plate scrapings carried to her by a kindly cat. Confined to the house, she was spared from the wind and the knife-sharp glass, but she saw how it poisoned folk, and she'd never been swayed by her mother's evil. But she was left-handed, and she bore the devil's mark on her cheek, and knew that if she ventured beyond her mother's house, the people would know her for a witch and strangle her at the stake."

As she spoke, the tang of smoke in the room intensified, and Maggie shivered beside me on the bench.

"Our young maid had seen such things, seen mobs drag women from their homes for pumping water left-handed or spitting on the Bible."

My hands were hot. Stinging, even. I set down my cup. Letting myself enjoy the tale was fine, but I'd already burned myself once tonight.

"There was no hope of drawing out the poison from afar, so the witch's daughter knew she must venture out. She brewed a potion of witch hazel, clear and sweet smelling. With that, she anointed her face and eyes, and washed the taint of evil from her hands. She took her lodestone, and slid it in her pocket, and walked down the mountain to the village below."

I frowned, because Cook's description of washing with witch hazel landed on my ears like a familiar chord, whole and familiar. Yet I couldn't recall inventing a detail like this one in any of the stories I'd told. Thomas favored tales of clever boys seeking adventure, knights and giants, dark forests and beasts with claws and terrible teeth.

"Mrs. Burnett, ma'am, would you like another slice of cake?" Cook asked.

"Thank you, Mrs. Williams. That would be lovely."

I pursed my lips, daunted by the warmth in their shared smiles and mystified at how to prevent it. While Cook dished up another slice of seedcake, and Maggie knit and wriggled with anxiety, I collected my sewing basket, hoping some handwork might tease apart my tangled thoughts. Witch hazel was a common enough remedy. Folk often used it, just as they wore goose windpipes around their necks to cure croup, and amber to ease pain.

It took four tries to thread my needle, but the other women were too caught up in the tale to notice my difficulty, how quiet I was, and how slowly my needle moved along the fabric.

Cook was telling her story again.

"The witch's daughter hadn't walked a quarter mile, when she chanced to meet a shepherd on the road, and though she drew her bonnet down and ducked her head, the man called out to her, demanding what business brought her and brandishing his stick. This was his family's land and they didn't like strangers.

"You must know that the witch's daughter had the sight, like her mother, though she was kind of heart. As soon as the man stepped near, she beheld the splinters of glass in his eyes and heart. But the man was angry, striking out with his knife, and though the witch's daughter reached for her lodestone, the blade would tear her throat long before she had a chance to free the man from the curse. So she looked into the hate-blind eyes, giving the fellow a full look at her face."

"And?" Maggie demanded, when Mrs. Williams paused to take a swallow of tea.

"And I'm a mite thirsty, child. Leave off a minute," Mrs. Williams said. She glanced at Mrs. Burnett. "I hope you don't mind these foolish tales, ma'am. I've always held that there's nothing like a good ghost story among friends around a fire, but I know some folk—"

She shrugged, took another swallow, and set down her cup. "Ready, Maggie? You know I only tell stories when I'm not surrounded by idle hands."

Maggie's knitting needles lurched into action. My own needle, pensive and slow, marched along a new hem, but my heart thudded in my chest, unusually fast. Unaccountably, I dreaded hearing what came next. "It's late, Maggie. You ought to be in bed," I said.

Mrs. Burnett was also knitting again, having finished her second slice of cake. "If you send the child to bed with the story undone, she'll have nightmares. You wouldn't know, of course, not having children of your own."

"No, I suppose I wouldn't," I murmured, and flinched as my needle slid wide, stabbing me in the thumb.

"Goodness. That looked painful," Mrs. Williams said, and fumbled for her handkerchief.

"I'm all right." I brought the injured thumb to my mouth and sucked away the blood welling from the soft part just beside the nail. I checked, once, twice, and again, but each time, there was more blood.

"I may have to bandage it," I said.

Mrs. Burnett muttered something under her breath—Gaelic again—and Maggie turned to her with anxious eyes. "Is this a bad omen, ma'am?"

"Might be," the old woman muttered. She set aside her needles and began winding her wool. "Change your task, child, and tomorrow, before you go out, throw a pinch of salt behind your back."

I wasn't putting up with such foolishness. "The bleeding's stopped." No one said anything, so I added, "I promise, I was just being clumsy. You tell too fine a tale, Mrs. Williams. My mind was miles away."

She laughed, dispelling the cloud that had settled around us. I rose to stir the fire, and the flames leaped obediently, brightening the room.

"Someone must warm the sheets upstairs and light the bedroom fires," I said, but when Maggie pushed to her feet, I waved her back. "No, you enjoy the story. I can tend to this tonight. Just tell me—" I turned to cook. "Did the spell fool the farmer?"

She winked at me. "Aye, it did. Without even knowing, the witch's girl invoked a powerful magic. She told the man she was his niece, and when she said it, he believed her. By the time he offered her bread and beer, she had the lodestone in her hand. She raised it and called the evil out of him. At once the man fell to the ground..."

I slipped from the room and hurried upstairs to ready the house for bed.

The next morning, instead of sending Maggie to do the marketing, I set out alone, with a shilling of my own in my pocket along with the household money. I could have bought a distillation of witch hazel from any number of apothecaries, but instead I bought the flowers from an herb woman in the Lawnmarket. If I was invoking superstition, there was no point in trying halfway. Tucking the twine-tied bundle of spidery yellow blooms in my pocket, I left the busy market. There was work to do, and tonight, when the household slept, I'd brew the concoction myself.

Vaguely I remembered my mother making such things, perfumes

and potions for her complexion. Or so I'd always thought. Mother had never told me what they were for.

I returned to the house in better spirits, breathing easier, no longer feeling pressed by the dark-walnut trim and crimson-papered walls. Mrs. Burnett disliked me as much as ever, but now I didn't feel her eyes following me all about the house. Perhaps it was remembering my mother. Perhaps in the was the sweet-smelling flowers safe in my pocket.

The precise reason didn't matter. It was all in my head.

Dr. Burnett had made it clear he didn't want Maggie cleaning his collection, which suited me perfectly. Still, my heart skipped unevenly as I unlocked the door the following Tuesday, two hours before Mr. Ferguson was expected to arrive.

I'd dabbed my face and hands liberally with the witch-hazel concoction I'd brewed days before. It stung my cheeks, and I wondered, for the twenty or thirtieth time, if I was completely unhinged, trusting fairy-tale magic, luck, and the lapses in Ferguson's memory. But I wasn't ready to give up, and that was my only alternative.

My head filled with a vision of Thomas, about three or four, healthy yet, smiling at me and offering a feather he'd found in the park. I stopped, caught my breath, and let myself into the drawing room. The house was unusually silent, and the fetal spine, shut up in its glass box, looked especially pitiful today. Poor thing. She'd never had a chance. I ran a duster of lambswool over the glass and wiped off the shelf and the nearby jars.

The "natural skeleton" was next. Facing this one was always a challenge, but I'd purchased a duster of brown ostrich plumes because it was softest and least likely to scratch. Working gently, I brushed from crown to toes, in front and back, wincing as I swept over the tiny hands and turned-up nose, hoping that in life, she'd been well loved.

The next set of bones, also human, were stripped clean, pale as ivory, and wired together, though still fragile. "I'm sorry for you too," I murmured, running over them with my duster, and straightening the nearby card. I'd been appointed their keeper, so I'd clean and care for these remains the best I could.

I refolded my cloth, hiding away the dust and exposing a fresh side, ready to polish the first cabinet with lemon oil. The sharp smell, mingling with the lingering scent of witch hazel, quieted the macabre thoughts lurking in the corners of my mind. Humming softly, I reached the duster to the top of the cabinet. There were plenty of shelves still to go.

Down one long wall, then on to the pedestal with the massive whale bones, then the rank of cupboards filling the wall across from the north-facing windows. Mr. Sibbald, that patient butler, had always said the best maids knew to clean a room from top to bottom. I carried over a short three-legged stool. Without it, I'd never be able to reach to the back of the highest shelf. My eyes were getting better at searching out fingerprints and dust, acknowledging then moving past the specimens of Burnett's collection, so when I first climbed the stool, I didn't register the jar on the second-highest shelf until I'd risen above it.

The jar. My knees folded, bringing me square in front of the heart. It was pushed to the back, slightly behind a wax cast of a pair of lungs that looked like a black tree. I gripped the shelf edge for support.

Thomas's heart was back. My breath slowed, and I focused on the card. The description was less specific now: *heart with defective valve*. I reached out and caressed a wide thumbprint off the glass.

Hello, dear one.

Tears scalded my cheeks. I scrubbed them away, then began furiously polishing the shelf.

*Da-di-*la. *Da-di-*la.

My hands went still.

Mam.

Thomas's voice, sweet and sleepy, rustled through my consciousness. But before I could catch it, the doorknob turned and Burnett's confident syllables swept up from behind me, filling the room.

{ 16 }

You should consider it," Ballingall said.

"It's a marvelous suggestion," Ferguson added, smiling enthusiastically.

Conall laughed. "I have. I'd add another two courses if I could, but—" He exchanged glances with the professor, then flicked his eyes to his housekeeper, busy dusting the shelves on the far side of the room. "You know the difficulties." There were never enough bodies, and Conall had built his school's reputation on the promise that pupils would have adequate learning and practice material.

Ferguson deflated a little, and Ballingall winked. "I do. You seem to handle them better than most."

Conall shrugged. "I try. It's never easy."

Ballingall set his bag down beside the sofa. "Well, if you find a way to do it, I fully support you. I see a real difference among my students in those who've taken your course. If I had my way, they'd all have to study with you before applying to me."

"You give me too much credit," Conall said. "Your students work hard."

"Some of them do." Ballingall rolled his eyes. "You know the difficulties there as well, I suppose."

"There's nearly a hundred students waiting for your next general anatomy course, Dr. Burnett," Ferguson said. "Dr. Balingall's idea is a good one. I often get requests from other students, asking me to recommend them."

"Don't raise any hopes," Conall warned. "You know I would if I could."

"I know."

"For now, it would be simpler to open the collection another evening, perhaps for medical students only—or prospective students. I could run some less formal teaching seminars with the specimens I have already," Conall mused. No need, then, to find and pay for additional bodies.

"That's a good idea," Ferguson said.

Conall grunted. "Only if you or Jones are available for an extra evening. I can't have just anyone managing things there. You remember what happened with that woman."

Ballingall nodded. "Yes. It's important to be mindful of public opinion."

"And the risk of theft," Conall added. Just to be cautious, he'd removed the heart temporarily from his collection, until talk had died down. Thankfully, it was back where it belonged: center place on an eye-level shelf. He didn't know of anyone else in the kingdom with such a perfect example of mitral valve scarring.

"I imagine you're safe enough there," Ferguson said. "Everything's under lock and key."

"Could you and Jones manage another evening, between the two of you?"

"I can't answer for Jones, but for myself—of course." As he

spoke, Ferguson moved backward toward the window, stepping inadvertently into the path of Miss Ross, who sidestepped just too late, dropping her duster.

"Miss Ross, forgive me. I didn't mean to startle you."

"Not at all, Mr. Ferguson. Good evening, Dr. Burnett." She brushed her face haphazardly with her sleeve, dabbing at flushed cheeks damp with sweat. "I expect I'm covered in dust. I-I was behindhand today, as you can see, but I've just finished. Everything is ready." On her way out of the room, she stammered, "Doctor, if you'd like your supper n-now—"

"Thank you, Miss Ross, Dr. Ballingall and I will be heading out again directly, but perhaps Mr. Ferguson—?"

"I'll see to it at once," his housekeeper said, and made to quit the room, gathering up her duster, broom, and pail.

Ferguson intercepted her, opening the door. "Thank you, Miss Ross. I'm sorry to give extra trouble."

The evening light, sweeping through the windows, flashed on her spectacles as she lifted her face to reply. Conall blinked and averted his eyes.

"It's no trouble, Mr. Ferguson. No trouble at all."

After she left, Conall ran a finger along one of the shelves. No dust, and the room smelled pleasantly of lemon. The curtains were pleated perfectly and tied back with tasseled cords; the lamps were burning but turned low, ready for the coming dark. Every surface gleamed, and Miss Ross had rearranged the chairs, grouping them comfortably for conversation and easier viewing.

"She really does treat them like art," Conall said, settling onto his heels and releasing a day's worth of tension from his shoulders. The room looked wonderful.

Ballingall nodded. "You've found a real treasure."

{ 17 }

That night, I didn't sleep, my mind filled with the shock of finding Thomas's heart again, and a chilling conversation with Mr. Ferguson. To my astonishment, he hadn't recognized me, but he did stop me as he was locking the drawing room door, when I was returning from running the bed warmer over Mrs. Burnett's sheets.

"Where shall I leave Dr. Burnett's keys, Miss Ross? Usually I give them back to him, but he's not returned from the club dinner yet." He held up a ring with differently sized keys—all silver and gleaming in the candlelight.

My breath caught and I stepped closer, stretching out a hand, searching for hints of recognition in his face. "Leave it with me." Maybe this ring held the key to unlock Burnett's desk, which I hadn't searched yet, in spite of a dozen attempts. It was always locked. Burnett had claimed to have records for the acquisition of each specimen, but I'd seen nothing like that, no matter where I looked in the house. I'd found the heart again, but with Burnett's keys, I might be able to learn more—if he'd really come by it years ago, as he claimed, or if it was a more recent acquisition, dating from Thomas's kidnapping.

The pulse—and Thomas's voice just hours ago in my ears—told me it was, but if I could be sure...

"May I trouble you for a cup of coffee before I go?" Ferguson asked, and my hopes shrank to the size of a thimble. "It'll chase away the evening chill," he added. "I've a long walk home."

I smiled thinly. "Of course. I'll bring it into the study." He'd probably prefer to read while he waited.

Down in the kitchen, Maggie and Mrs. Burnett were spellbound by another of Mrs. William's tales. Maggie was polishing Dr. Burnett's shoes this evening. He was particular about the shine on the rich brown leather. He had two pairs almost the same, with narrow square toes and silver buckles worked to look like twining vines. Tonight, Mrs. Burnett had switched to knitting stockings in matching brown wool.

While Cook brewed a pot of coffee, I went over tomorrow's lists with Mrs. Burnett.

"And here's next week's menu."

"Beef is so expensive!" she said, glancing over it.

"Yes, ma'am, but your son particularly requested it. If you prefer, I can have Cook make something else for you, more in line with your tastes. I believe he intends to host some colleagues that evening."

"All I need is bread and butter and broth," she said.

"If you wish it." I penciled a note. Mrs. Burnett never criticized her son, but had no such scruples when it came to me.

"Tray's ready," Mrs. Williams said.

"Thank you." I hurried away with it, hopefully putting an end to the skirmish.

Mrs. Williams had supplemented the coffee with a wide slice of cake, which I set beside Ferguson with a nod. I'd leave him to pour for himself.

"Cake too? Thank you, Miss Ross. You're kept very busy."

"That's just what I like." A lie, but it seemed the sort of thing a housekeeper would say, and came easier to me now than things I might have said to someone who truly knew me. A good house-keeper was expected to be brisk and efficient, not a well of dark and troubled feeling, so it was much simpler in this role to hide mine away. "I'm sure there's not more work here than any other household."

Ferguson raised his eyebrows, so I amended hastily, "Well, I take particular care with the specimens, and mornings can be busy when there are patients, but I confess, before I came here, I thought there'd be more of them."

Ferguson nodded. "There's less time for clinical practice because Dr. Burnett runs his own anatomy school. The demand for his courses is such that he could give up seeing patients entirely, but he says if a doctor doesn't actually doctor, he's like a knife left out to rust in the rain."

"I hadn't realized teaching took so much of his time. But I know little of these things."

He gave a short laugh, cutting off as his immature voice rock-eted up to the ceiling. Blushing, he stirred a lump of sugar into his coffee. "Well, there's no reason you would know anything about it. But teaching is where his money is. Over five hundred students any given term."

My hands, loosely clasped at my waist, knotted tight. *Five hundred?* "How long have you been his assistant?" Did he work for Burnett last year? Had he helped extract a small boy's heart?

"Two years this September," Ferguson said. He hardly looked old enough to shave.

"You like the business?"

"Very much. I'm fortunate to work with Dr. Burnett. Someday, I hope to open my own school—not in Edinburgh, unless Dr. Burnett invites me to join him, and there's a score of older men who'd give their left legs for the opportunity. No, I'll probably end up in England somewhere."

I smiled mechanically, shifting my feet.

"Burnett himself was once assistant to Dr. Barclay, and he was one of the first, you know, to begin a private anatomy school offering courses to supplement the teaching at the university. He was also a student of natural history, so there was considerable interest in his animal collection. Dr. Burnett was quite unknown then, if you can believe it. But after he joined Dr. Barclay, first as assistant, then as a partner, and began enriching the courses with his expertly prepared human specimens..."

I interrupted. The way my head was spinning, it was simply impossible to wait until he finished. "You'll let me know if I can bring you anything else?"

He nodded, blushing again, and I hurried from the room on legs as brittle as twigs.

Five hundred students, I thought, rolling over, trying to find a comfortable place on the mattress. All wanting to learn from human bodies. Burnett's reputation, according to Ferguson, was enhanced because he always had enough.

And scores of specimens lining his walls.

I still had Burnett's keys. Pushing back the covers, I slid my feet into slippers and wrapped myself in a thick shawl, though neither gave any warmth. Tiptoeing through inky dark, I felt my way up the narrow wooden stairs, testing every footfall and freezing whenever the floor creaked, until I reached Burnett's consulting room to rifle through his desk.

A delicate silver key unlocked the previously inaccessible drawers. By the light of a lone candle, I combed through a journal and some folders of papers, finding only routine correspondence, unintelligible notes, and something that looked like a calendar without any months, with numbers that couldn't possibly represent dates. The last folder, of soft brown leather, was larger than the others. Inside were thick sheets of artist's paper with detailed ink drawings—a hand with a missing thumb, a drooping eye so lifelike I nearly dropped the page. I pushed it hastily back into the folder, safe from the wavering candle, and found another paper, face down, folded in half, and tucked between layers of the leather cover.

Careful not to tear or crease the edges, I slid it out and unfolded it.

I leaned onto the table, my free hand pressing my stomach. No one could forget this face, even rendered in ink, but I knew this man well, a longtime inhabitant of my worst nightmares.

This was a drawing of Eoin Brennan, Thomas's monster man, hidden and locked away in Burnett's desk.

Thomas?

I heard nothing, but the air stirred around me, cold and tangible as the brush of silk on skin, setting my hair on end, just like in stories—mine, Mrs. William's, and the macabre serial tales in Mrs. Burnett's magazines.

Ghosts.

No, that was impossible. Slowly, methodically, I put away the drawing, but this didn't chase away the chill in my stomach or the faint pressure moving over my skin. I locked the drawer and blew out the candle.

I'd questioned whether I could really hear Thomas's heart thudding, whether I'd simply imagined his voice. But a heart with Thomas's condition was rare. Only Dr. Burnett, Mr. Craig, and I knew the exact details of his condition. Now, it seemed, Burnett knew Eoin Brennan too.

My fists tightened at my sides, remembering Burnett and Ferguson talk about "valuable specimens," the parts I regularly cleaned and cared for. Thomas was irreplaceable.

But if I brought this drawing to them, the police wouldn't take it as proof, and I was tired of hearing my suspicions dismissed as coincidence or hysteria.

And month after month, term after term, Burnett accumulated more specimens and supplied his hundreds of students.

I couldn't prove he'd taken Thomas, but the heart had come here and I thought I understood how. Once he'd known of it, Burnett must have wanted it, and someone was in the habit of bringing him bodies.

Mrs. McPherson and I had both seen Brennan, and he'd left Edinburgh with convenient speed as soon as Thomas was missing. Either he knew he had reason to be shy of the police or someone had warned him they were looking.

Brennan wouldn't have known about it on his own. It couldn't have happened without Burnett.

I stood there by the desk, listening to the ticking clock.

Burn-ett, Burn-ett, Burn-ett.

I'd seen a book here while dusting the shelves, and the title had stuck in the back of my brain like a burr. As I thought of it now, the air around me condensed into icy dew.

Suspended in the dark, I reached for the book unerringly, up on the highest shelf, four in from the left, between a small green volume and a thick brown one. My fingers closed on the spine and the book jumped toward me, flying to my chest, where I cradled it with my arms, heart thudding. Soundlessly, I descended from the step stool—I couldn't recall climbing it—and returned it to the corner of the room. Then I slipped away, pursued by the pulse in my ears and, it seemed, the protesting cries of my better angels.

Safe again behind my bolted door, I waited for my hands to stop shaking so I could light a candle. The wick caught on my third try, surrounding me with a yellow glow that steadied after I sat down on the bed. I tucked my freezing feet beneath me, pulled the blankets over my shoulders, and settled the volume on my lap.

The tan leather was cool in my hands. Pink and green marbling adorned the cut edges of the pages. It was a beautiful book with a harrowing title:

A Treatise on Poisons, by M. P. Orfila

I smoothed a hand over the volume like I was calming a troubled horse. Then I opened the cover and scanned the table of contents.

Poisons of Copper—followed by page numbers for a series of nine separate "*Observations.*" And under that:

First case—the patient is living: the rest of the poison can be acted upon

Second case—the patient is living: the whole of the poison has been swallowed: the matter vomited can be acted upon

Third case—the patient is living: the whole of the poison has been swallowed: the matter vomited cannot be procured

Fourth case—the patient is dead

I turned to page 233.

Next morning, Orfila's textbook rested demurely back on the shelf, as I fastened the parade of small brown buttons marching up the front of my dress, and listened to the sounds of Maggie carrying out the slops.

Someone began beating on the door.

"Doctor! Is the doctor home?"

Bloody hell. The sun wasn't up. I wasn't close to ready. Abandoning the last four buttons, I splashed my hands with witch-hazel distillation, patted it onto my face, and slid the wax inserts into my cheeks. I slashed the usual black onto my eyebrows, fumbled for my spectacles, and struggled into them and a cap and dashed for the stairs.

"What do you suppose—"

"I'll see to it," I said, waving away Cook's question.

Someone—Burnett, hopefully—was stumbling around upstairs, but I was alone when I reached the hall.

"Coming!" Hurrying forward, I opened the door before the man on the steps could bash his way through. He stumbled inside, a gasping child in his arms, sending an avalanche cascading down my spine.

"The doctor—"

I intercepted him with one arm and her with the other, though his haste almost took all three of us down to the floor. I didn't know whether to usher him in or warn him away, but before I could decide, Burnett's feet thundered down the stairs and he reached over my shoulder, lifting the child's face.

"My daughter. She can't breathe!" The man said unnecessarily. The wild-eyed girl was fighting for breath, her lips blue and wide open, her chest heaving with enough force to shake the earth.

Burnett snatched her up, carrying her with surprising strength into the consulting room. "I need you, Miss Ross."

The girl was small, much the same size as Thomas, thrashing just like he had when the fever delirium was at its worst.

"Miss Ross!"

My limbs were unresponsive, my body unraveling.

"I'm coming!" I uprooted myself just as Burnett set her on the low couch, elevating her head and tilting her chin back.

"There. Any better?"

She nodded, her storm of thwarted breaths subsiding.

"She was playing with a pebble in her mouth," the pallid father said through a fit of trembling. "Something startled her, and she accidentally breathed it in. I was trying to help her cough it out, but then she started sputtering and turning blue."

"I need my stethoscope," Burnett said. After a heartbeat, I realized he was talking to me. "My bag's in my bedchamber," he added.

I galloped for the stairs. Of course he meant me to fetch it. There was no one else.

When I returned, the curtains were open, the lamps lit. Burnett snatched the stethoscope from his bag and bent over the child's chest. I reached for the back of the couch, before vertigo pushed me down.

"What will you?"

"Collect yourself, sir," Burnett said, quieting the father at once. Then his eyes swept to me.

"I can hear it in the lungs, on the right," he said. "I can invert her, which may help her cough it out, but it might also bring back the suffocation. In that case, I'll need to cut it out."

"No!" The father reached for the child. "No cutting."

"What's her name?" Burnett said, as if the man hadn't spoken.

"Rebecca," the man whimpered.

"All right, Rebecca," Burnett slipped another cushion beneath her head. "Stay loose, like a doll, and let's see if we can't get this pebble out of you."

He lifted her until she was draped, face down, over the back of the couch, his movements sure but unexpectedly gentle. Rebecca's breath went shallow, then she was gasping again. He knelt down beside her, looking into her mouth.

"Nothing yet. Thump her back, Miss Ross," he told me.

I complied, wincing as my palms struck her between the shoulders.

"No, harder than that." I smacked down as hard as I dared. The poor girl's feet kicked and writhed, but she didn't make a sound. Burnett had her wrists tight in one hand, his other steadying her head.

"Again."

I tried twice more. He shook his head. Rebecca's struggles were fading. "Turn her over! Quick!"

He moved so fast there was almost no time to assist, but at this point he seemed to be talking to himself as much as anyone. He reached for the lamp and looked once more down her throat.

"It's stuck." Quick as a cobra, he reached into the bag, drawing out an ivory-handled scalpel.

"No!" The father shouted, lunging forward until Burnett changed the direction of his knife. Less than a yard hung between them.

"She's dead if I don't," Burnett said, and the man retreated, sobbing. "Sit her on your lap, Miss Ross, and hold her head against your right shoulder. I need her neck long, in a straight line. No, use this chair."

I scooped her body up and settled us both into the ladderbacked chair Burnett pulled forward from the wall beside the window. The child was lifeless as a bolster.

"Is this right?" My voice shook.

Burnett didn't answer, frowning at the girl's neck, like a scholar with a geometry problem, one hand reaching blindly for another ivory-handled instrument.

"Hold her arms behind her," he told the father. "Quickly!"

Jolted into action by Burnett's command, the father, still weeping, took up the place behind me, one hand on each of the girl's arms.

Burnett raised the knife, hovering a few inches in front of us, Rebecca's body on top of mine. Swooping like a hawk, he drew downward on her throat. His other hand darted forward with a long slender spoon.

"Hold still, Miss Ross." The warning was not a moment too soon. In the same instant, Rebecca dragged in a breath, her muscles tensing. "She mustn't move."

My arms tightened like fetters, and my head swirled in a fog of fear and blood. Hot liquid rolled down my right arm, the one braced across her chest.

Please God, please God, please God.

Rebecca forced out a breath and Burnett's hand gave a quick jerk, followed almost at once by a shake of his head. "Missed it. But I can see it rise when she exhales." He raised his voice. "Rebecca, if you can, breathe out harder next time."

I couldn't tell if she heard him, but I could tell that he was ready, tensing like a cat as the flow of air inside her slowed, turned, and began pushing out of her.

"Damn."

Rebecca's breath was a choppy sea; Burnett's hand, obscured from my view by her cloud of untidy hair, darted and twisted again.

"Have you got it?" the desperate father asked.

"I did. It slipped. Here." He groped in the bag, pressed a new tool into the father's hand, and carefully positioned it. "Hold this here. Don't move."

Into the bag again, this time for a pair of tiny pincers. Rebecca squirmed. "Miss Ross." Burnett sent me a warning look.

"I know. I'm trying." My arms burned with fatigue.

Don't move, Isobel. Don't shake.

But her frantic breaths, her writhing arms, the way her skin went from red to white to blue-tinged and back again had me thinking of Thomas—his faintness and spells. The room blurred, my skin slick and cold.

"Don't faint now." Burnett's hand on my cheek, almost a slap, pulled me back.

"I won't," I gasped, "I just—" My arms were about to fall off, but he wasn't minding me anymore. His eyes narrowed, then his hand dove and rose again, blood smeared and triumphant. A small stone, obscured by a trail of frothy mucus, was grasped tight in his pincers.

Behind me, the father shuddered. "Thank God—"

"Keep her still, fool!" Burnett yelled. "I haven't even stitched her up yet!"

Even Rebecca stilled, allowing me to slacken my hold a little.

Burnett worked, talking to himself under his breath, and the haze around me cleared, the sharp edges of furniture returning. I could see the weave of Rebecca's father's coat sleeves, and the light hairs on the back of Burnett's knuckles. I averted my eyes as he worked with the needle, but a moment later, he returned it to the table and began affixing plasters.

"Speak for me," he commanded, and Rebecca answered with a whimper, then a whisper.

"Is—is it done?"

"Yes." He smiled. "Such a brave girl you are. A true champion."

He wiped his hands on a cloth in his bag, then proceeded to instruct the father on her care. I was the last to leave the room, tottering on unsteady legs, as Burnett escorted Rebecca and her father to the front door, promising to come around in the next day or so, to give further instructions and to check Rebecca's wound.

"Send for me at the first sign of any swelling, coughing, or difficulty breathing."

"And no more playing with pebbles." The father was almost giddy. "Ever."

Rebecca smiled wanly as she shook Dr. Burnett's hand.

"I'll see you shortly." He closed the door. I was almost to the kitchen stairs—nearly out of sight, but Burnett saw me as he turned. "Don't leave."

I froze midstride, flinching at his narrow-eyed scrutiny. Had I given myself away? Did he remember my face?

"I must thank you. You did very well, Miss Ross, but I think a stiffener is in order. You're very pale."

I nodded without turning around. "I'll ask Mrs. Williams."

"You need whisky, not a cup of tea. Come," he said, and walked into the drawing room.

I lingered a moment, wondering if it was possible to refuse. I needed a moment alone—or a month. Rebecca would have died, if not for Dr. Burnett. Could my conclusions be wrong?

By the time I followed Burnett into the drawing room, he'd opened a cupboard and poured a finger of whisky into two glasses. "Here."

I took the glass and wet my lips, ignoring the nervous tremble in my hands and the ashy tinge of my skin.

"I'm glad you were able to save her." Uncertain and uncomfortable, my gaze flew sideways, landing almost by accident on the heart, floating in the jar just behind his shoulder. As I reread the altered placard and remembered the drawing of Brennan, locked away in a drawer, a lump of ice congealed amid my confusion: cold, solid, sure.

"Finish the glass, please. You need it," Burnett said.

Obediently, I took another sip.

"I have to thank you for rising to the occasion, Miss Ross. Without your help, we'd have lost her."

I pressed my lips to the rim of the glass. "Please don't be offended when I say I hope I'm not needed again."

Burnett chuckled. "A tracheotomy can be quite harrowing. Don't worry, Miss Ross. The trembling will pass. Should you be on hand in another crisis, you'll find it easier—but we won't talk of that today. For now, accept my congratulations on a job well done."

I dipped my chin, hiding my eyes. He seemed only concerned with my symptoms. He hadn't recognized me. "I think congratulations must go to you, sir."

He reached into his pocket and held something up to his eye. The pebble. At some point he'd wiped it clean, and it shone in his fingers now like a dark gray pearl.

"On its own, it isn't very dramatic." He smiled. "But when you know the story, it's a worthy addition to this room. What do you think, Miss Ross? Displayed in a velvet box next to an account of the surgery..."

As he spoke, he moved closer to the window. He seemed to have completely forgotten the girl. I couldn't see his expression, and I didn't want to. Nor did I want him to see my face or the gooseflesh climbing my arms—my sleeves only came to my elbows.

He pulled back the curtains, siphoning golden light into the room and transforming himself into a flat black shadow. Squinting against the brightness, I turned away.

Rebecca breathed again, but Thomas and I had only wanted what this man had given us to expect—a few more months together, maybe a year. In spite of what he'd done for that girl and her father, I couldn't dismiss the conviction that he'd robbed Thomas and me.

"I'm sorry, doctor, but I must ask you to excuse me. I think I should lie down."

"Of course. Of course." He came to my side and reached for my half-empty glass. "You've been through an ordeal. You must take care of yourself."

{ 18 }

Adam pushed open the apothecary door, jangling the bell overhead. The man behind the counter looked up with a practiced smile that disintegrated the moment he recognized Adam.

"Afternoon, Mr. Mitchell," Adam said.

Wearily, Mitchell reached below the counter and offered the ledger. "Arsenic purchases are in here, along with everything else."

Adam grimaced. "I was hoping you'd look them up for me." Mitchell ran a good business; there would be pages of transactions to sift through.

"I have a shop to run, Detective Kerr. No one's paying me to chase down murderers. That's your job."

Fair enough. Adam leaned against the counter, admiring Mitchell's tidy shelves, the brass pill press, and the delicate set of scales. Just now, Mitchell was compounding a paste that smelled of citrus and cinnamon, rolling it into a long string. "What about those thefts you had last year? You were happy to see me then."

Mitchell gave a reluctant laugh. "Was it you that fixed that? I thought I owed my run of better fortune to Detective Fraser."

Adam pressed his lips together. He and Hugh had worked the

case together, but he was the one who'd kept on until they found the brother and sister who were responsible.

With a sigh, Mitchell abandoned his pill paddle and pushed the gold spectacles off his high forehead down onto his nose. "Where was it? The death," Mitchell explained.

"Two streets away. You're the closest apothecary, I'm afraid."

Another sigh. Mitchell wiped his hands and opened the book. "How far back?"

"Start with last Sunday," Adam said. "I reckon she bought the arsenic after that."

Mitchell's eyebrows, nearly as sparse as the top of his head, rose inquiringly. "You have a suspect?"

Adam nodded. Truth was, he disliked these visits as much as Mitchell. Poison was a terrible way to die.

"The victim might have died naturally," the apothecary suggested.

"Not according to Dr. Chistison," Adam said. He'd collected the poor fellow's vomit and passed it to the University of Edinburgh's chief of forensic medicine.

In cases of suspicious death, police used to have to feed the vomit or stomach contents from victims to a dog, but these days doctors could test for poisons instead. Adam had no interest in toxicology, but he was grateful for the science, if only for the dogs' sake. What he didn't like was discovering how commonly people solved difficulties with doses of arsenic—something science was making increasingly clear.

"Could be a suicide," Mitchell argued half-heartedly, running a lean finger down the entries on the right-hand page.

"Could be," Adam agreed. But he didn't think so.

"Here." Mitchell tapped his forefinger and Adam leaned across the counter to read the name.

"Any more?" Hannah Clark wasn't the name he was looking for. "Patience, detective."

Adam grunted. Though it was best to know when and where a suspected murderer had bought her poison, it wasn't necessary. Sometimes he could frighten a suspect into confessing, just by explaining what the doctors could learn from a victim's stomach. But not always—he'd confronted some hard-bitten creatures over the years.

He hadn't seen enough of Mary Fisher yet to know if she'd surrender or stand her ground, but he was reasonably certain she'd killed her husband. Predicting innocence or guilt was easier than guessing what a suspect might do, because the guilty guess was almost always right.

"Here's another." Mitchell pointed to a line at the bottom of the page.

P. Fisher, 2 bottles Fowler's solution, 3s on account.

"That's enough to kill?" Adam asked.

Mitchell nodded. "In small doses, it's good for headaches and fevers. I don't generally sell more than one bottle. But this handwriting is Hill's—my assistant."

Adam copied the entry into his notebook. "Take care of this book, hmm? Prosecutor will want a look."

Though this should be enough to wrangle a confession from Mary—her thirteen-year-old son had bought the arsenic, and nobody had even paid for it yet.

Except Mr. Fisher.

Adam closed his notebook, slid it into his coat pocket, exited the shop—

"Watch it!" he snapped, as a grimy figure collided with him on the pavement.

"Sorry, sir." The child was breathless but quick, easily eluding his grasp.

"Wait." He knew those clear blue eyes, the warm brown of that cropped head of hair, though last time he'd seen her, she'd worn her tresses long and in plaits. "Nan."

What was she doing here?

The girl's eyes widened, round as twin moons in her hollow-cheeked face.

Adam reached again for her shoulder. "How—" His fingertips brushed her shawl, a dirty blue thing he'd used to wear as a scarf.

"Fuck off!" she spat, loud enough to stop the passersby.

Adam flinched. Before he could recollect himself and grab her, she wheeled and ran.

{ 19 }

I studied Burnett's poison manual in secret for weeks after the tracheotomy, weaving plans and unraveling them, determined to stop him myself, since I couldn't expect help from the police. They'd never believe me.

Verdigris would be an effective poison, and easy to blame on Mrs. Burnett's history of shoddy housekeeping—a meal cooked in a seldom-used pot or the slow accumulation of years of trace poison. Until I read that it would be impossible to administer a killing dose of verdigris all at once because of the poison's color and metallic taste. Burnett knew this book better than I did, and if I tried to poison him slowly, he'd recognize the symptoms in himself.

I needed something he wouldn't detect until it was too late, and I needed to keep him from dosing himself with purgatives or sending for help until the poison's work was done.

Nighttime, then, and Mrs. Burnett would need a sedative.

My next half day, on my afternoon off, I walked past Surgeon's Square to an unfamiliar apothecary in the Cowgate, and bought a box of sleeping powders. I tested them on Mrs. Burnett the next day, and found they were easily stirred into her evening porridge.

She retired to her bed promptly and didn't complain of strange tastes.

Two hours later, I went into her room and listened to her snore for a good two minutes. Then I dropped the coal scuttle. She barely stirred.

On my next half day the following week, I fixed a veil to my bonnet once I was well away from the house and walked toward the West Port, a squalid neighborhood, passing over a dozen dry goods shops and pharmacies. I went into three of them, but I wanted one far away and busy with customers. These were all too quiet.

The fourth shop, a dusty cupboard-sized place selling bottles of cloudy patent medicines and cheap household goods, had three customers waiting at the counter, one picking through a basket of mismatched buttons, and most importantly, a jar of white powder labeled *rat poison* on the shelf behind the shopkeeper. I joined the queue at the counter.

"How can I assist you?" the gentleman wheezed when my turn came.

"I'd like this, please." I pushed a metal rat trap forward, then angled my veiled face to the jar behind him. "What's in the poison?"

"Pure arsenic, ma'am. Perfectly effective."

"A box of that too, please."

He reached below the counter and brought out two pasteboard boxes. "I have two sizes."

"How much?"

He told me two sums.

"The larger, please."

I knew how much I needed to kill a man, but not the rats.

According to *A Treatise on Poisons*, arsenic acted quickly.

I did not. I needed to administer Mrs. Burnett's dose in advance, on an evening when Burnett was home without any company, and that opportunity was proving scarcer than expected.

But I was ready, with both powders measured into twists of paper, one white, one brown, and kept in my pockets. Twice I dosed Mrs. Burnett, only to have her son depart soon afterward without any warning—dining with a club of medical men at a fashionable hotel, tending a wealthy patient, returning to his anatomy school to prepare the next day's dissections.

The other complication was the risk of being caught.

If there was one thing Orfila's textbook made clear, it was that poison left evidence, and Dr. Burnett was friends with the university's chair of forensic medicine, who'd dined here just last week. Dr. Chistison would distill the toxin from the contents of Burnett's stomach. He'd tell the police, and I couldn't count on luck or witch-hazel magic to protect me from them. They knew my story and my face too well, especially the detectives.

I'd have to run the moment Burnett died. Meanwhile, I saw to his laundry, ran the bed warmer between his sheets, and polished the glass in his specimen collection, wondering how long it would take, and why Thomas wasn't speaking to me.

For days now, I'd heard nothing—no pulse, no whispers to his mam. It was troubling, because this was for him, after all, him and the others Burnett sacrificed to his five hundred students.

I had to believe his spirit had reached out to me, because the alternative was unthinkable. One, I was mad, and two, when it came to Burnett, I was wrong. I didn't want to contemplate that, not with poisons in my pocket.

"Anything else with today's marketing, Miss Ross?" Maggie glanced at me as she tied her bonnet, eyes contrite.

"Just the things on the list. Don't forget to stop at the candle-maker's." My head hurt, but I smiled as if it didn't. I owed Maggie some kindness for snapping at her yesterday. She'd forgotten to buy a lemon.

Mrs. Williams had managed her spice cake without it, and neither Burnett nor his guests had noticed the omission. I couldn't let Maggie suspect I was fraying under the pressure of waiting for an opportunity that stubbornly eluded me. And she didn't read, so it was unfair to expect her to remember everything when even the grocer missed an item from my list.

I reached into my pocket and drew out a penny. "Buy yourself a bun. There're so many errands today, you'll be hungry long before you're done."

Her face lightened, and I glimpsed her chipped front tooth in the quick flash of her smile. "Thank you, Miss Ross."

"Wait a moment." I closed the distance between us and straightened the tie of her bonnet. "Take my shawl, Maggie. It's on the hook by the kitchen door. Nippy out there today."

Lately, her shawl had been looking worn and thin. When she left, her brow was unfurrowed and she looked both comfortable and smart. I let out a breath—one without the usual constriction in my chest.

Before I settled in with the weekly household accounts, the snap of the front door knocker summoned me. Leaving my room, the narrow desk, and the neatly ruled ledger, I hurried to see who was calling on a Tuesday, because this wasn't one of Burnett's usual mornings for patients. He wasn't even here this morning, and Mrs. Burnett never had visitors.

Hopeful patients who didn't know his consulting hours, occasionally presented themselves at the house, but generally they were content to leave their names to schedule a later appointment. I was used to the routine, but today, the woman on the doorstep wasn't satisfied with that offer. She was slender, with an enviable complexion, sleek chestnut curls, and a stubborn expression that didn't augur well for me.

"No, I'm not a patient. And I'm not ill," she said crisply. "I'll wait until Dr. Burnett comes back."

Her dress, though expensive, wasn't particularly clean, and while I chided myself for making assumptions (I didn't hold up well to close scrutiny myself), there was something suggestive in the defiantly jaunty feathers of her hat, something I couldn't ignore.

I licked my lips. "I'm telling you the truth, Mrs. Dove. The doctor isn't here. I believe he's giving a guest lecture at the university today. I can't let you in to wait. You'll be here for hours."

This wasn't the kind of home where she could be shoved into a parlor with a servant to watch her until she confronted "the master" and stated her business.

"I need to see Dr. Burnett," she insisted.

"But if you aren't a patient—" I fumbled for words, finding none. I didn't know anything about Burnett's romantic inclinations or entanglements, and though I doubted he'd appreciate me foisting "Mrs. Dove" on him, I recognized her sharp-edged vehemence—the kind honed to a point by indifference and exclusion.

I lowered my voice to a whisper—the servant girl from the

house next door was sweeping the adjacent steps and I didn't want to be overheard. "Honestly, it's probably easiest if you say you're a patient and make an appointment, unless you'd like to leave your card, and—"

I broke off as she leveled a look at me. We both knew she wasn't the kind to carry cards.

I cleared my throat. "Mrs. Dove—"

She lifted her chin. "My name's Jenny."

My throat tightened, and I wondered how many times I'd looked as stubborn and lonely as that.

"I'll put you down as Mrs. Dove," I told her. "Don't argue. You'll get in to see him faster. Wait here." I shut the door, retrieving the diary I kept inside a drawer in the hall table, flipping through pages with the neat tables I'd drawn to better manage Dr. Burnett's appointments. I found a blank line, scribbled *Mrs. Dove, malady unknown*, and then reopened the door.

"Nine o'clock next Monday," I told her. "Don't be late."

I went back to the account books, but after an hour, I'd only gone through half the week's transactions, and my heart was running much too fast for simply playing with a pen and sitting in a chair.

Mrs. Burnett's bell rang, and I quit my desk with a sigh of relief.

Sunday evening, I was blessed with a miracle. Burnett arrived home unexpectedly, sullen faced, in time to dine with his mother.

Carrying in the main course, I gathered he'd been snubbed by a colleague, Munro, a man even his mother seemed to have little liking for. From her frequent nods and pointedly expressed sympathy, I gathered he wasn't a new topic between them.

With trembling hands and fraying resolve, I slipped down the hall to add a dissolved solution of arsenic (which Orfila had inadvertently recommended) to the whisky in the consulting office, knowing Burnett would retire there after the meal to read and drink a glass. My stomach churned as violently as if I'd already drunk a dose myself.

Burnett has Eoin Brennan's portrait, I reminded myself, *and you never saw Brennan hanging about until after you brought Thomas to Burnett.* He'd gone out of his way to poison the public against me and undermined my credibility, calling me emotional, as if that quality couldn't exist alongside perception or cleverness. Easy for him to malign me, with his university degrees and an honorable career. Easy because I was merely a woman, and he was a man, and his fame was more important than the last days shared by a child and his mother.

By the time I slipped the empty vial beneath my bodice, my hands were steady. Death by poison was far less than he deserved.

That done, I doctored Mrs. Burnett's cup of tea and swept in with the tray. She'd retire to bed within an hour. If Burnett drank his whisky soon, he might be dead by midnight. As soon as his heart stopped, I'd take Thomas's and run.

I'd lay him to rest in a sunny churchyard in a pretty village somewhere he might have gone if he'd lived to go adventuring. Someplace clean and new, with no scenes or inhabitants who might frighten him.

Down in my room, I began folding clothes into my box, rolling up stockings to line the corners, adding my warmest nightdress, my ebony comb and brush. But the tidy placement of these few possessions didn't stop me from thinking—after Burnett died, after Thomas had the best justice and peace I could give him, then what?

You don't have to know now, I told myself.

My box was only half-full when there was a muffled knock from the front door. I shoved the box under the bed, glanced at the palm-sized looking glass—eyebrows still thick and black, spectacles straight on my nose—and hurried to the hall, Burnett and his mother appearing a half second behind me.

It was a messenger, a breathless boy holding out a card with a penciled summons on the back.

My wife has had another seizure. Please come.

"Sir William Rae begs you to hurry, doctor," the boy said, clutching the stitch in his side.

"Yes, at once." Burnett vanished into his consulting room and returned with his bag in hand.

I ran my tongue over my teeth, a sour taste filling my mouth.

"Forgive me, mother," Burnett said, reaching for his coat. "Don't wait up."

I wondered if he'd ever called her Mam.

After he was gone, I composed my face, and turned to Mrs. Burnett. "What a shame he's been called away this evening."

Bland words. In truth, it was diabolical. I was so close. "Would you like to join Mrs. Williams and me in the kitchen?" I asked.

She'd probably already started another story for Maggie.

Mrs. Burnett hesitated, then shook her head. "Not tonight, Miss Ross. Just send Maggie to turn down my bed." She hid a yawn behind her hand. The dose was taking effect—again, for nothing.

I nodded, and went to tell Maggie, then returned to the dining room to clear, waiting until it would be safe to switch out the poisoned whisky. I could keep it in an empty bottle until I had another chance—

You make your own chances.

I spun around, but there was no one in the room, certainly no one to match the unfamiliar woman's voice I'd heard behind me. A coal slipped in the grate, and I started like I'd been shot.

Stop imagining things, I told myself, and stacked the dirty plates and smeared glasses resolutely onto the tray. Deliberately, I marched from the room without looking back.

But it was too soon to give up. There was still a chance Burnett would take some whisky when he came back.

Best to leave the poison for now, and wait and see.

Alone in my room, I paced from the door to the bed. My box was ready, but it was almost midnight, and Burnett hadn't returned. My eyelids dragged toward my cheeks, but I couldn't give in to sleep.

Then I heard stirring in the next room. Retching. The sound of falling crockery.

I flew to Maggie's room and barreled through the door.

"Sorry, Miss Ross," she mumbled. "I'm sick."

Oh, dear God.

Wait—was I allowed to pray anymore? This was my fault.

"Quick." I gathered her up and carried her to the kitchen, to the remnants of the day's fire. She was pallid and loose in my arms, with vomit on the front of her nightdress and in her hair.

I never imagined that Maggie would nip into Burnett's whisky, and I couldn't ask anything without revealing my complicity. *She'll live through this*, I promised. *She can't have drunk much*. Mrs. Burnett didn't trust me, and monitored liquor consumption along with other household supplies, raising her eyebrows and questioning expenses.

Later, I'd run upstairs and see how much Maggie had drained from the decanter. For now, I hauled her to the sink and pumped a glass of water.

"Quick. Drink this." Her hands shook, so I steadied the glass, trying to keep the water from spilling out her lips. She choked and sputtered but emptied the glass.

"Here." I deposited her in cook's chair, closest to the hearth. Orfila said—when the patient was living—to keep them warm, force them to vomit, and glut them with water and milk. Maggie had managed the first round of vomiting already, but yesterday's milk was gone. We'd have no more until morning. I dipped a ladle into the pot of hot water that was always warming over the coals. At this hour, the remaining embers still gave off some heat, and this water might be easier for her to drink—in some of the cases I'd read, they mixed in treacle or honey.

I prepared a second cup, this one sweet and steaming, and set it on the table. I dipped a towel in the hot water, and washed Maggie's hair, hands, and face.

"I'll fetch you a clean nightdress in a minute," I promised. "After you drink this."

"I can't." Her voice was rough and faint. "It hurts."

"I know." I pushed the wet hair off her forehead. Her skin was still cold. "But we must purge the—the sickness out of you."

"Is Dr. Burnett—?"

I shook my head, a fresh layer of frost climbing my arms. "He's not back yet. Take another sip."

I coached her until she drained half the cup. "Keep drinking," I ordered, vanishing into my room, and returning with every blanket from my bed—these were warm and fresh. I needed to clean Maggie's before Dr. Burnett came back, in case he thought of testing her vomit for poison.

I also needed to throw out the whisky.

With Maggie cocooned in half a dozen blankets, and her

half-full cup of honey water cradled in both hands, I was ready to risk the stairs. "I'll be right back," I promised, throwing another glance over my shoulder.

The whisky decanter was slick and cold in my hand when I snatched it from the sideboard. I wanted to vomit myself, but kept everything down except a jagged laugh that burned my throat and ears, as I fumbled with the stiff window catch.

Please, please, please.

At last, the frame swung open. I hurled the liquor outside, trusting the misty night would eventually wash all traces away. Shielding the bottle with my body, I carried it back into the kitchen and furtively rinsed it in the sink.

"Maggie?"

Her eyelids drifted open.

"Another sip?" I asked, framing her hands in my own and gently raising the cup. She took a swallow, but immediately began retching. I pried her from the blankets and carried her to the sink.

Halfway to emptying her stomach, I felt a hand on my shoulder. I tensed, but it was only Mrs. Williams.

"What's the matter with Maggie?"

"Sick. It'll pass," I said, radiating false confidence.

"What do you want me to do?"

"Sit with her once she's done. I'll look after her sheets."

Cook nodded, and if she was pleased I'd given her the better job, she was good enough not to show it. I couldn't tell if she'd noticed the whisky decanter next to the pump handle or divined the emotions stirring beneath my immediate worry: horror, panic, and guilt. The room was dark.

"I'll light a candle," she offered.

"Help me settle her first."

Together, we helped her to the chair and heaped her again with blankets.

"Let's build up the fire," I suggested. "Then we can find a light and mix her another posset of honey." Leaving Mrs. Williams to place the coals, I darted to the sink, snagging the empty decanter and vanishing in the direction of my room—and the cellar. There, I refilled the decanter to the previous level, taking note of the label on the bottle so I could replace the missing whisky later, before the loss was detected.

I covered the decanter in my arms with the pillow from my bed, carrying both back to the kitchen. "Maybe the doctor has something we can give her," I suggested, on my way to the stairs.

"Calomel, if you can find it," Cook called after me.

I returned the bottle to the sideboard and glanced about the room, but as I expected, Burnett's remedy chest and his black bag were gone.

I returned to the kitchen. "He took his medicines with him."

"He'll be back soon," Cook said, coaxing Maggie into another sip. "I've some licorice. Why don't you add that to the next cup of water and honey?"

I lit candles and brewed another concoction, adding honey, licorice, and mint, hoping the scent would bring comfort, and handed it to Cook, unable to meet Maggie's gaze.

"Keep drinking," I begged, recalling what I'd read of Orfila's methods, and the appalling number of dogs he'd tested his remedies on—most of them dying in states of heartrending distress. I'd wondered what kind of dispassionate man could exterminate so many animals in the name of science. The same kind of man as Burnett, I supposed, and I'd felt justified in killing him because it wasn't murder—it was an execution. A necessity, cutting away a diseased branch to make a healthier tree.

Now, another woman's child might be dying.

"As soon as we can, we must give her some milk," I whispered hoarsely.

Mrs. Williams nodded. "Aye, that's a sovereign remedy. Don't be afraid, Maggie. We'll have you turning cartwheels soon enough."

I set to scouring Maggie's room, removing every trace of illness—the scent, the slime, the stickiness—and prayed Mrs. Williams would be right.

{ 20 }

Dawn light frayed the edges of the sky by the time Conall arrived home in Sir William Rae's best carriage. Lady Rae was sleeping, having lived out the night. Conall suspected apoplexy, not a seizure, but it was too early to know if she'd make a full recovery yet.

He was tired, sustained through the night by only a bite of bread and a pot of coffee while bleeding, blistering, and listening to the lady's pulses. His brain was dull and sluggish, his eyes blurring and crossing whenever he relaxed his focus, and he wanted nothing but his own bed.

Now it was within reach, just beyond his front door—if he could manage the key. Why wasn't—oh.

Conall swore. He was trying to jam in the wrong one. Scowling, he fumbled for the correct key on the ring and unlocked the door. His servants must have been listening for him, because Miss Ross appeared immediately in the hall, carrying a coal scuttle. His cook, Mrs. Williams, was only a few seconds behind her, popping out from the door to the back stairs like a jack-in-the-box, wiping floury hands on her apron.

"What's this?" Conall asked. Carrying coal scuttles was the

kitchen girl's work, and both women looked nearly as weary as he felt. "Miss Ross, why are you—"

"Maggie took sick in the night, sir," Miss Ross said in a dull voice. "She's much improved now, but if you can—"

Conall closed his eyes and circled his shoulders. "How's her breathing?"

"Quite easy, and she's kept down half a bowl of broth and a cup of milk—"

"Still pale, but not at all feverish," interjected the cook. "We've given her licorice and..."

Conall turned a stern gaze on her and she pinched her lips shut. "I was under the impression that I'm the doctor here. Is she sleeping?"

Miss Ross and the cook nodded.

"She's been very unwell," the cook said, more subdued now.

"But she's sleeping. There's no better tonic than rest." He was in no state to tend to her now, and she could sleep for another hour. "I need some myself. If I tried to bleed her now, I'd probably miss her arm."

"You do look exhausted, sir," his cook conceded. "Will you take breakfast?"

"After," Conall said. Right now, sleep's call was overwhelming. Dropping his bag by the door, he detoured into his office, seeking the one thing he could pause for just now, because it would send him more quickly on his way.

He poured out a large whisky and carried it up to his bedchamber, passing Miss Ross along the way. She looked thinner than usual, and gray as a shadow.

Conall shook his head. A doctor's work was never done. He drained his glass, and stretched out face down on the bed.

After a hasty breakfast, Conall looked in on Maggie, the maid. Blessed with the sturdy constitution of most of her class, she was sitting in bed, drinking a bowl of broth.

Her breaths were even, her pulse regular, her stomach pain was diminishing, and though her face was shadowed and pale, he felt there was no cause for serious concern. His cook and housekeeper had provided her with surprisingly excellent care, and it was heartening to see the attention paid to every part of his house. The girl's room was scrupulously clean in spite of the night she'd passed, the dirty linen already boiling in the laundry.

"No need to bleed you." Conall patted the girl's hand. "You're doing very well all on your own. Rest, take a cup of milk or broth every hour, and you should be back on your feet in a day or two."

He turned to the two women. "You are both well?"

They nodded.

"My mother?"

"Perfectly well, sir," Miss Ross said. "She finished breakfast an hour ago and is knitting in the small parlor."

It would take a day or two to be certain there was no spread of infection, but this was encouraging. "You did well, both of you." He smiled. "If you show such skill again, other doctors will want to recruit you to the hospital—and then where will I be?"

Cook grinned and flustered. Even Miss Ross, normally cool and unflappable, was sufficiently disconcerted by the praise to flush and avoid his eyes.

"We're just glad Maggie's recovering," she said. "You're sure there's no danger?"

"None at all, I should say," Conall said. He consulted his watch and grimaced. Only another ten minutes before this morning's first patient.

"I'll take a pot of coffee, Mrs. Williams. Miss Ross, you'll bring it to the consulting room?"

"Of course, doctor."

Alone in his office, he unpacked his bag and inspected his tools, sharpening the finely wrought blades and polishing the ivory handles. He reviewed the contents of his remedy chest, taking note of supplies that were low. Just as he latched the box, the knocker sounded. Right on time. It was exactly nine o'clock.

He positioned himself behind his deck. Seconds later, Miss Ross ushered the patient in. "Mrs. Dove to see you, sir."

He waved the patient to a chair, noticing as he did so the coffee Miss Ross had brought earlier, which he'd been too distracted to drink. "Take that away, will you?"

She complied with a nod and swept away with the tray, a model of soundless efficiency. It was always satisfying, watching her at her work—quiet, calm, and organized—a credit to him, much more than the slatternly day servants his mother had employed before.

The door closed and he folded his hands on the desk. "How can I help you, Mrs. Dove?"

It wasn't common for women to see him alone. Many came with fathers or husbands. Those who could afford to came with a maid, and those who couldn't brought a female friend or relative. Mrs. Dove sat across from him on her own, straight-backed and sharp-eyed.

"I'm not here on my own account, doctor."

Conall tapped a forefinger on the blotter, holding back a sigh. This happened from time to time—patients approaching him through intermediaries, usually because of an unwanted pregnancy, syphilis, or maladies of that sort.

"I'm afraid I can't—"

"My sister consulted you two weeks ago about a lump in her left breast. She is tall, about my height, but with lighter hair. Do you remember her?"

Conall blinked, smoothing the frown from his forehead. "I see a great many patients, Mrs. Dove."

"I was told you spend most of your time teaching. Her visit wasn't that long ago—"

"I cannot reveal a patient's private medical information, I'm afraid." Conall rose from his chair. "I suggest you ask your sister about my advice."

"Believe me, I meant to." Mrs. Dove gripped the arms of her chair and leaned forward. "She never came home after her appointment with you. No one's seen her. Lizzie wouldn't leave without telling me. She wouldn't have gone anywhere without her things."

Conall turned his attention to his cuffs, concealing a sharp, almost painful tightening in his lungs. "People change their minds and do completely inexplicable things. It's not unusual, especially after receiving a disheartening diagnosis—which may have occurred, though I can't really remember."

"Check your notes," the woman said, and Conall looked up, unwillingly, in surprise. Her eyes, meeting his, were challenging.

"I don't write up all my cases. No one does. Most of a doctor's work is quite uninteresting," he said, embellishing the syllables of the last word. "You say your sister came to see me, but I've no memory of the woman you describe. If she did intend to consult me, instead of one of the many other doctors in town, she might not have kept her appointment."

"I walked her here," Mrs. Dove ground out. "All the way from Lady Wynd in the West Port. We planned to meet after I finished work, but Lizzie never came. No one's seen her since I left her here with you."

Conall glanced behind her, at the door. He smoothed his waist-coat. Mrs. Dove presented well, in an expensive dress, but she wasn't quality, not if she worked, not if she'd come from Lady Wynd. "I don't know what to tell you. I may have prescribed her a tonic. I may have referred her to Mr. Craig, the surgeon, especially if you say she had a lump on her breast. I'm not responsible for every patient who crosses my door, and I can't tell you when or where she may have gone when she left, since I don't make a practice of escorting patients to my door, let alone to whatever brothel they lodge in."

The woman didn't flinch. "It's no business of yours where Lizzie stays or how she makes her living."

"It is when her *work*"—the word was laced with irony—"puts her in need of a doctor."

"She paid your fee—I counted it out with her that morning. What's the rest of it to you?"

"Nothing, at all." Conall leaned forward, pressing his hands on the desk. "I'm sure you know better than I the dangers confronted by working women, and while I can treat disease, I cannot predict or protect her from the hazards of her profession. I suggest you contact the police."

Uncertainty flickered in her eyes. Conall smiled.

"Have you already? Or is it that they might be unduly interested in you?"

She stood up and smoothed her skirts, almost hiding the trembling of her fingers.

"I'm afraid that's all the time I can give you. I'm a busy man." He glanced down, arranging the papers atop his desk, a calculated move, and a risk. Without looking up, he gauged the air around him like a sailor feeling for a coming storm, the pressure around him rising for a moment, then dissipating swiftly. He'd won.

"You're an evil bastard," she whispered. "And you won't get away with this."

He looked up, and she took a step back.

"With what?" he asked softly.

Her mouth twisted, but the words she wanted must have eluded her. She spun away and fled the room, banging the door.

Conall let out a breath.

The name she'd given was almost certainly false, like the one offered by Lizzie, her sister. But he'd bet she was speaking true about Lady Wynd.

I jerked away from the keyhole with only a heartbeat to spare, barely avoiding Jenny on her headlong flight. Catching my movement from the corner of her eye, her head swiveled to me, her eyes rounding even wider.

"Get out," Burnett shouted from the study. "Or I'll send for the watch. They must know you well enough."

"Not as well as the police are going to know you," she muttered.

We were both out of sight of the open door, for now. I reached out a hand and nudged it gently—too gently. It stopped an inch from the frame. Close enough, probably, though it was foolish to trust my luck.

"You have to go," I mouthed, striding past the gap, touching her softly on the arm, before she did something drastic, like throw a vase through a window.

"Did you see her?" Jenny whispered. "My sister?"

Not that I remembered—I hadn't heard every word between

her and Burnett, and I feared her sister had come on a day when I'd gone marketing instead of Maggie, wanting to escape the oppression of the house.

But I had an idea where Lizzie might be, though I hoped, fervently, I was wrong. "I can't talk here."

"You're his housekeeper," she said with a scathing look. "You must have seen her."

I started to shake my head, but stopped when I met her eyes. I'd worn that desperate look, worn it threadbare.

"Please. Something's happened to her."

I swallowed. "You have to go," I said loudly, propelling her out the door. Under my breath, I mouthed, "Greyfriar's Kirkyard. Tomorrow afternoon."

{ *21* }

Adam stretched his neck inside his shirt collar and glanced once more at the clock on the mantelpiece. Though considerably more spartan, the Home for Foundling Girls—cold, smelling faintly of carbolic, and unnaturally quiet—reminded him of school.

He'd hated it. With his skin darker than everyone else's, still unaccustomed to Edinburgh, (gray skies, gray streets, gray houses, filth, and too many people), his only friend there had been Hugh.

Adam shifted irritably. The matron couldn't expect him to wait much longer. It almost seemed like she was punishing him, leaving him cooling his heels longer every time he came.

He tugged his coat straight, took out his notebook, and opened it atop his bouncing right knee. He flicked through scribbled entries—four pages, all under the heading *Nan Burt*. It was weeks since he'd spotted her.

"The girls often run away," the matron had told him. "We do our best." If anything, she seemed annoyed he wasn't as fatalistic about it as she was.

Nan had been spotted at least twice by the watch, once in Grassmarket and once in the West Port, thanks to the drawing he'd made of her face and posted at the station. Unfortunately, she was talented at eluding police officers.

Hugh thought he was making too much of it. So did most of the men at the station. This wasn't a police case, and Adam knew perfectly well not to involve himself in hopeless, heartbreaking situations, at least not more than the job required. But he wasn't about to lose Nan, too, not when she was still alive.

Between sightings, Adam questioned his tribe of informers. They didn't need to know this wasn't a police matter. In Adam's mind, it ought to be. But their information was useful only for the negatives—Nan hadn't joined the guild of urchins knocking doors and prowling the streets, scavenging bits of old iron. She hadn't taken up begging, a blessing, because the local beggar chieftain would have blinded or crippled her first. And though it was impossible for Adam to gain entrance to Edinburgh's houses of ill repute (his unusual coloring made disguise far too difficult), so far as he could learn, she hadn't been inducted into any of the brothels, an assertion he was confident accepting, since she'd been seen twice. Children in brothels were worse than prisoners. If Nan had been lured or forced in there, she wouldn't have the liberty of walking about the streets.

A small comfort. There were still innumerable sweatshops fueled by the busy hands and spent lives of small children. Adam intended to find Nan before she vanished into one of them or was taken up for thieving. He wouldn't be able to help her, then.

She should have been safe enough at the orphan's home. Why the hell had she left? He should have visited more. He'd meant to, but—

Adam shook his head. There was no excuse. Life was hard for a child on their own, and he'd never been as alone as Nan.

"Good afternoon, detective."

Stout, stern, and cagey, the matron swept into the room. Adam started, like a boy caught stealing jam from the pantry.

"Miss Oliphant. I'm still looking for Nan Burt."

Her eyelids, weighted by a double portion of the usual flesh, dropped dolefully. "I'm afraid we've seen no sign of her. And she must know we'd take her back. This is all her choosing."

"Can you—"

"Detective Kerr," the matron interrupted heavily. "I've already promised to inform you the moment we discover anything. Coming here is not a wise use of your time."

Clearly not, but he had no place else to look. "I'll be on my way, then." This was clearly what she expected from him.

He was not overfond of Matron Elizabeth Oliphant.

{ 22 }

The next afternoon wasn't my half day, it was Maggie's, but she was in no state to walk home and visit her parents. Instead, her mother and younger brother came to see her, sitting with her through most of the morning. I managed the greetings with wooden lips and a tight chest, looking away when Mrs. Hope, Maggie's mother, crooned sympathetically and gathered her daughter in her arms. Maggie downplayed her illness and—guiltily—I did the same, tending to her work and mine, scowling and scrubbing until my hands were raw.

Once Dr. Burnett and his mother finished their luncheon, he set off for the anatomy school, where he lectured every afternoon, except for Saturdays and Sundays.

"I'm taking my half day today, ma'am," I told Mrs. Burnett. "So that Maggie can have hers after she's fully recovered." In case she felt like arguing, I added, "Mrs. Williams has agreed to see to anything you need while I'm out. She says, if you wish for company—"

She nodded acceptance to Mrs. Williams's invitation before I could finish, so I retreated, leaving her gathering her knitting to carry belowstairs.

In front of my looking glass, I splashed my face with cold water and witch hazel, avoiding my eyes. I didn't need to see them to know they looked bruised—too little sleep, too much stifled crying, and a head full of recriminations.

"Going out already?" Mrs. Williams asked, as I cut through the kitchen, concealed behind my bonnet. "You haven't eaten!"

"Not hungry," I replied.

"You're not ill? None of Maggie's trouble?" Her brows creased with worry. Mrs. Burnett's needles paused.

"No—" I hesitated, not sure what to say, and finished by grabbing an apple from the bowl on the kitchen table.

"Take this too." Mrs. Williams cut off a wedge of cheese, then returned to her carrots and onions, the knife moving almost of its own accord.

I escaped outside, nodding at the neighbors' maid as she hurried to her kitchen door, arms laden with two baskets of marketing. She smiled at me through the railing. "How's your Maggie? Mrs. Williams said she took ill?"

"Mending. She'll be fine," I said.

"She's a good girl."

The words echoed in my head in time with my retreating footsteps.

The day was gray and wet, making the grass at Greyfriar's Kirkyard lank and slippery. I circled the kirk, unwilling to go inside unless I had to. I'd chosen to listen to my ghosts, and that made me reluctant to kneel in one of the pews, putting myself under God's eye, especially since I'd nearly ended up with Maggie's blood on my hands. So I walked outside, up and down rows of graves, looking for Jenny and ignoring the leering gazes of the skeletons carved into the stones, at least one every few yards:

above the locked iron gate guarding a family's mausoleum, on a stubby grave marker half-fallen over, on a stately plaque installed on the kirk walls.

Bony faces, bony hands, dead leaves, carved hourglasses warning of imminent death. I'd chosen a wretched place to meet. But it was quiet, far from Burnett's house, and a place two lone women could meet without being bothered or attracting notice. The place was almost deserted.

I spotted a hooded woman and started toward her, then realized not only was she too short, she was walking purposely toward a large monument and carrying a bouquet of flowers. Next I saw two boys with pocket catapults and cunning faces, hurrying toward the lower gate, undoubtedly about to ambush someone.

I walked for an hour, brooding and reading the inscriptions on the stones. Finally, Jenny appeared as I rounded the corner again onto the north end of the kirkyard. She was waiting under a spreading tree and wore no cloak today, only a green wool jacket.

"Where were you?" I asked.

"I'm sorry," she said at the same time. "I couldn't get away."

"I didn't think you'd come," I said.

"I have to. You're my best chance. Did you see her?"

"No," I admitted reluctantly, pained by her pinched and worried face. "I wasn't in the morning she came."

She swore in Gaelic, a curse that made me flinch, and whipped out a flask. A long swallow restored her, at least enough to ask, "So why'd you bring me here?"

I held out my hand, stalling for time. She passed me her flask but the rough liquor made me choke. I delved into my pocket for the apple and took a bite.

"Hungry?" I asked.

With a nod, she relieved me of fruit and flask. I hitched my cloak tighter. "I want to help."

"Why?" she demanded.

I jerked my shoulders in an uncomfortable shrug, and we walked down the row of graves, Jenny making quick work of the apple. I passed her the cheese as soon as she tossed the core away.

"Something's happened to her," Jenny said, her voice thick. "Lizzie wouldn't leave without telling me or without her good clothes." She rubbed the green wool of her jacket sleeve, her voice dropping to a whisper. "These are almost new. She has a skirt to match—I sewed it for her."

"Was she wearing it?"

Jenny nodded. "And a brown cloak, plain brown bonnet, gold earrings—she'd just got them back; they've been pawned twice—black boots, red stockings."

Not much to go on. I was wearing nearly the same, minus the red stockings.

"There was a little boy," I said, forcing my voice to remain steady. I couldn't put this off any longer. The cheese was gone, having vanished as quick as the apple. "He went missing fourteen months ago, a few weeks after seeing Dr. Burnett." I swallowed. "A while ago, his mother came to the house. She thought Dr. Burnett might have paid for her boy to be taken."

"Why?" Jenny frowned at me.

I let out a long breath. "His heart had a defect," I said. "Dr. Burnett collects those kind of things. He has one like the missing boy's displayed on his shelf."

Jenny stopped midstride, her widening eyes devouring the rest of her face.

"I'm guessing," I blurted, a desperate edge in my voice. I wasn't just confessing to her. "I don't know. Dr. Burnett claims the heart was a gift from another doctor, that this woman was imagining things and overset by grief."

He needed a constant supply of bodies, but I didn't know if there was anything about Lizzie that might make killing her worth the risk. She hadn't been seen since coming to his house. Why so quickly? Thomas had been left alone for those last precious weeks. But he hadn't visited Burnett alone. Mr. Craig and I had both been present.

"Was there anything—unusual—about Lizzie?" My heart sped as Jenny's pause lengthened. If my guess was right, looking for her was dangerous.

"Most people don't know about it," she admitted slowly. "She hides it in the way she holds her hand. Or conceals it in a muff."

I waited, terrified what it would mean if I was right—if there was something *collectible* about Lizzie.

"She has an extra finger on her left hand," Jenny said.

We parted soon after. "Don't wait. It may not be too late to find her," I urged. "You have to go to the police station by St. Giles. Ask for Detective Adam Kerr." He may not have believed me about Burnett, but at least his efforts at finding Thomas had been real. If Lizzie was alive, there was no time to lose. "Don't talk to anyone else. It's too dangerous. And you can't tell anyone about me—I'm in his house."

Jenny nodded. "But will you be safe? If you're right, you're taking an awful chance."

I replied with more confidence than I felt. "I make my own chances."

Jenny's mouth twisted. "Lizzie was always saying that. Take extra care. If Dr. Burnett learns you told me..."

"He won't," I said. "Not unless you tell. Not a word about me, not even to the police. They won't ask too many questions. What I've said is common knowledge. And Detective Kerr was looking for the missing boy. He came to the house," I said, inventing quickly. "He's your best hope." And as hopes went, a very slender one, but I couldn't tell Jenny that.

"All right," she said. "You'd best hurry back before anyone starts wondering."

I nodded and moved away, but she stopped me, catching hold of my arm. "Thank you." Her eyes were grave.

I nodded. "See you next week."

Detective Kerr wouldn't ignore another missing person, I told myself. Not one connected to Conall Burnett.

{ 23 }

Conall breathed on his hands, rubbing them together to work up some warmth. The two overhead lamps gave excellent illumination, but their heat and the warmth outside was counteracted effectively by the low roof, thick walls, and wide blocks of ice.

"This one's fleshy," Ferguson lamented, slipping his hands into the wide oak barrel, looking for leverage. The body folded inside was mottled as a tortoiseshell cat, splotched black, bone white, and purple. He was also, as Ferguson said, rather stout. Difficult to get him into the barrel, never mind pulling him out. Ferguson tugged, freeing an arm, which he draped over the side. Conall grasped it with one hand and reached into the barrel with the other, eyes closed against the sting of the alcohol spirits bathing the corpse. Trawling over the waxy flesh with his fingers, looking for leverage, he found the crook of a knee.

"Ready?"

Ferguson grunted an affirmative and they heaved.

"Again," Ferguson gasped.

On the third try, they raised the shoulders past the barrel's rim. From there it was easier. Grunting, the two of them pulled the corpse free and laid it on the marble table.

Ferguson wiped his forehead. "It'll take Jones and me twice as long to get him ready."

He was underestimating, as he often did, not liking to complain. Conall guessed it would take both assistants a day or more to remove the subcutaneous fat from the back and buttocks of this fellow—if they recruited a pair of senior students to help. Well, no reason why they shouldn't. Lately that was a coveted invitation. "Ask Mr. Henry and Mr. Paterson to assist," Conall suggested. "I can help for the next hour, and tomorrow I'll manage the evening tour."

Ferguson would be exhausted by then, and he'd smell terrible. Conall's visitors might enjoy frightening themselves, but they liked their spectacles dried, bleached, or jarred, so it was important to maintain the correct intellectual atmosphere, something he understood more acutely since hiring Miss Ross. The dishes of potpourri in the hall, the lush potted plants spaced throughout the salon, and the unrelenting cleanliness of the house elevated the tone more than he'd thought possible.

It was almost unfair, that such mundane things made so much of a difference, even among the best medical minds. Considering the lengths he'd gone to acquire his specimens, you'd think they'd speak for themselves. But people liked to be comfortable. Even him.

It was a pity they had to work in the icehouse. Unfortunately, preservation was quite impossible out of it.

"Here you are, sir." Ferguson slid a piece of leather across the table, with Conall's tools arranged from smallest to largest across it. Pins, probes, forceps, four scalpels of varying sizes, shears, two saws.

"We'd best get to it." Conall sighed and reached for his favorite knife.

The skin was peeled back, pinned to shoulders, buttocks, and flanks, and the fat partly cleared away, giving a view of the scapular muscles and the upper fibers of the latissimus dorsi, when Ferguson cleared his throat. All Conall's students knew better than to nudge him in the arm.

"Dr. Burnett? Someone's here."

Following Ferguson's gaze, Conall turned around and recognized an unmistakable silhouette.

"I'm afraid I have to leave you," he said, and wiped his hands on his apron. "A patient needs me."

"No matter. Jones will be here soon," Ferguson said. "Tomorrow I'll recruit Paterson and Henry. We'll have everything ready."

"I'll come back at noon tomorrow to help with the delicate parts," Conall promised. "Don't let the students wreck anything." Granting them experience was one thing, letting inexperienced hands spoil his teaching materials quite another.

"Of course not, sir."

"Good night, Ferguson."

Though his assistants were familiar with most aspects of the body trade, there were some conversations, like tonight's, that his assistants couldn't be allowed to hear. He stepped out of the lamps' illumination, into the unlit yard.

"Evenin', doctor."

"Good evening, Eoin."

They left through the alleyway, avoiding the lights in the square, Conall stretching his strides to match Eoin Brennan's. He didn't like it.

"I expected you yesterday," he said. "And not empty handed."

"She's not easy to get, this girl you're after," Eoin said. His voice was unexpectedly clear, despite his stretched lips and scarred and distorted face. A slight lisp marred his words, but not more than his Irish accent did. "Been following her, but she's never alone. Sent my cousin Will to her place. It's been a good while, but I still don't like showing my mug about. 'Sides, some of them tarts are particular."

Conall grunted. He didn't like Eoin delegating more specialized work, but his appearance did present some limitations. "So why didn't Will get her?"

"She's not working. Not seeing nobody."

That wasn't good. Jenny Dove suspected him. If she was on her guard...

"What about your other friends?" Conall asked, like a cautious player unsure of his cards. Eoin didn't wear a green ribbon in his buttonhole, but he was a Ribbonman nonetheless. Across the water, the Irish secret society was infamous for murdering tithe men, for violent and deadly riots, and for their merciless treatment of turn-coat Catholic informers.

Fleeing English law, Eoin and his brethren had joined the Irish migration to Scotland, working in factories, digging canals, and resorting to old contrivances when circumstances demanded or the work gave out. The body trade was lucrative business, so it was natural that unemployed laborers found their way there—and even more natural that a business as necessarily secret as graverob-bing had fallen almost entirely under the Ribbonmen's control. The brotherhood was known to be extremely loyal and merciless.

"Surely you have associates who could take care of her."

Eoin shrugged. "Wasn't sure if you wanted others knowing your business. It's one thing to for me to ask Will, but you said you wanted our side contracts kept secret."

Years before, Conall had discovered Eoin's readiness to take on special commissions. But he was a dangerous man, with dangerous friends, who all had to be handled carefully.

"Will's been told off by the bosses already," Eoin said. "They didn't like that you tried to make him renegotiate the fees. Reminded him he works for them, not you."

Conall grunted, realizing this "reminder" was probably the cause of Will's recent bruising. Last time he'd come, two days before, someone had clearly taken their fists to his face.

"Will's mad enough at them he might be fool enough to find that girl for you," Eoin admitted, "But you don't want that. He's all right for simple jobs. But if anything went wrong, you couldn't trust him to keep your secrets. He'd spill."

Conall's jaw tightened. "I want Jenny Dove gone. Quickly. I don't care about the condition of the body, so the job should be easy."

"Well—" Eoin scratched the weblike scarring on his neck. "It isn't. Yesterday I followed her to the police station. You know I can't be seen there. They'll haul me in for questioning about that boy."

Conall sent him a look. "You got away safely." Someone within the police—probably connected to the Ribbonmen too—had warned Eoin, who then came to Conall for help. Sending him to Ireland for six months had been a costly maneuver, but necessary. "That was well over a year ago. It's out of people's minds."

"Some of the police have long memories," Eoin said, shaking his head. "I can't count on my friends for help again if there's police involved. 'Twould get me in trouble."

They crossed a wide street, then strode along a narrow wynd, toward the shops and public houses of the Canongate. Eoin probably expected him to buy drinks.

"I doubt your friends' niceties are so well developed," Conall said evenly. "I'm willing to pay for extra trouble, but I don't like to ask twice."

Eoin stopped on the pavement, studying him. With all his scars, it was difficult to make out his expression.

"Is that understood?" Conall asked.

"Right." Eoin gave a curt nod and touched the brim of his hat. But instead of leaving to tend to the business immediately—"How much extra?" he asked.

"Double." Conall spat and told himself the cost was not as reckless as leaving Jenny free to petition the police.

"Double it is." Satisfied, Eoin walked away, sliding between the sweaty shoulders of a pack of laborers in the next street. The next second, he vanished.

Eoin Brennan was good at that.

"That's it, then?" Adam uncrossed his legs and made to rise from his chair.

"Yes, I think we can say this one's finished." Behind his desk at the Crown Office, John Stevenson set aside his pen. "Mrs. Fisher will plead guilty to poisoning her husband in exchange for a reduced sentence of transportation. Thank you, detective."

Adam nodded, plucked his overcoat from the stand, and let himself out, satisfied with the conclusion to the case, but not with the man who'd done it. And really, it was no good allowing John Stevenson to get to him—the man was an able prosecutor, handling the Fisher murder most adroitly. But Adam disliked Stevenson's straightforward success, his uncreased forehead, and his easy tone. Thomas Tait deserved some tired shadows from beneath his father's eyes and more streaks of gray at his temples. There ought to be traces of his life and death on his father's face.

Adam was certain Isobel wouldn't look so unchanged. Not that she or Stevenson were any of his business, though he'd done the difficult work telling both of them there was little chance of finding the boy. Still, every time he spoke with Stevenson, he couldn't help thinking the man should have tried harder.

Back at the station, Adam collected his messages.

"Fellow to see you," said the desk sergeant, jerking his chin at a rumpled-looking man with greasy hair, sipping from a flask and occupying himself watching the crowded occupants of the station's holding cell. Not one of his usual informers, and there was no sympathy in this man's face; he wore a look of canny appraisal Adam saw too often and always found distasteful.

"Give me two minutes," he said to the sergeant. "Then bring him up."

Fortified by a biscuit and a nip from his own flask, Adam greeted the man Stevenson-style, from behind his desk without offering a chair.

"Sergeant Gray said you want to speak with me," he said, not wanting to waste time with preambles.

"Been waiting since noon," the man said. "It's important."

Assuming this was merely a ploy for more money, Adam raised his eyebrows.

The man leaned on the desk, his dark-rimmed fingers perilously close to Adam's stack of pristine papers. "I hear tell you're looking for someone," the man whispered. His eyes were steady, fringed with eyelashes so pale they'd disappear at any greater distance, and his cheeks were burnished with streaks of grime and glittering stubble. "A child."

"What can you tell me?" Adam reached into his pocket, noting the flicker of disappointment in the man's face as he extracted a pencil and notebook instead of his purse.

Most of the time, Adam received good value from his informants, maybe because he looked different from the other police. Try as he might, he couldn't completely inhabit the role of officialdom. Looking at this man, Adam promised inwardly not to overpay.

"Found her. Stole her from a workshop making silk flowers yesterday. Me and my woman have her safe—but you can't have her 'less I get some reward."

The last sentence, almost a threat, overrode most of Adam's questions, but he forced himself to speak deliberately, to act unconcerned.

"You are talking of Nan Burt?" He'd been thinking of Thomas Tait, so naturally his mind had gone to him first.

The man nodded.

"And you are?"

The man hesitated, loathe to give up his name. "Will Brennan."

"And how do you know I've been looking for her?"

Brennan shrugged. "I got friends. Didn't know it was a secret."

"It's not. I have nothing to hide," Adam said.

"D'ye still want her?" Brennan couldn't have been more unconcerned about Adam's motives.

"Yes."

"I want five pounds."

It was a ludicrous sum. "You can't be serious. What is she to you?"

Brennan straightened. "I had to break her out of that

workshop. There's risk involved in that. Could still be, if word spreads around."

Adam tilted his head, narrowing his eyes. This man was just as likely to have plucked Nan off the street to sell to a workshop or worse. Adam wouldn't have trusted him with his stepmother's flatulent pug, let alone a child.

Brennan didn't fluster under his stare. "Can't trouble myself for nothing."

Adam stood. "Let me see her. Then I can judge what your trouble is worth." If Brennan was expecting payment, he probably hadn't mistreated her. Still, there was no saying what might have happened before, assuming Brennan was telling the truth.

On the way out of the station, Adam glanced at Gray, the desk sergeant, and straightened his collar, lingering by the door until Gray returned his sign. Foolish to follow Brennan anywhere without a couple of constables tracking behind.

Brennan was wrapping a muffler around his face, though the day was warm.

"Where have you got her?" Adam demanded.

"West Port. My woman keeps a lodging house there."

Probably nothing more than a few unlit rooms filled with straw.

"Let's go," Adam said.

The distance wasn't far, and the house was just as wretched as Adam imagined, with dark-stained walls, papered windows, and a rickety flight of stairs zigzagging up the outside wall, over the front door, up to the second floor. Adam glanced back, locking eyes with a young constable in plain clothes, before following Brennan inside.

The room was dark and so pungent, Adam blinked his eyes. A quick scan revealed a smoking fire, a pig, and a piss pot, but no Nan.

"Ellie! I brought him!" Brennan shouted, and the stairs out-side groaned beneath a cascade of quick feet. A second later, Mrs. Brennan—if that's who she was—hurried into the room, skinny and snub nosed, with hair as lank as her man's. She scratched her neck, gray with dirt, and peered at Adam.

"He paid up?"

"I want to see her first," Adam interjected. Futile quibbling. He'd have to pay, even if the girl they had wasn't Nan. He wasn't leaving any child here.

"I'll bring her." Brennan darted outside and up the stairs, no doubt anticipating his money. Adam tensed, hoping the constables were out of sight.

Brennan returned, and any relief Adam might have taken in his unconcerned demeanor was destroyed when he saw Nan, towed along by bound hands. There were marks on her cheeks, and welts on her ankles. Her eyes widened at the sight of him, but he couldn't give her more than a glance.

He glared at Brennan. "Why are her hands tied?"

"Knew she was important to you. Couldn't risk her running off." Brennan grinned appeasingly. Behind him, Ellie shifted on her feet, edging toward the poker propped near the fire. "Go on and take her," Brennan said, holding out his cupped hand.

Adam floated a hand to his pocket, judging the seconds between him, Ellie Brennan, and the iron poker. There had to be enough. "Now Cathcart!" he shouted and lunged for Nan.

Whistles shrilled. His hands closed on birdlike shoulders, and he and Nan crashed to the floor, rolling over wet straw to the wall, out of reach of the poker, which whooshed past his head and thud-ded into the ground just as Cathcart and the other constable, clubs raised, burst through the door.

Nan cried, but she didn't say anything until they were back at the station, and the Brennans on their way to Calton Hill Prison.

"What happened?" Adam asked.

"She said she had a job for me, washing clothes. But she took me to a house where we were locked in, making velvet roses all night and day."

Her fingers were red and callused, and the easiest things for both her and Adam to look at. It was hard to meet the girl's eyes.

"Can you show me where it is?" he asked.

She swallowed. "I think..." She dropped her voice. "The foreman there buys protection from the Ribbonmen. Because nobody comes to the place who's not supposed to."

"Adam, you better speak with Fra—" Cathcart, cutting in, was quickly silenced by Adam's sharp glance. Raiding the place might not be the wisest move, but it was better than knuckling to criminals. The superintendent and Fraser were meeting with the lord advocate today, leaving Adam as ranking officer. He could arrest the people who'd stolen Nan even if he paid for it later.

"If we don't act now, they'll clear the place," Adam said, and Cathcart sighed.

"I can show you," Nan said, her interlaced fingers blanching at the knuckles.

"Good lass." Adam smiled but didn't touch her. He'd seen how she flinched when Cathcart had patted her shoulder.

"I'll assemble the men," Cathcart said, resigned, as he heaved out of his chair.

They were at the house within half an hour, but the door was unlocked, the rooms swept bare, the place empty. And Nan, insistent this was the place whenever she managed to move her compressed lips, was pale and sweating, even across the street where Adam had stationed her, hand in hand with Constable Craigie.

"What will you do with her?" Cathcart said in an undertone, though they wouldn't be overheard, not here on the same side of the street as the house. "You need her as a witness if you're going to prosecute the Brennans for kidnapping."

Cathcart knew he'd taken her to the orphanage already—and how that had ended. For a moment, Adam thought of his stepmother, Emily. A difficult proposition, but not impossible. She was a kind woman, with charitable impulses.

Then he looked at Nan, a mouse of a girl he couldn't lose again.

"If Nan will come..." Adam swallowed, wondering how on earth he'd persuade her. "I'll take her home with me."

{ 24 }

I refolded my duster and reached back behind the jars to the far corners of the shelf. "The police will come soon," I whispered to Thomas.

This time, I'd be ready. Burnett wouldn't be able to intimidate Jenny into silence or suborn the law with lies. I'd contradict his evidence, with lies of my own if I must, but hopefully with proof. The circumstances of Lizzie Dove's disappearance were too similar and too suspicious, the pattern as plain as the repeating melody of a Bach fugue.

To me at least. Burnett hadn't yet added a six-fingered hand to his collection. The nearest thing to evidence I'd found was the drawing of Eoin Brennan, and that was locked in Burnett's desk.

I needed the keys, but once again, I had to wait for a careless moment from Burnett. Suppose it didn't come?

My cloth showed only the faintest traces of dust, but I refolded it once more, exposing a pristine patch of cotton. I stepped back, surveying the shelf, then the room, looking for streaks on the window, for fingerprints on the doorknob or cabinet handles. Nothing. The room was immaculate, just like the eighty-seven human specimens on display. Some, I knew, Burnett had inherited from his mentor

Dr. Barclay, but even so. There was a great difference, a grave one, between finding and taking.

He must be stopped. *Help me*, I pleaded silently. No answer came, so ignoring the aches in my tired arms, I drew the curtains and locked the room.

Next morning, I searched Burnett's bedchamber and his mother's, while he saw patients and she met with the ladies of the Episcopal congregation of St. Peters on how to improve the lot of Edinburgh's poor. She didn't seem particularly prone to charity, but her son was encouraging it, so she went. I wondered what the ladies thought of her, if she said much or if she concealed her scanty education by stitching studiously while others traded gossip and household recipes.

Cook had offered to send preserves for the ladies' hampers, but I was keeping out of it. Mrs. Burnett and I managed best when we stayed out of each other's way. Any offers I made would be swiftly rejected, even if I'd wanted to earn her approval.

Her room was prettier now, with lighter curtains and new sheets, but I didn't find extra keys. It was the same in Burnett's, though his washstand was more disordered, the basin filmed from his shaving water, his used towel tossed onto the floor.

I wiped the basin, straightened his razor and shaving brush, and hung up the towel, then swept the room with a disappointed glance. No keys. No specimen records. Nothing.

And the police didn't come.

On my half day, I returned to Greyfriars Kirkyard—where I'd arranged to meet Jenny, in case she needed help. This wasn't the first or even the second time I'd looked for her again. After walking the paths for an hour, the verger braved the rain, abandoning his room in the little gatehouse and approaching me through the drizzle.

"Can I help you, ma'am? Is there a grave you're looking for?"

"No, thank you." More explanation seemed necessary because he studied me with a puzzled frown. "I'm just—just organizing my thoughts."

I left soon after, crossing the Mile to brave a walk down Lady Wynd, reminding myself there was no reason to be squeamish. I cleaned a room full of body parts, but it was still necessary to press my lips together, to look past the poverty and pretend I was impervious to the smells. Jenny said her house was ninth from the corner. Next to the others, it appeared of sound constitution and reasonably clean.

A woman sat on the step, smoking a pipe, saving me from knocking on the door.

"Do you live here?"

She nodded, blowing a long stream of smoke. She might have been forty or eighty—her face was brown as shoe leather, and though her eyes were clear, the crisp curls peeking from beneath her bonnet were white as winter frost.

"I'm looking for Jenny."

"Not here. Left a week ago at least. Took her clothes too."

I frowned, stepping closer. "She's gone?"

"Said so, didn't I?"

I couldn't argue with that. "Did she say—"

The woman rolled her eyes at me. "For the last time, she didn't. And you might as well tell whatever man it is that sent you that none of us has the least idea where that girl's gone."

The skin on my arms prickled. I licked my lips. "What man?"

She took a long draw from the pipe. Shrugged.

"What did he look like?" I glanced over my shoulder, but no one was paying us any mind. "I'm trying to help her. I'm worried she isn't safe."

She seemed to consider, squinting at the space behind my shoulder. "Hard to say what the fellow looked like."

I reached into my pocket, drew out a coin without looking at it, and pressed it into her swiftly appearing palm. Just as quickly, her hand curled into a fist and vanished. "Was he dark? Tall?" I asked.

"Might have been. Not so dark as me, but not many are," she said, and coughed a laugh. "He had his coat turned up and his hat low. Didn't stay once I said the girls were gone. Wasn't interested in any of the other ones."

"You knew Lizzie?"

She nodded. "Know 'em both. Fine girls. This is my house."

I nodded, uninterested in the property or the character reference. "No name?"

She gave me a pitying look. I tried again, guessing names didn't mean much here, where folk probably offered false ones simply from habit. Jenny and Lizzie's surname almost certainly wasn't Dove.

"Was his voice—" I hesitated, wondering how to describe Burnett's baritone. "Pitched between the low and high tones," I said. "And—" I circled a hand. "Carrying."

This time her expression suggested I was taking leave of my senses. "I'm just trying to explain," I said.

"I know. I wish I'd paid more mind. I didn't know—" She shook her head. "Jenny said she'd find Lizzie. And she was being careful. Wasn't working at all. Barely left the house—nearly always had me walk with her. She said someone was helping her. But I don't think she'd have stayed away this long, not if she had any say in the matter."

She stared at the pipe, turning it round in her hands. "I wish I had more to tell you, but—" Her hands turned upward, and her shoulders sagged.

"If you notice something or remember anything else—" I stopped. I couldn't give my name or leave an address. "I'll come back and ask again."

Again, the eyes were pitying.

"Just be on the watch, will you?"

She nodded, but I could tell she didn't think it would help.

That night, when I carried the coffee tray into the consulting office, Burnett was deep in a newspaper, his stocking feet propped on the footstool, his coat tossed on the opposite chair.

I set down the tray, poured him a cup, and stirred milk and sugar into it.

"Thank you, Ross." Lately, he'd taken to referring to me by my last name only, like the gentry tended to do with their housekeepers. Yesterday, Maggie had said he was acting "like he's born to the purple," which had earned her a swat from Mrs. Williams.

I crossed in front of the fire and shook out the discarded coat so wrinkles wouldn't set into it. No keys jingled, but there was a weight in the right-hand pocket.

"This is a little damp, sir. And there's a spot on this sleeve. I'll just sponge it off, and hang it in your bedchamber—there's a fire going, so it'll dry just as quickly up there."

Maggie would have said "in a jiffy," but these days Burnett didn't like his servants using slang.

He nodded. No thank-you this time. I gathered the coat, and hurried away as if I had wings on my heels.

I dipped my hand into the pocket the moment I gained the hall. Burnett's ring held four keys—one to the front door, one to his collection, one to the consulting office, and the smallest one for the drawers of his desk. I had my own copies of the first two. Only the sharp-edged consulting office key and the dainty silver one held me back. I slipped the key ring into my pocket, plotting out my surreptitious search as soon as Burnett quit the room, when he called me back, freezing me on the stairs.

"Ross?"

"Yes, sir?" Like any good servant, I would normally have returned to the room with my answer, but I could barely force the words past my seizing throat.

Burnett didn't notice the omission. Instead of waiting for me, he went on, his voice even and unconcerned. "I believe my keys are in the pocket. Bring 'em back, will you?"

Weight settled on me, a giant hand trying to squash me into the steps. The metal keys burned inside my tightly closed fist.

Think like a thief, lassie.

I didn't know this voice, and though it sounded only in my head, I swore the breath of a conspiratorial whisper swept past my face, stirring the loose strands of my hair.

With my free hand, I reached into my mouth, pulling the pads of wax from my cheeks. Warm and wet and slippery, I wrapped them around the two keys that stymied me, then carefully pried them loose and slipped the wax impressions into my pocket, praying they'd survive intact until I could hide them in my room.

Drying the keys with my skirt, I waltzed back to Burnett, wearing my calmest smile, trying to hide the natural contours of my face. The room was brighter than before—my imagination, unless he'd actually turned up the lamp.

"Here you are, doctor."

I placed them in his outstretched hand, and he nodded, eyes still on his book.

Now I just needed to find a locksmith who thought like a thief too.

Unfortunately, I spent the next day settling accounts, writing lists, and negotiating with the woman who came two days a week to do laundry. Mrs. Burnett had hired her at the urging of a newfound acquaintance among her church ladies. A pleasant enough soul, but she wouldn't have been my pick, and her cut-rate prices were contributing to Dr. Burnett's unhappiness regarding matters of starch. Last week's cravats hadn't been crisp enough; he was turning finicky just as my patience waned and my preoccupations grew.

So before I could puzzle out a plan to locate a willing locksmith, I found myself cleaning the drawing room again, running my duster over the shelves with a new mixture of polish I'd concocted myself with witch-hazel extract instead of lemon oil. The scent was clear and piercing, not dissimilar from my previous recipe, but it soothed me in a way the other could not. Maybe the polish or the care I took with this room would also comfort any troubled spirits lingering here.

As I rubbed a high gloss into the walnut table supporting Mr. Grant's femur and its enormous osteoma, the voice of an earlier whisper floated up to me, raising the hairs on my neck as the words climbed my spine.

You make your own chances.

My hands didn't slow. I simply nodded, barricading the way to thoughts that might question my judgment or wonder from where this counsel came.

"My own chance," I murmured.

"What *are* you talking about, Ross?"

I set down the bottle of polish and turned to face the grumbler behind me. "Good afternoon, Mrs. Burnett. I didn't realize you were back."

I'd been too wrapped up to hear either door, and—I frowned, studying her more closely. "Are you well, ma'am?" The sweat beading on her forehead argued against it. So did the pale cheeks and graying lips.

"Please sit down," I said, quickly taking her arm.

"Don't touch me!" She crossed herself, stepping away from me and closer to the settee in the middle of the room. "Hurts like fire."

"Let me get you some sherry." Cook had some in the kitchen. It might be the thing to restore her. She looked like a drawing, faded from too many years spent facing the sun.

"No, just some—" She broke off, her face contorting with pain.

I rushed to her, plucking at the buttons of her coat. "You're not well, ma'am."

She must have been too frightened or too pained to contradict me. This time, she didn't even swipe at my hands. "Mrs. Williams!" I called. "Tea and sherry for Mrs. Burnett. Quickly!"

She arrived as if I'd conjured her, drying her hands on her apron, the bottle of sherry tucked under one arm. Breathless from her dash up the stairs, she thrust the bottle at me. "Maggie's coming with tea."

I looked around me for a glass, but Mrs. Williams hadn't carried up any. I uncorked the bottle and brought the rim to Mrs. Burnett's lips.

She moved her face away.

"Just a wee stiffener, ma'am." Mrs. Williams urged. "Your color is dreadful. Why those ladies would expect you to walk to the church on such a hot day—"

I righted the bottle, afraid Mrs. Burnett would sputter on her two small sips, but she downed both.

"Let's take off your coat." I set aside the bottle and tugged at her sleeve. Mrs. Williams took the other side, and we soon had her out of it.

"I'm feeling better," she said, expelling words between shallow breaths.

"Don't stand yet, ma'am. Give yourself another moment or two."

She had a little color in her cheeks by the time Maggie arrived with a tea tray. "We should send for the doctor," I said.

"Rubbish," Mrs. Burnett said. "No need to trouble him. He's lecturing."

Mrs. Williams didn't argue, though I could tell from the set of her chin she agreed with me. "Let Miss Ross and I take you upstairs. Rest is what you need after a spell like this. Maggie can bring up the tray."

Mrs. Burnett rose to her feet unaided, with no sign of pain. Still, Mrs. Williams and I stayed close beside her as she climbed the stairs.

"See, it's nothing," Mrs. Burnett said, when she gained the upstairs floor, though she was quite short of breath.

"Just the heat," I agreed, and offered my arm, but she looked away, taking Mrs. Williams's.

When we reached the bedchamber, Mrs. Williams decreed it was necessary for Mrs. Burnett to change into comfortable clothes. While she and Maggie divested the mistress of her dress with its rows of hooks and tiny buttons, she mouthed to me over the lady's head.

"Fetch the doctor."

I nodded.

It was relatively quiet in Surgeon's Square when I crossed over to Burnett's Institute of Anatomy. A placard hung from the closed door.

Lecture in session. No latecomers admitted.

I knocked. Twice.

Finally an elderly porter in a new-looking coat opened the door.

"Ma'am?" He seemed astonished.

"Janet Ross. I'm Dr. Burnett's housekeeper. His mother just had a spell. I thought—"

The man's forehead creased. "Dr. Burnett's in the middle of a lecture. I can't—"

"If you just let me into the room, he'll see me and understand that something's wrong. She's recovering in bed, and the cook is watching her, but he'll want to examine her."

He hesitated.

"I clean his specimen room," I said. "I'm his housekeeper. I won't be distressed by the lecture."

"All right," he said. "This way."

Compared to this building, Burnett's home was extraordinarily modest. Our feet tapped a brisk tempo down the long-tiled corridor, lit by a wall of long windows facing the square.

"That's the laboratory," the porter grunted when I veered to the first door. "Next one's the theatre."

He stopped outside it. "Don't talk to anyone. Don't interrupt the lecture. Wait for the end or for Dr. Burnett to come to you. And stay at the back."

I nodded. Unwrapping his hands, tangled together with misgiving, he turned the knob and ushered me in.

At first all I saw was a dark wall, but when I turned my head,

I discovered a narrow flight of stairs. Soft-footed, I climbed them, timing my steps to a steady bass rhythm of muffled words. Above, the place opened to a brilliantly lit theatre, obscured by a barricade of closely packed shoulders. Burnett's voice, clearer now, marched relentlessly, accompanied by a furious scratching of pens.

I stepped closer, looking for a gap, skirting the ranks of pupils, two and three deep, pressed against a railing. At the end of the row, I saw that there were four U-shaped tiers, arranged in widening, ascending arcs, from a central area holding Burnett, Ferguson, the other assistant, Jones, and a partially disassembled body stretched out on a table. I stepped closer, and the nearest student—he was taller than the ones beside him—looked over his shoulder. Immediately I retreated, pressing my back against the wall, but he studied me for a moment from the corner of his eye. I retreated farther, edging back to the middle of the curve.

Burnett's voice followed me.

"Thanks to the excellent work of Mr. Jones, I'm able to present you with an unparalleled view of the arm and shoulders before we turn our attention to the feminine organs—here, on the left, when we retract the"—in my mind's eye, I saw him gesturing with a baton, like my father had, leading an orchestra—"the lower branches of the bronchi."

I glanced up, at the windows, but though all were open, the room was unpleasantly warm. A few of the students looked back at me, but none were willing to spare more than a glance from their notes and the body below, intent as vultures on the feast lying on Burnett's demonstration table. I pressed my hands to my stomach and leaned against the wall, disappearing into the sound of Burnett's voice: sonorous, controlled, regular. He'd never see me back here. I'd have to wait until the end.

Stay calm, Isobel.

The minutes stretched unbearably.

Finally there was a surge of motion and sound: students talking, chuckling, closing their books, and preparing to leave. I caught plenty of askance looks, but most passed by without pausing. I was out of place, but I didn't look important.

Then, I caught a pair of dark eyes in a face higher than most, coming toward me from the far edge of the row. I turned away, sheltering behind my bonnet, convinced I'd been mistaken. Counting silently, I waited for the man who looked like Adam Kerr to pass by me.

At fifty, I glanced up and saw I'd judged wrong. He was almost in front of me, frighteningly close. I thought of my eyebrows, my padded cheeks, my strange but seemingly effective herbal charm. Uprooting my feet, I pushed away from Kerr, into the flow of students pouring toward the lower tiers, the stairs, and the lecture theatre door. Until I lost Kerr, I couldn't be seen by Burnett. No one could be allowed to piece my two lives together.

I veered between two students, talking earnestly and gesturing with their hands, and darted for the stairs. Out in the hall, I hurried away from the students crowding around the cloak room, toward the doors at the end of the hall. I'd hide someplace until the crowd was gone, then find Burnett.

"Watch out," someone said, and I stepped aside, half stumbling when I turned and saw that two students were propelling the body just used in the demonstration toward me on a wheeled table, without any covering sheet. When I'd glimpsed her from above, naked and largely deconstructed, I'd missed an important detail. Her face was intact, waxen and bruised, but with a lovely profile, and a head of fine flax hair.

A pair of hands caught me as I swayed on my feet.

"Careful, madam. I don't think you're meant to be here."

I glanced up. Kerr.

I stepped out of his grip, dropping my eyes to his shoes. "You're mistaken. I work for Dr. Burnett. I'm here with a message for him."

His hand reached out, closing hard on my arm. "Is that so?" He stepped closer, whispering angrily. "What are you doing here, Isobel?"

"You aren't a student," I countered.

"I am for this course," he replied.

"Gynecology?" I said, incredulous. I'd understood enough of the lecture to glean that much.

"I'm following up on a tip from an informer. She came to me, recommended by—she said—the doctor's own housekeeper, but I didn't imagine—"

"Not here." I silenced him with a quick sideways jerk of my head. He took a long breath.

"Tonight's lecture was very informative," he said. "You didn't notice?" He motioned with his eyes to the table, receding down the hall.

I frowned.

"Look closer," he commanded under his breath.

I forced my gaze back to the exposed body as the table turned right and disappeared through a door. The arm nearest us stopped at the wrist. "Wha—

"Left hand," Kerr muttered.

I bit my lip, confused for a slow, stretched second. Then comprehension seized me, sharp, ice-cold, and bitter.

"It's missing."

"Exactly."

Lizzie. Her hand with the extra finger.

"She could be our missing girl," Kerr whispered.

I was going to be sick.

"Quiet. He's coming." Kerr didn't wait to see if I listened. As he spoke, he slipped away into the crowd. I spun around and found myself face-to-face with Burnett.

{ 25 }

Conall frowned at his housekeeper. "Miss Ross? What are you doing here?" His eyes flicked to the man who'd just left her. Detective Adam Kerr was completely humorless, rumored to be part Indian, and memorable for the simple fact that, not so long ago, he'd questioned Conall with insulting persistence about a juvenile heart in his collection—a remarkable specimen and a valuable instructional tool, though Kerr hadn't seemed to see that.

So why was he here? And why was Miss Ross?

"Do you know that man?" Conall demanded. The police barely troubled to work themselves, nearly always relying on informants, so—

"I don't know him," Miss Ross denied sharply. "He—he was—" She swallowed, cheeks burning. "I suppose I shouldn't be here."

"Was he disrespectful?"

No admission, just a heightening of the color on her face.

"Wait here." Conall strode after the detective, relishing the thought of taking him to task—what business had he here anyway? He wasn't a student. He shouldn't be allowed.

But it was unexpectedly hard to find him, even in the thinning crowd. Conall frowned and quickened his pace, scanning both sides of the hall, finally catching him just as he slipped out the door, his shoulders hunched and his hat pulled low.

"Kerr!" Other students stopped and stared, but not the detective. Conall darted after him, shoving his way through the door. "Kerr!"

Already the man was halfway across the square. Conall broke into a run, pelting after him and grabbing his shoulder.

"Hey." Kerr wheeled around, brushing his coat and looking offended.

"Detective Kerr."

He didn't deny it, and there was something both infuriating and unsettling in his stare.

"What are you doing in my school?" Conall demanded, face heating, annoyed he'd had to run.

Kerr reached into his pocket and held out a card identical to the ones the other students carried—an admission ticket to the current gynecology course.

Conall snatched it, turning it over in his hand. Not a fake. The Institute's seal was engraved clearly above the penciled registration number, and the porter's signature was written boldly across the back. "I've paid the fee," Kerr said laconically.

"Why haven't I seen you here before?" Conall demanded.

Kerr shrugged. "The others make me stand at the back."

"Yes, but why come at all? This isn't your line of work." Conall tugged his coat, tired of sparring from the wrong foot. He was on firm ground here. A police detective might attend forensic lectures, though this was stretching the point.

Kerr flexed his mouth into a mechanical smile. "Heard you put on a good show. I've taken an interest. Forgive me, but I can't stay. Have another appointment." He touched the brim of his hat and walked away with such an air of purpose, Conall didn't dare follow. He'd only look ridiculous, chasing him. Choking back a mouthful of profanity—words beneath his station—Conall marched back inside.

"Take that man's ticket away," he snapped at the porter. "I don't want him here again."

"Certainly, Dr. Burnett."

"Sir—"

"What?!" He rounded on Miss Ross, and she shrank, her eyelids dropping and her lips pressing together.

"I'm sorry," Conall said. God, he was making a scene.

"It's your mother," Miss Ross murmured, so quiet he had to strain to hear. "She had a spell. I came to fetch you."

Bloody hell. And he hadn't even readied tomorrow's specimens.

"Perhaps I shouldn't have interrupted you, but we thought it best. She's never taken faint before," Miss Ross added.

"No, no, you did right," Conall said, deliberately loosening his jaw. "I'd best hurry back." Sam, the porter, held out his hat, stick, and coat. Conall was halfway out the door before he realized Miss Ross wasn't following.

"You might as well ride in the carriage with me," he said, and she scurried after him.

His usual hired driver was waiting at the end of the square, and though she hesitated before joining him, she climbed inside without a word. They lurched into motion, and Conall turned his face to the window and his mind to the previous scene, studying his housekeeper from the corner of his eye. Kerr had been standing extraordinarily close to Miss Ross, close enough to trade whispers. At one point, his hands had been on her arms—though she'd looked startled by the body on the stretcher passing by. Maybe he'd simply taken the chance to manhandle her.

It was unlike her, though, to be upset by the tangible efforts of his work. He couldn't think why the body on the cart today had distressed her, when she'd always exhibited admirable composure.

He tilted his head at her. "You're certain you haven't seen that man before?"

No flushes this time. She was her usual self, untroubled as a painted madonna. "Quite sure, doctor. He didn't impress me as a pleasant fellow, but I doubt our paths will cross again."

Conall shifted in his seat. "Well, you're right, I'm afraid. He isn't pleasant. Not at all the type you'd wish to know."

"Then how does he know you?" she asked. "Is he training to be a doctor?"

Conall snorted. "I doubt it."

"Then why is he interested in you?" Something in her level stare unsettled him.

"He's a half-breed. Works for the police." But instead of looking repulsed, her eyebrows rose.

"The police? What do they want from you?"

Mentioning that was a mistake. Now he was compelled to explain.

"Our paths crossed some time ago," Conall admitted. "There were some unpleasant rumors. A professional matter."

"So Mr. Kerr was a patient?" Her eyes held his, as if she was divining his thoughts instead of waiting for an answer.

"Not exactly… no," Conall said, adjusting his cravat. "Suffice it to say, he didn't impress me as a genteel kind of person."

"I see." Her hands traded places on her lap, right over left. "And he didn't think you'd done anything wrong."

A half second's pause, as Conall fumbled for his best world-weary sigh. He supposed he was grateful for her hard work, and that made it harder to prevaricate. "I don't know. I was hoping you might help me understand that, but if he didn't say anything to you…"

"Nothing," she said, and his shoulders eased, until she glanced up at him. "At least, nothing that made any sense."

She shifted her hands, left over right this time, arranging them like she was waiting to be sculpted. "Your mother will be very glad to see you, doctor. She doesn't like to admit it, but…"

Smiling mechanically, Conall let her continue, nodding at intervals yet examining a very different problem internally—ways to make the police dismiss Adam Kerr.

{ 26 }

I stared out the carriage window, my breath leaving in a rush. Kerr believed me. In spite of what he'd said when I told him about the heart (cautions and excuses, mostly) he must have questioned Dr. Burnett. My whole body tingled, as if I'd just touched one of those glowing blue jars charged with vital electricity. It was hard to keep still, and even if my hair wasn't actually standing on end, surely Burnett would notice the effort to restrain my restless hands or the color flooding my face.

Luckily, there was his mother to discuss, and once we returned home, to tend.

After a thorough bleeding, Dr. Burnett informed her (and Mrs. Williams and me) that she needed a few days in bed and to carry some smelling salts. Horrified at the suggestion, she took some cajoling from her son before accepting this as a legitimate treatment for spells of faintness and pain, not merely a fashionable affectation.

Still, the salts disappeared into a drawer every time she was left alone in her room. Lightheaded and fretful from the cupping (Burnett's leeches had taken a surprising amount of blood), she was edgy with everyone, even Mrs. Williams, who thankfully took on most of her care.

We were all tired, she and Maggie and I, spending much more time abovestairs, though things were not so behind that Burnett was required in the kitchens. But I found him there when I returned downstairs to fetch more hot water.

"Doctor? Can I help?"

He started, then smiled sheepishly. "Peckish, I'm afraid. Was hoping to find some bread and butter."

I pointed to the shelf behind him, and the loaf, wrapped in a green oilcloth next to the crock of butter.

"You really should let us fetch it for you," I said, with just enough edge to raise a blush. "If you moved one of Mrs. William's saucepans, she might never forgive you."

"You're right. I just—you've all been busy caring for my mother. I didn't want—"

"It's our job." I waited, and a moment later he realized I wanted him to move away from the shelf. He scooted to the other side of the table.

"Jam too?" I asked, knowing his liking for it.

"If there's more of the strawberry…"

"Of course." I added the jar to the tray, then sawed two thick slices off the loaf. "I suppose there's no law against you eating in the kitchen, but it is startling to find you here, sir, if you'll forgive me for saying so."

He smiled. "N—yes, I mean. And I'm happy to take it upstairs."

He held out his hands, and I surrendered the tray. When he quit the room, I walked around, wondering what he'd really come down for. Everything looked undisturbed, and my bedroom door was always locked. I frowned at it, thinking of the wax impressions of his keys still hidden behind the folded stockings at the back of my drawer. I thought I had all the household keys except his, but now I wasn't sure.

I wasn't the only one capable of snooping. Burnett could order extra keys much more easily than me.

I couldn't afford to be careless.

It took only a second to unlock the door and retrieve the wax impressions. But the stone-flagged floor, the painted brick walls, and simple furniture left few options for concealment. My eyes landed on the washstand, and the silver snuffbox that had been my father's and now held my pins and a lock of Thomas's hair.

I unsnapped the lid and tipped out the pins. But Thomas's hair... I crossed the room to the little writing desk and tore off the bottom of a greengrocer's bill, folding the soft golden lock into the paper and wedging it into the snuffbox lid. Then, half-afraid they were already gone, I reached into the drawer for the wax imprints of Burnett's keys. They were still behind my stockings and just fit inside the box.

From now on, I'd carry them with me.

Sunday evening, Maggie was busy at Cook's elbow, helping her with tomorrow's baking and listening raptly to another ghost story. The fire was warm, my feet tired, and I ought to have found the room inviting, but I felt off-kilter around Maggie, especially times like now, seeing her healthy and happy, knowing how disastrously different things could have been.

And I was still unsettled about Burnett's foray to the kitchen, by his questions about Adam Kerr. Judging from his presence in the lecture, and what he'd said, he must have spoken to Jenny. But after being chased away by Burnett, would he keep looking? Or was I on my own? Jenny was missing now, too, and I shrank at thinking what might have become of her.

I couldn't count on Kerr's help or hers, so my best way forward was still Burnett's keys. I had to take the wax impressions to a lock-smith, but if I approached the wrong one, he might report me to the police unless I had enough money hidden away to buy silence.

Wishing I'd learned less music and more about bribes, I carried the broom outside. The August days were warm and dry, with no rain to rinse dirt from the street or dust from the doorstep. I smiled at the maid from next door, busy polishing the knocker, her sweeping already finished. Never one for idle chatter, she only smiled back, leaving me free to attack the grime lodged in the corners.

When these were clean I stretched my back, catching a glimpse of the brown spaniel and retired Navy lieutenant who lived across the street. They proceeded down the close, on their usual after-dinner stroll. The dog glanced my way, but I was beneath the notice of the naval officer. Finished with the front door, I began sweeping my way down the servant's steps, putting off the moment when I'd have to return to Maggie and Mrs. Williams through the kitchen door.

"I see you decided not to be careful," a familiar voice said. I looked up, because down here, I was six steps below the street, my eyes level with Adam Kerr's boots.

"I can't talk here," I said tightly, and turned away, chasing dirt from the corners with my broom.

"I can't understand why you are here at all. I nearly died of sur-prise when I saw you get into a carriage with him. He's dangerous. You know that. You've got to come away."

"No." I might not know precisely how to do it yet, but I had a partial plan, and Burnett had to be stopped.

"I've been watching for you," Adam said.

"Don't. He asked if I knew you. I said I didn't."

His throat bobbed and his eyes flicked to the windows.

"When's your half day?" he asked.

"Tuesday."

"And you go out? Where?"

I thought about turning my back, marching into the kitchen, and slamming the door, leaving him with a stymied face and nothing to say. My belly warmed with satisfaction. But he might just come back. I didn't want that, and maybe...

Adam Kerr must know all kinds of locksmiths.

I jerked my head right, wordlessly indicating the craggy mount that overlooked the city. "I take Piper's Way."

"I'll meet you there," he murmured, and walked away, giving me no chance to reply.

A new specimen arrived without warning the following afternoon, in the arms of Burnett's porter, the same man I'd seen guarding the door of the anatomy school.

"For the salon, ma'am. Dr. Burnett said to bring it right inside."

"He didn't say anything to me about this."

The porter shifted, so I could see more of his face behind the wooden box. "Well, he forgets sometimes..."

"And what's that?" I motioned at the wicker hamper sitting on the step beside him.

The porter shrugged. "Grocery delivery?"

I shook my head. Groceries came Tuesdays and Fridays, save for the odd things Maggie and I went out for.

"Dunno," he said. "But I didn't bring it. So will ye keep me waiting or—"

"Bring it in." I stepped away from the door and he carried in both box and basket while I unlocked the salon. Leaving the unknown delivery in the hall—a puzzling find, since we weren't in the habit of receiving unlabeled packages—the porter preceded me into the salon, setting to work immediately on the cords tied around the crate. Inside, swaddled in a bed of straw, was yet another jar.

I turned my face to the window.

"I'll just pull it out for you."

"Yes, put it on the table. I'll find a place for it." I pressed damp hands to my skirts, unable to look or think of anything but Lizzie Dove's missing left hand. I could almost hear Burnett telling his visitors about it.

"You all right, ma'am?"

I mustered a smile. "Of course. Please tell Dr. Burnett the specimen's arrived safely and—"

"They've arrived," he corrected, smoothing back his greasy hair.

Frowning, I glanced without thinking and gasped.

The porter grinned. "Something, aren't they?"

This jar was much smaller than the box that held it and far too small for an adult human hand. Inside was something quite different—two mismatched eyes, one brown, one green, set alongside each other on some sort of glass frame inside the jar.

"You wouldn't think it, but they came from one woman. That's what the doctor told me."

I swallowed, telling myself these eyeballs couldn't possibly be scanning the room. It was just my imagination or the movement of liquid in the jar. "I haven't seen eyes as specimens until now," I said, my voice high and thin.

"Maybe you should sit down," the porter suggested. He seemed to enjoy my distress, and that rallied me, even if it didn't cure my churning stomach.

"Not necessary," I said firmly, to make it true. "Did Dr. Burnett want anything else?"

"No, nothing else."

I hurried the porter out of the house and was bolting the door when Mrs. Burnett exclaimed behind me, "Oh, good! They're here."

I'd have liked a cup of tea or a splash of cool water on my face. Instead, I composed myself again and turned around. "Do you mean this hamper? Is it yours, ma'am? I wasn't at all sure what to do about it. It seems to have simply appeared, and you can see there's no label."

"Donations," she explained hastily. "I'm bringing them to the parish, but it won't hurt to take a look first. There may be something Mrs. Williams might like." She hesitated, adding grudgingly, "Or you, I suppose."

I almost suggested she go through the basket first, and I wouldn't have put it past her. Instead, I produced a hard smile—so many in so short a time made my face ache—and said, "That's very thoughtful of you, ma'am."

"Maggie!" Mrs. Burnett called. "Come help Ross carry this down to the kitchen!"

Just get it over with, I told myself. *It won't be worse than eyeballs.*

Maggie, of course, was too young and from too poor a family to have scruples against picking the best from a basket of donated clothes.

"Oh, how pretty!" Face alight, she held up a tartan shawl, then, not wanting to look greedy—"It would look lovely on you, Miss Ross."

"My old one is fine, but you could use one for cold days." Seeing her smile, I chided myself—I had no right to be sanctimonious. "It brings out the color of your eyes," I told her.

Maggie carefully folded the shawl and set it aside before diving back into the basket. She was so excited, it was easy for the rest of us to sit back and watch her, letting her judge what might suit each of us. It was a motley collection, including a repulsive pair of old trousers, some crumpled hair ribbons, stockings in need of darning (Mrs. Williams offered to fix those so they'd be fit to wear by some poor soul), a velvet jacket too small for any of us women, and too large and far too fine (so Mrs. Burnett decreed) for Maggie. A feathered bonnet, only slightly battered about the brim, was quickly appropriated by Mrs. Burnett herself.

"And why not?" said Mrs. Williams quickly. "None of us should be too proud to make use of something that still holds use in it. Isn't that right, Miss Ross?"

I couldn't agree with her heartiness, but I did produce a nod, busying myself refolding a pair of trousers.

"Look at these gloves, ma'am," Mrs. Williams said to Mrs. Burnett. "They're in very good repair."

"Might I give this to my brother?" Maggie asked, holding out a knitted cap. "His is getting worn."

"Of course you can," Mrs. Burnett said, setting the gloves beside her new bonnet. "He's a hardworking boy. Deserving."

"And look at this—see how lovely?" With a flourish, Maggie held up a green wool skirt. Her glance, quickly flying between the three of us, revealed that, too late, she'd seen her error. It was a fine skirt—but it would only fit my waist, not Mrs. Burnett's or Mrs. Williams. "I'm sure it could be altered," she added.

"May I have a look?"

Maggie thrust the skirt at me gratefully, pleased to have it out of her hands before anyone else said anything. I held it up, examining the weave and color of the wool in the light from the kitchen window. In spite of myself, my hand ran along a well-turned seam.

"It's very—" I broke off, remembering another voice.

Almost new. She has a skirt to match—I sewed it for her.

Green wool. Just like the jacket Jenny wore, which she swore her sister Lizzie would never leave behind. Lizzie had worn the matching skirt to her appointment with Dr. Burnett.

The light in the room dimmed, retreating beneath a black wave. I reached out a hand to steady myself. In front of me, Maggie's mouth moved, but I couldn't hear. My ears were stopped by the sound of someone's labored breathing.

"I can't see," I said, as everything went dark.

But I could still hear the breathing.

Blurs came back to me, swirls of brown and orange, surrounding a bright blaze that might have been a lamp—if my eyes were clear enough to make sense of things. I thrashed and kicked, for although those panting breaths filled my ears, my lungs burned and ached to the point of bursting. I couldn't move my head, but the rest of me writhed, needing freedom, needing air. For a half second, I jerked away, and though I gasped a mouthful, I got no more than that, pinned again by the weight on my mouth, and the mass holding tight to my green skirts.

"Janet! Janet!"

"I'm here," I croaked, hoping this would convince Mrs. Williams to stop slapping me. "I'm awake."

"Drink this."

There was nothing wrong with my eyes now. The kitchen was exactly as it was, strewn with clothes, lit from the window, not some hideous blur of a lamp.

I swallowed and coughed. "Can I have tea?" I didn't like sherry.

"Don't let her faint again," Mrs. Burnett warned, and attacked with her smelling salts.

"I'm all right." I recoiled as far as I could (not much) into the back of my chair, pushing her hand away.

"You were having some kind of fit," Mrs. Williams said. "Kicking and shaking. And all without making any sound."

"It's nothing," I said. "See?" I pushed out of the chair, in spite of their restraining hands, and though they were surprised, I could see all of them wanted to believe me. Maggie was white as goose down, Mrs. Williams wrung her hands, and Mrs. Burnett was crossing herself and praying in Gaelic.

I crossed the room and unlatched the window. "I just need some air. These clothes are terribly musty."

Somehow, I wasn't even trembling, aware I couldn't alarm anyone, least of all Dr. Burnett. Returning to their circle of gaping mouths, I picked the skirt off the floor. "I like this very much. Do you think it suits me?"

Mrs. Williams gave a dumbfounded nod.

"I may have to raise the hem," I said, holding it up to me for a critical inspection.

"Just a little," Maggie said, glad to fall in with my assertion that nothing was wrong. "No more than an inch."

"I thought an inch and a half."

"I agree with the girl," Mrs. Burnett said, her gaze disapproving.

I nodded, as if the matter was settled. "I'll do it tomorrow," I said. More than anything, I wanted to grab the skirt and run, but I had a role to maintain, so I folded the skirt into my lap and myself into another chair, one closer to the breeze from the window.

"How much more do you have in there, Maggie?"

{ 27 }

I hope you think this is worth it," Fraser grumbled, watching another pair of constables setting out from the station. Though they'd never found the people running the workshop where Nan had been imprisoned, the Brennans' kidnapping trial was looming, and Adam was trying to be content with that. But earlier today a constable had been set on and beaten in the West Port—Cathcart, who'd been with Adam when he found Nan.

Adam hoped it was a random attack, but if Cathcart had been targeted, it didn't bode well for him, the girl, or the coming trial.

It might be a warning from the workshop owners—or the Ribbonmen—that they were fighting back.

"Our men will be fine in pairs," Adam said, for himself as much as Fraser. The Brennans might be crooked as the path to Hell, but they couldn't be important enough to warrant this kind of trouble. Cathcart's beating had simply been rotten luck, and his bruises and cracked ribs would heal. For now, increasing the number of constables in the West Port would keep everyone safer—and make certain this kind of thing didn't happen again. Everyone, Ribbonmen included, would learn not to trifle with the police.

Adam checked his watch. Nearly seven. Nan would be expecting him. "Once the trial's done and the Brennans awarded long sentences, the Ribbonmen—if they're connected to this—will know we won't be intimidated."

Fraser grunted. "If Stevenson doesn't back down."

"You think he will?" Adam frowned. "He didn't give me that impression when he agreed to prosecute the case." If anything, he seemed anxious to correct the perception that Ribbonmen could evade justice in the West Port.

"Since when have you had anything kind to say about Stevenson?"

"I don't have to like him to trust he'll do his job," Adam retorted. "It's a straightforward case."

And we'll be in the soup without him, he added silently. Stevenson wouldn't give up, not when they were this close to convicting Will and Ellie Brennan. Fraser was just broodier than usual, upset about what had happened to Cathcart.

"I should go. Getting late. Surprised you're still here." Adam forced a smile but couldn't quite keep the edge from his voice. "What will Sarah say?" Fraser's early departures from the station were starting to needle him.

His friend gave another grunt and a wry smile. "Nothing good, I promise you that. But listen, I've been thinking about that girl, Nan Burt. Where did she end up?"

"My stepmother found a place for her," Adam said, used by now to the lie. He wasn't taking chances with Nan's whereabouts, not until after the trial, even with Fraser. Their straightforward case would come to nothing without her testimony. "I forget the details."

"Hope she's all right. Poor thing."

Adam nodded. "Me too." He put on his hat. "Evening, Hugh."

"Give my best to Emily."

Adam just rolled his eyes.

It was dark by the time he returned home, but there were lights waiting. He still wasn't used to it. As he drew nearer the house, he noticed something different about his front door.

He broke into a run.

The door was shut and locked, just as it should be, but there was a message scrawled on the panels—*Beware halfbreed.*

"Nan!" he shouted, pulse climbing into his throat. He was used to casually delivered insults and snide whispers, but not this. Not right on the heels of Cathcart's beating. The Brennan case might be at the root of this trouble after all.

"Coming!" Nan's voice, muffled by the door, was untroubled. Relief seeped into his palms.

"Wait there. I'll be right in." He whipped out a handkerchief and scrubbed at the words, but only succeeded in smearing them, staining his handkerchief a rusty brown.

Blood.

A bead of cold sweat rolled down his spine. Nan couldn't stay here. It wasn't safe.

Clumsily, he stuffed the handkerchief into his coat pocket and unlocked the door. Nan was waiting for him inside, grinning like a monkey and bouncing on her toes.

"Did you find them?" she asked.

He'd completely forgotten. The blood on the door had driven everything else from his mind. On reflex, he patted his pocket. His finds from the pawnbrokers were still there. "Maybe." He peered back into the empty street, then locked and bolted the door.

"You were gone so long, I was sure you'd found them. Let me see."

Nan wouldn't talk about her mother's disappearance, but when she'd learned he was on the trail of another missing woman, she'd developed an interest. Adam wasn't sure it was good for her, but what did he know about children?

"Once we're in the kitchen," he said. "I'm starving." A lie. His appetite was gone, but the fire, the smell of soup, and Nan bustling about like she'd been keeping his house for years instead of a month eased his tension a little. He reached into his pocket, past the bloodstained handkerchief, retrieving the results of this afternoon's searching. "Here."

He set three pairs of simple gold earrings into her outstretched hand.

"These all look the same," she said.

"Nearly," he agreed. "It's what makes detecting so hard." It took persistence, patience, and time, narrowing the range of possibilities and chasing down leads. "We'll send these to Mrs. Dove and see if any belong to her missing sister."

"And if they don't?" Her voice caught; she wasn't just asking about earrings.

"We keep looking until we find her. Or until we find who's responsible."

And take care of you in the meantime, he added silently. "You stayed indoors today?" he asked, hiding his concern by tugging lightly at her ear.

"I always do," she said, ladling a bowl of soup from the pot over the fire. "I'm quiet, and the curtains stay shut."

"We should think again about school—"

She froze, ladle poised in midair. "Please. Please let me stay."

His stomach twisted. "It might be dangerous to stay with me. After the trial—"

"Did the Ribbonmen mark the door?" Caught off guard by her question, his face gave away the answer.

Nan cursed under her breath. She'd lived all her life in the West Port, even before her time on the streets. He'd no hope of hiding the truth from her.

"Someone did," he said uneasily, forcing the tension from his hands by pressing them flat on his knees.

"They don't know I'm here," she insisted, and set a bowl in front of him. "Marking the door is just a warning. You've upset them, is all. I'm safe here."

Adam wasn't as confident. But would she be any safer at a school? The trouble was, he was gone far too much. "Sit down," he said, nudging out the nearby chair with his foot.

"In a moment." Taking two mugs—he'd had to buy a second, smaller one for her, because he'd only owned the one—she filled them with ale and carried them to the table, setting them down without spilling a drop. Adam shifted guiltily in his seat and reminded himself at least her fingers weren't bleeding and scabbed from overwork now.

"School is important," he said. "More important than waiting on me."

Her hands tightened on her mug, the knuckles blanching as she lowered herself into her chair.

"Were *you* happy there?" she asked.

"I hated school," he admitted. Nan was afraid of being left again, so he took his luncheon at home every day now, and left his father's watch with her when he departed for work to help her keep time and trust he'd come back. He even slept on a pallet on the floor next to her bed, because it was the only way she could sleep.

But he wasn't much of a guardian: out at all hours, inexperienced, never mind the latest threat imposed by his work. And Nan would never manage school, not with the condescending attitudes or outright bullying that would come her way as surely it had to him. A child of Nan's class would be nearly as foreign and despised as he'd been.

He needed help, but there was no one to ask. Not if the Ribbonmen were after him.

Someone rapped on the door.

Adam jumped, but recovered quickly, reaching across the table and turning down the lamp. "Into the cupboard," he whispered.

Nan was usually painstakingly obedient, but her speed surprised him. She vanished in a blink. Moving slowly, without any sound, Adam left the table and closed the kitchen door. There was a pistol hidden in the hallstand. With that reassurance resting comfortably in his hand, Adam went to the door.

"Adam! Let me in!" A woman's voice. A familiar one.

Adam tucked the pistol in the back of his trousers and opened the door.

"What are you doing?" His stepmother demanded, stepping inside. "You never came to dinner. We were all expecting you. Your house is dark as a tomb and—"

She was small, barely up to his shoulder, red-haired and freckled, like both of her boys. Adam was the only one of the family who didn't look like he belonged. But even after his father died, nine years ago, Emily refused to let him loose, expecting him to dine once a fortnight, and forcing him into company with her sons, his half brothers. She was only six years older than Adam, and he'd never quite kicked his boyhood habit of standoffish resentment.

"Hello, Emily," he said.

She turned her cheek, and he bent to kiss it.

"I'm sorry," he said. "I completely forgot about dinner."

"It's not hard to remember. Every second Wednesday. I—" She let out a shriek, clutching his arm at a sound from the kitchen. A cupboard door opening. So much for obedience.

"Who's that? Who's here?" Emily demanded, alarmed by the noise in his darkened house, and perhaps a glimpse of his pistol.

Adam fumbled for words, and Emily's cheeks went scarlet.

"Holy Jesus. You're not alone. I mean—well, why should you be? I'm sorry. What a busybody—" Spinning on her heel, she practically lunged for the door.

Adam stopped her. "No, it's not what you think. I—I'm having some trouble at work." And a pushy stepmother might be just what he and Nan needed.

"Come into the kitchen, Emily," Adam said. "I'll explain everything."

Conall had felt only pride and satisfaction toward his housekeeper until he realized how much power she carried. It was a trifle disconcerting. She moved through much of the house unobserved, and had found her way inside the school and into conversation with Detective Kerr.

And Kerr didn't like him, not since they'd met over the matter of that hysterical mother's claims. He'd put them to rest quite efficiently—at least, he thought he had, until now.

Twice now, he'd seen the same man, a dirty organ grinder, within eyeshot of his house, watching the comings and goings. Even if the man was what he appeared, his presence put Conall on edge. He might notice things.

It ought to be a simple matter to stifle any qualms about Janet Ross's loyalties, but he couldn't get into her room. His mother didn't have the keys.

"You took them," she reminded him with a sniff. "I didn't want to give them to her."

His thumb twitched, a nervous habit he'd long since repressed, impeding both a surgeon's work and an anatomist's. Weaving his fingers together, he studied his hands, following the tendons to the tips of his fingers, visualizing the delicate architecture beneath the skin: the sheaths that allowed his tendons to glide and move and grip, the threadlike nerves and blood vessels, the bands of ligament that fastened bones together. In combination, a perfect miracle.

"You are always so pleased with her," his mother said waspishly, snaring his attention again. "I suppose she's been thieving."

"No, I don't think so," Conall said, alarmed at where this conversation might take him. Chances were, there was nothing to fear from Janet Ross. He valued her, and didn't want to rouse anger or suspicion if nothing troubling was there. "But some of my colleagues' wives told me they inspect their homes every so often, just as a matter of practice. Prevents carelessness and—and other things."

"Pity you didn't think of it earlier," his mother said. "I can't help you."

Mother's sitting room was much prettier now, though sadly deficient in keys. Conall drummed his hand on the occasional table at his elbow, topped with a lace-trimmed tablecloth.

He couldn't even have a locksmith in, because during the four hours or so Miss Ross had off each week, his other servants were here, and news of that kind couldn't be kept quiet. They'd probably all be offended.

"There's no money missing, is there?" his mother asked.

"No, no. I wouldn't stand for any of that," he assured her.

She set down her knitting, something lacy in fine burgundy wool. "I don't like to nag..."

"But..." he filled in, sure of what was coming.

"There's something not right about her," she insisted. "Something in the eyes."

"They seem to work just fine to me," he said, suppressing a smile. His mother's suspicions were always vague and unfounded. *Miss Ross has an odd face. Her hands aren't as plump as her middle. She buys bunches of odd flowers and uses scissors with her left hand.* As if he would ever worry about nonsense like that. "Try to like her," he said, for probably the twentieth time.

"She hired a wonderful cook for us," his mother said, in the tone of one making concessions. "Mrs. Williams is a treasure, and Maggie is hardworking, in spite of her sickly constitution."

"She's only been ill the once," Conall said. "You took sick yourself not long after." Seeing the beginnings of an affronted frown, he added, "Is the tonic still agreeing with you?"

She nodded, her face clearing. "Yes, and I do much better with it than my evening cup of tea, though I don't sleep as soundly."

"Well, if that's a trouble, I can prescribe some powders for that."

She tilted her head. "Can you?"

"Of course. Would you like some?"

She tapped her lips with her finger. "You haven't already tried them with me, have you?"

"Of course not!" Conall said, affronted. "But if you need them—"

"You know, I think I might. As long as it's no trouble—are they expensive?"

"Not at all," he promised.

"They aren't dangerous?"

"Not with me measuring them out for you."

"Thank you, Conall. You are very good to me."

She'd said the same words when he presented her with a silver medal from school, his first prize and his first real step forward. She'd sold it to pay the landlady, and to buy his next term's books.

"I'd be nothing without you," Conall said, as he bent to kiss her cheek. "Don't worry about the keys. It's not important."

He'd think of something. Already, the germ of an idea was taking root. There were other ways to test his housekeeper's loyalties.

{ 28 }

Tuesday afternoon couldn't come fast enough. Mrs. Burnett lurked everywhere I went, watching me sideways, but she only made excuses when I asked her what she wanted, and muttered in Gaelic more than ever. So as soon as she took her luncheon, I left Newington Place at a pace that quickly carried me beyond the houses to the base of the hill. A pair of gentleman were far up the path; another party of walkers was visible moving along the top of the crags. I waited, fidgeting with impatience, expecting to see Kerr, but the only person who appeared was a sandy-haired man with a pointer dog and a walking stick.

After about a quarter hour, I started the climb myself.

Had Kerr changed his mind? I couldn't believe it—he was investigating Burnett, just as I'd hoped, and he wouldn't want to miss our meeting, even just to scold me again. But I had a use for him, and if he didn't come—

"Afternoon, Isobel."

I yelped as Kerr emerged from a brush-filled dip in the ground, my hand flying to my throat. "You didn't have to ambush me," I snapped, once my heart steadied. "I waited for ages at the bottom of the track."

"I know. Didn't think you'd ever start climbing up."

"You were watching? Why didn't you—"

"Couldn't. I can't meet you in the open, not after Burnett saw me talking to you at the school. He might have seen me on your street and out there"—he motioned with his chin—"we're visible to anyone with a telescope."

I stared at him. "Are you mad?" No one in their right mind would do such a thing.

His lips thinned. "It's a reasonable precaution, if you and I are right about Lizzie."

"Ah. So now you believe he might be guilty of *actual crimes*?" It wasn't kind, hurling back his words, but they'd festered for a long time.

"Yes, I do. You're *in his house*, Isobel. That's worse madness than I've ever seen or heard."

"What else was I supposed to do?"

"Not that. The longer you keep on, the greater chance that you'll be the next body on his table."

I shook my head, cutting short the argument by holding out the basket on my arm. "Here. You said you need proof."

He took it gingerly, as if it might explode. Lifting the lid, he let out a sigh and drew out the skirt. "If you're expecting me to cry, 'Aha!' and run down to Newington Place shouting for the constables—"

"I think it's Lizzie Dove's," I explained.

He grunted. "And here I was, thinking you'd brought me her hand."

I shook my head. "I haven't seen it. But I'm watching. I met her sister, Jenny, after she came to the house, asking questions. She told me Lizzie was wearing a skirt this color when she went missing. It appeared at our house in a hamper of old clothes. The porter denies it, but I think he brought them over from Burnett's school."

Kerr folded it up, unimpressed. "Lots of people wear green."

"It's more than that. The sister, Jenny. She spoke to you, aye?"

He gave a reluctant nod. "I take it you sent her to me?"

I nodded. "She sewed this, and a matching jacket. She was wearing it when I met her, and so far as I can see, the fabric is the same."

I took a deep breath, crossing my fingers. "Do you know what's happened to her? I tried to find her again, but—"

"She's fine. She's in Leith. I gave her some money. Didn't want her disappearing too. Someone was following her. Come on, sit down." He motioned just beyond the brush, where his cloak was draped over one of the larger rocks.

I wanted to protest, but my calves were aching.

"It's a steep climb," Adam said apologetically. "But it's your usual route, as well as the least used path."

His makeshift bench was wide enough for two, but not comfortably. As I sat, he folded easily onto the ground, examining the skirt again, rubbing the wool between his fingers.

"You're sure we're safe from telescopes?" I asked.

He nodded, refusing to treat the question as a joke. I sighed, and tucked a loose strand of hair behind my ear.

"I don't know if he's killing people himself or paying others to do it, but he's dangerous, Isobel. You can't go back."

I reached down and picked a burr off my stocking. "Is the skirt proof enough to stop him?"

His breath left him in a gust, swirling up to join the birds circling the hill. "I'll show it to Lizzie."

Not a straight-out refusal, but definitely not a yes.

"I've been looking in local pawnshops, hoping to find Lizzie's earrings," he said. "Figured there was a decent chance of them turning up. If we had both—"

"You and I both saw the body," I put in. "So did all those students."

Kerr rubbed his cheek. "But we never met Lizzie, and the students are all loyal to him. So are most of the doctors in the city. Even the few that dislike him wouldn't go against him. Not for accusations like this. They look after their own."

"What about the rest of us? Lizzie. My Thomas? He can't just take people. If people knew, they'd—"

"Even if Jenny can identify the skirt and earrings, we have to prove they've been in Burnett's possession. It's not impossible, but it won't be easy."

"There's the hand," I suggested. Burnett had it somewhere. "If police search the school and I search the house—"

He shook his head. "I'd search both—if I had a warrant. Doubt we'll get one, if all we have is this." He touched the skirt, folded in a neat square on one of his knees. "I had to register for his course just to get inside."

"There's more evidence. I can find it."

He shook his head before I even finished speaking. "I don't want you to." He saw my look and sighed. "It's too great a risk."

"I won't need to stay much longer." I reached into my pocket for the silver box. It was warm in my hand. "Look."

I passed it to him and he flipped the catch.

"They're impressions of his keys, for the only places in the house I've been unable to search. But I unlocked his desk once before." I swallowed and busied myself smoothing the cuff on my wrist. "He had a drawing of the man with the scars. Eoin Brennan. The one I think took Thomas."

His head lifted. "Do you have it?"

I shook my head. "Saw it months ago. I didn't want to take it in case..." I'd planned on killing him then; a missing drawing would have made him suspect me.

Kerr winced. I reminded myself there was no way he could guess my thoughts. "Isobel..."

"Can you get me copies of these keys?" I interrupted, not wanting to hear another warning.

He hesitated. "I know a fellow," he admitted reluctantly. "But—"

"I'm not leaving. This is the best way for us to get proof. How many more will he kill if we wait to do things your way?"

I almost smiled when he had no answer for that.

"Two days," he said finally. "They'll come in a delivery of candles. You can get them before anyone else?"

I nodded.

He closed the box with a snap. As he carried it to his pocket, my heart lurched. "Detective."

"Hmm?" He paused and looked up.

"The paper in the lid. It has a lock of Thomas's hair."

"Oh. I'm sorry." He fumbled with the box—

"No, leave it there. Just—just keep it safe."

"Of course." For a moment he held it in both hands. Then, instead of reaching for the side of his coat, he slid it into his breast pocket. "It's safe with me, Isobel."

I reached for the empty basket, wanting to shift his gaze off me. In my life as Janet Ross, no one knew about Thomas or looked at me with painful pity, which made it easier to talk and eat and go about my days. My throat thickened. I didn't know if I wanted easier anymore.

"I should go." I picked up the empty basket. Twenty yards or so away, I looked back, but I couldn't see Kerr. Maybe he was concealed again by the brush. Maybe he'd already gone.

{ 29 }

A s soon as he came down from the hill, Adam sought out John
 Stevenson. It wasn't possible to go to anyone else, not for this.

He's doing a decent job with the Brennan trial, Adam reminded
himself. Because Stevenson hadn't given up. Since Cathcart's injuries, he'd been questioning the Brennans so relentlessly it was a
wonder they hadn't pled guilty yet. The trial was just two days
away.

Adam didn't find Stevenson at his home. He wasn't even in the
Crown Office, behind his desk. Following the advice of his clerk,
Adam found him walking off Bruntsfield Links after a game of golf.

Though surprised to spot Adam, Stevenson greeted him with a
smile. "Hello, Kerr. I didn't know you play."

"Once in a while," Adam admitted. Only rarely since the death
of his father, but he owed Emily for watching Nan, and she wanted
him to teach his brothers the game in exchange. A poor trade, since
he figured they'd all enjoy it, but Emily seemed happy enough to
have Nan about during the day, now that his brothers were away
at school.

"Finished your game?" Adam asked, looking at Stevenson's
companions: other lawyers, talking a few paces away.

Stevenson nodded. "We're headed to the Golf Tavern for a drink, if you'd like to join us."

"I'd like a word, if I may. Privately."

Stevenson's eyebrows lifted.

"It's important," Adam said.

"All right. Be right with you. Just let me leave my clubs at the pub."

He was wary now, because in less than a minute, they were walking away through the park, though there must have been plenty of Stevenson's acquaintances talking and drinking in the taproom.

"You heard about Brennan, I suppose," Stevenson said with a sigh, squinting into the distance like a sailor assessing the wind.

"No, I—what happened?"

"Yesterday he agreed to plead guilty. I've been speaking to him. Suggesting his sentence could be reduced if he were to give up some names. Help us root out the trouble in the West Port. Those Ribbonmen."

Adam nodded, pretending that his breath wasn't catching in his throat. So there was a connection. And if Brennan was ready to break faith with his brothers—

"He died last night in prison," Stevenson said. "So did his wife. No one saw anything."

"Of course not. Bloody bastards," Adam muttered.

Stevenson nodded. "Still, I think it's an overall victory for our side. At least we know we got two of them. Probably wise if you and I take a little extra care this next while." His hand flew to his hat as they rounded a corner, into a gust of wind. "So what did you come about?" His voice dropped. "Is it Thomas?"

Adam shook his head. "No—"

"Forgive me. I don't know why I thought—" Stevenson broke off, extracted a small engraved flask, and took a swallow. Almost as quickly, the flask disappeared again. "There was just something about your face."

Adam cleared his throat. "Actually, I was going to say, no, not entirely."

Stevenson stopped, tensing as if expecting a blow. "Well?"

Since Thomas's disappearance, Adam had thought and held in any number of pointed comments, building an arsenal that made it surprisingly difficult to begin. He needed Stevenson on his side.

He tugged at his cuff. "Have you heard from Isobel Tait?"

Stevenson started walking again. "I don't hear from her," he said sharply. "That was our arrangement. Only when Thomas—"

"She left her lodgings months ago," Adam said, taking long steps to regain lost ground. "No one knew where she went. This was right after she came to me, suggesting Dr. Conall Burnett kidnapped Thomas. I thought it was suggestive. I made some discreet inquiries. She'd withdrawn all her money, and simply disappeared."

Impossibly, Stevenson's face became even harder. "I heard about that. Not that she changed lodging, that's news to me, just that—what she claimed about Burnett's collection."

"Did she go to you too?" Adam's voice was tight, forced past the prickly, unspoken comments stuck to his tongue.

Stevenson shook his head. "I heard through my wife. Her brother is a doctor. We dined with him, and Burnett was there. The conversation was—" He swallowed. "Quite warm in his defense."

"You didn't think Isobel might be right? His ownership of the heart is at least an interesting coincidence."

"But wildly improbable!" Stevenson tugged his coat, moderating his tone. "I'm sorry for her. You know I am, and though there was some sympathy for her around the table, what was I supposed to do? I can't stick my neck out again."

"Did you before? I didn't much notice," Adam said, sharp enough to draw a glance.

"I don't expect you to understand the difficulties of my position," Stevenson muttered, barely audible above the leaves crunching under their feet. The path was strewn with them, harbingers of an early autumn, and perhaps an especially cold winter. "But I do expect you to explain why you are here."

Adam shoved his hands into his pockets, the familiar fabric prickling against his skin.

"If the superintendent didn't think her claims warranted investigation back then, you're acting outside your authority," Stevenson said. "I can't—"

"I had to do something. I couldn't find her son," Adam spat. "No one else was helping."

"So you made 'discreet inquiries.' If that's supposed to convince me to help you talk yourself out of trouble, you'll have to do better," Stevenson said.

"I'm not in any trouble," Adam began.

"So what did you do?" Stevenson asked, before he could elaborate.

"Then? Or now?"

Stevenson's face darkened. "Start at the beginning."

"After Isobel told me about her suspicions, I called at Burnett's house. I may have exaggerated and said there were concerns from the public."

Stevenson snorted.

"I may also have suggested Burnett could dispel any trouble that might be brewing by being forthcoming—"

"And was he?"

"Two days later, he invited me back. Said he'd reconsidered and would take my advice. He showed me a catalog of his specimens. Acquisition dates, what he'd paid for them. It all looked correct," Adam said.

"And?"

"All in the same color ink. And I didn't see the variations I'd expect to see in records assembled over time using a variety of pens."

"That's not evidence," Stevenson said. They were nearly at the end of the park, where a palisade of houses fronted the green and lined the road up the hill. Stevenson might not give him much more time.

"It's suggestive," Adam argued. "You didn't think to see her then? Write to her and ask?"

Stevenson scowled. "I did think of writing, as it happens, but since there was nothing to accomplish by it, I—"

"You might have stopped her," Adam snapped.

Stevenson turned a blank face to him. "Stopped her from what?"

You need him on your side, Adam reminded himself. *It won't help if you kick him.* "She's gathering evidence against Burnett."

Stevenson's eyes narrowed. "Are you saying there is evidence?"

"Some," Adam said, unwilling to reveal his hand. Jenny Dove hadn't even confirmed the skirt and earrings were her sister's yet. "I'm working on it."

"Does anyone know you are?"

"Isobel does. I spotted her during one of Burnett's anatomy lectures."

At this news, Stevenson's eyebrows climbed to his hairline. "I'm afraid to ask why, but—"

"I was there looking for someone. A body. Another person who's disappeared."

"Aye?"

Adam started walking again, unable to push the suppositions and fears out his throat without the lubricant of motion. It took a few strides for Stevenson to catch up. A petty win, but Adam enjoyed it.

Quietly, their heads bent together to keep their words from passersby, he told Stevenson about Jenny Dove's missing sister, Lizzie, and why no one in authority had been persuaded to care.

"That kind of woman often goes missing," Stevenson said. Noting Adam's scowl, he added, "I'm not saying I'm glad of it, just that it happens, and—"

"She had an extra finger. Within a month, I saw Burnett dissecting a body with a missing left hand." Adam kicked a pebble off the pavement into the gutter. "There are other disappearances too. The child who was kidnapped—"

"Nan Burt." Stevenson seemed wary now. "Is she—"

Adam interrupted. He didn't want to talk about Nan. The less attention on her, the better. "Her mother went missing earlier this year. And there's others. Here." Adam passed the prosecutor a folded list, seven names he'd culled from three years' worth of investigations, and all still missing. Thomas Tait was written across the top.

Stevenson's lips thinned.

"I don't know anything of what's happened to them," Adam said. "But I've talked to the family or friends who initially spoke to police. All these people"—he cleared his throat—"are unique."

He pointed at the paper at the second column of writing. Across from Thomas's name he'd penned *mitral valve defect*. Across from Elizabeth Dove—

"Polydactyly. I looked it up. Means extra fingers," Adam said. Unusual in humans, apparently, but common enough in cats. And at the bottom of the list, across the name of Mary Burt, Nan's mother, *mismatched eyes*.

At some point, he'd have to tell her, but he couldn't face it yet.

"Burnett's colleagues defended him because they all use human specimens. They buy stolen bodies from resurrection men and talk about the needs of science to improve medicine anytime someone objects or turns squeamish." Adam tapped the list. "But this—"

"Might be something different," Stevenson said quietly. He looked older since taking that list, as if his face were made of the same building stones as the city.

"There's more," Adam said, reluctant because this was even more tenuous. But the connection was there, and it wouldn't stop tickling the back of his brain.

"The burned man. The one Isobel thought kidnapped Thomas."

"Eoin—" Stevenson stopped.

"Brennan," Adam finished.

"You think there's a connection between them? The kidnappers of Nan Burt and—" His voice broke.

"They're cousins," Adam said. "I asked."

"I meant between the Ribbonmen and Burnett," Stevenson said slowly. "Is he one of them? Hiring them to help him collect—oh, God." Stevenson put a hand over his eyes.

"I don't know," Adam admitted.

Stevenson shook his head, as if to clear it. "You can't—" He stopped, his eyes falling once more on Adam's list. An inch below the others, Adam had penciled in one additional name. Now he regretted it. "That's just a guess," he muttered.

"Another? Guesswork isn't policing." But Stevenson stopped walking, his forehead creasing. "I knew John Barclay. He taught my brother-in-law."

"Burnett was his pupil too. Joined him right after he left the army. Barclay started the school and the collection. He offered Burnett a partnership."

"Aye?" Stevenson eyes were riveted to the paper.

Adam cleared his throat. "Barclay died a month after they signed the papers. And Burnett was the doctor who registered his death."

Stevenson grunted.

"It fits," Adam argued. "If I'm right, it fits. He's bold with his murders. He's an opportunist."

"I want to help." Stevenson hesitated. "You know I do. For the son I lost, if nothing else. But this isn't enough."

"I know. I'm looking." But it was a daunting prospect. And if Burnett was allied with the Ribbonmen...

Stevenson combed his fingers through his hair, then replaced his hat. "Guesses and accusations and even a few trifling proofs won't do it. We need irrefutable evidence of wrongdoing so terrible his colleagues won't risk protecting him. As it stands, if a whisper of this gets out, they'll jump on you. Have you dismissed."

"Like what happened to Isobel," Adam said.

"Mrs. Tait," Stevenson corrected, then dropped his eyes at Adam's incredulous snort.

Stevenson glanced aside, at the dome of the university. "If you're right, these are terrible crimes."

Adam nodded, but there was one more terrible thing he hadn't touched on yet. They walked silently up the hill, past university bookshops, medical instrument makers, and student lodging houses.

"John." Adam stopped walking. "There's something else. I'm even less certain of it than the rest." But Will Brennan and his wife had just died in prison, and by unlucky coincidence, Adam knew three men from the station who'd visited Calton Hill yesterday. And Stevenson had heard him out so far.

"Tell me," Stevenson said.

Adam hovered a hesitant hand over the waistcoat pocket where his private notes were folded away. Notes with all three names on them, even before he'd heard about the Brennans dying at Calton Hill.

If he gave them to Stevenson, there'd be no going back. "I'm not sure," he said again, almost pleadingly. "It's just some observations of mine. Possibilities."

Assumptions, really, and Adam was relying on a particularly common one about the Irish—a prejudice he particularly despised, because it was a variety of the prejudice folk applied to him, when they called him half-breed and Indian, and treated him like he was less.

But Stevenson was waiting, so Adam reluctantly surrendered the much-creased bit of paper, filled with penciled lines he'd written, crossed out, then rewritten.

As Stevenson read, slowly enough he must be perusing it more than once, a stone grew in Adam's stomach. Would Stevenson dismiss him for this? Or just laugh and call him a fool? But too many things had gone wrong. These days, he was always looking over his shoulder.

Stevenson's lips pressed together. "I'll come with you to the station," he said. "I'd like to look over the records myself."

Adam didn't know if he should scowl or sigh with relief. He settled with something in the middle. "Thank you, John."

"And Adam?"

"Aye?"

Stevenson slipped the paper into his own waistcoat pocket. "If you're right, I'm behind you."

Adam turned his face so Stevenson wouldn't see his rapid blinks. But the fact was, no one had said words like these to him, not in all his years on the force.

"Appreciate it," he said curtly, and they resumed walking, turning eastward toward the station.

"You haven't told me what Isobel is doing," Stevenson said.

Something must have shown in Adam's face, because Stevenson's voice sharpened. "Kerr? Where is she?"

"I'm thinking," Adam said, but he was still unsure what to tell him, even when the pavement leveled at the top of the hill.

"I can't tell you," he said finally. If the least suspicion crossed Burnett's mind, Isobel would never escape that house. "It's too dangerous for her. Suffice to say, she's gathering evidence."

"You didn't—" There was a tightness around Stevenson's eyes that hadn't been there before. "Is she—"

"She's alive," Adam said. "But she isn't safe. I didn't urge her to do anything. Her actions are all her own. I'd have dissuaded her, given the chance."

"You have to stop her," Stevenson said. "If you're right about Burnett, he'll—"

Adam huffed. "Tried. Don't think anyone can." He hoped to God this didn't end badly for her.

Stevenson opened his mouth, prepared to argue.

"Use your imagination, Stevenson. If Burnett has committed—or paid for—half of these disappearances, think of the risk. There's danger to you and me, but multiply that by a dozen, and you'll have an inkling of the risk she's facing. No one can know. Not my superintendent, even if he'd support us. Not your clerks. Not Detective Fraser. Not any constables. If I didn't need your help, I wouldn't have told you."

Stevenson looked ill. "Another dram?" Adam suggested, reminding him of his pocket flask.

The prosecutor shook his head, then changed his mind, downing a long gulp and wiping his mouth on the back of his hand. Usually, Adam begrudged this man's well-kept fingers, his old gold ring with a family crest, his pale coloring and classical profile—a face any woman would find handsome. Adam saw them as much as ever just now, but for once he noted these advantages more ruefully than resentfully, which surprised him.

Stevenson stoppered the flask, giving no sign he'd noticed any change in Adam's thinking. "Bring me the evidence, Kerr." He was frowning, his jaw tight. "As soon as you possibly can."

After bidding good evening to the constables on duty and to Fraser (who was headed to the pub because of a quarrel with his wife) Adam walked to his family's home, a three-story town house on Clarence Street. Though no one was visible through the windows, it was a good bet that, by now, Nan was watching. A retired constable, Emily's new manservant, admitted him.

"Any progress?" Emily asked, coming down the stairs.

"Possibly. Hard to say. Meeting with the prosecutor went better than I expected." It was strange, to have confided so much to Emily, and once begun, he hadn't quite known how to stop. But her help certainly made life simpler, and he couldn't have taken it without explaining all the risks. It shouldn't have surprised him that Emily, who'd thrived in her marriage to his much older father, hadn't quailed an inch.

She'd always been the type to take charge of things, while Adam had been the kind who wouldn't let her.

He smiled past Emily at Nan. "How was your day?"

"She's making beautiful progress with her letters," Emily reported. Nan made a face.

"And I learned how to make silk flowers today," Emily added. "See?"

She held up a lopsided yellow blossom, then tucked it behind the wide ribbon of Nan's bonnet. "Not as nice as the one you made me, but the color suits you."

Nan had her cloak on already. Though she was always anxious for Adam to collect her and for the two of them to leave, she thanked Emily with a perfect dip of a curtsey.

"I'll see you tomorrow, Nan," Emily said. Over Nan's bonnet, she mouthed, "Be careful."

Adam nodded.

The two of them slipped out the back door, soft shadows in the dim evening. A block away, Emily's carriage waited to drive them home.

"May I speak to the prosecutor?" Nan asked.

"Why?" She'd already given a statement when her kidnappers were arrested—upsetting to her and to him. He didn't understand why she'd want to go through that again.

"I want to help," she said. "We'll be safe, then."

Adam squeezed her hand and said nothing.

Once they were home, they sat down to supper—bread and cheese and beer—deplorable food, but the kind they both enjoyed. Adam brewed coffee afterward and Nan munched an apple, practicing writing vowels on a slate.

"I can write fifteen different letters now," she said. "And I know all of them."

Adam nodded.

"So did you find out anything today?" Nan demanded.

"Found some clothes that might have belonged to Lizzie Dove."

Nan stirred uneasily. "You said she was special too. Like my mam."

It was pure chance that had made Nan mention her mother's eyes. Unfortunately, it put a new and sinister light on her disappearance. Warily, Adam nodded. "Aye, she is."

"What about you?" Nan asked. "You're different."

Adam bit his lip. "Don't worry about me," he said. "I'm not—" He stopped. With black hair and russet-toned skin, he didn't look like a typical Scot, but that wasn't nearly enough to attract an anatomist's interest. But how could he possibly explain that to her?

"If anyone kills me, it will be because I'm a detective, not for my looks."

Abruptly, Nan got up and stirred the fire.

He'd muffed it again. "*Nitânis*," he said, and her stiff shoulders softened, just a little. "It's sad for me to sit alone."

"What does it mean again?"

She liked his pet name for her and couldn't possibly have forgotten, but Adam liked that repeating his explanation seemed to reassure her. He'd remind her a dozen times, if that helped.

"*Nitânis*? It means you're mine to look after," he said. "Remember?"

Nan nodded, and his chest eased as she came back to the table, sitting down with her feet tucked under her knees. Wary of her feelings, he hadn't used Scots or English words for *daughter* around her. *Nitânis* meant the same thing, but she didn't know that, and conveniently, it shared some of the sounds of her given name.

It was strange how this word, and so many others he'd forgotten, were inexplicably coming back.

"I'll look after you as long as you want me to," Adam told her, offering her another apple from the bowl on the table. "Here. You need fattening."

She took it and turned it in her hands, choosing where to take her first bite. "You'll tell me about the people again?

The *ayisînôwak*. That word had come back to him too.

He didn't talk of them, too used to people not caring to know, but Nan, for some reason, couldn't hear enough.

He set down his spoon. "There's many different peoples there."

"In Prince Rupert's Land," Nan said, adding, as Adam raised his eyebrows, "Beyond Upper Canada. Aunt Emily showed me an atlas today. With your da's maps."

"Aye. Well, he, as you know, was Scots. He went to make maps for the company. My mam—"

"Was mixed," she inserted, then added, "That's why you're darker than I am."

Something wistful in her tone made Adam pause before replying. He put down his coffee cup and picked up Nan's hand, stained with sepia ink. Not, he realized, from a mishap during writing practice.

"Nan."

She looked up at him.

"You didn't smear this on yourself practicing vowels, did you?"

She flushed.

"Good thing you started with your hands instead of your face."

Nan sent him an injured look, then relaxed into a smile.

"It was a silly idea," she admitted.

"And it won't work," he told her. "It doesn't have to. You're just right the way you are, and so am I." He wove his fingers between hers and laid their clasped hands on the table. "We mix together fine."

She nodded slowly, then let his hand go and picked up her apple again. "Did you go to school there too?"

Adam shook his head. "There weren't any. My grandmother taught me to hunt and trap and fish. Over there, that's how you do housekeeping." At least, that was what she'd had to do, after the Nor'Wester men, passing traders from a rival company, had burned their settlement, killing Adam's mother and grandfather and leaving Adam in her care. His father had been away on a mapmaking expedition during the massacre.

Nan's eyes widened. "I probably wouldn't be able to do it."

He thought of her, escaping the bigger girls at the children's home who stole her food, beat her where it wouldn't show, and lied to the matron about it. After her mother vanished, when she lived rough in the streets and toiled in the workshop, she'd kept body and soul together. She was canny, tough, and also appallingly young and fragile.

Kanapawamakan, his grandmother, would have loved this child.

It frightened him a little, after so many years alone, that he was remembering her, just as he was needing help from the ones he had here, who'd tried to be family to him, but couldn't.

He couldn't imagine what his grandmother would have made of Emily. But then, he'd always been hard on her since she'd stepped into his dead mother's place, only six years older than he was. Kanapawamakan might have liked Emily, if only for her kindness to him, clumsy though it was, at least in the early days.

His grandmother had carried more than her share of grief, but she hadn't let it get in the way of living. She'd brought Adam to her people, and taught him to smile and laugh again, until Adam's father found them. By then Jock Kerr had decided to return to Scotland and work for the company there. He'd done well for them in the New World, and they were offering a promotion.

Naturally his son would go too.

She'd argued long and hard, and lost. But she hadn't let that break her either. She'd just hugged Adam hard, gave him gifts and blessings, and let him go. They would be brave, both of them.

Adam studied the shape of Nan's head, the shine on her smoothly brushed hair, the fullness and healthy color reestablishing itself in her cheeks.

"*Nitânis*, I'm sure you'd master my grandmother's lessons just fine."

{ 30 }

Dr. Burnett was at the window when I returned to the house, smiling at me as I descended to the kitchen door, acting like this was ordinary for him.

I nodded a hasty acknowledgment, let myself inside, and hung up my shawl. "Why isn't the doctor at the anatomy school?" I asked Maggie. Usually he and his assistants were busy in the laboratory at this time, something I knew from the extra laundry.

"Dunno." Maggie didn't look up from her scouring.

"He didn't mention anything to me," Mrs. Williams said. "Took tea with the mistress and ate four lemon biscuits." Like this was some accomplishment. Well, maybe it was hers. The biscuits were excellent. I'd eat four myself, if I could do it without earning a stomachache.

"He did say Mr. Ferguson is taking leave for a day or two. Visiting his family. Someone's unwell, I think," Maggie said. "So maybe none of them are working this afternoon."

"Wouldn't that be nice," grunted the cook, scraping peelings into the rubbish pail. Her half day wasn't until tomorrow.

I considered Maggie's theory as I drank a cup of tea and helped myself to bread and butter. No use touching the biscuits yet. Mrs. Williams wouldn't let us have any until after supper.

No use either taking fright at every change in Burnett's schedule, because an afternoon at home with his mother probably meant nothing. Except when I carried my lists upstairs to present to Mrs. Burnett, I found the doctor in the hall.

Was he trying to make me trip? He was ubiquitous as dandelions today, popping up everywhere.

"Afternoon, Ross. Did you enjoy your half day?" He looked suspiciously genial—unless my uneasy mind was affecting my temper.

"Yes, very enjoyable sir."

"You took a walk? It's a fine day for it. Back early, though, aren't you?"

"The breeze is a little chilly today. It gets lonesome up on the hill." I smiled like there was nothing in the world to trouble me. "Besides, I like the kitchen chatter."

He nodded, seemingly satisfied, but I'd have given a pound to be sure.

Why did it take so long to make keys?

That night, I couldn't sleep, no matter how I arranged the bedcovers or reshaped my pillow. Eventually, I got up and paced, giving rein to the wild thoughts chasing through my head. I couldn't let Burnett catch me off guard. Even if nothing was wrong, I wouldn't go on unprepared.

Brimming with the resolve of midnight decision, I crept to the kitchen and felt my way to a meat fork and the file Mrs. Williams used for sharpening knives. Back in my room, I sawed off the hook on my window catch with anxious, chilled fingers, until the sash popped free at a nudge. The easiest place to hide the meat fork was under the mattress. I'd prefer a blade, but Cook would notice and complain about the absence of one of her knives.

That done, I returned the knife sharpener to the drawer, more awake than ever. My bed was cold. Still unable to settle, I prowled upstairs. There was no noise in the house but mine; everyone else was asleep, and the nighttime hours were lonely.

Unlocking the specimen room, I passed the vague shapes lining the walls, nodding greetings to the odd-colored eyes and the femur, the adult skeleton and the tiny child's. Then I lifted onto my toes and breathed against the jar holding Thomas.

"I think I've found a way," I whispered. Not much longer. In two days I'd have the keys. I'd comb through Burnett's papers every day if I had to. I'd take the drawing of the man with the burns. There would be something, because there had to be. Once Burnett was arrested, the police would extract the truth and then I'd know Thomas's story, so much worse than any fireside tale. Only happy people wanted frightening for fun.

My eyes stung, and I didn't touch them. It was a relief to feel warm tears run unimpeded down my cheeks. Real crying, silent or not, always takes ages.

I picked myself up off the floor when I was done, reaching for the shelf because I couldn't rely on my knees, which were protesting after all that time folded on the rug.

The carved shelf edge moved beneath my hand.

Unsure, I pressed again, and the molding slid another fraction of an inch.

No, I thought, licking dry lips. It couldn't be as easy as this.

I pulled, and a narrow drawer slid open half a foot. Too dark to see inside—I looked with my fingers, closing them on a bundle of papers.

272 † JAIMA FIXSEN

"Is this it?" I asked Thomas.

Nothing. I glanced around the room, then shook my head at the folly of waiting for an answer. I didn't need ghosts to tell me what my skin knew already. The papers pricked like shards of glass.

Seizing them, I pushed the drawer shut and hurried back to my room.

Just before my candle expired, I found it—an entry on the day Thomas and I had visited Dr. Burnett.

Suspected mitral valve defect, underlined. And on the next line, my old address. Penciled faintly in the margin was a check mark and the words: *delivery via E.B.*

Eoin Brennan. The scarred man.

I didn't read anything else. I stuck the pages under my mattress, next to the meat fork.

When the police arrested him, Burnett would learn how lucky he was that I'd taken these pages to them, instead of tiptoeing, prongs in hand, to his bedchamber upstairs.

{ 31 }

I woke late, with eyes coated in sand, a pounding headache, and Maggie at my door, telling me not to worry, she'd already done the rooms. "Aren't you well today, Miss Ross?"

"Just tired. Poor sleep," I mumbled.

"Cook said you've been looking peaky and I should let you lie abed this morning."

"What time is it?" I asked, squinting at the window. It was far too bright for my usual rising hour. I stood up quickly, light-headed and swaying on my feet. Closing my eyes to steady myself, I missed Maggie's reply. "I'm fine," I said. "Tell Mrs. Williams I'll be right out."

"She's not here, Miss Ross," Maggie said, twisting her fingers. "Received an urgent message from her sister, and Dr. Burnett said she could take the day. She left half an hour ago, before breakfast was done. Dr. and Mrs. Burnett have both eaten, but Mrs. Burnett just rang her bell and..." Maggie grimaced. "I'm sorry to wake you in such a hurry."

"You did right, Maggie." I hurried to the washstand to splash my face. The water was so cold I gasped, but it sharpened my thoughts, dispelling most of the cloudiness brooding above my shoulders. "Tell Mrs. Burnett that I'll be right with her." She didn't like to be waited on by Maggie.

I jammed the spectacles on my nose, hurrying through the rest of the usual modification to my face. Maggie might comment about the change in my appearance when I finished, but I didn't intend to remain here much longer. I had my proof; the sand in Burnett's glass had nearly run out. As soon as I was ready, I'd take my stolen notes and Thomas's heart and go straight to the police.

If only my buttons weren't so troublesome this morning. It was like they'd been bewitched and were trying to thwart me.

Tugging on my stockings, I heard voices from upstairs. Maggie's was conciliating beneath the strident and authoritative tones of both Burnetts. I stumbled into my shoes, anxious to relieve Maggie of Mrs. Burnett's displeasure—this wasn't her fault.

Smoothing my collar, I jogged up the stairs, just in time to see the front door swing shut. The hall looked empty. Had Mrs. Burnett left? But why would she take Maggie?

I stepped toward the door to see who'd left, when—

"Don't worry, Ross."

Dr. Burnett's voice was unsettlingly close.

I spun around. He was an arm's length away, poised on the balls of his feet.

"Doctor! I thought that was you who'd just left," I stammered.

"No, my mother has an appointment this morning. I suggested that someone go with her, so she wouldn't be alone." Again, his face was unsettling, friendly but opaque, the gaze too intent for me to meet with composure.

"Is that why she wanted me? I'm so sorry I didn't come up earlier,"

I said, smoothing my perfectly starched collar again. "Things were in a bit of a crisis downstairs after Cook left unexpectedly."

"It's no matter. It's best this way. Maggie can be spared, but I'm sure you have plenty to do." He came a step closer, and the hairs stood on the back of my neck.

Everyone's gone. Burnett and I are alone in the house.

I retreated a step, a split second closer to the door. He wouldn't be able to block me. But then I remembered the papers stuffed beneath my mattress.

Adam's warnings clanged in my head. Burnett was a killer. But with the means to stop him finally at hand, I couldn't afford to guard my life. Stopping him was more important. I stepped forward. "Is there anything you need from me, doctor?" I asked with as much coolness as I could muster.

"No, I'm leaving directly."

I nodded. "Then I'd best look after things downstairs." Muscles tight, breath locked inside my chest, I slipped past him, my steps quickening as I lengthened the distance between us, as I grasped the door to the servant's stairs and to safety. Out of his sight, I raced downstairs to the kitchen, snatching up my cloak and fastening it on my way to my room.

I dropped to my knees and pushed one hand beneath the bed, my breath easing as my fingers brushed the papers. Why had I shoved them so far back?

I reached further, straining my shoulder, fingers closing on a folded edge just as my head slammed forward in an explosion of sparks. I cried out and slid to the floor, helpless against the foot that rolled me onto my back.

"No!"

Burnett had followed me. Still smiling, he plucked the papers from my hand. "I thought you might take these. They'll be no good to you. I didn't even write them. Give them to the police, and they'll identify them as a forgery."

I pushed against the floor, struggling to get up, but he shoved again, dropping on top of me, fracturing my scream with a scythe-like slap that made the room go dark.

Before I blinked my eyes clear, his hand mashed over my mouth, his thumb a vise against my chin, his fingers clamped against my nostrils. I thrashed like a beetle on my back, desperate for air.

"Who sent you?"

The hand on my face loosened as the other tightened around my throat, giving me just enough to breath to rasp, "I'm not—you can't—"

"You took the bait."

"I didn't—" I stopped for want of air, not persistence, but it was useless to lie. He'd seen me with the papers.

"Someone sent you here to spy on me. Who?"

Black spots danced in front of me. I could barely see. "Thomas."

"Who?" he demanded again.

"My son," I gasped. "You took him for his heart. Thomas Tait." My son's heart. Lizzie's missing hand. "When he was alive, you taught me to hear his arrhythmia, remember?"

His grip slackened a little, his eyes narrowing.

"I hear his pulse when I'm in your specimen room. I know you killed him, and that he's not the only one you've taken. The victims speak to me. Your collection is witnessing against you." Speaking it aloud, for the first and probably only time, I was sure of it, more sure than I'd ever been of anything. If that made me a madwoman, so be it.

He blinked once, but then his hand closed again on my nose and chin. "I don't think so."

I battered his arms with my fists and tried to catch his skin in my teeth, feebler at each attempt from lack of air. I condemned him with my eyes, but he wasn't looking at me, his gaze fixed on his hands like he was trying to shove me right through the stone floor. My lungs ripped and burned, my hands dropped to my sides, as his face disappeared in a whirl of night specked with stars.

Lub-dup.

Lub-dup.

A pulse, but this slow, stumbling beat couldn't be mine.

Da-di-lah.

Fainter than I'd ever heard it before, the pulse skipped along, borne on the line of music that had first helped me detect the cadence, back when Thomas's heart was still inside his chest. Vivaldi. Such beautiful music to hear while dying. The sound grew in my ears.

I smiled. He was here. Thomas. My hand flopped out, reaching, but instead of a soft child's fist, I felt the side of my bed.

The fork.

Blind, moved along by fragile puppet strings, I probed beneath the mattress and wrapped muzzy fingers around the handle, hefting an impossible weight with muscles of air.

The music in my head whirled faster, pushing my hand, lending it strength. Quickly now.

I plunged the fork down, and a scream like a gale tore past me.

Burnett was on my belly, howling, both hands pressed to his thigh. I pushed up on my elbows and filled my lungs with air.

"Witch!" His leg ran with blood, but the way he writhed, I didn't think he was bleeding enough for the wound to kill him.

"I know your secrets." My lips moved; I couldn't tell if I made any sound. "Their ghosts tell me."

I brandished the fork, and he lurched back, scrambling out of range.

My free hand came to my face, touching the indents he'd left. "Is this how you kill? Is this what you did to my son?"

His hand moved sideways, to the rolling pin he must have collected on his way through the kitchen. I lunged forward, forcing him back, and scrambled to my feet, kicking his improvised club to the wall by the door.

I staggered, catching myself with an outstretched hand. The dark spots were bobbing around me again. Though I could have sworn the window was shut, a wind circled around me, buffeting me from side to side.

Run, Mam, Thomas shouted. *Run now.*

Clutching the fork in my fist, I stumbled past him, through the kitchen and out the kitchen door.

Cold air struck my face. I glanced back, heard Burnett howling, then hauled myself up the steps using the iron railings. At the end of the row of houses, an alley, narrow enough to touch the walls on each side, ran into a busy thoroughfare, full of people and carriages and wagons. Bolting into the bustling crowd, I tripped on the pavement, falling headlong into the street, almost beneath the hooves of a horse, who instead of trampling me, whinnied and reared. Amid curses and shouts, creaking wheels and panicking horses, I heard Burnett yell, "Thief! Stop her!" Back in the dark recesses of the alley, I glimpsed a rounded form, limping.

I don't know how I stood up. I simply arrived on my feet. A high wind, plucking off hats and whipping up cloaks and skirts on its headlong course down the street, pushed me hard in the shoulders. *Run.*

{ 32 }

Slowly, I walked the streets of the city, the fire in my lungs cooling to a bed of ash. People gave me strange looks, and every few steps, I glanced behind my shoulder. I never saw Burnett. Empty-handed, with only a cloak and the clothes I stood in, nothing in my pockets, I trembled incessantly, unable to tell if my quaking was leftover fear or cold. The usual tethers between mind and body were slack as the strings of a broken violin.

You're a mother, not a murderer, I told myself regretfully.

I should have aimed for his heart.

It wasn't safe to remain here. Burnett had money. His hirelings or his students would find me. If he hadn't already, he'd teach them to close my nose and mouth until darkness swallowed me, like it nearly had before. Just like it had swallowed Thomas and so many others.

I sank into a doorway and rested my forehead on my knees. I'd planned on finding Kerr today, victorious, not shattered by defeat.

"You all right, lass?"

I glanced up, and the man who'd paused beside me flinched, reminding me that my face was throbbing. "You'd better—" He swallowed. "I don't know if—"

He rummaged in his pocket and thrust a coin at me. "Is there a friend you can go to?" he asked.

I nodded. There was one.

"Do you need help to get there?"

"I can find my way," I said hoarsely, and the man nodded, lingered, then shuffled off.

Could I find him? I needed Kerr, but I couldn't go to the police station, not with Burnett calling me a thief. Burnett might already be there, and I knew who the constables would want to believe.

I needed help, just not the kind that man could have given me. I picked myself up and hid my face in the hood of my cloak. Kerr had a home somewhere. I just had to find it.

I took my coin to a taproom near the station, bought a mug of ale, and waited for the right kind of person to walk in, someone familiar with the place, who greeted the barmaids and the other patrons by name. Though hungry and thirsty, I rationed my drink, making it last.

A brown-skinned man with an accent knew Kerr but changed seats and moved away from me the moment my talk nudged to where Kerr lived. I couldn't pry information from either barmaid. They eyed me with growing impatience, measuring the inch of ale left in my glass. I was about to down it in a swallow and give up, when a tired-looking errand boy sat down with a mug and a pie on the opposite end of the table.

"Busy at the station today?" the barmaid asked him.

He nodded, gulping food in enormous bites. His fingers were red from cold.

"Where you off to next?" the barmaid asked. They had similar profiles, but different coloring. Maybe she was an aunt or an older sister.

"New Town."

"That's all right, then," she said.

"Been there twice already," he grumbled. "Andrews and Gibson and now I've another for Detective Kerr."

She patted him on the shoulder and picked up the empty mugs left on the table, humming as she disappeared into the kitchen.

I wet my lips and slid a little closer on the bench. "I can carry it for you. Give you a chance to get warm."

He looked affronted.

"Please," I asked. "I—"

"I deliver important messages," he said. "You'd just throw it away."

"No, I won't. I know Kerr. He's the tall one. Dark eyes and hair. Doesn't like talking much."

He tried to look deeper into my hood. I shifted on my seat, reluctantly drawing it back an inch. His eyes widened when he saw my face. "I'm not paying you until you come back," he said.

"That's fine. Give me the letter. I'll be back before you've finished your supper."

He hesitated. "You'd better be quick."

I nodded. "New Town isn't far. But you'll have to tell me his house."

"Dean Bank Lane, right by Leith water," he said, and gave me a number as he laid the letter in my hand.

Most of New Town was houses like Burnett's—identical boxes built in long rows of gray stone. I knew the district well—most of my former pupils lived nearby—but I didn't recognize Kerr's address, and had to ask directions to the street, counting out house numbers until I spied a short square house with a steep slate roof, tucked into the space left at the point of two converging streets. It was tiny, but that seemed right for Kerr. He'd want a place on his own, not the comfort or convenience of a suite in a gentleman's lodging house.

I drew a breath, telling myself to look like I belonged here, so that the carriages and muffled pairs of pedestrians wouldn't have reason to take notice.

Night was falling, and a woman alone at this hour, in this neighborhood, drew notice no matter what.

His door was painted green, a noticeable exception among neighbors dressed all in shiny black. And a threat—*'ware red man*—was scrawled across it. A chill ran up my arms. So much for my safe harbor.

But I had nowhere else to go, so I knocked.

And waited.

Maybe he wasn't home. I turned away, when a movement at the window caught my attention—a blur ducking behind a swinging curtain. I'd have missed it if I wasn't practiced at searching out a child's face.

She was older than Thomas, more guarded in expression, even in a brief glance. I rapped on the glass, but there was no sound from the house. I pictured her, resolute and crouched in a corner. No chance she was letting me in, not with that warning written on the door. She'd learned not to trust strangers. And if I lingered outside the house, some passerby would question me or summon a constable.

I walked around to the back of the house, into a small garden and away from the light, and stationed myself on the step, pulling my cloak tight around my shoulders. I could be resolute too.

Since I had nothing to do but sit, shiver, and listen, it wasn't hard to hear when Kerr approached the house. He cursed, and then I heard him run up the steps and jostle the key into the door. I imagined him rushing inside, anxiously holding the child—his daughter? But why was she alone?—then frowning as she recounted the visit of a filthy-looking stranger, knocking at the window and the door. What if he refused to help me?

Light bloomed in the kitchen window, falling on my feet. I edged closer, preparing for another try at the door, when it swung open, revealing Kerr, holding out a lamp.

"Isobel. Thank God you're here."

He glanced behind me and pulled me inside.

The room was cramped but comfortable, with a fire burning and a tea tray on the table. The girl was perched on a chair, eyeing me disapprovingly over the rim of her cup, and Kerr was in his shirt-sleeves. He looked me over as soon as he bolted the door behind me, recoiling even more than the man who'd given me the coin had done.

"You've blood all over you," he said.

"It's Burnett's."

"Sit down." He waved me to a chair.

"I'd rather warm myself," I said, and moved to stand by the fire. My fingers and feet had lost feeling ages ago.

"I'm sorry you couldn't come in sooner. Nan isn't supposed to open the door to strangers."

I nodded, wishing others had been so wise.

"I've explained that I know you. And that you'll be staying with us for a while."

I wanted to protest, but had nothing to say. I had nothing and nowhere to go but here, so I nodded, unable to cough out even the roughest thanks.

"Someone's threatening you," I murmured. "There was a message on your door."

"I know. I'm taking care of it," he said, and turned his attention to the child, sitting down with her and sharing a slice of bread. He cut one for me, so I sat down and ate it a crumb at a time, as she showed him a slate of letters and he praised her wobbly attempts. He wasn't, I gathered, her father, and yet—

"Time for bed, Nan," Kerr announced.

"Is she—" The girl glanced at me and looked away. She hadn't spoken to me at all, though she watched whenever she thought I wasn't looking.

"Mrs. Tait can have my room," he said, and before I could interject—I'd take his bed only if he wasn't in it—he added, "I'll be in the truckle bed next to yours, same as always."

By the time he returned, alone, my face was perfectly composed again.

"Nan has nightmares," Kerr explained. "So I can't leave her for long. Did you get enough to eat?"

I nodded.

"We can talk now," he said. "I don't want her upset. What happened? Did you find—"

I dropped my gaze to my hands. "He tricked me. Left some papers where I'd see them. Payment records, for 'deliveries.' One was the day that Thomas disappeared. And there were other entries matching specimens he has in his collection. When he saw that I'd taken them, he knew I wasn't only a housekeeper. The worst part is that it was fake. He had someone else write it. Said if I brought it to the police, it would have been proved a forgery."

I rubbed the back of my hand over my mouth.

"He told you that?"

"As he was trying to kill me. He sent everyone else away, followed me to my room, and stopped my nose and my mouth—" I broke off, swallowed, and said in a breaking voice, "I think that's how he killed Thomas."

I thought of the suffocating faint when I'd picked up the skirt that had belonged to Lizzie Dove. Burnett's consulting room had bright lamps. He could have smothered her right there, with Mrs. Williams in the kitchen and his mother upstairs.

"Did Jenny identify—"

"The earrings and the skirt. But I spoke with one of the prosecutors, and it's not enough."

I swallowed, dreading his reply but needing to ask. "What about my testimony?" I gestured vaguely at my face. "All this?"

He shook his head. "Burnett summoned the constables to his house this morning, claiming his housekeeper and a rough-looking man attacked him."

I choked out a laugh that sounded like a bellows breaking. He couldn't even allow me the revenge of being accused of stabbing him.

"He says you stole money, and a valuable human heart."

Mine stopped. "You didn't see it?"

"I wasn't at the house, but Fraser was. They went over the whole place, taking notes."

I reached for the half-eaten loaf of bread and cut another slice. One morsel reached my mouth—it tasted like dust, so I shredded the rest with my fingers, as Kerr tried to explain the limitations of law.

"—so the burden of proof is on us."

"I know that very well. Better than you," I snapped.

Kerr stopped pacing and slumped back in his chair. "I'm sorry.

I'm trying, for you, for Thomas, for Nan..." He sighed and shook his head.

Why her? Was she also connected? I remembered the comment about nightmares. "Isn't Nan your daughter?"

Kerr hesitated. "I hope she will be, but—"

"What happened to her?"

He leaned his elbows on the table, weaving his hands together and resting his forehead there. "Guess."

"Another disappearance?"

He nodded. "Her mother. We thought she must have abandoned her to go off with a new man—it happens, you know. Some fellows will take a woman on, but only if she leaves her children behind. This was after Thomas's disappearance, so I should have put two and two together."

He shook his head. "I didn't. I brought her to an orphanage, but she ran away and was living rough. Found her again." One side of his mouth hitched up, but the half smile faded as he rubbed a tired hand through his hair.

"We investigate a fair number of disappearances, but there is a worrying number with the same pattern—sudden, unexpected, and we never find any real leads. They're always the kind of people who aren't missed beyond their family, and there's often something unusual about them. I have a list." He met my gaze, and nodded at my unspoken request. "It's in my room. Come on. You must be tired."

He helped me stand, my aching muscles protesting.

The rooms we passed were small, matching the size of the house. His bedchamber hardly looked inhabited—there weren't any clothes lying out, and the washstand was empty.

"It'll be over here." He thumbed through a stack of papers on a table that served as a writing desk.

"Is that mine?" I reached past him for the silver snuffbox next to the inkstand. He nodded absently, still searching. I flipped open the lid, unfolded the paper, and lightly touched the lock of Thomas's blond hair.

"Thank you for taking care of this." If I'd had it with me, it probably would've been left behind with all my other things. "Didn't you get the keys made?" Besides Thomas's hair, the snuffbox was empty.

"They're in the drawer. Not that they'll be any use to us now. Burnett said because of the thefts, he's changing the locks." He grimaced. "Here."

I took the paper from his hand. He glanced about the room and seemed to find it wanting. Like the rest of the house, it was practically bare: bed, table, stool instead of a chair, a plain wooden box with his initials burnt into it, and six books arranged on a shelf mounted to the wall. He didn't own much more than I did, but there was a pleasant scent in the air and I didn't see any dust in the corners.

"Are you cold? Shall I light the fire?"

I nodded, since it seemed likely to put him at ease again, though what I really wanted was a flannel and some hot water. As Kerr bent over the wood laid in the grate, I turned my attention to the list.

I recognized his handwriting—the letters were compact and written firmly, with more pressure than could be good for his pens. Thomas's name was there, and Lizzie's, but the rest were unfamiliar, though I recognized two of the peculiarities written in the second column on the sheet.

"Which is Nan's mother?" I asked, scanning further down.

He pointed to the line at the bottom, and my breath stopped.

"Isobel?"

I'd put them in the room myself. Mary Burt's mismatched blue and brown eyes.

"He has these in his collection," I said. At least, he had last time I looked. But if Thomas's heart had been "stolen" from him, he might have taken the precaution of hiding other trophies. I didn't believe he'd get rid of them, though, not after risking so much to collect them. He'd hide them away for six months or a year, then bring them out again, when suspicion ebbed, just like he had when I'd made my first accusation.

"You can go look. The next tickets are for Tuesday next week. Bring Nan. Maybe she can recognize—"

"No." The word was unnecessary. The expression on his face said enough. "Nan doesn't know yet, and I need time to tell her. Even then, she's to be left out of this. Burnett isn't fool enough to let me through his door, and I'm not fool enough to try it, especially not with a child in tow. What would it do to her, seeing her dead mother's eyes on one of his shelves?"

"How else are we to stop him?" I demanded.

"We don't have to plan anything now. Better if we don't. We need to think, and just now, you aren't—" He licked his lips, choosing his words carefully. "He nearly killed you today. I can't look at you without my face hurting. Fraser promised to assign extra constables on the street for the next week at least, so Burnett won't be able to—"

"I know what he can do better than you," I insisted. "Constables outside won't stop him. We can't afford to wait."

"Believe me, I'd like nothing more than to march over and arrest him right now. And maybe we'd put up a fight with the things we know, but we can't prove anything. I don't want to fight him, Isobel. I want to win."

"Fine." I rubbed the back of my neck.

He looked around the room, a little helplessly. "You really should rest. Can I—"

"I don't have a nightdress."

"I'll give you one of my shirts," he said, relieved at solving such a simple problem.

"Some hot water?"

"I'll bring everything you need," he promised.

Soon I had a can of steaming water, a flannel, a towel, and a pair of leather slippers embroidered with roses, ready for my soon-to-be-clean feet. A nightshirt waited on the bed, and a comb lay on the washstand.

"Do you need anything else?"

He looked tired, too, so I shook my head, but a scent creeping into the air with the steam of the water made me ask, "Did you scent the water?"

He dropped his eyes, gave a half-hearted shrug. "Old habit. Something my grandmother used to do."

I sniffed again. "Is it—"

"Bergamot. It's the closest I've found to the plants she used. And witch hazel. My own addition, but I'm fond of it. Do you not like it? I can bring up more." Without waiting for an answer, he started for the stairs.

"No, please—" I stopped him. "I like it. I just—it surprised me. But it smells refreshing."

He smiled, surveying me again, top to toe, in a way that was hardly flattering. "I hope so. I really do."

{ 33 }

S he likes children, *Nitânis*," Adam said again, then wondered if
he'd made a faulty assumption. Isobel loved her lost son, but that
didn't mean she'd take to Nan, and Nan was cool with strangers. But
the next few days—crucial ones, if he was going to corner Burnett—
would be much simpler if he could count on Nan and Isobel to watch
each other.

He switched tactics. "I have to work. Would you like to go to
Aunt Emily's tomorrow instead?"

She nodded, and Adam sighed. Half-solved was better than not
at all, and he could figure out the rest in the morning. "Lie back
down, then. It's late. You should be asleep."

She snuggled back under her covers, a bit of rabbit fur from an
old mitten beneath her cheek. She liked the feel of it against her skin,
and stroking it seemed to help her sleep. At least, she was having
fewer nightmares since Adam dug it out of an old box.

"I heard you talking to her," Nan announced to the ceiling.

Adam turned his head on the makeshift pillow. He'd had to
leave his behind for Isobel. Emily always said his housekeeping was
impossible, and it seemed she was finally proved right. He didn't
own nearly enough cutlery, comforts, or linen, not for three.

He propped himself on an elbow so he could see her better. "What did we say, then?" His stomach tightened.

"You can't trick me. I know my mam's dead."

The words seemed to press him into the mattress. Adam stretched out a hand in the dark, but instead of laying it on her arm, he set it next to her, on the sheet. "I'm not trying to trick you. But I want you to feel safe and—and not sad."

He didn't want to burden her with expectations of happiness, like his father and stepmother had wanted from him.

Her head rolled sideways. Their eyes met in the dark.

"But it's all right to be sad," Adam added quickly. "I was sad when my mother died. My grandmother said I didn't speak for a long time after." A whole winter, if what she'd told his father was true, when he finally caught up with them, two years after the massacre of their family, and the burning of the house where Adam had been born.

He hadn't expected to ever see his father again. Kanapawamakan had told him Jock Kerr was probably dead too, what with Nor'Wester men pursuing Hudson's Bay Company surveyors like his father. Out in the wilderness, it was all too easy to make rival company men disappear.

Adam often thought about what his life would be like, how different it would be, if he'd stayed on the other side of the Atlantic. Even there, being mixed was different, but there were others like him, plenty of them, and being Michif was its own way. He wouldn't have grown up surrounded by Scots, every one of them convinced their language and traditions were better. Even his father never understood that Adam might have wanted something else.

But this wasn't the time for poring over fading dreams. Nan wanted the truth, and he owed it to her, even if he feared she wouldn't understand. "I planned to tell you, as soon as I was sure. I wanted to be sure first."

"Other policemen aren't so picky," Nan said with a sniff. "And I'm sure. I told you she wouldn't have left me."

"I know. I'm sorry." Even so, it seemed too cruel to say that Mary had been murdered for her eyes. "Did you hear everything?" Adam asked.

She nodded. She was staring at the ceiling again, but he could see a silver trail running from the corner of her eye to her hair.

"Try to be kind to Mrs. Tait," Adam said. "The same man took her son."

A quick look, a quivering lip, swiftly stilled, and a nod. Throat tight, Adam swept a hand over her forehead, smoothing her hair. "We'll stop him, Nan," he promised.

{34}

Kerr must have spoken to Nan about me, encouraging her to be less shy. Today, she responded to all my conversational sallies at breakfast, in between bites. Her face was full enough now, but when Kerr found her she must have been troublingly thin, because he kept urging her to eat more. I chewed slowly, my face and jaw still too sore for larger bites.

"I thought you might like to spend the day at my stepmother's house," Kerr suggested as Nan rose to clear our porridge bowls. "Nan usually visits there."

I held back a grimace. "Have you thought of a plan?" I asked, voice low, hoping Nan was out of hearing distance.

"Not in my sleep."

"I have one."

He looked at me warily. "Let me see which way the wind is blowing today first."

"Is that code for speaking with the prosecutor?"

He gave a reluctant smile. "Aye. Whether a court accepts your testimony or not, we still should record a statement. Your version of what happened, not Burnett's tale. It should be recorded by someone you haven't met before. Not me, and not"—he cleared

his throat—"not this particular prosecutor. Maybe the superintendent. I'm not sure yet. And I'll call on Burnett today for another
statement—he's lying, so it'll be harder for him to be consistent. If
I catch him in a lie on record, your statement will be more credible
by comparison."

It was one way of going about it, I supposed—hand picks and
shovels could undermine a fortress. I wanted gunpowder.

"You're lucky to have escaped," Kerr reminded me. "Rest for a
day at least. And you'll be safe with my stepmother."

Maybe he didn't want to leave me unattended in his house. After
all, he didn't really know me. But I preferred a dull day hiding here
to being foisted on another woman's company.

I straightened the cuffs of yesterday's dress, the only thing I
had to wear today. It was still damp from sponging, with Kerr's list
tucked out of sight inside my sleeve. "I'm not at my best," I said,
thinking of the bruises that had bloomed even larger across my face
overnight.

He frowned, turning thoughts over in his mind, but these were
opaque to me. Finally, he turned to Nan. "I'll take you to visit Emily.
Mrs. Tait will be more comfortable here."

Nan flashed me an unreadable glance. "I don't mind staying
here, if Mrs. Tait is agreeable."

"I don't th—"

"Perfectly agreeable." I responded quickly, impulsively, without
examining why.

"You might help me with my letters?" Nan suggested. I worked
to keep the surprise from showing on my face. I'd spent much of the
night thinking about letters, the carefully crafted ones I intended to
write today.

Of course, Nan meant practicing the alphabet, but—"I'd be glad to," I said. The smile she gave me in return was so demure I distrusted it immediately, unsettled that she seemed to perceive my thoughts.

"If you're certain." Adam glanced between us.

"Quite certain." My plan—really just some stirring ideas—and the letters I wanted to write didn't add up to much. Picks and shovels, just like Kerr's next moves. But these tools could strike a spark, and sometimes one spark was all you needed to start a fire.

Not everyone, I hoped, would be as hard to convince as the law.

After Kerr left, Nan brought me a stack of writing paper from the hall cupboard—a strange place to keep it, but this wasn't a typical house.

As I wrote, discarded, and rewrote my letters, Nan stubbornly formed bent-backed *k*s and misshapen *g*s. It was easy being in company with a child again, so easy it made me uncomfortable. I knew just how to help her rearrange her slate and her left hand to better manage her stick of chalk, and when her fingers grew tired, it was my idea, not hers, to share a story.

"Does Mr. Kerr have any books?" I asked, terrified of what I'd just done, without even thinking. All my stories were invented for Thomas and—I swallowed hard—he wasn't here.

"Some, but I like the ones he tells about the New World," Nan said.

"He's been there?" My eyebrows rose, a new idea nudging my consciousness, one that might explain his singular looks. Dr. Burnett had called him a "half-breed," but I'd interpreted that to mean part Greek or perhaps even part Arab. I hadn't considered he might hail from someplace even farther. When Adam spoke, there were no foreign traces in his speech. He sounded like anyone else who'd grown up here.

"He has," Nan nodded earnestly. "It's his home. It's where his people are. His mam's lot anyway. But his da took him away."

They were both transplants. Maybe that was the similarity knitting them together.

"We don't have to have a story," Nan said. Then, when I didn't reply, she added. "I'm sorry for your son."

I thought of the blue and brown eyes in Burnett's drawing room, my heart twisting. "Did Mr. Kerr tell you mine?" I asked.

She nodded. "What's your plan?"

To my horror, I laughed, unnerved by her matter-of-fact tone, her calm expression.

"You told Adam you have one," she said, before I could deny it. "What are the letters supposed to do?"

Kerr would kill me for this. He'd spent twenty minutes with me before he left, explaining the risks he took as a police detective, and how that endangered people around him, like Nan. I was not to talk about her mother's fate. I was not to let her leave the house or even stand near the windows until he'd arranged for a trustworthy servant of his stepmother's to come protect us.

"It's not just letters, Nan." I reached into my pocket and took out the pair of copied keys I'd taken from Kerr's room.

Not having spent time in the Burnett household, he assumed Burnett would change all his locks, but Mrs. Burnett never paid twice when once sufficed. Why trouble with more than the front door?

That single lock would have stopped me, even with these illicitly acquired keys—if I hadn't prepared an escape route through my bedroom window. Now it was my way in, so long as no one had found it.

"You've seen Mr. Kerr's list?" I asked. She was just learning to read, but a sharp mind like hers would understand its significance.

"He's been working on it a long time," Nan said. "These people aren't just taken, like I was." She swallowed. "They aren't coming back."

"No," I admitted, my stomach heavy, because I knew where their unique oddities were displayed, had cleaned and polished them. Before Nan asked something I couldn't bear to answer, I said, "But I know where their bodies are. I'll go back for them."

And then I'd tell everyone.

That night, Nan rapped softly on the wall between our rooms as soon as Kerr was asleep. I rose, still dressed, and crept out of the house following the route I'd practiced with Nan, avoiding the creaking spots on the floor.

There should have been a moon, but rain clouds hid the lady in the sky, rinsing the roofs, the church spires, the streets. By the end of the block, my toes were wet in my shoes. By the time I crossed the Royal Mile, wet hair clung to my forehead, beneath my heavy cloak.

The lantern in my hand, though safely shuttered, surrendered and went out. No matter. I knew the way. Edging out of passing carriage lights, skirting huddled figures sheltering beneath eaves and covered doors, I ghosted through Surgeon's Square, down sloping streets with running gutters, and peered around the corner into Newington Place, just as a cloaked police constable strode into the weak light puddled beneath a hissing streetlamp. Three steps, and he vanished into the dark.

I walked past the house at the corner, the bookend to this long gray row, and into the alley running parallel to the street, until I came to the back of Burnett's house. Crouching down, I pried at my old window with my nails, tearing them in jagged flakes and bruising my fingers, until it finally budged enough to slip one of my keys into the gap. The latch hadn't been repaired—thank God—but I should have greased the casement hinges. Lucky for me, I hadn't actually resorted to this avenue when I escaped. Even a second or two of delay, and Burnett would have grabbed me before I clambered free.

I nursed my hands for a moment, then wrestled the window open and pushed inside, discovering more flaws in my earlier plan—my skirts and cloak caught on everything.

I dropped onto the floor with my skirts around my shoulders and the lantern clamped between my teeth. Striking a spark proved nearly impossible with my numb, mashed fingers, but eventually I coaxed a light into being and persuaded it to stay, fiddling with the lantern shutters until only the slimmest beam escaped to show the way.

Keys in hand, I stole into the specimen room. The place had grown larger in the dark; I felt half as tall, ranged against cabinets and shelves twice their usual size. Beneath the swaying beam of my light, the ears and intestines, the cancerous testicles and curled-in feet churned slowly inside their jars. My breath was the only sound, but it echoed heavily, as if these stolen bones and bits were grasping at me, trying to share breath and life again. Though I expected it, the empty space where Thomas's heart used to be made my hands twitch.

A reckoning falls on everyone, I reminded myself, and Burnett's was coming, a whirlwind stirred up by the thieving of hands and eyes and hearts. I would call it down and open the door to the blast.

Beneath my cloak, I'd slung a loose satchel over my shoulder. I didn't need to retrieve Kerr's list from the hiding place inside my sleeve; I walked without hesitation to the shelf by the window with Mary Burt's eyes and unstoppered the jar—too large, too heavy, too prone to clink.

Lifting tenderly, I extracted the eyes, wrapped them in a handkerchief, and stowed the damp bundle in my bag. From my pocket, I took out a card, replacing the one next to the empty jar. MARY BURT, it read, in Nan's wobbly block capitals, instead of Burnett's neatly penned Latin.

The femur with the osteoma was too big for me to carry away, but I tore up Burnett's label, replacing it with a name: OLIVER GRANT. I wrapped and pocketed the tiny curved leg bones of a woman with osteomalacia from Adam's list and opened the shutter of my lantern a little wider, so I could search for Lizzie Dove's hand. She'd disappeared nearly two months ago. By now Burnett might think he was safe. Or maybe I looked because of a premonition, a sense from Lizzie herself that her hand would be here—because there it was, floating as delicately as a rose blossom inside a blown glass jar on the far side of the room.

"Hello, Lizzie," I murmured.

"That's not my name," said a voice behind me.

I leaped and spun, confronting the living body that had followed me into the room, a dark shadow outlined in the wildly swinging beam of my lamp—Mrs. Burnett.

"Don't scream," she whispered, thrusting a pistol into my belly. "I'll shoot. There's constables patrolling the street."

"Don't!" I gripped her forearm—realized what I'd done—and breathed out because she didn't fire. "I'm not a thief. These are from people he's murdered." I licked dry lips. "Please, I know it sounds crazy, but if you just listen to me—"

"You stabbed my son when he caught you stealing—"

"That's a lie!" My voice punched through the air between us, making her flinch. "He came to my room. He tried to smother me. If I hadn't fought back, he'd have killed me too. Like the owner of that hand. Like my son, Thomas. He was only seven."

Her eyes widened and her lips, pale in the uncertain light, fell open half an inch. "No."

"It's true," I countered mercilessly. "The police suspect. It's only a matter of time before they bring proof against him. His victims are here, and their names—"

"Stop." She pushed the pistol deeper, forcing out my breath. But she was rattled. Convincing her was my only chance.

"Thomas had a damaged heart. Your son diagnosed it here, then had him kidnapped a month later. Elizabeth Dove had six fingers. She also disappeared after visiting this house." I expected an explosion after each word, but she was transfixed by my recital, name after name. I pressed on, desperate to make her understand and dreading the moment—seconds away—when my names would run out.

"And that's not all," I said, drawing the moment out, hoping to delay our reckoning. "There's suspicion over the unexpected death of his mentor, John Barclay. He died—"

"I know," Mrs. Burnett interrupted. "I remember."

"—practically as soon as he signed the partnership. Don't you see—"

She prodded with the pistol, and I stepped back, the lamp swinging. In the erratic beam, her eyes glinted with unholy light. "You're the blind one." She giggled, the lace at her neck trembling against sinewy skin. "I killed John Barclay."

Recoiling, I stumbled, caught by the leg of a chair that had crept up on me while I'd inched away from Mrs. Burnett. The lantern fell from my hand, and she sprang, knocking me back to the floor.

"Conall needed the chance. He'd worked for so long already, and as a junior partner, everyone credited Barclay for Conall's work. But it was simple. I read how in one of his books. And you thought I couldn't manage things."

I'd spent hours studying Orfila's *Treatise on Poisons*, but never considered whether someone else had already put the information to practical use. Senseless, stupid, foolish...

She motioned with the pistol. "Lie back."

Eyes on the gun, I lowered my shoulders to the floor, the room spinning above me, a hot scratchiness at the back of my throat. With the gun pointed at me, there was nothing else I could do.

She straddled my chest, just like her son had, and reached for my face. I turned away, but my lungs were burning already, as if in anticipation. Her hands weren't strong, but she'd have little trouble smothering me. Why couldn't she just shoot instead?

Then, I smelled it, and understood the heat in my lungs, the rasp in my throat. As her hand smashed onto my face, fingers seeking out my nostrils but jabbing my eyes, I gasped, "The carpet is smoking. My lamp."

She flew off me with a speed that would have been disorienting, if I'd had a second to waste. Instead, I struck out, sending the pistol spinning to oblivion in the corner of the room. She fought back, clawing, biting, and battering me with fists, but age told, and I forced her back. She thrashed beneath me, nearly oversetting me onto the smoldering rug. I silenced a yell with a jab to her stomach, then clapped my hands to her mouth, terrified she'd alert the constable outside.

My overturned lamp lay just past her shoulder, and my eyes

stung and watered from the rising smoke. If I didn't beat out this fledgling fire, this house, the next—whole streets could burn. Almost unbidden, my thumb slid down to clamp her mouth shut as my fingers closed her nostrils.

Just until she stops fighting, I told myself.

For ageless seconds I pressed, my own chest too tight to breathe. Finally her shoulders relaxed, and I freed my other arm, righted the lamp, and began flailing against the carpet, striking it with my flat palm for lack of anything else, the heat scorching my skin. She tossed, and my left hand gripped harder, as I battled the rug and her, trying not to be thrown off. I couldn't let her scream. I couldn't let her escape.

In the dark, I couldn't see if I'd extinguished the embers, and it was impossible to judge by the smell of the smoke. I fought until I was sure, and Mrs. Burnett was limp beneath me, then rolled off, desperate to get away from her. Everything hurt, from my eyes to the tips of my fingers, and I moved heavily, stumbling about the room. The hand. I couldn't go without that.

After several clumsy attempts, I extricated it from the jar and slid it into my bag, twitching at each imagined sound and every sway of my skirts.

Why just Mrs. Burnett? How come I hadn't been attacked by the doctor?

I glanced at her, splayed on the floor, unmoving, and the prosaic information returned to me—this was the last Friday of the month. Burnett was dining with the Aesculapian Club.

I shuddered and looked away from her, drawing a long breath of relief. I had to get out of here.

I'd never manage to hoist myself through the basement window. My limbs were as shaken as laundry left out on the line, buffeting every which way as I stumbled through the hall to the door. I cracked it open and peered down the street, waiting for the sentry outside to walk to the bottom of the close.

Then, burdened by the remains of Burnett's victims and an additional, unaccustomed load on my soul, I escaped into the wet street.

{ *35* }

Good night, John." Conall touched his hat and climbed from
Ballingall's carriage, stepping awkwardly over a pooling gutter.
"Thanks for bringing me home." The wound on his leg made it
impossible to walk far.

"I'll see you next week at Mrs. Stevenson's," Ballingall said.
"Unless you want me to take another look at that injury of yours."
He'd stitched the twin punctures closed yesterday and applied
fomentations to the skin.

Conall eased the weight off his injured thigh. The wound still
hurt like hell. "Thank you. I'll give it a couple of days."

Ballingall nodded and rapped his stick on the side of the carriage, signaling the driver, who flicked the reins. The carriage rolled
off toward the end of the close, where a hunched and miserable-
looking constable prowled the pavement.

If he was lucky, they'd stop patrolling here tomorrow. Though
Conall was glad to have convinced the constables of his story, it
wouldn't be convenient, having sustained scrutiny on this street. Not
even Isobel Tait would be fool enough to come back.

He limped up the steps, wishing he'd taken the time to buy a
stick. Ballingall took his everywhere he went, and there was nothing

wrong with his legs, so carrying one wasn't conceding weakness. It looked quite distinguished, in fact. He could have one made, with something appropriate fashioned into the handle—a snake referencing the caduceus perhaps.

He'd drunk more wine than usual tonight to combat the pain in his leg and mute his frustration with Brennan—Eoin still hadn't found the sister of that six-fingered woman—so he applied extra focus to the extraction and selection of his keys. He wasn't used to finding the new one yet by touch.

He brought it to the lock—and discovered the door was open, ajar by half an inch. His pulse jumped tempo and he glanced over his shoulder. The constable was within hailing distance now, and he caught the look, raising a hand in half-hearted salute.

"Evening, doctor."

"Good evening, constable." The face was familiar, but for the life of him, Conall couldn't recall his name.

"Everything all right?"

"Perfectly," Conall said. "Just a little the worse for wear this evening."

"I'm right here if you need anything," the man said, with an edge in his voice that spoke more of irritation than solicitude.

"Much appreciated." Unable to put it off any longer, Conall pushed his way inside, bracing for anything.

The hall was dark and empty, with nothing disturbed, no felons, no additional police. His tight-strung muscles eased; with a sigh, he removed his coat and hat and limped toward his study and the decanter of whisky beside the window. Halfway to the door, he stopped and sniffed the air. It smelled like smoke—not just the traces of a hastily extinguished candle.

His wine haze retreating behind a wave of apprehension, Conall applied flint to steel, sparked a flame, and lit a candle, raising it high to inspect the hall. Shadows fled from his light, and he saw what he'd missed before. The drawing room door was unlocked and open, just as the front door had been. And for this door, he had the only key, save for the one kept by the Tait-Ross woman. Somehow she'd found a way past the new wards on his doors.

A chill crawled up his arms and he reminded himself the murmuring heart was safely away at the school, but his blood congealed when he thought what she might have done to the rest of his collection. He rushed into the drawing room, nearly extinguishing his candle, and stopped dead on the threshold, swaying on his feet. His mother lay supine on the carpet.

He clutched the doorframe, but was too used to bodies to stop the swift and automatic cataloging of her urine-stained skirts, blue-tipped fingers, and staring eyes. Swallowing twice, he glanced away from her face and set down the candle, just in case, though shock was passing, and his hands now felt steady enough.

His mother must have confronted Ross—no, Tait, he corrected. He examined her face and throat, checking for bruises, finding only the hint of one beneath his mother's chin. The bitch had used his method of asphyxiation.

Conall sat back on his heels, drumming the fingers of one hand on his good thigh in time with the blood pounding in his ears.

He knew—who better?—that his mother's murder might pass as a natural death, but was that a risk he could afford to take? Definitely not. There were rumors enough already. If he didn't call in another doctor to register the death, it would excite comment, and suppose Ballingall or one of the others noticed the bruise? He couldn't sacrifice his hard-won respectability for this.

Dear God, what was he to do? That constable was right outside, and it was astonishing this could have happened without rousing anyone. He only had a few hours until the little maid, Maggie, would be rushing about with the coal scuttle.

Mother wasn't large, luckily. She'd fit in Eoin Brennan's tea chest, but at this hour, with the constable patrolling the close, Conall couldn't see how to get a message to him. He'd have to fetch him instead, an awkward journey at the best of times, let alone at this hour, on an aching leg.

Impossible. He'd have to wait until morning. *This room is always kept locked*, he reminded himself.

No, that wouldn't work either. He was forgetting about rigor. If he waited, he and Brennan would never be able to fit her in the truck, and he couldn't very well keep her in the salon until rigor mortis wore off. That would take a day and a half.

He needed to consider calmly. Mother wouldn't want him to be so overset. He bent down and straightened her legs, crossing her arms across her chest.

Then it came to him. Simple, and perfectly believable. His servants would think little of it, and there'd be nothing to alarm the police. Catching hold of his mother's heels, he dragged her to the edge of the damaged rug, then rolled her up inside. He'd send for Brennan in the morning; until then, he'd lock the room. He'd tell the servants he'd dropped a candle, and have a new rug here by the end of the week.

As for his mother...

She wouldn't be wasted, he decided. One of the barrels at the school would do for six months or a year, in which he'd track and kill Isobel Tait. That was certain. Eoin and his ilk would find her, if she didn't try her luck here again. He almost hoped she did—because he'd be ready.

Meanwhile, he'd tell people his mother had gone on a spa holiday. They had enough money for it, and his mother had been ill. Many women went from one spa town to another, testing the different treatments on offer. It might seem like a hasty decision, but he'd make it convincing.

Locking the door behind him, Conall limped up the stairs to pack a valise for his mother. Once he had done that, he'd take a dose of laudanum for the leg and to put him to sleep.

{ 36 }

I debated whether I should return to Kerr's place, but there was no place else to go. I'd have to chance it.

Kerr was asleep. There was no reason he'd ever know I'd left, and if he suspected me tomorrow, when the police were summoned to Burnett's—well, there was a difference between knowing a thing and proving it.

I told myself that every dozen steps or so, until I stood, shivering, outside the house.

Unfortunately, there was a light in the upstairs window. Flight was the sensible option—Kerr was a police detective, and though I didn't think he would see me charged with murder, I couldn't count on it. But I was tired, cold, rattled—and I wasn't finished with Burnett yet.

I let myself inside as quietly as I could, but I must have made more noise than I knew. The moment I latched the door, Kerr confronted me, speaking from the stairs.

"What the hell were you thinking?"

"You're dressed?" I asked, blinking to accustom myself to the light.

"I was about to go after you. I woke up in the night, found you gone, and when Nan finally admitted what you were up to—" He raked a hand through his hair. "Saints above, Isobel. You might have been killed."

"Well, I wasn't," I snapped tartly, hating the way trembling took hold of my limbs again.

Kerr's eyes narrowed. "What happened?"

I winced, reliving Mrs. Burnett's waning struggles, and the smell of burning wool.

"Come into the kitchen."

I was in no state to argue. By the time I considered taking issue with his autocratic tone, I was relieved of the satchel and wrapped in a blanket, while Kerr fussed over laying and lighting a new fire.

Nan was out of bed, too, though still in a nightdress, and the way she flitted about, assembling tea, never in Kerr's direct line of vision, I could tell she intended to stay. Once the flames caught, though, Kerr turned on her. "*Nitânis*, get to bed."

She flashed me a wide-eyed glance and left the room. She even closed the door, but Adam seemed to listen to her retreat anyway, counting each creak of the stairs.

"I'm sorry. I shouldn't have involved her," I began.

"No, you shouldn't have," he agreed. Ignoring Nan's pot of tea, he went to the cupboard and fetched a bottle of whisky, pouring out a dram. He drank it down, poured another, and passed the glass to me.

"You need something," he snapped. "A dose of sanity mainly, but—"

I picked up the bag from the floor. "Lizzie Dove's hand is here."

For a full minute, he said nothing. Then—"What happened?"

I was so weary, such a shadow of my usual self, that any attempt at defensive jockeying was beyond me. In spite of my misgivings, I told him.

I told him everything.

Long after I finished, Kerr paced out the room from sink to fire to window and back again. My unease grew with each second he frowned and said nothing.

"Will you arrest me?" I finally asked.

"It's not murder," he said, surprising me with the speed and certainty of his response. "But Burnett will make it look that way. So we'll have to handle this carefully."

He was still frowning, probably sorting through different scenarios. I sank deeper in my chair. Just this once, it was nice not to have to think. I was warm again, and my head pleasantly muzzy from whisky.

I woke in bed without knowing how I'd arrived there, with an aching head and new bruises. My clothes were gone and I was clad, once again, in one of Kerr's shirts. Frowning, I checked myself, then realized it was a little late for suspicion—I'd already confessed to killing Mrs. Burnett. For whatever reason—and I really couldn't think of a decent one—last night I'd decided to trust him.

Today, that felt like a mistake.

I glanced about for my clothes and saw an unfamiliar dress alongside a folded stack of stockings, shift, and stays. Someone—Kerr, as little as I liked to think of it—had laid out a comb and a toothbrush.

I was afraid to face him today, afraid of seeing suspicion, dislike, the same barriers I put between myself and killers, and couldn't reasonably believe in now. I feared he'd reconsidered in the night, and that Detective Fraser and a pair of constables would be waiting in his kitchen.

Someone scratched on the door.

"It's me," Nan called. "I can help you dress."

Now I saw that, unlike my housekeeper's garb, these clothes fastened in the back. I let Nan inside, and tried to act like I wasn't bothered by the brush of linen I hadn't bought against my skin. These stays were stiffer than I was used to, with a wide wooden busk inserted in the front. I'd worn similar undergarments before, but lately grown used to more flexibility around my middle.

"Where did he find these?" I asked dryly, sounding much more confident than I actually felt.

"Emily's," Nan informed me. "She sent them over this morning."

"Must have been early."

Nan shook her head. "It's past noon. Adam said we weren't going to wake you."

My stomach twisted into double knots. "Is there any news?" Was Kerr still here? What about the stolen specimens left in my satchel—and the letters I'd planned on delivering today?

Nan, balanced behind me on the chair, brushed the loose hair over my shoulders and set to work on the last buttons. "Fits nicely," she announced. "Emily said it would."

I grunted.

"Breakfast?" she asked.

It seemed that no matter how I felt, I was expected to eat. I trailed her down the stairs, until I froze three from the bottom. There was, after all, a policeman in the kitchen.

Neither Nan nor the constable acted like his presence was in any way remarkable. Without speaking, Nan dished me up a bowl of porridge and beckoned me to the table. I crossed the kitchen on stiff legs and sat down next to her, but I couldn't take my eyes off the uniformed man at the other side of the table, dipping toast into a cup of tea.

"Excuse me, but why are you here?" I asked. There was nothing to gain being coy, but my skin itched as I waited for him to swallow and offer an answer.

"Kerr said he's worried about Ribbonmen." His eyes swept to Nan. "On account of the girl. He's got some inquiries to make, but he'll return as soon as he's able—I'm to take you to his stepmother's."

He dabbed at his mustache. I tried to decide how I felt about this, but my head was too sore and my stomach too uneasy to tease apart this tangle. I looked away, colliding with Nan's watchful eyes, and picked up my spoon with a sigh.

Would Mrs. Burnett's ghost follow me now? Would she speak to me in the night or over my morning cup of tea?

I brought the napkin to my mouth and took a deep breath.

"Not feeling the thing?" The constable appraised me sympathetically.

I smiled weakly in response. *Not at all, constable. Not at all.*

I walked to Emily Kerr's house as slowly as I could, like Thomas had when I used to pull him unwillingly from the park. But the house was closer than I expected, only two streets away. Dawdling didn't help.

I had no idea what Adam had told her or what she must think of me. For months I'd lived someplace in between, but I was myself now. Back where opinions mattered.

We were admitted by a manservant, who smiled and greeted Nan by name, and nodded at me while looking over my shoulder. Emily Kerr wouldn't be the only one with opinions. This man probably had some too. I didn't like his sideways glances. Nothing marred my hands, but I felt like *murderer* was branded across my forehead. How could anyone see me and not know?

Then I remembered. He was probably just noticing the bruises, lightening to green today but still stamped firmly upon my face.

The lady of the house was in the parlor, along with Kerr. "You're back. What news?" I blurted.

He pinched his lips together, and I glanced at the woman beside him. Sensing the pressure of things unsaid, she motioned Nan to the writing desk and asked to be shown her letters, so Kerr could leave his chair and confer with me privately.

"There's been no summons to Burnett's house," he said.

I frowned.

"But—"

"Until there's a reasonable pretext, I can't appear to know more than the next man. So our best chance is to use an informer, not a constable. See if she can find out anything from Burnett's servants."

She? I cocked my head.

He nodded slightly. "I thought we could ask Jenny Dove. We can trust her. She'll want to help. So long as she avoids Burnett, there isn't too much risk." Again, the dark look. "You and I can speak to her later today—she'll want to know what you found."

I swallowed, catching the unspoken words. I didn't want to think about explaining how I'd found her dead sister's hand, and paid for it with dearer coin than I'd ever spent before.

It was self-defense. The words came to me in Adam's voice. He'd said them more than once last evening. But maybe I could have stopped sooner. If not for the threat of fire, if I hadn't been so terrified, would I have stayed my hand? Tried to revive her?

I didn't think so, and that, in its own way, was as frightening as being smothered.

She'd killed John Barclay. She might have helped Burnett with the others. She might have conspired in the murder of my son. I'd tell myself so until I believed it, and make myself content with that.

"Won't you have a seat, Mrs. Tait?" The question, from Mrs. Emily Kerr, almost made me laugh. It seemed far too genteel and ordinary. I couldn't sit here, on a sofa with doilies on the armrests and *converse*.

I glanced about, seeking escape, and my eyes fell on a pianoforte, glowing in the slanting light from the window. Astonishing that I hadn't seen it before, that my eyes hadn't lighted on it as soon as I entered the room. "Do you play?" I asked, as if this was as miraculous as her speaking Bulgarian.

"Not well," she said, her eyelids dropping in the usual female response. At once I knew she was a competent musician at the very least.

"May I?" The instrument was irresistible—more than anything, this was the salve I wanted. I'd avoided music, run from it before, but now I longed for that line of Vivaldi, the one I'd heard as Burnett smothered me, that sang new strength into my hands.

But I hadn't played in so long. My fingers were bruised, my nails broken. Suppose I no longer knew how? It seemed fitting, like the prices paid by witches in Mrs. Williams's tales, that my hands would lose their gift after dropping poison into a whisky decanter, after stabbing and smothering.

"Of course you can play it," Mrs. Kerr said, leaving me no choice but to seat myself before the keys.

"Do you wish to be left alone?" My hostess looked slightly anxious, as any good musician might. I hoped I could still play.

I shook my head, lifted the cover, and adjusted the seat while Mrs. Kerr fluttered in my periphery, adjusting curtains, offering sheet music, and simultaneously apologizing for her collection. It was all highly technical.

That was a jab to my pride. I pretended to study the scores as she, Kerr, and Nan settled themselves on the other side of the room. Clearly, this wasn't what Kerr had in mind, but he could have intervened, had he really wanted to stop it. And whatever was happening, whatever I—we—chose to do next, I needed this first.

I let out a sigh, wondering if this instrument would hate me, if the blood on my hands made me unworthy of coaxing it into speech, let alone song. My fingers, resting lightly on the keys, were stiff and clammy, but right now, more than anything, I wanted a song. A spell of forgetting.

I began with a scale—the melody I craved was too demanding to simply fall into. I flinched at my first errors, but soon they slipped past without causing pain. I picked up the first piece of sheet music, fumbled my way through, and had the satisfaction of doing better the second time through the repeats.

"You said you were out of practice, Mrs. Tait," Mrs. Kerr said, with the fading of the last chord. I glanced back, saw the three of them and an untouched plate of sandwiches I hadn't noticed arrive.

"Oh, I am," I said.

Her eyebrows lifted.

I blushed and stretched my fingers. "Perhaps I should have told you that my father was something of a musical celebrity. I learned from him."

She nodded, as if she now understood.

"You don't mind if I continue?" I felt better playing, but not whole yet. Maybe that was too ambitious.

"Please," she said.

I bowed my head over the keys and took a deep breath. No more practice scales. I was ready.

La-di-da, di-da, di-da...

Quietly, my left hand picked out the syncopated pulse that haunted me, the melancholy measures that were the foundation of everything. Then my right traveled up the keyboard in slow, sad melody—Vivaldi's largo written for spring, my song for grief and loss, played above the tempo of my lost boy's injured heart. The melody climbed, high, piercing, trilling with pain.

The piece was slow, accommodating my hesitations and stumbles, the places where I stretched notes long to draw uneven breaths. I let the music lift me, a fathomless tide to draw out my own river of heartache—rising, rising, to a tormented fluttering, a high note of pain that faded to silence above that low, uneven pulse. My shoulders curled. My left fingers slowed. One measure. Two. Another four, which Vivaldi hadn't called for.

I lifted my hand and brushed my wet cheeks. The music stopped.

"Isobel."

I stiffened. Kerr's voice was kind, but unexpectedly close, right at my shoulder. He might have heard the song, but I didn't intend to share my tear-streaked face. Shrugging as if he'd touched me, I rasped, "I'm not finished yet."

Shutting him out, I plunged my hands into the keys.

There was sad music in me, but it wasn't my only song. I wanted volume, rapid tempo, a minor key. Something too fast for me to think, a whirlpool of notes to carry away everything else. Lost in the torrent, my fingers moved like Father's had, unerring, with a will of their own, striking a fusillade of sound.

This wasn't a song for mourning or forgetting. I'd erred, but this was still the music of forging blades, of witch hazel and whisky, of unheard voices and winds with unseen hands.

My skin prickled, but I kept on, waiting for my hands to stumble, but they didn't, accelerating and landing with a crash that should have exploded the windows from all the force it carried.

I sat on the piano stool, breathing like I'd run a mile.

Tentatively, Kerr stepped into my field of view. "Isobel?"

"I'm here," I said. A strange response, but he nodded as if it made sense to him.

"Are you all right?" he asked.

"I think so." I glanced over my shoulder. Nan's mouth was open. Mrs. Kerr couldn't have stared any wider if I'd sprouted wings.

I let out a breath. It almost felt as if I had.

Kerr leaned in close. "I don't know what will happen," he whispered. "But I am sure of this."

He paused, so I prodded with a hum for a question.

"Burnett had better watch out."

I smiled and stood, acknowledging the astonished applause from Nan and Mrs. Kerr, my minuscule audience. "Thank you."

And then I bowed.

We left Nan with Emily and set out for Jenny's lodging after stopping at Kerr's to retrieve the hand, resting in a stoneware jar with Nan's mother's eyes and as much whisky as Kerr had left after last night. Not a drop remained in the bottle, but there wasn't enough to cover everything in the jar. When I peered in, three fingers curled above the liquor's surface.

"If you don't mind..." Kerr swallowed. "Putting them in here was almost too much for me to manage..."

I used to be squeamish. Not anymore. I picked out the hand and laid it in the towel Kerr held out to me.

"We have to tell Nan," I said. Another necessity that couldn't be avoided.

"Let me do it," he said quietly. "In a day or two. I'm afraid the news will hurt more than she thinks it will."

Nan was a hardy soul, and a brave one. I trusted her to bear up under the news, but the sight of her mother's eyes might very well shatter her. "Will you show her?" I asked.

"If she wants to see, I'm afraid I might have to. But I don't—" He rubbed his mouth, speaking through his fingers. "Was it better or worse, seeing Thomas's heart?"

I bit my lip. "Worse. Then better. But I don't know what will be right for Nan."

Adam sighed.

"Don't wait too long," I suggested. It was the closest thing to advice I could think of and the only point I felt any certainty about. Nan deserved answers, kindly given, but clear. To me, nothing was worse than the unknowns surrounding the known.

"This visit will be hard enough," he said. "You remember everything?"

I nodded. I was ready, wearing my disguise, my statement carefully rehearsed.

Even so, cold crept into my hands and feet the closer our carriage drew to Leith, biting sharper than it should, given that the chill outside wasn't unseasonable, and I wore thick wool stockings and a cloak.

Kerr stared out the window as we wended seaward and down-hill, letting me study him without interruption.

"What's your name?" I asked without thinking, flustering when his eyebrows drew up.

"Not Adam," I said, desperate to explain, knowing it was too late to extricate myself. "Nan told me about your mother's people. She said that's where your name for her comes from. *Nitânis*. Do you have one in that language too?"

"*Nitânis* isn't a name." He smiled self-deprecatingly. "It means *my daughter*. At least I think it does. After my father brought me to Scotland, I forgot the language, so I may have made it up."

I waited, but he didn't elaborate. We rumbled along the road, bouncing over ruts so large I gripped the seat to steady myself with one hand, and used the other to push Janet Ross's mistreated spectacles up my nose.

"I haven't explained the exact meaning to her yet," Kerr admitted.

My gaze snapped back to him. "You should. Nan ought to feel wanted."

"I hope she does," he said.

"Wouldn't you rather be sure?"

"It's not my way to presume," he said, sounding needled.

"She's a child," I snapped, my breaths inexplicably fast. "Don't make her wonder. Let her feel loved and safe. *Presume*." I spat the last word, baffled that he couldn't see how much Nan already loved him, and how much happier they would both be when—

Adam let out a long breath. "I've never done this," he said. "It's not easy, finding my way." He dropped his voice. "My mother called me Pchi Wezoo."

I frowned at him. "Chee Wizoo?" My mouth couldn't quite reproduce his syllables.

"She spoke a different language than my grandmother's," Kerr explained. "A mix of Cree and French."

I parsed the name, then my brow cleared. "Little Bird?" I hazarded. It sounded a little like *petit oiseux*.

He nodded.

Huh. I measured him against the name, unable to see a likeness. He had been little once, but I couldn't imagine it. And Kerr was remarkably contained, with a capacity for stillness that was almost uncanny—not at all like the quick, chirping child who'd suit that name.

"When did you lose her?" I hated that word. There was a difference between lost and stolen, and it was easier to be angry than bereft.

"Four, I think."

Younger than Thomas.

"I'm sorry."

He shrugged. "You learn to carry on."

He had. I suppose I had, too. Sort of. I had a purpose at any rate, and I didn't often think beyond that.

"Why didn't you tell me you believed me? When I first told you about finding Thomas's heart?" He'd said nothing then to indicate he'd even considered further investigations into Conall Burnett. And yet he'd kept on searching. If I'd known, the fight wouldn't have felt hopeless for so long.

Kerr picked at the fabric of his trousers, fussing with an invisible spot on one knee.

"I've been honest with you," I reminded him.

He sighed. "It will sound ridiculous."

"I hear disembodied hearts," I said, and he smiled tightly.

"My mother and grandmother had different traditions," he began uneasily. "People tend to think them strange, so I don't mention them. But I remember some of the stories."

I stared at my hands. "Thomas had a favorite story. He called it 'the one about the blood that speaks.'" I swallowed, hesitant to say what I scarcely dared to think aloud. "And then, after he was murdered, I could hear him. I suppose if it comes right down to it, it must be madness or magic," I finished, under my breath.

Of course he heard. His ears were sharp. He smiled slightly. "Kanapawamakan—my grandmother—told stories about spirits. Maybe she heard them too. I don't remember all the details, but she told me the ways to know the *Wihtikiw*. And she acted like being able to see them for what they were was important." His eyes were pinched around the edges, his gaze far away.

"What's a *Wihtikiw*?"

He hesitated. "Like a bogeyman. But…" He swallowed, and my attention sharpened. "They start as men. They become monsters as a punishment for misdeeds. My grandmother said there were warnings, if you knew how to watch. And listen."

He didn't say more. He didn't need to. I was the listener, and the *Wihtikiw* was Burnett. But most people didn't believe in bogeymen, and they certainly didn't think much of Adam's people—unfamiliar, strange even, and living far away. So Adam had learned to keep his thoughts to himself, something I never had.

I'd thought it unkind and unjust of him, not being forthcoming. But if I'd spent most of my life under his burdens, I didn't think I'd have chanced my arm.

"I'm sorry," I said quickly. "I only understood my own pain over it, and you've done more to help me than I have any right to expect." Much more than anyone else.

"Some right," he corrected. "After all, I'm a detective with the police."

I snorted.

"And, forgive me for presuming, but I felt there were things that I understood about you." He let out a breath and shifted his eyes from me to the window. "Loss, certainly. Maybe a willingness to cling to a bit of magic."

My lips twitched. No matter who your people were, everyone had stories about evil and magic, *Wihtikiw*, witches and bogeymen, monsters and incomprehensible things. I'd rather think of myself as a witch than a lunatic.

Maybe that was just madness of a different kind, because thinking a thing didn't make it so. But I heard heartbeats and whispers, and had felt the touch of wandering spirits. Lizzie Dove had seized me with her memories, and in all the months I'd anointed myself with witch hazel, hoping it might help me stay unknown, only Adam Kerr had recognized me.

"I think I might be a witch," I said, waiting for him to laugh.

Instead he nodded. "I think you might be too." The air between us thickened, until he freed us both by cracking a smile. "I noticed right away that you're left-handed."

"My mother was, too. No red hair, though."

Now he laughed, and I joined him, softening with relief.

"Maybe only half a witch, then," he said.

I grinned. "Maybe."

The carriage stopped, and I remembered we weren't here to talk about monsters, constrained by matters of law and evidence. I picked up the carefully wrapped parcel and whispered a prayer for Jenny Dove.

Adam helped me down from the hired carriage, in front of a cottage not far from the shore, wrapped in a vine of fading autumn leaves, rustling beneath the cries of gulls and the shushing wind. The air was fresh, and there were potato plants, carrots, and onions still belowground in the garden.

It was a lovely place, and I said as much to Adam, but he just shrugged. "She's safe here."

I meant to ask more, but had to hurry after him into the house. Jenny Dove was inside, sewing, and she wasn't alone. Before my eyes could adjust to the dimmer light, a man's dark shape rose from his chair.

"Afternoon, Kerr. Miss Ross."

I knew that voice. I smoothed my face and held out a hand in greeting. "It's Miss Ross. Good afternoon, Mr. Stevenson."

Adam had said there'd be a prosecutor here, but he hadn't mentioned John, who clearly expected me, and knew quite well there was no Janet Ross. I cut my eyes in Adam's direction, but he stood perfectly straight and impassive, even more contained than usual.

John took my hand gingerly, releasing it almost immediately—not nearly fast enough. "How nice to see you," I said, then regretted it, as I intercepted a rapidly assessing glance from Jenny. She was no fool, and I was here for her.

John cleared his throat. "I've been recording Mrs. Dove's statement," he said. "If you'll look it over and make sure I haven't missed any important points..."

As Adam moved to look over the papers, Jenny motioned to the place beside her on the settee, which I took, taking time to arrange my skirts.

"You know Mr. Stevenson?"

"Long ago," I said.

"I just met him today." She rolled her needle between her thumb and forefinger. "He said you have something for me."

I glanced at the parcel in my lap. "Only sadness," I whispered. "I wish—"

Jenny interrupted me with a shake of her head. "No. Please don't mistake me. I know the dangers you've faced. Kerr told me. I've wanted to thank you."

My hands clenched on the box, but Jenny wasn't looking at it. Her gaze was on her knees, draped in a familiar green wool. She was also wearing the jacket.

I didn't know what to say.

Jenny reached into her sewing box and pulled out a handkerchief that had been pressed and neatly folded, stitched with some excellent white-on-white work. Jenny's probably. I'd seen the quality of her stitching before, on the skirt she'd sewn for her sister and was now wearing. "This was in the pocket," she murmured. "Lizzie made it. I want you to have it."

"I can't," I said, eyes filling, but Jenny pressed her lips together and set the white square down beside me. She drew a deep breath. "The prosecutor told me you found her hand. He said it was my decision, but he hoped to have it as evidence. I said yes."

"It's very brave of you, Mrs. Dove."

I stiffened. I hadn't noticed John sit down again or slide his chair closer.

He picked up his lap desk again, setting it on his knees. "Whenever you are ready."

I had to remind myself he wasn't talking to me. He was here to take evidence, nothing else, and he must have agreed with Kerr that it was safer not to taint my evidence by revealing I wasn't really Janet Ross. To stop Burnett, he'd agreed to our conspiracy, even facing Burnett's fame and popularity, and the blind eyes of Edinburgh's medical community.

The John I'd known was clever and careful and selfish. He didn't stick his neck out, at least not very far, but he was doing that now.

Too late, as always. I scowled, watching him put Jenny at ease, chronicling the remaining events of her sister's disappearance, scratching down her exact words in black ink. "I'm not as quick a recorder as my clerks," he said apologetically, "but Detective Kerr and I think it's best to keep information within as small a circle as possible, for your protection."

His eyes darted up from the paper, giving me a brief, unreadable look. I didn't know whether to snort or to snap at him, for acting like he cared or had any right to. Letting out a breath, I reminded myself of the litany of strengthening words I'd silently recited to myself when it became clear I'd have his child and he still wouldn't choose me. That was the point I always pressed, when we'd argued, until he conceded that I would choose everything else.

"Miss Ross?"

I came back to myself, facing three sets of eyes. I'd missed my cue. I surrendered the box into Jenny's hands, leaving mine uncomfortably empty and cold. I picked up the handkerchief, wanting the distraction of something between my fingers, something to rub away the pricking sensation sparking in my fingertips.

I let out a cry, drawing my hand back like it was burned.

"What happened?" Kerr demanded, as Jenny's face creased with concern. I stuck my finger in my mouth, tasted blood, and drew it out. More blood swelled from a pinprick on the tip of my forefinger and rolled down the side.

At once Jenny was searching for the handkerchief that I already held, for whatever it was that had stung me. "I'm so sorry. Must be my needle. No—" Because there it was, tucked plainly and carefully in her sewing. "What could it have been? I must have dropped a pin."

She searched the cushions on the settee. "I can't find it," she said, a little desperate.

"Probably on my lap somewhere." Without thinking, I wrapped my finger in the handkerchief I'd meant to refuse, blood spreading through the cambric. "I'll find it."

Jenny relaxed, leaving me to look half-heartedly for the errant pin. Somehow, I knew there was nothing to find.

Jenny twitched her shoulders. "When you cried out, I had the most awful feeling. Like a goose walking over my grave."

"Understandable." I glanced at the box, which John had taken during the upset.

"I suppose so."

"I can open it for you, if you like," John offered.

"I can do it." But she took the box slowly this time, and paused before plucking at the knot in the string, steeling herself. I squeezed my wounded finger tighter.

She opened the box and lifted out the jar I'd selected, sealed with cork and wax, and packed in a protective layer of straw. The six-fingered hand floated inside, as clean and undamaged-looking as I could make it.

Her face crumpled, and the handkerchief she should have reached for was already twisted tight around my hand. Adam came forward with his.

"Do you recognize the hand?" he asked.

"It's Lizzie's," Jenny said, her hands tight on the jar. "I didn't think—" She gulped, and turned it around, studying it for at least a full minute. "I recognize so many things," she said softly. "That freckle, just above the wrist. The bitten nails. She was always doing that." Her voice steadied and strengthened as she looked up at John and Kerr. "I don't need the extra finger. I'd know her from either hand."

How did Burnett not understand how easy it was to recognize the pieces of people you loved? They announced themselves in a thousand different ways, in a living voice, in a handwritten word, in the blend of browns in a lock of hair or the precise shape of an ear. This blindness would be his undoing.

Jenny and I would bring it about.

John bent again over the sheets of paper covering his lap desk, scribbling ferociously. Without looking up, he said, "Now we come to your testimony, Miss Ross. Mrs. Dove has identified this hand as her sister's. How did you come by it?"

I cleared my throat.

"I'm sorry." John licked his lips, visibly nervous again. "I forgot to put you under oath."

The wound in my finger pulsed a little when I raised one hand and laid the other on his bible, but I repeated his words without blinking.

"Until recently, I worked as Dr. Burnett's housekeeper," I began. "I met Jenny when she came to the house, looking for her sister. And I'd heard about the woman who accused him of having her son's heart in his collection."

"That would be the Thomas Tait case, sir." Adam inserted.

"Yes, I remember it." John dipped his pen, tapped it four times, and dipped it again. "Nothing was proved." His voice shook.

"Mrs. Dove told me about her sister—what she was wearing, what she looked like. She would be easy to know, because she had an extra finger. You don't forget a thing like that, Mr. Stevenson."

I waited until his hand stopped moving across the page, each word committed to paper.

"I was worried. A short time later, a basket of clothes arrived at the house. The doctor told me they were for the parish, but there was a skirt like the one Mrs. Dove had described. I brought it to the police."

"Me, in fact," Adam said.

"Detective Adam Kerr," Stevenson said, timing his syllables with the contortions of his pen. "And?"

I adjusted my spectacles. There was no reason why these lies should feel weightier than any of my others. Mistaking my hesitation, Jenny shifted like she meant to reach out and pat my arm and then thought better of it. I bridged the distance instead, capturing her hand in my handkerchief-bound one, glad of the contact, the company. She didn't know how much Burnett had taken from me, but she understood we both had scores to settle.

I cleared my throat. "One of my duties was cleaning Dr. Burnett's collection of medical specimens. He acquires new ones frequently, and soon after this, he added a six-fingered hand." I squeezed Jenny's lightly, offering what I could in comfort and apology. "I took it from the room, knowing it would interest the police."

"Aye?" John didn't lift his eyes from the paper.

"Burnett came to my room later. He confronted me about the theft. I didn't think of it as stealing, Mr. Stevenson. I was concerned a crime had been committed."

Adam stepped in. "What did Dr. Burnett say to that?"

"Nothing, detective. He tried to smother me. If I hadn't managed to fight him off—"

The pen was still, and now the pressure on my joined hand came from Jenny.

"How did you do that?" Adam prompted, since John couldn't.

"I managed to stab him in the leg."

"With what?"

330 † JAIMA FIXSEN

"A kitchen implement," I said.

"A knife?"

I shook my head. "A meat fork."

John's lips moved, but without any sound. He tried again. "Forgive me. I need a minute."

Slowly, scrupulously, he wrote down the words, composing himself. "What happened next, Miss Ross?"

"I ran away."

"With the hand?"

I nodded. "But I heard that Dr. Burnett had accused me of stealing. He said I'd attacked him, and that made me too afraid to go to the police."

"Luckily, I located her eventually," Kerr said.

When Mrs. Burnett's body surfaced, no one but Adam would know I was responsible.

John set down his pen and rubbed the tightness from his hand. "That should do it," he said. "I think we've got what we need."

They had Jenny's evidence. They had the hand, and a sworn statement of its provenance from Burnett's former housekeeper, Miss Janet Ross.

"I'll apply for the warrant today," John said, tidying his papers.

They'd have to collect more evidence, but I knew it was there to find, enough that when "Miss Ross" left Edinburgh before the trial, it wouldn't bring a halt to proceedings. A statement was one thing. I couldn't appear in court.

Jenny licked her lips. "If I can ever help you, Janet..."

The name caught me off guard. I wished I could give her my real one. Instead, I unwrapped the handkerchief from my hand, but she stopped me. "No. I want you to have it."

It was dotted with my blood, so there really was no way to

refuse. I spread it on my lap, smoothing away the creases, trying to think of something to say.

"Look. You made a pattern," Jenny said.

I glanced down. Besides a few smears, the blood had concentrated in one place, soaking through the cambric and leaving a dark spot perfectly placed in each of the four corners.

Magic to protect you.

Though I'd always told the story, the words came to me in Thomas's voice. I swallowed.

"You have to keep it now," Jenny said. "Maybe it will be lucky."

"I'll be more careful with it from now on," I said slowly.

Jenny lips twitched. "From what I heard, I don't think you know how." Her mouth firmed into a frown. "I hope his leg still hurts."

I lowered my voice. "You should have heard him bellow." I focused on folding the handkerchief, so she wouldn't see my suppressed shudder, and tucked it beneath my sleeve, next to my wrist.

"I'm afraid you and I have to hurry," Adam said, standing beside me like he'd offer his hand if I didn't immediately rise to go. I stood and drew my hood.

"A moment, Miss Ross." In his hurry, John dropped one of his papers. Adam stepped aside, resigned to the interruption, but when I looked at John, with his rounding shoulders and flushed cheeks, I shook my head.

"Another time, Mr. Stevenson. You have some important work to do."

And so did I.

{ 37 }

Conall limped into the laboratory with a mere twenty minutes to spare, but today's specimen wasn't waiting under a sheet. The body was almost as he'd left it yesterday, with the ribs still intact, and his assistants, instead of frantically sawing to expose the lungs, were hunched over an open newspaper.

"What's going on?" Conall asked.

Their heads snapped up guiltily. Only Ferguson had the grace to flush.

"We're terribly sorry, sir."

"Sorry? I'm supposed to be lecturing on the lungs in fifteen minutes." At least half his students were already gathered in the theatre, with more arriving every minute—an impossibly vexing situation on a good day, never mind this wet, windy one, after three unexpected cancellations from his morning patients *and* a late and most unsatisfactory luncheon. When he'd expressed his displeasure, Mrs. Williams had only shrugged, saying that with Miss Ross gone, it was impossible for Maggie to keep up with the house and the marketing, especially with the mistress away.

Then she'd stared at him, waiting for him to offer some news of his mother.

"Is she enjoying Harrogate?" Her question was sulky, almost demanding, so Conall stammered a response, saying that if he didn't have a letter from Mrs. Burnett soon, he would visit her. The opportunity for the trip had arisen so unexpectedly, and she was probably having such a wonderful time she'd simply neglected to reply to him.

"Have you written? Maggie hasn't posted any letters to her," Mrs. Williams said flatly, folding her arms.

"I write her from the school," Conall explained hastily. "So naturally I give the letters to the porter."

Mrs. Williams grunted and returned to the kitchen, but her stares and questions were becoming so problematic, it might be necessary to dismiss her, but if he did that... Conall stared at the unfinished corpse and rubbed his forehead tiredly.

His skin was warm. Warmer than was healthy, and his leg hurt. He shucked off his coat and looked around for his apron.

"Right here, sir." Jones thrust it into his hand. "We weren't sure you would wish to proceed with the scheduled lecture and—"

"Why wouldn't I?" Conall tugged the ties around his waist. "My classes follow a set schedule for good reasons."

Jones licked his lips. "You didn't—?"

"There's something in this morning's paper, sir," Ferguson interjected. "Perhaps you should take a look."

Conall stumped to the newspaper splayed open on his workbench. The headline leaned out and struck him from two yards away: *Mysterious Disturbances! Are Edinburgh's Missing Bodies in Famed Anatomist's Collection?*

"I'll sue them for libel," Conall spat, snatching the paper close. A wasted effort. He'd eat his hat if his assistants hadn't read the thing half a dozen times already.

Conall scanned the lines, his stomach shrinking like a punctured bursitis. He could almost hear the writer clearing his throat self-importantly in the opening sentence.

Most, if not all, of Edinburgh's doctors, surgeons and medical students have viewed the curiosities in Dr. Conall K. Burnett's Medical Museum, and probably half this city's polite society as well. In this scientific age, an educated man can hardly call himself complete without a visit, nor can the fashionably daring lady—a troubling phenomena, given the disturbing delivery received by this paper yesterday.

Conall looked up. "Did you send this rag anything?"

"I never read the *Edinburgh Courant*," Jones protested. "Another student showed it to me. We live in the same lodging house."

"Keep reading," Ferguson muttered.

I would venture, in my term as editor, that this newspaper has never reported anything quite so horrifying before.

Halfway through a dismissive snort, Conall read:

I received a letter, accompanied by a glass jar containing two human eyes, one blue, the other brown. Here is the text of the letter, which the directors of this paper have decided to reproduce in full.

Here the print changed, the letters becoming larger and more emphatic.

Dear sirs—

Again, it is time to draw attention—or try—to the gross crimes perpetuated in this city in the name of science, because yet again, a so-called specimen in Dr. Conall K. Burnett's Medical Museum has been connected to a missing person. Earlier this year, Mary Burt, a milliner's assistant, mother to a young child, went missing for no apparent reason. Police

*investigations, half-hearted at best, proved fruitless, and it
was generally assumed that Mrs. Burt had abandoned her
child and left town.*

*Mrs. Burt was known for having mismatched eyes, like
these ones which I now send you, having liberated them from
the museum in question. Or perhaps your paper doesn't
consider murder a newsworthy concern.*

*Mrs. Burt was well known by her neighbors. It should not
be difficult to have these eyes identified. It should not be hard
to find among the many museum visitors at least one who
remembers seeing them in the collection.*

*It will not be hard for a person of ordinary curiosity and
average conscience, if Edinburgh has any of those.*

Junius

"Junius?" A drop of spittle flew onto the newssheet, which
shook slightly in his hands.

"A pseudonym, obviously," Ferguson said. "I asked my father.
It's a reference to another anonymous letter writer."

He took the paper from Conall's hands and smoothed the wrinkles from the edge of the sheet. "Sixty years ago, in London. The
Duke of Grafton had to resign as prime minister because of Junius's
letters, and the author was never found. You could almost call it a
compliment?" His feeble attempt at a smile vanished.

"They ought to have contacted me before printing this trash.
My lawyer will—"

"That's why we didn't think you'd lecture this afternoon," Jones
said quietly. "This isn't like last time—" He faltered beneath Conall's
stare. "You know, that hysterical mother." He waved his hands

helplessly. "I wasn't there, but Ferguson was, and you had to send a letter to the newspaper."

Conall nodded, quelling the lightning flash of pain in his leg with a slowly exhaled breath. "I remember." He straightened his shoulders, keeping his weight on his left. "The unlettered will always try to hinder progress. I won't let my lectures be interrupted by scandal mongering. Tonight I will call on this *editor*." He lashed into the word, almost trilling the *r*, there was such heavy contempt in his voice. "And both of you, right now, will compose letters to the *Edinburgh Courant* and the *Caledonian Mercury*."

He'd contact Ballingall, and the other members of the Aesculapian Club. He'd enlist his students and the university's deans. They wouldn't stand for this. They couldn't afford to. There wasn't a man among them who hadn't worked on illegally acquired corpses.

He set down the paper, though there was still a full column of additional remarks, and seized the corners of the wheeled table burdened with the ill-prepared corpse. "I'll apologize to the students. Explain why we are not perfectly ready."

Ferguson looked satisfied, but Jones was still wide-eyed and sweaty. "Sir, about those eyes—"

Conall fixed his own sternly on the wavering apprentice.

"Never mind, sir."

Masking his limp, Conall propelled the demonstration table into the theatre. The murmured tumult died beneath his confident gaze.

{ 38 }

A dam escorted Isobel home from the cottage in Leith, then returned to his office at the station. It was too early for Stevenson to have obtained a warrant, but there was another matter he must tend to. Nodding at the desk sergeant, Adam took the stairs two at a time, pausing only to look inside Hugh Fraser's empty office before disappearing into his own.

Everything looked just as he'd left it, but he checked anyway, leafing through the papers on his desk and unlocking the side drawer. The neatly penned notes he'd left underneath the biscuit tin were missing.

Adam sighed and slumped into his chair. He'd learned wood-craft from Kanapawamakan—and she'd always praised his ability to set traps.

The house was in the opposite direction from his own, nearer the university. And though on a perfectly respectable street, it was also nearer to the West Port.

It took him twice as long as it should have to walk the distance.

Adam knocked, then waited on the front step with his hands in his pockets, afraid of what might happen if they were left free. Or that he'd betray himself with visible trembling.

"Who's there?" Through the door, he recognized her warm Irish lilt, the *th* sliding into a cheerier *d*.

"It's Adam."

The door swung wide. "Well, what are you doing here, then?" Hugh's wife gave him a broad smile, her eyes as bright and her cheeks as round as her baby's. Wee Sarah smiled, too, comfortably balanced on her mother's hip.

"Come in, come in, Adam. You haven't been round in ages."

"Evening, Sarah." He resisted the urge to caress her daughter's chubby fist. "Hugh in?"

"Just sat down to supper. You'll join us?"

As she led him inside, not waiting for a reply, Adam picked up the leather briefcase resting by the coat stand, beneath Hugh's hat and overcoat. Both were new.

Adam's feet were slow, but his fingers were quick with the case's buckles. He pulled out the contents as he came into the kitchen, where Hugh was sitting at the table, in his shirtsleeves and apparently unarmed, though there was a knife resting between his hand and a plate of meat and potatoes.

"Adam, what are you—"

"I'm looking," he said curtly, as the welcoming smile slid off his friend's face. "Yes, it's here."

He laid the duplicate notes, written much more neatly than his first version, out on the table. "These are my notes about the influence of Ribbonmen in the force. Why did you take them from my desk?"

In the past week, he'd afforded all three of his suspects an "accidental" glimpse of the document, with *RIBBONMEN* in capital letters writ across the top. Bait. An idea he'd stolen from Burnett, but a good one, apparently. Hugh had taken it as quickly as Isobel.

"It's good work." Color rose in Hugh's cheeks, but he spoke with almost his usual tone. "Though I can understand why you were hesitant. Thought I should help. Show it to one of the prosecutors. We can't take it to Maxwell, you know that." He nodded at the sheet, where Maxwell's name was written in the middle.

"And this?" Adam reached out a forefinger to Hugh's name, last of all, at the bottom.

Hugh shrugged. "We both know you're the better detective. You consider all the possibilities, even the absurd ones. Gave me a start, it did, seeing my name there, but I suppose you're just doing your job. If Ribbonmen are bribing the police—"

"I think it's more than that," Adam said, and the flow of words stopped from Hugh's throat.

"Adam, what are you talking about?" Sarah asked, her arm tightening around the baby. Adam took a step back, his right hand ready to reach for the pistol waiting snug in the small of his back.

"Where are your people from again, Sarah? Louth? Some awful murders there, as I recall, about ten years back."

Her lips pressed shut.

"Rough justice, there too. I think the magistrates hung nearly thirty people for those crimes, after trials that make a mock of law and justice. Did you know about these happenings, Hugh? When you and Sarah married?"

Hugh's face was too guarded to read, but he was tense as a cat ready to spring. Countering, Adam moved his hand to his waist. Against the two of them, a single-shot pistol might even the score—if neither were armed, at least.

"Knew Sarah was Irish. Wasn't time for much more—" Hugh began, trying to divert them with a joke.

"Quiet, Hugh," Sarah snapped.

They'd married quickly, these two, with wee Sarah arriving not long after that. Adam knew Sarah had brought more money than one would expect to the marriage, including this house, but had Hugh never thought about where it came from?

"Let me hold her," Adam said, nodding at wee Sarah, who was gurgling on her mother's hip. When Sarah's arms tightened, he slid his fingers onto the pistol and pulled it out from under his coat. "I want to hold my goddaughter."

No one moved, except wee Sarah. Frozen in place, they weighed each other's glances.

"Let him hold her," Hugh said.

Sarah's eyes darted from her husband, to Adam, to the gun. She blinked as her eyes filled, and whispered, "You wouldn't—"

"No tears, Sarah. You let me in because you trust me. Just like I trusted you."

"Adam—"

Silencing Hugh with a jerk of his pistol, Adam held out his free arm and Sarah passed him the baby, moving like her bones were grinding together. Wee Sarah whimpered once, then closed a fist around Adam's shirt.

"Good lass," he murmured, settling her with a bounce. "Now we can talk."

"Don't hurt her," Sarah blurted.

Adam sent her a look that made her catch her lip in her teeth. "Sit down, both of you," he said. "Hands on the table. You can knock the knives onto the floor."

Hugh huffed. "You're holding our child. You can't think we'll—"

"I thought I knew what to think. I was wrong," Adam snapped. "So push the knives to the floor, and listen."

Both blades landed with a clatter.

"Sarah, you told me your father and brother were in the masonry trade."

She nodded reluctantly.

"They do have a storefront," Adam admitted. "But not much stonecutting happens there. So where does the money come from? Growing it in the ground out back with the potatoes? Because they own a prodigious lot of shovels."

Husband and wife exchanged glances, and Hugh's shoulders drooped. "I didn't know, Adam. Not until months after, and by then—" He swallowed. "By then we had our baby."

Wee Sarah sneezed. To keep her settled, Adam began walking back and forth. "Selling bodies is good business," he said. "Lots of money to be made, especially if you're Irish, and last on the list for most other kinds of work. Or if you already have differences with the law."

Sarah lifted her chin. "You want to watch yourself, Adam."

He huffed a laugh. "I certainly do. Tell me, Sarah, when did Hugh begin giving you information?"

No answer, so Adam prodded. "If I don't know, there's only one thing for me to do next." He adjusted wee Sarah's soft weight, fitting her closer in his arm, praying her parents wouldn't call his bluff.

Sarah's shoulders crumpled, and her eyes dropped to the meat congealing on the table. "Right from the start," she whispered.

Hugh flinched.

"Not on purpose, not then," she said quickly. "When he was with me, not working, I'd tell my da. And then I'd visit Hugh at the station. See who was there. Who wasn't. Who was in the cell."

"Quick worker," Adam said.

"And then I began asking things. Hugh—"

"Don't, Sarah." Hugh's face twisted, but she went on as if he hadn't spoken.

"I told him there was money in it. And there was."

Hugh gave Adam a stricken look. "What was I supposed to do? My own wife—?"

"Tell me about the Brennans," Adam said, his eyes on Sarah.

"They worked for us. Digging up bodies. Selling them."

"To Conall Burnett?"

"And others." She let out a long breath. "I didn't know Eoin had extra business with him. Not until Hugh saw your drawing of Eoin's face during the case of that missing boy. But he came home and told me right quick."

Adam's gut clenched. Believing a thing and knowing it were very different. "And you told Brennan."

She nodded. "I had to protect Hugh. If you'd found Eoin—"

"We might have found Thomas. The missing boy." Adam's muscles drew so tight, wee Sarah bleated. He forced down a swallow, softened his grip, and gave her another bounce, but his next words emerged in as rough a tone as ever. "You're a mother too, Sarah, for God's sake. Didn't you even think of that?"

She lifted her face, the shine of tears marring her cheeks, and answered in a smothered voice. "Aye. I did. I made Brennan tell me everything before he left town, but he'd already taken him to the doctor. He said—" She choked, "He said the boy would be dead by now. There was nothing I could do."

"That's not true." Adam breath fluttered through Sarah's soft curls, his heart a battering ram against his chest. "You could have told me. We could have made a case. We could have arrested Burnett and stopped him from killing at least two others. And the Brennans? Do you know what else they were up to?"

Sarah licked her lips.

"They kidnapped Nan Burt and put her in a grimy workshop, Sarah, to work out her days, unpaid, underfed, never seeing the sun." Only a fool would believe Will and his wife only tried that trick once, but both Brennans were dead now, so there was no way to find out. "If you hadn't—"

"We know," Hugh said. "We—"

"Stopped them?" Adam asked. "Someone did. Because they were about to testify. Against people like you."

"Not us." Sarah shook her head. "My father takes protection money. He runs the grave robbing. That's all."

"I don't believe you," Adam said.

"You have to," Hugh said. "Please, Adam. It's the truth."

Adam's fingers tightened. If it weren't for the child in his arms, he'd pull out his gun and smash his friend across the face with it. Hugh deserved at least that much.

That's not the plan, Adam reminded himself. He settled his weight on his heels and let out a long breath.

"What are you going to do with Sarah?" her mother asked.

"She's coming with me." The words vibrated in his chest.

"You can't—" Sarah clutched the table. Swearing, Hugh half rose, but Adam warned him back with a lifted brow and a shift of his grip on the gun. It took a few heartbeats, and a tightening of his finger on the trigger, but then Hugh subsided in his chair.

"She's my goddaughter," Adam said. "She'll be cared for. Better than Nan Burt and Thomas Tait."

The muscles in Hugh's neck snapped tight.

"How long?" demanded Sarah.

"That depends on you." Adam tucked the baby closer, tilting his head toward her cheek. "Don't think about coming after me. She's going to a family of gentry where she'll be safe and out of your reach. I've reported you both to the prosecutor, and he's willing to offer a deal."

A better one than they deserved.

"You have six months," Adam said. "Six months to provide me with proof against the Ribbonmen or whoever is running the workshops in the West Port. If there are orphaned or kidnapped children in any of them, I want them back. I want details of the body trading, proof that your family are digging bodies up, not killing for corpses, and evidence against Eoin Brennan and anyone in the West Port that is. You'll get your daughter back once I have a case. And then you get to leave Edinburgh. No charges."

For a moment, Hugh looked about to choke, blood rushing to his cheeks. "You bastard," he breathed in an undertone.

"Not at all." Adam smiled. "But I am a half-breed. And I was your friend."

Hugh lurched to his feet, but Sarah halted him even before Adam stepped back.

"No!" She leaned her shaking arms onto the table. "No, Hugh. He'll shoot!" She swallowed. "This is business. And Adam is being more than fair."

Her husband sat down.

She looked at Adam. "We'll get what you want."

Adam nodded, and began backing toward the door. "See that you do."

"Just—" Sarah's voice broke, so Hugh finished for her.

"Please take care of her."

Adam nodded.

He'd taken no blanket, so Adam wrapped wee Sarah in his overcoat, quieting her surprised cries, and walked with her to the end of the street where a carriage was waiting. The door opened as he approached, and Adam climbed inside.

"They agreed," he said.

"Good," said John Stevenson. "This is the girl?"

Adam nodded. "You'll keep her safe?"

"She's going to my grandmother's. Out in Lomond. I'm sending her with a footman and a nurse, as well as the coachman and outriders."

Adam nodded. Across from him sat a neatly garbed woman in a frilled cap. She smiled at him and reached for the baby.

"This is Sarah," he told her.

"She's a pretty one."

"Like her mother," Adam said, with a tight smile. *You have to do this,* he told himself. *Or what will happen to other children like Nan?*

"I'm sorry it was Fraser," John said quietly. "I know you were friends."

Adam tried to speak, failed, then settled for a nod and studied his hands in his lap, folding his fingers together to still their shaking.

At the Royal Mile, John signed for the carriage to stop. "I'm going back to the Crown Office," he said. "Working on that warrant. My coachman will continue on to Lomond. Care to join me?"

Adam considered. He didn't exactly suffer from too many invitations. This probably meant Stevenson was starting to see him as a friend. So he paused and chose his words carefully before shaking his head.

"Thank you, but I have to say no." He softened the words with a smile. "I'm going home to Isobel. There're things I need to tell her."

Stevenson gave him a long look, and finally nodded. "Wise idea. I'll send you word when I have the warrant."

Adam brushed a hand across wee Sarah's face and smiled at the nurse.

"I'd best go."

Following John, he climbed from the carriage. Easy to walk home from here. "Good night, John."

The carriage rolled away.

"Adam?"

He turned and looked back. Stevenson was smiling lopsidedly at him. "Best of luck."

{ 39 }

"Where's Isobel? Why isn't she back yet?"

Adam held in a sigh, meeting Nan's anxious eyes. "She can't be still yet."

It had been a difficult conversation, but he'd told Isobel everything Sarah said.

Isobel hadn't slept. He'd heard her crying intermittently all night, and come morning, she'd gone walking, not even waiting for breakfast.

She'd returned midday, terse and pale, but only long enough for them to deliver their next parcel to the *Edinburgh Courant*. Nan had joined them, and she had as much reason to be fretful as anyone. But though Nan had settled after the delivery, Isobel had not, prowling about the house until finally she took to the hills again, trailed by the constable assigned to protect her from malice and mischance. She hadn't even returned for the delivery of the evening papers to see the results of their work.

"I'm worried," Nan said.

Adam dropped a kiss on her forehead. It eased his heart, seeing Nan's courage grow as their snare drew in on Dr. Burnett.

Maybe, for Isobel, it still wasn't enough.

Nan sighed, prompting him to shift in his seat and draw her a little closer. "I'm sorry about your mam," he said quietly.

Nan only nodded, and when she finally spoke, she first gave a little shake. "If she's not home soon, will you fetch her?"

"Let's finish reading," Adam suggested, wary of making any promises. Whatever drove Isobel was too murky for him to measure.

He'd read Junius's second letter to Nan already, published in the evening edition, but like the paper two days ago, this one had additional commentary from the newspaper's editor.

"It is time for our people and our police to earnestly consider how much confidence can be laid on these physicians. With opportunities for riches and fame riding solely on reputations for learning and discovery and not at all on what you and I consider basic scruples and common decency, can we trust we are safe? Or do their so-called resurrection men restrict themselves to stealing the bodies of the dead? Do they think science excuses murder?

"Readers are invited to turn the page, and examine Dr. Burnett's response, along with those from other notable doctors. While full of indignation and fury, I find them lacking in reassurance and proof. Because this writer spoke with a dozen residents of the West Port yesterday—"

Adam broke off.

"Please finish." Nan's voice was soft, her body still.

Adam cleared his throat. "—spoke with a dozen residents of the West Port"—he swallowed, and closed his fingers around Nan's tightly fisted hand—"who all claim to recognize Mrs. Mary Burt's eyes."

"I'm glad I did it." She blinked twice and looked up at him. "When Isobel comes home, I'll tell her."

Adam nodded, insight chilling him, reasons why Isobel walked and walked, even in the rain. She wasn't merely struggling for her own peace. She was leaving room for Nan to find hers, with Adam the first and only one to turn to.

"That will ease her mind somewhat, I'm sure," Adam said, with more hope than confidence. "This hasn't been easy to ask of you, for either of us." He smoothed the hair from her forehead. "You know how much I wish I'd helped you better, right from the first. I'm so sorry, Nan. And I'm very, very proud of you."

She squeezed his hand back and, with the peculiar blend of bold shyness that only belongs in childhood, brushed the tears from his cheeks.

"Are you going to adopt me?" she asked. "Now that we know?"

"Absolutely." He caught himself, steadying his voice because it was on the verge of breaking. "That is, if you wish it. We can wait if you aren't ready."

She considered, brows tilting up and down, then rebalancing. "I'm ready."

An hour later, Nan was in bed, after subsiding to sleep faster than Adam had seen before, her breath deep and even, when he heard the sound of Isobel's key in the lock. She was soaked through, and though Adam had a hundred rehearsed lines to say to her, he only offered a blanket, tea, and a chair by the fire.

"They printed my letter again?"

"In four different papers this time," Adam confirmed. "Not just the *Courant* and the *Mercury*."

"The commentary?" Her hands were clenched.

"On our side," Adam said. "Not Burnett's."

She relaxed only a touch.

"Nan confided in me," Adam said, probing gently without questioning. His answer came in the loosening of her knitted brows. "She's happy with her choice." He brushed at nothing on the back of his hand. "She's letting me adopt her."

"I'm glad." Isobel nodded, then leaned back in the chair and closed her eyes. "I thought of another letter while I was walking."

"I might have to ask one of the constables to deliver it," Adam said.

Her eyes snapped open.

"I just had a message from John Stevenson." Adam measured her face carefully, but her expression remained inscrutable. "They've approved his search warrant."

A day later than he'd hoped, but they finally had it.

Now her eyes lit up.

"We're standing by you. Of course we are," Ballingall repeated. But he'd been shifty this whole interview, glancing away from Conall, at the wallpaper, at the windows, and the door.

Conall pried his teeth apart. "So why are you asking me not to come?"

Instead of answering, Ballingall applied his lancet, releasing a trickle of blood from Conall's left arm. "You're overwarm," he reminded Conall. "A trifle feverish, even. You should be in bed, not gallivanting to dinners."

If Ballingall had fought half as hard as Conall had for admittance to the Aesculapian Club, he'd understand why nothing but death would stop Conall from attending tonight's dinner, even though it wasn't their usual meeting, just a gathering hosted by one of the senior members. "I'll be much better after this," Conall insisted.

"The wound has an encouraging amount of pus," Ballingall

temporized. "Bodes well for healing. But I don't think—" He changed tack as Conall drew breath.

"Kellie insists on it. He says if you want to continue with the club, you must let this fracas resolve itself first." There was a mulish set to his mouth.

Conall scowled at the blood pooling in the basin. "Not too much, mind."

"I know my work," Ballingall said. Again, he glanced at the wall behind them. Conall followed his gaze, landing on a shelf of specimens.

"Have you considered...?"

"Considered what?"

"Your resurrection men. Your dealers. What if they—" Ballingall cleared his throat. "What if they're anticipating?"

"I don't know what you mean."

"Yes, you do." Ballingall reached into his bag and pressed a wad of gauze with unnecessary firmness to Conall's arm. Though he pressed his lips together, Conall refused to flinch.

"It could happen innocuously enough," Ballingall said, his cheeks reddening with every word. "Maybe your assistants contribute, willingly or not. No one would deny that Ferguson is ambitious. He and Jones know the needs of your school—how many bodies, what sort, when you have to have them in the curriculum, and they are intimately familiar with your museum. Most of the time they lead the tours. We all deal with unsavory types. We have to, or we'd never have any bodies at all. Suppose Ferguson let it slip that you were interested in acquiring some particular specimen or—or item of interest." He set aside the gauze and wiped his forehead.

"Item?" Conall raised his brows.

"You know what I mean," Ballingall muttered. "And you must have better—I mean bolder—resurrectionists than anyone else. No one has finer specimens."

Conall fought through a wave of lightheadedness and reached for his tumbler of whisky. Maybe Ballingall was offering him an out.

"You know I don't like to get too involved," he said slowly.

"Of course not," Ballingall nodded, his forehead smoothing.

"Ferguson and Jones deal with most of that," Conall said. "Sometimes it's better—"

"We all understand," Ballingall said. "But just now, it puts all of us in an impossible situation."

Conall took another sip from his glass, swallowing back the retort that sparked on his tongue. No one was more impressed than Ballingall by his collection. Did he think it just came to him without any effort? But then some men did have success given to them. And, like Ballingall, these ones frequently fell into a dither at the first show of opposition. They didn't know the first thing about staying the course.

"I heard a rumor—"

"Not another one," Conall said.

"Not about you," Ballingall put in hastily. "About the man you use. Brennan, I think he's called."

"Not the most savory character," Conall agreed.

"Irish, isn't he?"

Conall nodded.

"Well…" Ballingall turned up his hands.

Conall sipped again, nodded again, more slowly. "Not really trustworthy, of course, but—"

"It's not as if you had any choice," Ballingall said in a rush.

"No," Conall agreed.

"Stay home tonight," Ballingall said. "I'll tell the others how you are doing. Kellie is really quite concerned for you."

Conall resisted the urge to snort.

"And I'll come around again tomorrow. To take your pulse, and—"

"And to tell me what happened at dinner," Conall said firmly.

Ballingall smiled, showing too many teeth. "Of course." He looked around the room. "What happened to your servants?" Quickly correcting—"I don't mean that awful woman who was posing as housekeeper, but—"

If he wasn't pale and short of breath from the bleeding, Conall would have flushed. Instead he flinched, watching Ballingall catalog the dust on the desk, tables, and window ledges, and the unswept grate.

"I sent the maid to Harrogate with my mother," he said stiffly.

"Ah. Would it help, hiring someone temporary? I can recommend a very competent sick nurse."

Conall snorted. "I don't need one of those."

Ballingall repacked his bag and, with one last caution to take some rest, left for the Aesculapian Club.

At midnight, someone knocked on the door. Conall set down his whisky and peered through a gap in the curtains, but whoever was on the step was keeping to the shadows.

Of course, that gave Conall an excellent idea who this might be. Heart sinking, he walked to the door.

"Who's there?" he called.

"Brennan."

As he'd thought. "What do you want?"

Brennan wasn't supposed to come here. They transacted business out of the shed behind the school. If not for the matter of his mother's body, he'd never have let Brennan know the location of his house.

"I've news. You want it," Brennan said.

Conall was quite sure he didn't, until Brennan added, far too loudly, "It's about the police."

With fumbling hands—Ballingall did tend to bleed patients enthusiastically—Conall unbolted the door.

"Quiet!" he hissed, then inventing rapidly—"You'll wake my servants." It wouldn't hurt for Brennan to believe Conall wasn't entirely alone, now that Mrs. Williams had walked off the job, taking Maggie with her.

As usual, Brennan was hooded, with a closely wrapped muffler concealing his face, but he unwound it when Conall brought him into the study. He, of course, seemed unmindful of the dust and sprawled into a chair with his dripping boots right where the carpet had been, before they'd moved it to fill the empty place in the drawing room.

"What news?" Conall asked.

"Can't I have a drink first?"

"I was about to go to bed," Conall said.

Brennan rubbed his chin—he didn't have facial hair, just thick ridges of scar that, he said, tended to itch. "Well, that plan's shot to hell, then." His mouth contorted—a cruel approximation of a smile.

"Why?" Conall still hadn't taken a chair, and now he hesitated between the smaller armchair (Brennan had taken his) and the sideboard with the whisky decanter, glowing in the candlelight.

"Heard a rumor."

Brennan was different tonight. Although he always had a

menacing edge, the deferential mien he usually adopted was gone. Conall's eyes narrowed. "I don't generally concern myself with gossip," he said.

Brennan laughed. "Well, good luck staying out of this one. From what I hear, there's a prosecutor just got a warrant with your name on it." He blew on his hands, red tipped and grimy, inadequately protected by a pair of worn fingerless gloves, and studied Conall from lashless eyes. "A search warrant, not an arrest warrant," he added coolly. "And so far as I know, there's nothing here the police shouldn't see. Not anymore."

Conall's heart resumed beating. Brennan noticed, judging from the quick quirk of his mangle of a mouth.

"But," Brennan added, "I imagine they'd be most interested to learn the whereabouts of your mother."

Conall's mouth went dry. His mother was at the school, packed in a barrel. "I suppose I do need your services this evening," Conall admitted tightly.

"You do." Brennan folded his arms. "My silence too. And that, my friend, is going to be expensive."

Conall crossed to the sideboard and carefully unstoppered the decanter, smoothing his movements purposefully to hide the twitching impulses of his hands. If promised immunity, Brennan would happily testify to anything—and lead the police right to his mother's concealed body. He might even admit to moving the body of the six-fingered woman and kidnapping Thomas Tait. "I was under the impression that I paid you very well," Conall said mildly. Sixty-two pounds this year already, a princely sum for a man in Brennan's class.

"I think you can spare more," Brennan said. "I want twenty."

Conall gasped. "Impossible."

Brennan said nothing, just studied his fingers.

"All right, maybe," Conall admitted. "What are your terms?"

"I guess that depends on what your life's worth, doctor."

He'd never subdue Brennan, not with his wound, not right after a bleeding. Conall cursed and protested, but Brennan was unmoved, even after a second glass.

Finally, Conall refilled both glasses a third time and carried them back to the fire. "Independence is worth a great deal to me, Brennan."

"Well, then..." The man took the glass and straightened in his chair.

"I have ten now. Come to the anatomy school tomorrow for the rest."

{ 40 }

"Y ou'll wait here?" Adam asked, for the third or fourth time.

I nodded, picking at my breakfast. Nan was still asleep. The warrant had come, but I was not allowed to witness the search of Burnett's house or even to accompany him to the police station. It was infuriating, but Adam had decided. Too much depended on my statement as Janet Ross to risk anyone guessing there might be any connection between her and Isobel Tait. And, as Adam had pointed out many times, we didn't know what Burnett might say, in perfect truth (for once) if they found his mother's body. Adam believed me that it wasn't murder, but why should anyone else?

I couldn't argue, but the strictures chafed.

"I don't think you should walk today," Adam said.

"Why not?" This was the first fine day in ages, and there was little to do at Kerr's house: no piano, only a small store of books, most of them travel accounts to the Americas. For lack of anything else, Nan and I occasionally helped with the cleaning, which seemed to make Kerr acutely uncomfortable, and irritated the daily woman who typically looked after things. "I thought perhaps Nan and I could walk together. We needn't go for long, and we'll be back in time for your return." Which wouldn't be for some time, if they found good evidence.

I hated waiting when there was so much real work to do, and though I was constantly composing letters and sifting through newspapers, gauging the public response, I felt unmoored, removed from the struggle to which I'd already given everything, my hands idle, and my mind spinning.

"You'd take Nan?"

"Why wouldn't I?"

"I'm never quite sure if you want to," he said, flat and forthright. "And it doesn't seem fair to ask you to look after her—"

I rolled my eyes, annoyed that he seemed to think I would mind helping her with her letters or dusting the shelves of his house, when what I needed more than anything else was something to do, but his sentence didn't finish the way I expected.

"—when I imagine it must be painful to you."

"It's not painful," I said, and stopped. The words surprised me, but it didn't hurt, spending time with Nan, especially now that Adam had settled the adoption question and was treating her like the daughter he intended her to be. Soon, he'd be almost as considerate a father as mine had been.

Papa had always wanted my company and kept me with him, even when perhaps he shouldn't have. He always said I wasn't to blame—that I couldn't have fallen in and out of love with John, if I'd been governessing somewhere or a pupil at a young ladies' academy. I'd always told him I was stubborn, and if it hadn't been John, it would have been someone else, because nineteen-year-olds are bound to fall in love with someone.

Papa, bless him, had never let me win that argument.

"You think too much," I told Adam, but the scold was meant for myself as well. I liked Nan and wanted her happy. No need to think further than that. "What's the harm in a walk? Even if I wanted to, Nan and I can't leave the house without the company of your constable."

"I hear someone smashed a window in Surgeon's Square," Adam said quietly. "And Emily told me on Sunday the vicar's chosen text was 'Thou shalt not kill.' Fellow went on about the sanctity of the body as the temple of the soul for twenty-nine minutes."

I didn't know Emily well, but she'd already made her opinions clear about brevity at church. I could just imagine her counting the minutes, as she must have done to end with a figure like twenty-nine. Stifling a laugh, I choked on a mouthful of porridge, coughing over my bowl until Adam passed me my cup of tea. A large swallow cleared my throat.

"Was the sermon well received?" I asked. My heart was racing. Though it was funny to think of Emily fidgeting impatiently in her pew, the congregation's reaction mattered. It mattered very much.

Adam cleared his throat. "She said there was a lot of 'Hear, hear!' By the end she said it felt more like a rally than a Sabbath meeting."

I stirred my spoon through the porridge.

"I'll be easier when Burnett's in jail and we've pulled this thing off," Adam said.

So would I. At least, I'd always thought so, and there was little point in anticipating it before it happened. I'd had too many disappointments.

Not this time, I promised.

Adam had stepped away, perhaps sensing me drifting from him again, deeper into my thoughts. I surfaced just as he was shoving his arms into his coat.

"Detective Kerr?"

"I wish you'd call me Adam."

I did, in my head, but there was no need for him to know that. I licked my lips. "You'll look for it today? Thomas's heart? It's small, about the size of his fist—smaller than Nan's. He—"

"I'll bring it back for you," he promised.

I nodded, dropping my eyes to the bowl on the table.

"You might visit my stepmother again," he suggested. "Play the pianoforte. This is a difficult time for you."

I nodded. "That's a good idea. And it gives us a short walk, at least."

He didn't roll his eyes with exasperation, as I expected. He just grinned and shook his head, conceding, "A short one is probably all right. And my stepmother would love to hear you play again."

We'd visit, I decided. And afterward Nan and I would take a walk into Surgeon's Square. It was short, after all—only a mile.

I wanted to see that broken window.

{ 41 }

Watch yourself!" Conall spat, and the sandy-haired constable who'd lumbered into him, trying to return the sofa to the place where it belonged, shied away.

"I'm sorry, doctor."

Conall knew he was overreacting, but the man's innocuous nudge had turned the world white with pain. After last night's bleeding—physical and financial—he'd slept poorly.

"Don't touch that," Conall said as Kerr, that bad penny, leaned toward an incredibly delicate natural skeleton. A juvenile specimen, perhaps three years old, in beautiful condition, and—"You're far too close," Conall snapped. "I'm holding you responsible for any damage."

Kerr snorted, but his hand drew back.

"Where did that one come from?" The prosecutor, a man named John Stevenson, demanded. Conall had dined at Stevenson's house, but today the man had refused to shake his hand, and when Conall mentioned the party given by Mrs. Stevenson, the prosecutor looked away with such cutting swiftness Conall hadn't dared offer regards to his former hostess.

"The natural skeleton? I inherited that one," Conall said. "From my former partner, Dr. Barclay. He didn't keep records of his acquisitions. People trusted him."

"You see?" Kerr muttered to Stevenson. "No accountability. The whole profession is in on it."

Conall prepared to launch a stinging retort, but Stevenson sent him a look that would have made him step back, if his throbbing leg had allowed it. Instead, Conall extracted a handkerchief and dabbed it against his forehead.

"Who's your dealer?" Stevenson snapped. "If you buy these instead of taking them, who sells them to you?"

Conall spread his hands. "My assistants look after most transactions. I'm afraid my lecturing schedule doesn't permit—"

"I'd like to speak to those gentlemen," Stevenson said.

"They're both working, I'm afraid. Like I should be," Conall said.

"You don't look well," Stevenson said.

Conall flushed. "Actually, I am under a doctor's care. This persecution isn't healthy for me. I'm trying to be helpful, but I really don't know what you expect to find."

"Really?" Kerr raised his eyebrows and stuffed his hands into his pockets. "What happened to the old rug, for starters? You used to have one with more blue."

Conall dabbed at his forehead again. He really needed to lie down, just for a quarter of an hour. "There was an accident. With a candle."

"Should you be out of bed, doctor?" Kerr asked.

"No," Conall retorted. "But I have you and your horde in my house, unannounced, I have an injury to my leg, my cook has resigned—"

Stevenson's eyebrows shot up. "Has she? Why's that?"

"I don't know. Doubtless some argument with my mother—" He

broke off to glare at Stevenson, because now he was prodding the natural skeleton with his forefinger.

"Who also is missing," Kerr informed the prosecutor.

"She isn't missing," Conall said. "Mother's gone to Harrogate."

Kerr's brows lifted—only a fraction, but with such skepticism Conall felt the hairs raising on his arms. There was no way this detective could know—

"Harrogate? Is that so?" Kerr asked, whipping out a notepad and pencil. "When did she go there?"

Conall's right palm began to itch. He stuffed his hand into his jacket pocket. "A fortnight ago? I haven't been counting the days exactly." Now Stevenson was moving jars, peering at the back of the shelf.

"I'd like her address, please." Kerr blinked about as often as a reptile, and his scrutiny was just as unsettling.

"Surely that's unnecessary," Conall said, as out of breath as if he were losing to the detective in a footrace. "She's unwell. She's taking a cure."

"All the more reason. You'll be relieved, I know, to have someone look in on her, busy as you are."

There had to be a way out of this, but his burning leg and clammy skin usurped too much thought for him to find it. His mother might have died or moved to a different hotel—there were plenty of possibilities, but for now he was stuck, afraid of trapping himself further.

Conall spat out an address, promising himself he'd think of a solution later, when he had time to plan it out.

"Are you finished here? I'm expected in Surgeon's Square."

Stevenson consulted his list, making Conall balance on his raw leg for a few seconds longer. "I wouldn't say finished, doctor, but we are done for now. You may complete your business at Surgeon's Square, but you may not leave town."

A syringe full of morphia eased his leg, even if it did little to clear his head, so he could cut a way through this thorny problem. Kerr knew more than he was telling. Had constables broken into the academy? Had his mother's body already been found?

Conall couldn't gauge the closeness of the surrounding dangers or count how many. *The point,* he told himself, *is that there's room to fight.* He just had to be clever in choosing how, same as before. He must make sure the cellar beneath the laboratory floor was secure. He must make sure Ferguson and Jones were blamed for everything found there.

He hailed a hackney carriage and settled himself in for the short ride to Surgeon's Square, keeping the window shades drawn, because the noise outside was louder than usual. When the carriage stopped unexpectedly before the last turn, he raised the blind and discovered why.

The square was full, but not with students arriving for his afternoon lecture.

"Sir?" The coachman called back hesitantly. "Do you wish to turn around?"

Conall's first thought was that it was lucky the man hadn't called him doctor. Then he remembered this driver knew him well. The omission was intentional.

He opened the door and leaned out, just as the rumbling clarified into a unified shout. "Burn it! Burnett!"

"Turn around," Conall said.

Children hurled clods of mud at the students trying to pass.

Women shook fists, and in the center of the square was a straw-stuffed effigy, slumped over a growing pile of scrap wood and torn books. Someone—Ferguson? The porter?—had boarded his ground- and first-floor windows, so they matched the other blindfolded facades fronting the square.

As he watched, the crowd shoved a young student from their disorderly ranks. The man sprawled to the pavement, crying out, his books and bag flying.

"Murderer!"

The student, hat gone, front dirtied, scrambled to his feet. He had spectacles and a weedy mustache—features Conall knew.

Jones.

"Burn it!" The crowd howled again.

Jones started for his bag, then, eyeing his attackers, abandoned it on the cobbles to wheel and run.

"Turn around," Conall said again, his voice hoarse.

"I can't without going forward," the driver said. "We have to go forward at least another twenty yards to make the turn."

Even with the blinds closed, it wouldn't be hard to guess who was coming if the carriage ventured that far into the press.

"I can back the horse," the driver said, "but I'll have to get down."

And it would take several minutes, in which they'd be practically motionless, here on the edge of the square.

"I'll get out. I'll walk from here," Conall said. He could let himself inside through the gate in back.

"Be careful, sir."

Conall edged out the door farthest away from the trouble, swearing as his foot landed on the pavement. Lowering his hat, he edged away from the hackney, fist tight on the handle of his bag. Just another doctor making a discreet exit.

"Burn it! Burnett!"

He glanced over his shoulder at the limp straw figure with his name painted across the tattered shirtfront in bloodred letters, an inexplicable chill running down his back. Tonight was All Hallows' Eve. He'd forgotten.

He forced the tension from his muscles, exorcising it with a long slow breath. Because of All Hallows', the police might stand aside so the mob could scream and sing and spend their rage with their bonfire. Bonfires were traditional, after all.

But constables would ring the square, probably in the next hour, so no more students were accosted. Tomorrow at the latest, they would clear this mess away. There'd been demonstrations against doctors caught stealing bodies before, and every time the storm had passed.

He needn't think this one would be any different, just because it was directed at him. Just because of a date, and the superstitions his mother believed in.

He straightened his shoulders, adjusting course for the offshoot alley that would conduct him safely to his laboratory. And then he glimpsed a familiar profile out the corner of his eye.

Like a puppet on a string, his head jerked sideways.

It was her. The Ross-Tait woman, a little way off from the crowd, watching a knot of adolescent boys tear apart Jones's books. A young girl stood beside her holding her hand.

This was all that woman's fault.

She gestured across the square and at the same moment, a rock sailed through the air, right into his second-story window. The pane cracked, and a cheer trumpeted from the crowd.

Ice spread up his spine. Had she directed the stone? Impossible.

But then he remembered her, panting and clutching a bloody meat fork. His eyes narrowed.

I know your secrets, she'd said. *Their ghosts tell me.*

This was all her fault. He dabbed at the sweat on his forehead and suppressed a shiver.

Witch.

He thought of his mother and the mutterings he'd long dismissed as superstition. He'd been wrong, and now she was dead, and he was on the back foot, wounded and hounded by police. His problems wouldn't be resolved with mere strategy.

He glanced at the pile of wood and dismembered books, and nodded. It was the same in every story, he thought, limping and bracing himself with a feverish hand on a soot-stained wall. Nearly stumbling, he righted himself with a moan and hobbled from the square.

Once, law had decreed it, but he didn't need legislation to tell him what needed to be done. It was written in the Bible: *Thou shalt not suffer a witch to live.*

He needed to kill Isobel Tait.

{ 42 }

I held Nan's hand tighter on the walk home, inexplicably uneasy. The tumult in the square was a wonder, a miracle I'd fought for but never seen foretold in the stars. Chills chased up and down my spine—after bearing my anger alone, it was dizzying to swim among a crowd carried by the same current.

Maybe I was just shaken. I glanced over my shoulder, earning a tolerant smile from Constable Gilmore, two paces behind. He'd been guarding us all day, and it had only taken a little cajoling to persuade him to allow us to walk to the edge—"only the edge, mind"—of Surgeon's Square.

"I wish we could see the bonfire," Nan said.

It would be a sight, but by nightfall the afternoon's disorderly, defiant throng might be a riot. Adam would never permit her to go. I wouldn't either. The mood was dangerous, as if someone—me, really—had untied the bag holding all the fiercest winds and loosed them into the square. I couldn't see what might come of this storm.

"I've been to bonfires before," Nan reminded me, reading some of my thoughts from my face.

"Not like this one. You and I have to stay in tonight."

"My mam used to let me go guising," she said.

It was All Hallows' Eve, but mask or no, Nan wasn't venturing out tonight.

"You and I can make neep lanterns and put them in the windows," I said appeasingly, recalling the basket of root vegetables in Adam's cellar.

She brightened at that.

I glanced back, but saw only ordinary people, in ordinary hats and coats. No ghouls. No monsters.

"Hungry?" I asked Nan, and she nodded, as always, and hopped over a cracked paving stone.

"Bread and cheese and apples?" she suggested.

I nodded. Constable Gilmore could eat with us. We'd bring out the toasting forks. The house was in sight, glowing in the afternoon sun, but I reached into my sleeve, reassuring myself that my handkerchief charm was still there.

Waiting for Adam to return home was a trial of patience and nerve. Nan and I carved our vegetable lanterns, played spillikins, and sewed, while I tried not to jump at every unexpected sound. Constable Gilmore departed, replaced by the older, gray-whiskered Sergeant Cathcart. Nan would have been happy with nothing but apples for supper, but out of consideration for her stomach, I insisted she work at eating a bowl of soup, and tried to set an example myself. Mostly, I just stirred it around. By now, Cathcart was lost in his book, and until Adam returned, I wouldn't have today's newspapers. A dozen times I resolved to walk out and buy even one, but when it came down to it, I was too rattled to even consider sending Cathcart. The light outside had been golden over an hour ago; now the sky was an indigo bruise and night was falling. And I didn't know, on this night of guising and bonfires, what the anger I'd stirred up might do.

My heart lurched in my chest when Adam appeared behind Nan in the kitchen, without any warning sound.

"I didn't hear you," I said, explaining the hand that had flown involuntarily to my throat.

"Sorry." His tired eyes matched the wilting points of his shirt collar. He bent to kiss Nan's head, then poured tea into a cup and himself into a chair.

"What happened?" I'd thought of two things today—the simmering crowd in Surgeon's Square, and Adam's search. He'd been gone so long, he must have news of both.

"I couldn't find the heart," he said heavily. "And there was nothing traceable remaining in his collection. But he's changed the rug in the salon. And he's lying about his mother. He says she's in Harrogate. It will take a little time, but we'll disprove that soon enough."

More time? When the poor on whom he'd preyed were shouting for his effigy to be burned in Surgeon's Square? Knocking down his students and tearing up their books couldn't satisfy them for long. Soon, they'd be lighting their bonfire and beating anyone foolish enough to be caught walking about. I glanced at the window, assessing the sky.

"If you won't be needing me, I'd like to return home, sir," Cathcart said. Adam nodded. Cathcart tucked his book under his arm, laid his hat on his head, and went out.

"Hungry?" Nan asked.

I hid a smile. She liked to copy me—a pity, really. Most men wouldn't be impressed by a curt offer of soup and apples or bread and cheese. But Adam smiled and reached for a toasting fork, and Nan bustled to dish up a bowl from the pot on the fire. I shifted in my chair, trying to adjust the lump, warm and uncomfortably heavy, that solidified in my stomach whenever I watched the two of them.

Adam's bundle of newspapers lay next to the tea tray. I picked up the one on top and tried scanning the lines.

Da-di-la.

I frowned, glanced right, and gave my head an imperceptible shake, focusing on a smudge through a line of dark print.

Da-di-la.

I lowered the page.

"He's got wicked eyebrows," Adam said, grinning at the neep lantern Nan was showing him.

"Look at Isobel's." Nan held up a turnip head with appallingly jagged teeth. I wasn't clever with a knife.

He laughed. "It's dark enough to put in the rushlights. Shall we?"

Nan seized her chance. "May I go guising? You could take—"

"Do you hear that?" I interrupted, but the pulse died before their voices stopped. "Listen," I urged.

Silence, and a pop from the fire like the firing of a gun. Nan jumped, then relaxed into a laugh. Adam gave me a look, and a barely discernible shake of his head, warning me away from ghost stories.

"I'm not—" I began, just as the beat sounded again. It was different, heavier, not so much a thud as a series of clunks, lacking the blur of the usual shushing. My eyes followed the noise, right to the kitchen door. "Don't you—"

Da-di-la.

Something was tapping against the panels.

Adam silenced me with a raised hand and sprang to his feet. Nan dropped the turnip lantern, sending it rolling across the stone floor.

They heard it too.

I lunged for the door, my skin burning. "Hide," I gasped. They couldn't—I couldn't let them face this danger, even if I had no time to guess what it might be. I clutched the bolt, but before I could slide it home, Adam pushed me aside.

"Stay back," he ordered, and braced himself against the door, firelight gleaming off the wide wicked blade clutched in his fist.

*Da-di-*la.

Adam threw open the door and vanished into the dark. I couldn't see anything in the back garden, but a thud reached my ears, some scuffling. As I seized a candle and threw myself outside, a shot rang through the room. I staggered, and the light winked out.

Not me. I was breathing. I wasn't hurt.

"Papa—" Nan scrambled over me, clawing and tearing in her haste.

"Wait!"

The monster was outside, and though a pistol held only one shot, suppose he had another? I darted after her, blind in the night. "Nan!"

Then I stumbled on a prone body, landing on the ground so hard I lost my breath.

I squeezed my eyes shut, gasping insufficient sips of air, nowhere near enough to restart my lungs. Above the rib-cracking wheezes shaking apart my chest, I heard a moan.

The body beside me was Adam.

My lungs eased as I pushed onto all fours and crawled to him, patting his arms and chest. "Careful," he gasped. "My leg. I'll be fine. You have to go back in the house."

It was too dark to see, and now I didn't dare touch. "You're shot! I can't—"

"Isobel." He pushed himself up on his elbows. "That tapping. He's hunting you. Get. Back. Inside."

A high scream answered him instead of me, coming farther away from the door.

"Nan!" But this shout was Adam's. I was breathless again, reeling from an invisible blow.

A curse. A grunt, but no more screaming. He had her.

I surged to my feet. I could make out shapes now, deeper wells of shadow, and motion, several yards from me—a hunchbacked form disappearing out the gate. It would take only a minute to smother her, so I had less time than that to catch him.

"Call for help," I told Adam, praying he wasn't bleeding fast. "I'm going after her."

{ 43 }

H old still!"

The girl writhed in Conall's arms, even with his hand clamped to her mouth. He shook her with neck-snapping force and limped to the end of road, where his hackney carriage was waiting, and bundled her inside. Gritting his teeth, he levered himself in after her, shouting commands at the driver.

The carriage lurched into motion spasmodically, as if it too was intent on disobeying him, and the girl squirmed free and bit his hand. Conall jerked away, sending another lightning bolt of pain from his leg to his head.

Bracing himself on the ceiling, Conall swung out a fist, knocking her back onto the seat, away from the door. The child whimpered.

No time to waste. As soon as he'd grasped her, he'd known this wasn't the witch woman, Isobel Tait. But he'd seen her holding the girl's hand. She'd emerged to the sound of his tapping, the beat of her dead son's heart. She'd come after this child too.

He'd be ready for her, but for now, he needed to quiet this one. He only had so many punches.

He dropped his good knee onto her chest and fumbled in the dark for his bag. Just as his hand closed on the syringe, the carriage turned, forcing him off-balance. He groaned aloud as weight shifted onto his wounded leg.

"Try not to pitch me into the street!" Conall shouted angrily.

"You said to hurry," the driver called back.

There it was. The steel syringe, filled with another dose of morphine to dull his pain. Conall slipped his fingers into the rings and his thumb on the plunger. In his current state, after lugging her down the street, he couldn't overpower her much longer.

"Keep still." He wrenched up her skirts, exposing a white swathe of thigh, and jammed in the needle. As if in protest, his leg quivered, another wave of pain overpowering her high scream. "Don't stop," Conall shouted at the driver, who must have heard him, because they kept rolling forward.

He yanked out the syringe, shook it once, stuck it through his trouser leg, and pressed the plunger the rest of the way home, eyes closing with relief.

Long breaths.

He tossed the syringe into his bag, where it landed with a clink. The girl wasn't screaming. Conall peered at her. It should have taken longer for the morphine to take effect. He'd been ready, now that the edge of his pain was blunted, to stop her nose and mouth.

He watched, while lights passed outside them, too worn and shaken to bother taking a pulse or counting her breaths. She was quiet. She wasn't going anywhere.

Conall let himself slump into the opposite seat.

{44}

I raced through the gate, and remembered Adam's knife, lying somewhere in the dark. My stomach twisted, but I didn't slow down or turn back. I ran down the road, hands empty.

At the bottom of the road, the lumbering shadow hailed a hackney carriage. I sprinted forward, shouting, but though the driver turned his head in my direction before he started his horses, he immediately slapped the reins, urging the beasts faster, and drove around the corner without looking back.

Please don't let him kill her, I begged, and ran on, my shadow swinging past me every time I dashed through the glow of a streetlamp. In spite of my pumping arms and pounding feet, my pace was much too slow, the carriage pulling farther and farther away.

I'd have to take a chance. Veering right, I dashed into the nearest close and up the steep stairs—a direct route not open to carriages. I'd not seen the attacker, but I knew it was Burnett. Who else would tap that exact cadence to lure me into the dark? And where would he go but south, to his home or to Surgeon's Square?

A gamble, and not one I could afford to lose. Pain ripped through my lungs, but I took the steps two at a time, pushing myself faster. I collided with a square set of shoulders, bursting from the close onto the Mile, but pushed free and ran on without a word, curses trailing behind me. Gangs of masked and hooded children wove along the street. I shouted for them to clear the way, but most only jeered at me, brandishing lanterns with evil faces.

And there were others about, full-grown men and women, carrying torches, wearing masks. Their flames glowed gold against the gray stone. One called for me to join them, but I swerved and kept running.

The road slanted downward now, and the wind was at my back, pushing seaward from high above the castle. My feet felt like they were flying. As I drew near Southbridge, I glanced right at the southbound carriages.

There—that driver, the one with hunched shoulders, a green muffler, and a dented hat. I was ahead of them, barely, but if I kept running, I'd be close by the time they reached Surgeon's Square. Except Nan had been in Burnett's hands for too long already. I sobbed, drawing a startled gaze from a fiddler on the pavement.

Something brushed against my neck, but it didn't feel like my hair, whipping about my shoulders. I glanced back and saw nothing, but between my frantic footfalls, I thought I heard pounding from other feet—a light skip, a heavy trot, and the easy stride of a born runner.

Once, this would have frightened me.

Come with me, I begged. There were ghosts and demons abroad tonight, and I feared that, alone, I wouldn't be able to stop him.

The hackney pulled ahead, but this time panic didn't close my throat. I followed as fast as I could, even when I lost sight of them a few blocks from the square.

I'd have run straight into it, but the way was blocked by a line of constables. Behind the barricade of their shoulders, the square was filled with people, visible only as black and amber outlines against a giant bonfire shooting a thousand sparks into the sky.

I smelled smoke and liquor, and the footsteps in my ears faded beneath shouts and songs, with "Burn it, Burnett," chanted loudest of all.

"Get back," the nearest constable snarled.

"I've business here," I said, and ducked under his outstretched arms. A club whizzed by my head, fluttering my hair. I ran as far as I could into the surging crowd surrounding the fire, jostled this way and that, until I lost the way forward and my stomach fell into my shoes. There was no way Burnett could have driven into this.

Should I have run to his house? Prayers were such slender things; I'd relied on them to keep Nan alive so long already that the thought of fighting my way out of the square and running another quarter mile extinguished all my hopes.

"Have you seen him?" I said to the man nearest me. He turned, so I repeated the question in a shout.

"Too much a coward," he said, shaking his head.

"Look!" His companion—freckled, with a crooked nose— seized his arm. The dummy, twice the size of Burnett, was almost on top of us, swimming on the raised arms of the crowd.

"They didn't burn it yet?"

"Any minute now," the freckled man shouted in my ear. "Waiting until midnight. Don't be afraid."

My lip curled scornfully. "I'm not here for children's games. I'm here to catch a monster. Burnett's taken another child. A little girl."

I nodded at the building. "You didn't see him?"

They shook their heads, eyes wide. The dummy passed over us, nearly dropping, since none of us raised our arms.

"Another child?" The woman beside me asked, clutching a young boy close.

I nodded, fixing my eyes on the lower windows armored by heavy planks. Above them, though, I could see the broken windows, three stories up, much too high to climb. They were all dark.

"A minute or so past, I thought I saw a light inside," the woman ventured.

My arms stiffened. He was here. "I'm going after her," I shouted, but my words couldn't have reached more than five sets of ears. "Will you help me inside?" A gust swirled around me, tossing my skirts and scurrying on icy feet up the back of my neck.

"How? Everything's boarded up," the woman said.

If two of us were lifted onto the portico, over the iron railing, the second person could lift me to the next floor, using the ornamental ledge, if he were strong enough. "Please. There's no time."

The woman edged away, but the two men must have had more to drink, because they didn't turn away. "He took my son's heart," I said desperately. "We have to stop him."

I wished they were as eager as my ghosts.

Another man, tall and unshaven, wearing a spotted neckerchief, shook his head. "You can't—"

"I can." I smiled without opening my lips. "Burnett doesn't know I'm a witch."

No way to know if they'd believe me or if they considered themselves superstitious. But I knew that tonight, with the fire burning, the crowd calling for blood, and tales of murder and stolen bones abounding, anyone would be tempted.

They glanced at each other. I raised my fist to the sky and opened my hand, and in exactly the same instant, the passing cloud blew away from the moon, washing us in blue light that froze me to my bones. It lasted only seconds—with renewed shouts, someone touched a torch to the dry straw body on top of the bonfire. Bright flames streaked into the sky, but no one circled around me heeded them. I laughed, because against all odds, I'd shown them *something*, and now their eyes were fastened on me.

"I'll stop him," I promised. "I'll save this child."

The freckled man nodded, and the three began shouldering away from the fire, nearer to the mud-splattered walls. I caught hold of one man's shirt so I wouldn't be torn away by the crowd.

"Quickly," I urged.

We reached the railing.

"Lift me up first. Then I'll need someone else to come up and hoist me to the upper windows."

"It's too high," the man with the neckerchief said.

"Do you want her to die?" I countered. The wind swelled, showering us with sparks from the fire, blinding me briefly with my own hair.

"The constables will see you," another warned. "As soon as we lift you up."

"By the time they reach here, I'll be inside. You can slip back into the crowd." It might work, if we did it in under a minute. The constables were sensible men, who'd run around the edge of the square instead of fighting through this crowd. I crossed my heart. "Get me inside. If I can't finish Burnett, I'll send him out to you."

"Burnett! Burnett!" The crowd shrieked.

"All right," the first man said. "We'll be watching."

"Be quick." The freckled man knelt down, cupping his hands. "We'll have to toss you."

I swallowed, but stepped onto his and his friend's hands, balancing myself with a hand on each of their shoulders.

"Ready?"

I wasn't. They hurled me up anyway, screeching like a hawk. Windmilling through the air, I had barely enough time to throw out my arms and grab the railing before I crashed into the wall. My face stung and my lungs had no air, but my hands held tight.

"Use your feet!" someone shouted. "Push up from the wall!"

"Help me!" I was too far up for any assistance from below, but the wind pressed me as my feet scrabbled against the stone, and I heaved onto the balcony, landing in a trembling heap.

Hurry. I picked myself up. My arms were as useful as frayed ribbons, and blood ran from my scratched face. If I couldn't help one of the men up and over—

Look.

I leaned closer. One of the boards hadn't been nailed to the window frame. I didn't stop to think if this was intentional or oversight. I tugged and discovered it was nailed—just only on one side.

I leaned over the railing. "Loose board. I can get inside. Keep watch."

Then I turned away, ignoring their protests.

I pried the board free, kicked away the pane beneath it, and groped for the window catch. It took two tries to slip the latch, and more attempts than that to slide up the sash until there was room enough to wriggle through. My clothes caught and tore, my skin, too, but I squeezed out my breath and inched forward until my shoulders were clear, then my chest. I had a bad moment, imagining myself stuck, but before I went mad with panic, I kicked the rest of the way inside.

Even with the broken window, the noise from the square was muted by the thick stone walls of the school and the thudding of blood in my ears. I checked each door, peering into the lecture theatre, the stairwell, the cloakroom off the ground-floor corridor, but all were lifeless and empty.

Then I heard the clink of glass. My head spun automatically. The laboratory door was open, with a weak glow spilling into the hall.

I stepped inside. Stopped. A cry tore from my throat because Nan lay in an untidy bundle on the floor, pale as wax.

And two yards in front of her, emerging from an underground cellar, was Dr. Burnett, clutching a jar. Though his hands obscured the specimen inside, the thud in my ears swerved to a different tempo. It had to be Thomas's heart.

"Stay there," he commanded.

"No." My skin prickled, the hair on my arms on end, and though his cool lizard's gaze tried to root me to the floor, I stepped forward, once, twice, like I was fighting a heavy wind. "No." I said it again, as if the word were a charm that could bring life and breath and color back to the girl crumpled behind him. As if it could rewind the clock through autumns and summers and springs, to one where Thomas fell asleep beside me and walked holding my hand.

Burnett fumbled with the jar, freeing one hand. Something gleamed between his fingers.

"That heart doesn't belong to you," I said, taking another step.

"I'll give it to you. For a price, Mrs. Tait." His hair stuck in clumps to his forehead. His cheeks had a high flush, like the one I remembered from Thomas's fever. The glittering thing in his hand—a scalpel—quivered.

"You're still limping," I said stupidly.

"Putrefaction. From you and that blasted fork," he said bitterly.

"I hope it hurts."

His fist tightened on the scalpel as, eyes on me, he set down the jar on the nearby worktable, slightly behind him.

"I'll trade it to you. For your blood. For another piece of flesh." His eyes shone in the lamplight.

Maybe I could have done something, but my hands were empty. I reached anyway, but nothing happened. There were no whispers, no icy touches, no lashings of air. The room was still, silent, and the jar stayed right where it was.

Burnett laughed. "I'm going to kill you," he said. "End what's left of your power. You'll never—"

"I accept," I said. He could have my blood. He could have my heart, too, but I didn't have to listen. His glassy eyes and burning cheeks and sweat-damp hair told me the truth. Burnett was dying. I'd already won.

I wished I could have saved Nan.

Adam would find me here with her. I wouldn't have to tell him, and Burnett wouldn't live long enough for the law to hang him. That would trouble Adam, but not me. Death from my hands was better.

I hadn't even had to conjure any magic.

"I'll pay," I said, face hardening. "Give me the heart." Victory, with Thomas's heart in my hands.

Burnett held out the knife, mouth flexing in a wolf's wide grin. "Come closer."

*Da-di-*la.

I took one step, then another, to bring my son and me back together.

Burnett lunged for my stomach—and screamed as the blade turned, tearing the cloth of my dress and slicing the side of his hand.

I'd forgotten about the busk tucked into my borrowed stays, beneath my borrowed dress.

Be quick.

I shoved hard, forcing him back, stealing a half second to

seize the jar. He recovered faster than I anticipated, slashing my arm, releasing a spout of blood into his face. The jar fell and shattered around my son's heart, exploding into shards. I fumbled at my bleeding arm, trying to stop the blood spurting through my fingers.

The room tilted, and I lowered myself to the floor. Above me, Burnett mopped blood from his eyes. He must have dropped the knife, but I couldn't see it, and I didn't dare let go of my wound. My head swam, and my nostrils filled with the smell of iron.

"The radial artery," Burnett said, with a satisfied nod at my blood-soaked arm. "You'll be dead in two minutes." He stooped to pick up the heart. I kicked out at him—a feeble gesture, but he straightened and backed away.

"I suppose you paid for it." He smirked. "Grab it if you can. Good night, Mrs. Tait."

I heard him go, watching crimson spill from my hand, staining my skirts, sleeves, and cuffs, but not, oddly, a tiny corner of white on my right wrist. The handkerchief.

I blinked hazily. The charm had failed. I'd earned revenge, but not protection. Nan was dead, and I would follow her, because no matter how I squeezed, blood pulsed out of me.

Hush. Hush. Hush.

Conall stumbled down the hallway, wiping her blood from his face. By now, the witch was breathing her last.

What a pity he'd had to split his dose of morphine. He hadn't saved nearly enough, and could scarcely think for the throbbing. Leaning against the walls, he slipped through the open back door, past the icehouse, into the alley that would take him safely away—if he could walk that far. The way was shorter if he just skirted the edge of the square.

No one would notice him, not in such a crowd, not in the excitement of the bonfires.

Conall turned up his collar. He didn't know what had become of his hat.

So painful was his forward shuffle, he didn't immediately notice the big freckled man.

"Oi! You!" A wide hand clamped down on his shoulder. "D'you just come from there?" His head jerked at the boarded building behind them.

"I—" Conall's words died on his tongue. There were three of them, hulking men with bulging forearms and heavy scowls.

"Whatdja do to that lassie, then?"

"The witch?"

The barricade of shoulders drew closer. Through the cracking of the fire filling his ears, Conall realized he must have spoken his thought aloud.

"Aye. Her, for starters. But she said there was a wee one you had with you."

"No, I only meant—"

"Are you that doctor, then?" This from the fellow with a neckerchief.

"No, I'm just—" Conall backed, looked sideways, but they hemmed him in, and more were joining them, studying him with frowns and curious stares, and moving inexorably closer. Nothing would escape from here, except the sparks streaking into the sky.

"It's him. Has to be," the freckled man said.

"I'm not! My name is Ross!" Conall shouted, but this assertion quailed under a familiar guttural laugh.

"Don't be fooled, men. It's Conall Burnett, all right." The wall parted, admitting a man in a low hat and heavy coat. His face was half-hidden by a brown scarf.

"You know him?" the man in the neckerchief demanded.

"I do." Gloved hands slid from Eoin Brennan's pockets, trailing a length of dark rope. "I know Dr. Conall Burnett right well."

Hush, hush, hush.

I blinked. I couldn't see Nan anymore. I couldn't see Thomas.

Tie up your arm! my brain screamed at me through numbing fog. The charm. Lizzie's handkerchief.

I let go of the wound, releasing a jet of blood. Clumsily, I tugged the handkerchief free with my blood-soaked hand, taking one corner between my teeth and wrapping it around my arm, looping it under, drawing it tight, then even tighter. The blood stopped spurting, slowing to a trickle.

I fell back as the room darkened around me, my breaths fast and shallow. My hand went to the wound, pressing hard. I swallowed. Blinked. *Maybe...maybe not yet, Thomas.*

I lay still. Maybe if I didn't move an eyelash, my body could knit itself together. But of course I had to blink. I couldn't fight the impulse down, though each fall of my eyelids seemed impossibly heavy.

I began to shiver, and couldn't stop that either, but the room seemed brighter. Maybe I really was dying. I turned my head, searching for the heart. It was there, sparkling on the floor beside me, pulsing gently. It must have closed itself when the jar broke, hiding the injured valve inside. Even the cut that had laid it open was no longer visible. I didn't dare touch it, but the sight drew warm tears from my eyes.

The haze around me cleared; it became easier to focus, and though my eyes only wanted the heart beside me, there was something behind it, something round and silver on the floor, teasing me with its unfamiliar shape. Finally, I let my eyes drift to it, in a place farther away. I squinted, trying to make sense of a silver cylinder, a sharp needle, two rings, and a metal plunger.

There was a word for this, but it took an age before I thought of a syringe, and longer again before I guessed what this meant. My throat burned.

I looked back at the heart, still sparkling, now still. I must have imagined it beating.

Morphia solution could be injected by a syringe. Even in a swirl of lightheadedness, my thoughts were quickening. But I was afraid to decide what a syringe that might hold morphia could mean.

Anyway, I was dying. I couldn't drag myself across this floor. I'd roll onto Burnett's knife or cut myself again on the bits of glass.

Maybe she's still breathing. In spite of the hazards, I rolled, expecting to fail or flop like a fish, but it wasn't half as hard as I was expecting. Hand on my arm, I heaved myself up, and began scooting across the floor, closer to the blue heap of Nan's dress and the tangle of her hair.

A loose strand of hair swayed back and forth in front of her parted lips.

I started to cry.

{ 45 }

I sobel."

It was Adam. I knew before I blinked my eyes clear. "Don't move," he said. "I've brought a doctor."

"Nan—"

"Yes. Her first. I'm to keep watch over you for the time being."

I turned my head sideways, wishing it didn't bob like a too-big flower on a too-thin stalk. My stomach flipped once, then settled. "Not a doctor. He's a surgeon." I knew the hands carefully turning Nan, and the balding head bent to her chest above the stethoscope.

"Slow, but steady," he said. "Regular."

I sighed. "Good evening, Mr. Craig."

He bandaged me up, fearing for my life and my arm, debating when and whether to cut off my makeshift tourniquet.

"Your father would never forgive me if I make it impossible for you to play again," he said, blinking, his voice rough. "But I've got to keep you with us yet."

"Please do," I said.

At last Mr. Craig said we could be moved. My arm was white

with bandages, and Nan was wrapped inside Adam's coat. Mr. Craig wanted her at home, next to a large fire, with hot broth ready as soon as she stirred.

Adam carefully picked the glass off Thomas's heart, and wrapped it in more of Mr. Craig's bandages. "Your leg?" I asked him.

His bandages were smaller than mine, and not nearly as clean. Nan's and my fault, I supposed. He was using a stick.

"It'll be fine," he said.

"It might turn putrid," I said, biting my lip.

"A clean wound, but I'll check it every day," Mr. Craig promised.

One of the constables picked me up and carried me into the hall. Mr. Craig brought Nan, her head cradled on his shoulder. Adam limped along behind us.

"Don't worry. There's a carriage," Adam murmured.

I frowned. "What about the bonfire?" The scores of shouting people? It was quiet outside, though I smelled smoke.

Adam's lips tightened. "I recommend you close your eyes."

Of course I didn't. I actually managed to lift my head and look around the square. There were constables everywhere, and most of the people had fled. The fire burned sulkily beneath the glares of the fire brigade, a third the size it had been before. They weren't trying to put it out, but I noticed they had a great many pails of sand.

"We mustered all the constables," Adam said. "But it took time to subdue the crowd."

"Why—"

Then I saw it, dangling like a discarded cloak from the nearest streetlamp. There was a cloak—but also hands and arms, and a pair of costly shoes. I couldn't recognize the face, it was too dark and discolored, but the shoes I knew. I'd seen Maggie polish them so many times. The body, beaten and strung up in the street, had once been Dr. Conall Burnett.

"What happened?" I asked.

"I don't think he was in his right mind," Adam said. "They say he walked right into the square. Some men were waiting. The story goes that he told them not to worry, that he'd killed the witch. They started beating him, saying that they'd better kill the devil then too."

His lips pressed together. "When we arrived, it was too late. They'd already strung him up."

"Don't upset her," Dr. Craig said. "I told you it's touch and go—"

"I'm not—" I stopped trying to shake my head, because the movement hurt. I swallowed. "A witch? What a strange story."

Adam shrugged. "I've heard stranger. He got what he deserved."

"That's enough for now," Mr. Craig said. "I don't want her spending her strength talking. She'll turn delirious."

So Adam pinched his lips together again, and the constable set me inside the carriage. The jostling hurt a little, and I closed my eyes. The fever hadn't killed Burnett after all, but this seemed just. I wasn't the only one with a score against him. Maybe there'd been others like me in the square.

"Will anyone be charged with killing Burnett?" I asked, earning a dark look from Mr. Craig.

Adam gave a tight smile. "One. I saw him when we arrived, holding the rope. The constables have arrested him. He has quite a memorable face. You know him."

I saw the answer in his eyes, but the name passed through my lips all the same, faint, half-believing. "Eoin Brennan."

"Yes. Him." His voice was perfectly even.

{ 46 }

"Your breakfast," Adam said, limping in with a tray.

I shifted on the pillows. The light at the windows looked like morning, but it was so hard to tell. My head felt full of cotton.

Nan was beside me, practicing letters on her slate.

"Eat it all," she told me severely.

I glanced at the broth, the bread, the pretty plates and silver spoon, the boiled egg standing in a china cup. "This will take me all day," I complained.

"That's why I brought the newspaper," Adam said, settling heavily into the chair. "I'll read to you."

"Are they still making guesses about Junius's identity?"

Adam nodded. "A good half dozen today. None of them close to the truth. I'll read them to you, but first there is something you need to see."

I raised my eyebrows. We both knew I was too weak to pick up the paper.

"Both of you," Adam said. "It's here, on the second page. There's a public demonstration tomorrow afternoon at the university. The body of suspected murderer Conall Burnett will be dissected by Dr. Alexander Munro."

My eyebrows soared. "Imagine that," I said.

Nan snorted. "I can imagine it. But I bet he never did."

Adam shrugged, setting aside the paper and bringing a cup of tea to my lips. "Thought you both should know. I don't imagine it will... Well, most fates are too good for him, but this seems..."

"Fitting," I said.

Nan nodded.

Nan was first to recover, and Dr. Craig remained satisfied with Adam's healing leg. After a week, he was back at the station, and—to my surprise—newly promoted to chief inspector. But I took a fever and had to be kept in bed for over a fortnight. Afterward, I was still breathless and feeble, but I began taking walks—and working at persuading Adam.

Nan only snorted, and said I was welcome to try.

"You'll never make it up the hill, never mind all the way to the top," Adam warned me.

"You'll hire a carriage to take me most of the way," I told him. "I'll rest when I need to. I can put one foot in front of another. I'll get there, even if it takes all day."

"All day and all night, more likely," he told me. "Isobel—"

I shook my head. "I'm not waiting. This isn't meant to keep." I gestured at the new jar, resting on the other side of the room. "Thomas and I have waited long enough."

He hesitated. "You need something to put it in."

He left me and went to his and Nan's room, still full of odds and ends packed in crates under the eaves, and though I heard a good deal of bumping about, he didn't return for almost a quarter of an hour.

"Will this do?"

He passed me a leather pouch, stitched with a sunrise pattern in bright threads. "To lift the soul and soothe the spirit," he said.

I swallowed. I thought I knew who made this, but I wasn't ready to ask. Not yet. "Are you certain?"

He nodded.

I stroked it with a finger. "I would be comforted by this gift, if you are truly willing to part with it."

"It will help," he said softly, and untied the pouch.

The next day, after Adam took Nan to church, I wrapped Thomas's heart in the torn and stained handkerchief that had saved my life, and wouldn't wash clean, no matter how I scrubbed it. Kerr held out the open pouch. I raised the package to my cheek, then slipped it inside.

"You can carry it around your neck," he told me. "It will be next to your heart while you climb."

That seemed right.

We were quiet in the carriage. Nan had stayed behind, and though I felt anxious leaving her, if I could have, I would have made this walk alone. It was slow, and both Adam and I had to lean on sticks, though I suspected he was using his in large part to humor me.

The sun was falling westward when we reached the top of the mount, and the wind was blowing.

Adam took out a spoon and I sat down to rest while he dug a hole.

I don't remember what I said, but I remember the sigh I felt as the pouch touched the earth. With cupped hands, I pushed a covering over it, concealing the bundle beneath a mound of earth. I was breathless again.

"We need stones. A little cairn to protect it and mark the place," I said.

Adam nodded. I watched him walk along the hill's edge, gathering stones, returning to me with his hands full and his pockets overflowing. Choosing from them, I began crying, remembering how Thomas had found stones, carried and thrown and stacked them, loving them like children do.

I assembled the cairn alone, and when it was complete, we sat.

"Can you make it back down?" Adam asked.

I gave a tired smile. "Eventually."

"And—then?"

He wasn't asking about supper or what I wanted to do this evening. I suspected he wasn't even asking about next month.

I hesitated. I wasn't certain. "You may, at some point, want your bed back," I suggested.

"I'm not set on it," he said. "But I understand—with so many memories here, you may not wish to stay. You could go somewhere else, give yourself another name."

I thought about that, drawing up my legs and resting my chin on my knees. Down by the crags, two boys, older than Thomas had ever been, were flying a kite.

"I always thought that was what I'd do," I said slowly. "Before."

"And now?"

"Burnett is gone," I said. "I held the ground. Edinburgh is my home, not his."

"So it is." Kerr leaned back, stretching out on the ground. He laced his hands together, putting them behind his head.

I followed the change of color in the sky, over the spreading rooftops below—blue to pink to gold. I took the bonnet off my head and let the wind weave through my hair.

Burnett had taken enough. I had more good memories than bad ones here.

"So it is," I repeated, like the words were a charm, and saying them would make a home for me, even if it was new and different. Because I suspected, somehow, that they could.

AUTHOR'S NOTE

This novel is based on true stories, though perhaps a more accurate way of putting it is this story grew from seeds of truth.

The most obvious seed is, undoubtedly, the infamous Burke and Hare murders in Edinburgh in 1828. William Burke and William Hare, two Irish immigrants, took up killing to supply the anatomy school of Dr. Robert Knox (who inspired Dr. Conall Burnett). I first examined this story in detail some years ago, while writing *The Girl in His Shadow*, and the facts are chilling enough that they stayed with me. Burke and Hare killed sixteen people in ten months, harvesting vulnerable people for Edinburgh's anatomy industry. Shockingly, their client, Dr. Robert Knox, was never charged. In fact, he was never even called to testify in their trial, almost certainly due to pressure by the medical fraternity, most of whom relied upon stolen corpses for teaching, study, and research.

Though Burke and Hare were undoubtedly guilty of ending many human lives, Knox's relative impunity (he was "disgraced" and left Edinburgh but practiced medicine for the rest of his life, and one of his assistants eventually became physician to Queen Victoria) sat ill with me, especially given these facts: a female corpse was recognized by one of his assistants as a sex worker, and another, a male called "Daft Jamie" who was well known for his intellectual and physical impairments, was only dissected after the removal of his recognizable feet. Bodies were carried to Knox's school while still warm, and some victims' bodies were stored for months, until searches died down, so it was easy to imagine the famous doctor as the true villain of the piece, leaping from a complacent, unscrupulous man to a trophy-hunting, murderous one.

Which brought me to his victims, and my protagonist, Isobel. In spite of my long-brewing thoughts about Knox, this was the real genesis, an imagined scene of a mother, viewing her dead child's heart on display in a medical collection. I wrote the scene down and began filling in the rest. She was broken and oppressed, yet challenge forced her to discover her strength, until she was Burnett's nemesis. I owe some of her to Matthew of All Star Guides. Following him about Edinburgh on a highly enjoyable and informative walking tour, he noticed my left-handedness and red hair and laughingly informed me of dangers I might have faced on the same streets, hundreds of years ago, had I forgotten myself and pumped water with my dominant hand. Between four thousand and six thousand witch trials were held in early modern Scotland, and 75 percent of accused victims were women. Though the last trial was in 1727, the legacy of judicial torture, executions, and superstition is hard to forget, and it would have colored nineteenth-century life in the city, as it still does today.

So Isobel, who I'd originally conceived as the daughter of a showman charlatan, with her own talents for illusion and sleight of hand, instead became a pianist and the daughter of a witch.

I have a sister and a niece who were born with heart abnormalities, and while my sister's corrected naturally, my niece underwent corrective surgery when she was a few months old. But there is more of myself in this story than Thomas's heart—or more correctly, more of the people I love.

I wanted an ally for Isobel, a detective who was also an outsider, and almost as soon as I thought of him, he was Métis. The Métis people of Canada are descendants of Indigenous and European ancestry, with distinct languages, traditions, and the often harrowing and troubling history that comes from being "in-between." My husband comes from a Métis family, a heritage they have always known but seldom admitted to others. Developing Adam's character through the window of my husband and children's heritage made me reflect on the many reasons why this might be the case and the pressures racism, erasure, and genocide put on individuals to conceal, deny, and assimilate, especially in the early nineteenth century, closer to the time when Kanapawamakan, a Plains Cree woman, raised a family with a Scottish immigrant from the Orkney Islands.

After a failed bid for sovereignty at the Red River settlement, Métis people, including this family, traveled farther west, settling and dislocating numerous times. My husband's family eventually moved to eastern Alberta, where they farm still. They are an incredibly loving bunch, and I am phenomenally lucky to have joined such a clan. I married at twenty and feel as loved by them as any daughter, niece, or granddaughter.

With his mixed Cree, French, and Scottish heritage, his careful and courageous detecting, and his longing for home and family, Adam was much more than the character I needed. He is (I hope) a tribute to Kanapawamakan and the family she created, to which I am fortunate to belong.

It might seem a liberty to put a Métis man in nineteenth-century Edinburgh, but without a Eurocentric filter, the reality of transatlantic movement is less unidirectional than many suppose. After reading

Caroline Dodds Pennock's *On Savage Shores*, it felt right and natural
to fictionally represent what could have been part of the narrative
of many Indigenous, mestizo, and mixed explorers who discovered
Europe and made homes there, bringing unfamiliar goods and traditions to those lands.

I am also indebted to the scholarship of Owen Dudley Edwards
in his book *Burke and Hare*, where he recounts the murders, investigation, and legal trial in fantastic detail and posits a connection
between Irish immigrants like Burke and Hare, Ribbonmen, and
the body trade.

David Barrie's *Police in the Age of Improvement* was another
invaluable reference that hopefully enabled me to write this story
with sufficient accuracy and realism. I also benefited from the
exhibit *Anatomy: A Matter of Death and Life* at National Museums
Scotland and the excellent exhibits on medical science at Surgeons'
Hall Museums. Walking among artwork and artifacts from the
Indigenous and Métis exhibits at the Royal Alberta Museum was
also an integral component of the inspiration for this story.

Oh, and in case you were wondering, the Aesculapian Club
is real and still in existence today. Burke and Hare's last victim,
Margaret Docherty, was murdered on October 31, 1828, All Hallows'
Eve. The next morning, her body was found by neighbors before
it could be carried away to Knox, sparking the police investigation
that led to Hare turning the crown's evidence and Burke's conviction
and execution. John Brogan, who was a victim of burns like those
I bestowed on Eoin Brennan, was a relative of William Burke (but
according to record, a harmless individual). After his death, his skull
was found by family members in a local anatomist's collection. They
sued for the skull to be returned, so they could bury it with the rest
of him, but when their suit was successful, they promptly sold it to

another collector. Today, the skull and a portrait of John Brogan are on display at the Surgeons' Hall Museums. You can imagine how surprised I was to discover that the experience I imagined for Isobel had actually happened to someone alive at the time.

Rioting did occur outside Knox's house and in Surgeon's Square, and the doctor was burned in effigy by angry protestors. Some sources say as many as twenty-five thousand came out to watch Burke's execution. His body was publicly dissected by Dr. Alexander Munro (a.k.a. Munro Tertius, who really was known for teaching from his grandfather's notes). It was quite satisfying to reassign the dissection fate to Burnett/Knox.

John Barclay, a famous physician and comparative anatomist, really did mentor Robert Knox and die within a year of their formal partnership. Suspicious as this seems, Barclay's murder is my own invention.

This book has been one of my most enjoyable writing projects. Thank you for joining me in bringing this story to life.

READING GROUP GUIDE

1. Isobel is convinced the heart in Burnett's collection belongs to Thomas. Why? Do you think supernatural elements are at play?

2. Discuss Adam's familial background. Who were his parents, and what happened to them? Before reading this book, what did you know about the Métis people?

3. In the nineteenth century, cadavers played a crucial role in educating medical students, but they were a finite resource. Do you think the actions of the resurrectionists can be at all justified? In what scenario would the ends justify the means?

4. Explain how Isobel's status as a single woman affects how law enforcement treats her. Why is that?

5. Isobel's choice to go undercover in Burnett's home is a dangerous one. Would you have done anything differently? Do you think she exhausted all other avenues of investigation before diving into the lion's den?

6. Who were the Ribbonmen, and what role do they play in this story?

7. How did Burnett pick his victims? Why do you think he was able to go unsuspected for so long?

8. Define Isobel and Stevenson's relationship. How do they seem to feel about each other now, given their history?

9. Toward the end of the story, Burnett accuses Isobel of being a witch, and Isobel herself suspects she might be one. Why do you think that is? Do you agree with them?

ACKNOWLEDGMENTS

There are not enough words invented for the thanks deserved by my agent, Jennifer Weltz, who was the first person to tell me to go ahead and write this book. I am beyond fortunate to have such a champion advocate, expert adviser, and patient early reader. I'm greatly indebted to her talented, enthusiastic team, including Ariana Phillips, who is kind of like a fairy godmother, generally emailing me with exciting news to do with audio and foreign language rights.

Because of Jennifer, I get to work with Jenna Jankowski, whose exceptional editing transformed this story into a book I am proud to share. I am grateful to Jenna for identifying so many unseen possibilities in the story and then letting me figure out how to use them. When I read her excitement (and occasional emojis—they are hard to earn, believe me) in the margins, I know I wrote some good words there.

Sarah Brinley is the smartest, fastest, and best developmental editor I know. She coached me through a ten-thousand-word day on this project in Nanowrimo 2022, kept me accountable as I reworked the resulting word salad, and provided invaluable feedback on early drafts.

Without Emily Engwall at Sourcebooks and Christina Morden

at Raincoast, this would be a book that no one knows about—so many, many thanks to them for their effort and enthusiasm. They also help me present myself as an author with functioning knowledge of the publishing industry and social media. When the nerd with an overactive imagination shows through, that's me, not them.

I'm thankful for the expertise of Teddy Turner, whose editing, metaphorically, stops me from smiling at the world with spinach stuck between my teeth. Also thank you to Heather VenHuizen for the beautiful cover design (and basically reading my mind for what I hoped for and then making it even better).

Thanks to the Daisy Chain Write-Nighters in Edmonton for tapping away on keyboards next to me at our favorite bookstore and in assorted cafes and for listening to me read some of the first bits aloud. Writing is fun, but it's more fun with friends.

It's not really fair that mine is the only name on this cover, but I suppose there has to be room for the picture. As I think of everyone on this list, and the family and friends who supported me throughout, my heart is full and my face is smiling.

Thank you.

ABOUT THE AUTHOR

© ALEXANDER AULENBACH

Jaima Fixsen is a *USA Today* and international bestselling author living and writing in Alberta, Canada. Her novel *The Girl in His Shadow* (co-authored under the pen name Audrey Blake) was selected as Libby's 2022 Big Library Read and has been translated into six languages.

Jaima studied occupational therapy at the University of Alberta, and her experiences learning anatomy and dissecting cadavers began her fascination with the history of science and medical ethics. She loves reading, snow, mountains, snow, history, and snow. And Diet Coke.